7/07

SACRIFICE

SACRIFICE

— KAREN TRAVISS —

 BALLANTINE BOOKS
NEW YORK

Published in the United States by Del Rey Books, an imprint of The Random House Publishing Group, a division of Random House, Inc., New York.

DEL REY is a registered trademark and the Del Rey colophon is a trademark of Random House, Inc.

ISBN 978-0-345-47740-8

Library of Congress Cataloging-in-Publication Data
Traviss, Karen.
Star wars : legacy of the force : sacrifice / Karen Traviss.
        p.   cm.
ISBN 978-0-345-47740-8 (acid-free paper)
1. Star Wars fiction.   I. Title.   II. Title: Legacy of the force.   III. Title: Sacrifice.
PR6120.R38S73 2007
823'.92—dc22   2007002756

Printed in the United States of America on acid-free paper

www.starwars.com
www.delreybooks.com

98765432

Dedicated to the memory of
Sergeant 1st Class Daniel Crabtree,
Company B, 2nd Battalion, 19th Special Forces
Group (Airborne)—father, husband, soldier,
police officer, and Star Wars *fan:*
one of our own.

acknowledgments

My thanks goes to my incredibly patient editors—Shelly Shapiro (Del Rey) and Sue Rostoni (Lucasfilm); comrades-in-plotting Troy Denning and Aaron Allston; my agent, Russ Galen; Mike Krahulik and Jerry Holkins, the Penny Arcade gods, for great *Star Wars* debate and good company; Ray Ramirez, *Mando* armorer extraordinaire, for bringing *beskar'gam* to life; my good friends in the 501st Dune Sea Garrison, for their insights into *Mando* culture; Jim Gilmer, who never fails to steer me back on course; and all the *Star Wars* fans who make this job worth doing.

Del Rey Books and Lucas Licensing Ltd. wish to thank Tawnia Poland, who contributed the name of our latest Sith Lord, and the thousands of fans who took part in the "Darth Who" contest.

You folks really do know the power of the dark side. . . .

dramatis personae

Ben Skywalker; junior GAG officer (human male)
Boba Fett; Mandalore and semi-retired bounty hunter (human male)
Cal Omas; Chief of State, Galactic Alliance (human male)
Cha Niathal; admiral, Galactic Alliance (Mon Calamari female)
Dinua Jeban; Mandalorian soldier (human female)
Dur Gejjen; Prime Minister, Corellia (human male)
Ghes Orade; Mandalorian soldier (human male)
Goran Beviin; Mandalorian soldier (human male)
Jacen Solo; Jedi Knight (human male)
Jaina Solo; Jedi Knight (human female)
Jori Lekauf; GAG corporal (human male)
Leia Organa Solo; Jedi Knight, copilot, *Millennium Falcon* (human female)
Lon Shevu; GAG captain (human male)
Luke Skywalker; Jedi Grand Master (human male)
Lumiya; Dark Lady of the Sith (human female)
Mara Jade Skywalker; Jedi Master (human female)
Medrit Beviin; Mandalorian soldier (human male)
Mirta Gev; bounty hunter, Boba Fett's granddaughter (human female)
Novoc Vevut; Mandalorian soldier (human male)

prologue

THE SKYWALKERS' BEDROOM,
ROTUNDA ZONE, CORUSCANT: 0300 HOURS

THIS IS GOING TO BE ANOTHER SLEEPLESS NIGHT.

But should I have killed him?

Maybe I should try some meds. Warm milk, even.

I've taken a lot of lives. Ever since Ben asked us how many, I've been counting. Maybe Luke's been adding up the tally, too. But he hasn't mentioned it since.

Where's Ben?

I was better placed than anyone to assassinate Palpatine. Now I look back on it and wonder how history would have turned out if I'd come to my senses and killed him when I had the chance. I'd have been a traitor then; I'd be a hero now. And he'd still be dead either way. Perspective is a funny thing.

How many people died because I didn't make that call? I didn't even realize that I could.

Ben, I feel you're alive. But where are you? It's been days.

So . . . how *would* I have known when it was the only option left?

When things had gone too far, and someone *had* to do it? And how come Luke is sleeping like a comatose nerf? I wish I could. If I switch on the holonews, though, even without the audio, it might disturb him. Meditation isn't working, either. Maybe I should just get up and go for a walk.

Ben . . . if Jacen *doesn't know where you are, what are you up to?*
I have to stop doing this.

He's a smart kid and he's been trained by the best. He'll be okay. And maybe he knows now that killing someone is a split second, a heartbeat, a thing you're trained to do until you don't stop to debate it, and then it can't ever be undone. Now that he's killed for himself, and knows the mark it leaves in your head, perhaps he won't judge me or his father harshly.

That's his legacy from Mom and Dad: assassin, freedom fighter, soldier, call it what you will. It all ends in a body count. Ben's joined the family business.

But I don't know what he's doing or even where he is right now. I'm worried sick. I don't care how strong his Force powers are. Jedi die like everyone else, and it's a big and pitiless galaxy, and he's just a kid. *My* kid.

Ben, if you can feel me, reach back. Let me know you're okay.

Luke never believes me when I tell him he snores. He snores, all right.

Ben . . .

"You okay?" Luke's awake. He can do that without warning. Bang—he just snaps alert. "It's the middle of the night."

"I know."

"You're worrying about Ben."

"No, he can look after himself." Why do I say that? Luke knows what I'm thinking. "I shouldn't have eaten so late."

"I'm worried about him, too." He punches the pillow into a more comfortable shape and buries his head in it. "But he's okay. I can still feel him."

Nothing is okay now.

Luke knows it. I know it. The whole family knows it.

There's a war going on across the galaxy, but it's the war within my family that I care about most. My son's a stranger most days.

And Jacen . . .

I don't think I know Jacen Solo at all.

And Lumiya . . .

She tried to kill my kid. For that, sweetheart, you're going to have to answer to me. I'm coming for you, and soon.

I think I can get some sleep now. I feel more relaxed already.

SACRIFICE

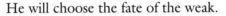

chapter one

He will choose the fate of the weak.
He will win and break his chains.
He will choose how he will be loved.
He will strengthen himself through sacrifice.
He will make a pet.
He will strengthen himself through pain.
He will balance between peace and conflict.
He will know brotherhood.
He will remake himself.
He will immortalize his love.

—*"Common Themes in Prophecies Recorded in the Symbology of
Knotted Tassels," by Dr. Heilan Rotham, University of Pangalactic
Cultural Studies. Call for papers: the university invites submissions
from khipulogists and fiber-record analysts on the subject of the remaining untranslated tassels from the Lorrd Artifact. Symposium
dates may change, subject to current security situation.*

SITH MEDITATION SPHERE,
HEADING, CORUSCANT—ESTIMATED

IT WAS *ODD* HAVING TO TRUST A SHIP.

Ben Skywalker was alone in the vessel he'd found on Ziost, trusting it to understand that he wanted it to take him home. No navigation array, no controls, no pilot's seat . . . nothing. Through the bulkheads he could see stars as smeared points of light, but he'd stopped finding the ship's transparency unsettling. The hull was *there*. He could both see it and not see it. He felt he was in the heart of a hollowed red gem making its sedate way back to the Core.

And there was no yoke or physical control panel, so he had to *think* his command. The strange ship, more like a ball of rough red stone than a vessel made in a shipyard, responded to the Force.

Can't you go faster? I'll be an old man by the time I get back.

The ship felt instantly annoyed. Ben listened. In his mind, the ship spoke in a male voice that had no sound or real form, but it spoke: and it wasn't amused by his impatience. It showed him streaked white lights streaming from a central point in a black void, a pilot's view of hyperspace, and then an explosion.

"Okay, so you're going as fast as you can . . ." Ben felt the ship's brief satisfaction that its idiot pilot had understood. He wondered who'd made it. It was hard not to think of it as alive, like the Yuuzhan Vong ships, but he settled for seeing it as a droid, an artifact with a personality and—yes, *emotions*. Like Shaker.

Sorry, Shaker. Sorry to leave you to sort it all out.

The astromech droid would be fine, he knew it. Ben had dropped him off on Drewwa. That was where Shaker came from, like Kiara, and so they were both home now. Astromechs were good, reliable, *sensible* units, and Shaker would hand her over to someone to take care of her, poor kid . . .

Her dad's dead and her whole life's upended. They were just used to lure me to Ziost so someone could try to kill me. Why? Have I made that many enemies already?

The ship felt irritated again, leaving Ben with the impression that he was being whiny, but he said nothing. Ben didn't enjoy having his thoughts examined. He made a conscious effort to control his wandering mind. The ship knew his will, spoken or unspoken, and he still wasn't sure what the consequences of that might be. Right then, it made him feel invaded, and the relief at finding the ancient ship and managing to escape Ziost in it had given way to worry, anger, and resentment.

And *impatience.* He had a comlink, but he didn't want to advertise his presence in case there were other ships pursuing him. He'd destroyed one. That didn't mean there weren't others.

The Amulet wasn't that important, so why am I a target now?

The ship wouldn't have gone any faster if he'd had a seat and a yoke to occupy himself, but he wouldn't have felt so lost. He could almost hear Jacen reminding him that physical activity was frequently displacement, and that he needed to develop better mental discipline to rise above fidgeting restlessness. An unquiet mind wasn't receptive, he said.

Ben straightened his legs to rub a sore knee, then settled again cross-legged to try meditating. It was going to be a long journey.

The bulkheads and deck were amber pumice, and from time to time, the surfaces seemed to burn with a fire embedded in the material. Whoever had made it had had a thing about flames. Ben tried not to think *flame,* in case the ship interpreted it as a command.

But it wasn't that stupid. It could almost think for him.

He reached inside his tunic and felt the Amulet, the stupid worthless thing that didn't seem to be an instrument of great Sith power after all, just a fancy bauble that Kiara's dad had been sent to deliver. Now the man was dead, all because of Ben, and the worst thing was that Ben didn't know why.

I need to find Jacen.

Jacen wasn't stupid, either, and it was hard to believe he'd been duped about the Amulet. Maybe it was part of some plan; if it was, Ben hoped it was worth Faskus's life and Kiara's misery.

That's my mission: put the Amulet of Kalara in Jacen's hands. Nothing more, nothing less.

Jacen could be anywhere now: in his offices on Coruscant, on the front line of some battle, hunting subversives. Maybe this weird Force-

controlled ship could tap in and locate him. He'd be on the holonews. He always was: Colonel Jacen Solo, head of the Galactic Alliance Guard, all-around public hero holding back the threats of a galaxy. *Okay, I'm feeling sorry for myself. Stop it.* He couldn't land this ship on a Coruscant strip and stroll away from it as if it were just a TIE fighter he'd salvaged. People would ask awkward questions. He wasn't even sure what it was. And that meant it was one for Jacen to sort out.

"Okay," Ben said aloud. "Can you find Jacen Solo? Have you got a way of scanning comlinks? Can you find him in the Force?"

The ship suggested he ought to be able to do that himself. Ben concentrated on Jacen's face in his mind, and then tried to visualize the *Anakin Solo,* which was harder than he thought.

The sphere ship seemed to be ignoring him. He couldn't feel its voice; even when it wasn't addressing him or reacting to him, there was a faint background noise in his mind that gave him the feeling the vessel was humming to itself, like someone occupied with a repetitive task.

"Can you do it?" *If it can't, I'll try to land inside the GAG compound and hope for the best.* "You don't want Galactic Alliance engineers crawling all over you with hydrospanners, I bet."

The ship told him to be patient, and that it had nothing a hydrospanner could grip anyway.

Ben occupied himself with trying to pinpoint Jacen before the ship could. But Jacen's trick of hiding in the Force had become permanent; Ben found he was impossible to track unless he wanted to be found, and right then there was nothing of him, not a whisper or an echo. Ben thought he might have more luck persuading the ship to seek holonews channels—or maybe it was so old that it didn't have the technology to find those frequencies.

Hey, come on. If it managed to destroy a freighter on the power of my thoughts alone, it can find a holonews signal.

Ah, said the ship.

Ben's mind was suffused with a real sense of discovery. The ship dropped out of hyperspace for a moment and seemed to cast around, and then it felt as if it had found something. The starfield—visible somehow, even though the fiery, rocky bulkheads were still there—skewed as the ship changed course and jumped back into hyperspace. It radiated a sense of happy satisfaction, seeming almost . . . excited.

"Found him?"

The ship said it had found what it was seeking. Ben decided not to engage it in a discussion of how it could find a shutdown Jacen hiding in the Force.

"Well, let me know when we get within ten thousand klicks," Ben said. "I can risk using the comlink then."

The ship didn't answer. It hummed happily to itself, silent but filling Ben's head with ancient harmonies of a kind he'd never imagined sounds could create.

COLONEL JACEN SOLO'S CABIN, STAR DESTROYER ANAKIN SOLO, EXTENDED COURSE, HEADING 000— CORUSCANT, VIA THE CONTRUUM SYSTEM

None of the crew of the *Anakin Solo* seemed to find it odd that the ship was taking an extraordinarily circuitous course back to Coruscant.

Jacen sensed the general resigned patience. It was what they expected from the head of the Galactic Alliance Guard, and they asked no questions. He also sensed Ben Skywalker, and it was taking every scrap of his concentration to focus on his apprentice and locate him.

He's okay. I know it. But something didn't go as planned.

Jacen homed in on a point of blue light on the bridge repeater set in the bulkhead. He felt Ben at the back of his mind the way he might smell a familiar but elusive scent, the kind that was so distinctive as to be unmistakable. Unharmed, alive, well—but something wasn't *right*. The disturbance in the Force—a faint prickling sharpness at the back of his throat that he'd never felt before—made Jacen anxious; these days he didn't like what he didn't know. It was a stark contrast with the days when he had wandered the galaxy in search of the esoteric and the mysterious for the sake of new Force knowledge. Of late, he wanted certainty. He wanted order, and order of his own making.

I wasn't ridding the galaxy of chaos then. Times have changed. I'm responsible for worlds now, not just myself.

Ben's mission would have taken him . . . where, exactly? Ziost. Pinpointing a fourteen-year-old boy—not even a ship, just fifty-five

kilos of humanity—in a broad corridor coiling around the Perlemian Trade Route was a tall order even with help from the Force.

He's got a secure comlink. But he won't use it. I taught him to keep transmissions to a minimum. But Ben, if you're in trouble, you have to break silence . . .

Jacen waited, staring through the shifting displays and readouts that mirrored those on the operations consoles at the heart of the ship. He'd started to lose the habit of waiting for the Force to reveal things to him. It was easy to do after taking so much into his own hands and forcing destiny in the last few months.

Somewhere in the *Anakin Solo*, he felt Lumiya as a swirling eddy eating away at a riverbank. He let go and magnified his presence in the Force.

Ben . . . I'm here, Ben . . .

The more Jacen relaxed and let the Force sweep him up—and it was now hard to let go and be swept, much harder than harnessing its power—the more he had a sense of Ben being *accompanied*. Then . . . *then* he had a sense of Ben seeking him out, groping to find him.

He has something with him. Can't be the Amulet, of course. He'll be angry I sent him on an exercise in the middle of a war. I'll have to explain that very, very carefully . . .

It had just been a feint to get him free of Luke and Mara for a while, to give him some space to be himself. Ben wasn't the Skywalkers' little boy any longer. He would take on Jacen's mantle one day, and that wasn't a task for an overprotected child who'd never been allowed to test himself far from the overwhelmingly long shadow of his Jedi Grand Master father.

You're a lot tougher than they think. Aren't you, Ben?

Jacen felt the faint echo of Ben turn back on him and become an insistent pressure at the back of his throat. He took a breath. Now they both knew they were looking for each other. He snapped out of his meditation and headed for the bridge.

"All stop." The bridge was in semi-darkness, lit by the haze of soft green and blue light spilling from status displays that drained the color from the faces of the handpicked, totally loyal crew. Jacen walked up to the main viewport and stared out at the stars as if he might see something. "Hold this station. We're waiting for . . . a ship, I believe."

Lieutenant Tebut, current officer of the watch, glanced up from the console without actually raising her head. It gave her an air of disapproval, but it was purely a habit. "If you could narrow that down, sir . . ."

"I don't know what kind of ship," Jacen said, "but I'll know it when I see it."

"Right you are, sir."

They waited. Jacen was conscious of Ben, much more focused and intense now, a general mood of business-as-usual in the ship, and the undercurrent of Lumiya's restlessness. Closing his eyes, he felt Ben's presence more strongly than ever.

Tebut put her fingertip to her ear as if she'd heard something in her bead-sized earpiece. "Unidentified vessel on intercept course. Range ten thousand kilometers off the port beam."

A pinpoint of yellow light moved against a constellation of colored markers on the holomonitor. The trace was small, perhaps the size of a starfighter, but it *was* a ship, closing in at speed.

"I don't know exactly what it is, sir." The officer sounded nervous. Jacen was briefly troubled to think he now inspired fear for no apparent reason. "It doesn't match any heat signature or drive profile we have. No indication if it's armed. No transponder signal, either."

It was one small vessel, and this was a Star Destroyer. It was a curiosity rather than a threat. But Jacen took nothing for granted; there were always traps. This didn't feel like one, but he still couldn't identify that *otherness* he sensed. "It's decelerating, sir."

"Let me know when you have a visual." Jacen could almost taste where it was and considered bringing the *Anakin Solo* about so he could watch the craft become a point of the reflected light of Contruum's star, then expand into a recognizable shape. But he didn't need to; the tracking screen gave him a better view. "Ready cannons and don't open fire except on my order."

In Jacen's throat, on a line level with the base of his skull, there was the faint tingling of someone's anxiety. Ben knew the *Anakin Solo* was getting a firing solution on him.

Easy, Ben . . .

"Contact in visual range, sir." Tebut sounded relieved. The screen refreshed, changing from a schematic to a real image that only she and

Jacen could see. She tapped her finger on the transparisteel. "Good grief, is that Yuuzhan Vong?"

It was a disembodied eye with double—well, *wings* on each side. There was no other word to describe them. Membranes stretched between jointed fingers of vanes like webbing. The dull amber surface seemed covered in a tracery of blood vessels. For a brief moment, Jacen thought it was precisely that, an organic ship—a living vessel and ecosystem in its own right, of the kind that only the hated Yuuzhan Vong invaders had created. But it was somehow too regular, too constructed. Clustered spires of spiked projections rose from the hull like a compass rose, giving it a stylized cross-like appearance.

Somewhere in his mind, Lumiya had become very alert and still.

"I knew the Yuuzhan Vong well," said Jacen. "And that's not quite their style."

The audio link made a fizzing sound and then popped into life.

"This is Ben Skywalker. *Anakin Solo,* this is Ben Skywalker of the Galactic Alliance Guard. Hold your fire . . . please."

There was a collective sigh of amused relief on the bridge. Jacen thought that the fewer personnel who saw the ship—and the sooner it docked in the hangar, to be hidden with sheeting from curious eyes—the better.

"You're alone, Skywalker?" Technically, Ben was a junior lieutenant, but *Skywalker* would do: *Ben* wouldn't, not now that he had the duties of a grown man. "No passengers?"

"Only the ship . . . sir."

"Permission to dock." Jacen glanced around at the bridge crew and nodded to Tebut. "Kill the visual feed. Treat this craft as classified. Nobody discusses it, nobody saw it, and we never took it onboard. Understood?"

"Yes, sir. I'll clear all personnel from Zeta Hangar area. Just routine safety procedure." Tebut was just like Captain Shevu and Corporal Lekauf: utterly reliable.

"Good thinking," Jacen said. "I'll see Skywalker safely docked. Give me access to the bay hatches."

Jacen made his way down to the deck, resisting the urge to break into a run as he took the shortest route through passages and down durasteel ladders into the lower section of the hull, well away from the busy starfighter hangars. Droids and crew going about their duty seemed surprised to see him. When he reached Zeta Hangar, the speckled void of space was visible through the gaping hatch that normally admitted supply shuttles, and the reflection he caught sight of in the transparisteel air lock barrier was that of a man slightly disheveled from anxious haste. He needed a haircut.

He could also sense Lumiya.

"So what brings you down here?" he asked, deactivating the deck security holocam. "Hero's homecoming?"

She emerged from the shadow of an engineering access shaft, face half veiled. Her eyes betrayed a little fatigue: the faintest of blue circles ringed them. The fight with Luke must have taken it out of her.

"The ship," she said. "Look."

A veined sphere ten meters across filled the aperture of the hatch, its wing-like panels folded back. It hovered silently for a moment and then settled gently in the center of the deck. The hatch doors closed behind it. It was a few moments before the hangar repressurized and an opening appeared in the sphere's casing to eject a ramp.

"Ben did very well to pilot it," Lumiya said.

"He did well to locate me."

She melted back into the shadow, but Jacen knew she was still there watching as he walked up to the ramp. Ben emerged from the opening in grubby civilian clothing. He didn't look pleased with himself; if anything, he looked wary and sullen, as if expecting trouble. He also looked suddenly *older*.

Jacen reached out and squeezed his cousin's shoulder, feeling suppressed energy in him. "Well, you certainly know how to make an entrance, Ben. Where did you get this?"

"Hi, Jacen." Ben reached into his tunic, and when he withdrew his hand a silver chain dangled from his fist: the Amulet of Kalara. It exuded dark energy almost like a pungent perfume that clung and wouldn't go away. "You asked me to get this, and I did."

Jacen held out his hand. Ben placed the gem-inlaid Amulet in his palm, coiling the chain on top of it. Physically, it felt quite ordinary, a heavy and rather vulgar piece of jewelry, but it gave him a feeling like a weight passing through his body and settling in the pit of his stomach. He slipped it inside his jacket.

"You did well, Ben."

"I found it on Ziost, in case you want to know. And that's where I got the ship, too. Someone tried to kill me, and I grabbed the first thing I could to escape."

The attempt on Ben's life didn't hit Jacen as hard as the mention of Ziost—the Sith homeworld. Jacen hadn't bargained on that. Ben wasn't ready to hear the truth about the Sith or that he was apprenticed—informally or not—to the man destined to be the Master of the order. Jacen felt no reaction from Lumiya whatsoever, but she had to be hearing this. She was still lurking.

"It was a dangerous mission, but I knew you could handle it." *Lumiya, you arranged this. What's your game?* "Who tried to kill you?"

"A Bothan set me up." Ben said. "Dyur. He paid a courier to take the Amulet to Ziost, framed him as the thief, and the guy ended up dead. I got even with the Bothan, though—I blew up the ship that was targeting me. I hope it was Dyur's."

"How?"

Ben gestured over his shoulder with his thumb. "It's armed. It seems to have whatever weapons you want."

"Well done." Jacen got the feeling that Ben was suspicious of the whole galaxy right then. His blue eyes had a gray cast, as if someone had switched off the enthusiastic light in him. *That* was what made him look older; a brush with a hostile world, another step away from his previous protected existence—and an essential part of his training. "Ben, treat this as top secret. The ship is now classified, like your mission. Not a word to anyone."

"Like I was going to write to Mom and Dad about it . . . what I did on my vacation, by Ben Skywalker, age fourteen and two weeks." *Ouch.* Ben was no longer gung-ho and blindly eager to please . . . but that was a good thing in a Sith apprentice. Jacen changed tack; birthdays had a way of making you take stock if you spent them somewhere unpleasant. "How did you fly this? I've never seen anything like it."

Ben shrugged and folded his arms tight across his chest, his back to the vessel, but he kept looking around as if to check that it was still there. "You think what you want it to do, and it does it. You can even talk to it. But it doesn't have any proper controls." He glanced over his shoulder again. "It talks to you through your thoughts. And it doesn't have a high opinion of me."

A Sith ship. Ben had flown *a Sith ship* back from Ziost. Jacen resisted the temptation to go inside and examine it. "You need to get back home. I told your parents I didn't know where you were, and hinted they might have made you run off by being overprotective."

Ben looked a little sullen. "Thanks."

"It's true, though. You know it is." Jacen realized he hadn't said what really mattered. "Ben, I'm proud of you."

He sensed a faint glow of satisfaction in Ben that died down almost as soon as it began. "I'll file a full report if you want."

"As soon as you can." Jacen steered him toward the hangar exit. "Probably better that you don't arrive home in this ship. We'll shuttle you to the nearest safe planet, and you can get a more conventional ride on a passenger flight."

"I need some credits for the fare. I'm fed up with stealing to get by."

"Of course." Ben had done the job, and proved he could survive on his wits. Jacen realized the art of building a man was to push him hard enough to toughen him without alienating him. It was a line he explored carefully. He fished in his pocket for a mix of denominations in untraceable credcoins. "Here you go. Now get something to eat, too."

With one last look at the sphere ship, Ben gave Jacen a casual salute before striding off in the direction of the stores turbolift. Jacen waited. The ship *watched* him: he felt it, not alive, but aware. Eventually he heard soft footsteps on the deck behind him, and the ship somehow seemed to ignore him and look elsewhere.

"A Sith meditation sphere," said Lumiya.

"An attack craft. A fighter."

"It's ancient, absolutely *ancient.*" She walked up to it and placed her hand on the hull. It seemed to have melted down into a near hemisphere, the vanes and—Jacen assumed—systems masts on its keel tucked beneath it. Right then it reminded him of a pet crouching before its master, seeking approval. It actually seemed to glow like a fanned ember.

"What a magnificent piece of engineering." Lumiya's brow lifted, and her eyes creased at the corners; Jacen guessed that she was smiling, surprised. "It says it's found me."

It was an unguarded comment—rare for Lumiya—and almost an admission. Ben had been attacked on a test that Lumiya had set up; the ship came from Ziost. Circumstantially, it wasn't looking good. "It was searching for *you*?"

She paused again, listening to a voice he couldn't hear. "It says that Ben needed to find you, and when it found you, it also recognized me as Sith and came to me for instructions."

"*How* did it find me? I can't be sensed in the Force if I don't want to be, and I didn't let myself be detected until—"

A pause. Lumiya's eyes were remarkably expressive. She seemed very touched by the ship's attention. Jacen imagined that nobody—nothing—had shown any interest in her well-being for a long, long time.

"It says you created a Force disturbance in the Gilatter system, and that a combination of your . . . *wake* and the fact you were looking for the . . . *redheaded child* . . . and the impression that the crew of your ship left in the Force made you trackable before you magnified your presence."

"My, it's got a lot to say for itself."

"You can have it, if you wish."

"Quaint, but I'm not a collector." Jacen heard himself talking simply to fill the empty air, because his mind was racing. *I can be tracked. I can be tracked by the way those around me react, even though I'm concealed.* Yes, *wake* was the precise word. "It seems made for you."

Lumiya took a little audible breath, and the silky dark blue fabric across her face sucked in for a moment to reveal the outline of her mouth.

"The woman who's more machine, and the machine that's more creature." She put one boot on the ramp. "Very well, I'll find a use for this. I'll take it off your hands, and nobody need ever see it."

These days, Jacen was more interested by what Lumiya didn't say than what she did. There was no discussion of the test she'd set for Ben and why it had taken him to Ziost and into a trap. He teetered on the edge of asking her outright, but he didn't think he could listen to either the truth or a lie; both would rankle. He turned to go. Inside a day, the *Anakin Solo* would be back on Coruscant and he would have both a war and a personal battle to fight.

"Ask me," she called to his retreating back. "You know you want to."

Jacen turned. "What, whether you intended Ben to be killed, or who I have to kill to achieve full Sith Mastery?"

"I know the answer to one but not the other."

Jacen decided there was a fine line between a realistically demanding test of Ben's combat skills and deliberately trying to kill him. He wasn't sure if Lumiya's answer would tell him what he needed to know anyway.

"There's another question," he said. "And that's how long I have before I face my own test."

The Sith sphere ticked and creaked, flexing the upper section of its webbed wings. Lumiya stood on the edge of the hatch and looked around for a moment, as if she was nervous about entering the hull.

"If I knew *when*, I might also know *who*," she said. "But all I feel is *soon*, and *close*." Something seemed to reassure her, and she paused as if listening again. Perhaps the ship was offering its own opinion. "And you know that, too. Your impatience is burning you."

Of course it was: Jacen wanted an end to it all—to the fighting, the uncertainty, the chaos. The war beyond mirrored the struggle within.

Lumiya was telling the truth: *soon.*

MEETING OF THE CLANS, MANDALMOTORS HALL, KELDABE, CAPITAL OF MANDALORE

A hundred or so of the hardest-looking males and females that Fett had ever seen were gathered in the stark charcoal-gray granite building that MandalMotors had donated to the community.

The hardest face of all was that of his granddaughter. Mirta Gev watched him from the side of the meeting hall with his father's eyes.

My own eyes.

Fierfek, she really did have the Fett eyes. Maybe he was seeing what wasn't really there, but the look bored through into his soul any-

way. It was a look that said: *You failed.* He didn't hear the murmur of voices around him, just the soundless accusations that his daughter Ailyn was dead, that he had never been there for her until it was too late, and that he might also be too late to start being a worthy Mandalore. His father had groomed him to be the best, and even if he'd never mentioned being Mandalore one day, it went with the legacy. *Jaster's* legacy.

Better be quick, then. I'm dying. I've got business to take care of. Priorities: a cure, then find out what happened to my wife, what happened to Sintas Vel.

It wasn't that Mirta wouldn't tell him.

She didn't *know*. She had the heart-of-fire gem he'd given Sintas as a wedding gift, but it had turned up at a dealer's shop. It was just bait. And he'd taken it.

But, Fett being Fett, it was more than bait. It was a motivator: it was another piece of evidence.

It's never too late to find out. I thought it was, but it's not.

The hubbub of the chieftains of the clans, heads of companies, and an assortment of veteran mercenaries faded voice by voice into silence. They watched him warily. Not all of them were human, either: a Togorian and a Mandallian, both wearing impressive armor, leaned against the far wall, massive arms folded across their chests. Species didn't matter much to Mandalorians. Culture defined them. Fett wondered what that made him.

"*Oya!*" It was muttered at first, then shouted a few times. "*Oya!*" It was a word with a hundred meanings for Mandalorians. This time it meant "*Let's go, let's get on with it.*" They always started their gatherings this way, and this was the nearest Mandalorians ever came to a senate. They didn't go in for procedural nicety.

A chieftain with an ornately shaved beard and an eye patch stood up to speak without ceremony. "So, *Mand'alor,*" he said. "Are we going to fight or what?"

"Who do you want to fight?" Fett noted that they reverted to Basic when addressing him, in deference to his ignorance of *Mando'a.* "The Galactic Alliance? Corellia? Some Force-forsaken pit on the Rim?"

"There's never been a war we haven't fought in."

"There is now. This isn't our fight. Mandalore's got its own troubles."

"The war's escalating. Their troubles might come and find *us*."

Fett stood by the long, narrow window that ran the height of the west-facing wall. It was more like an arrow loop than a view on the city. Mandalorians built for defense, and public buildings were expected to serve as citadels, even more so now. The Yuuzhan Vong had wreaked terrible vengeance on Mandalore for its covert work for the New Republic during the invasion, but the carnage had just made *Mando'ade* more ferociously determined to stay put. The nomadic habit was still there: it was more about a refusal to yield than love of the land. But they couldn't lose a third of the population and shrug it off, not while many still remembered the Imperial occupation.

Sore losers, the Vong. But it's not like I had any alternative. Better the New Republic than the crab-boys.

Fett scanned the hall, aware of Mirta's fixed and almost baleful stare.

"What's the first rule of warfare?"

On seats, on benches, leaning in alcoves, or just standing with arms folded, the leaders of Mandalorian society—or as many as could get to Keldabe—watched him carefully. Even the head of Mandal-Motors, Jir Yomaget, wore traditional armor. Most had taken off their helmets, but some hadn't. That was okay by Fett. He kept his on, too.

"What's in it for *us*," said a thickset human man leaning back in a chair that seemed to have been cobbled together from crates. "Second rule is *how much* is in it for us."

"So . . . what *is* in it for us this time?"

Us. Fett was *Mand'alor*, chieftain of chieftains, commander of supercommandos, and he couldn't avoid the *us* any longer. He didn't feel like *us*. He felt like an absent husband who'd sneaked home to find an angry wife demanding to know where he'd been all night, not sure how to head off the inevitable argument. They made him feel uncomfortable. He examined the feeling to see what was causing it.

Not up to the job.

He might have been the best bounty hunter, but he didn't think

he was the best Mandalore, and that unsettled him because he had never been simply adequate. He expected to *excel*. He'd taken on the job; now he had to live up to the title, which was much, much easier in war than in peacetime.

Fenn Shysa must have thought he could do it, though. His dying wish was to have Fett assume the title, whether he wanted it or not. *Crazy barve.*

The thickset *Mando* shrugged. "Credits, *Mand'alor*. We need currency, in case you hadn't noticed."

"To spend on importing food."

"That's the idea."

"I suppose that's one way of balancing supply and demand."

"What is?"

"Back one side or the other in this war. That'll reduce the number of mouths to feed. Dead men don't eat."

There were snickers of laughter and comments in *Mando'a* this time. Fett made a mental note to program his helmet translator to deal with it, and that felt like the ultimate admission of defeat for a leader: he couldn't speak the language of his own people. But they didn't seem to care.

"I'm with the *Mand'alor* on this," said a hoarse male voice at the back of the assembly. Fett recognized that one: Neth Bralor. He'd known a few Bralors in his time, but they weren't all from the same clan. It was a common name, sometimes simply an indication of roots in Norg Bral or another hill-fort town. "We lost nearly a million and a half people fighting the *vongese*. That might be small change for Coruscant, but it's a disaster for us. No more—not until we get *Manda'yaim* in order. We'll eat *bas neral* if we have to."

A murmur of rumbling agreement rippled around the hall. A few chieftains slapped their gauntlets on their armor in approval. One of them was the woman commando Fett had met in Zerria's on Drall, Isko Talgal. Her expression was still as grim, graying black hair scraped back from her wind-tanned face and braided with silver beads, but she banged her fist on her thigh plate in enthusiastic approval. Fett wondered what she looked like when she was unhappy.

"You wanted a decision from me. You got it." Fett felt time accelerating past him, and it eroded what little patience he had. Every bone in his body ached right through to his spine. "Galactic Alliance or Confederation—you think it's going to make any difference to us?"

"No," said another voice, thick with a northern Concordian accent. "Coruscant won't be asking us to disarm anytime soon. They might need us if they get another *vongese* war."

"*Chakaare!*" someone laughed. But the debate picked up pace, still mostly in Basic.

"And what if the war comes too close to home? What if it spreads to a neighboring system or two?"

"Even if we side with the Alliance, what's to say they won't turn on us and expect us to toe their nice tidy disarmed line?"

"It's not disarmament they want, it's pooling every planet's assets into the GA Defense Force, and we all know how slick and efficient *that's* going to be . . ."

Fett stood back and watched. It was both uplifting and entertaining in its way. It was the kind of decision-making process that could happen only in a small population of ferociously independent people who knew immediately when it was time to stop being individuals and come together as a nation.

Funny, that's the last thing Mandalore is: a nation. Sometimes we fight on different sides. We're scattered around the galaxy. We're not even one species. But we know what we are and what we want, and that's not going to change anytime soon.

The arguments were all coming down to one thing. A lot of people needed the credits. Times were still tough.

Fett brought his fist down hard on the nearest solid surface—a small table—and the crack brought the hubbub of discussion to a halt.

"Mandalore has no position on the current war, and there'll be no divisions over it," he said. "Anyone who wants to sell their services *individually* to either side—that's your business. But not in Mandalore's name."

He braced for the eruption of argument from the sudden silence, thumbs hooked in his belt. His helmet's wide-angle vision caught a fully armored figure standing at the rear of the hall. It wasn't always possible to tell if a *Mando* in armor was male or female, but Fett was sure this was a man, medium height and with his hands clasped behind his back. The left shoulder plate of his purple-black armor was a light

metallic brown. It wasn't unusual to see odd-colored plates, because many Mandalorians kept a piece of a dead loved one's armor, but this was striking for a reason Fett couldn't work out. Something glittered in the central panel of the man's breastplate, a tiny point of light as the sun cut across the chamber in a shaft so sharp and white that it seemed solid.

I should do that. I should wear a piece of Dad's armor with my own, every day.

He felt bad that he didn't, but jerked his attention back to the meeting.

"That's okay, then," said a cheerful, white-haired man sitting a few paces from him. A dark blue tattoo of a vine emerged from the top of his armor and ended under his chin. Baltan Carid, that was his name. Fett had last seen, him dispatching Yuuzhan Vong with a battered Imperial-era blaster at Caluula Station. "That's all we needed to know. That there's no ban on mercenary work."

"I'll make it clear to both sides that there's no official involvement in their dispute," Fett said. "But if any of you want to get yourselves killed, it's your call."

"So we might see *Mando* fighting *Mando* in this *aruetiise*'s war." Everyone looked around at the man in the purple armor. Fett saw no need to learn the language, but there were words he couldn't avoid: *aruetiise.* Non-Mandalorians. Occasionally pejorative, but usually just a way of saying *not one of us.* "Hardly conducive to restoring the nation, is it?"

"But fighting's our number one export," said Carid. "What do you want, make Keldabe into a tourist spot or something?" He roared with laughter. "I can see it now. Visit Mandalore before Mandalore visits you. Take home some souvenirs—a slab of *uj* cake and a smack in the mouth."

"Well, our economic policy right now seems to be to earn foreign credits . . . get killed . . . and neglect the planet."

Carid had a magnificent sneer. He was far more intimidating without a helmet. "You got a better idea? Oh, wait—is this going to be the all-day diatribe on *kadikla* self-determination and statehood? 'Cos I ain't getting any younger, son, and I'd like to be home in time for dinner, 'cos my missus is making pea-flour dumplings."

That got a lot of laughs. Carid generally did. There were shouts and guffaws. "Yeah, we know about the dumplings, *Carid* . . ."

But . . . *kadikla.* So the Mandalore-first movement had a name now, even its own adjective, too. He hadn't come across Kad'ika yet, the man they said was driving the new nationalism. Fett thought that was remiss of the man, seeing as he'd done just what was asked of him and returned to lead Mandalore.

"Critical mass, *ner vod.*" Purple Man ignored the howls of laughter. His voice had the tone of someone who'd argued this many times before. "We have a population of fewer than three million here, and maybe as many as three times that in diaspora. We lost a lot of our best troops, our farmland's been poisoned, and our industrial infrastructure is still shot to *haran* after ten years. So maybe this *is* the ideal time to bring some people home. Gather in the exiles while the rest of the galaxy is busy."

Carid was focused on the debate now, and Fett was temporarily forgotten. "Yeah, group up to make a nice easy target. All of us in one place."

"Nobody except the *vongese* has attacked us in a long time."

"The Empire gutted us. You've got a short memory. Or maybe you were still in diapers when Shysa had to kick some pride back into us."

"Okay, so let's abandon Mandalore. Go totally nomad again. Keep moving. Rely on the whim of every government except our own."

"Son, we *are* the *shabla* government," Carid said. "So what do you want to do about it?"

"Consolidate Mandalore and the sector. Bring our people home, and build something nobody's ever going to overrun again." Purple Man had a faint accent; a little Coruscanti, a little Keldabian. "A citadel. A power base. So we *choose* when we stay home and when we go expeditionary."

"Funny, I thought that was just what we were doing."

Fett watched the exchange, fascinated. Then he realized everyone was staring at him, waiting for him to respond—or at least to call a halt. So *this* was leadership off the battlefield. It was just like running his business, only more . . . complex. More variables, more unknowns— he *hated* unknowns—and something that was utterly alien to him: re-

sponsibility for other people, millions of them, but people who could take care of themselves and ran the place well enough without any bureaucracy.

Or me. Do they need me at all?

"What's your name?" Fett asked.

Purple Man was leaning against the wall, but he pushed himself away from it with a shrug to stand upright. "Graad," he said.

"Okay, Graad, it's policy as of now. I'm asking for two million folks to return to Mandalore. How many you think we'll get?" It made sense: the planet needed a working population. It needed extra hands to clean up the soil that the *vongese* had poisoned and to cultivate the land left fallow by dead owners. But every Mandalorian in the galaxy didn't add up to a single town on many planets. "We're still short on credits until we become self-sufficient in food production again."

"We'll contribute half our profits," said the MandalMotors chief. "As long as we can sell fighters and equipment to either side, of course."

"Business is business." Fett gave him an acknowledging nod. "I'll chip in a few million creds, too."

Carid looked around him as if to single out anyone mad enough to dissent, but everyone had what they wanted from the meeting. Mirta still managed to look baleful. The slice of her mother's heart-of-fire stone dangled on a leather cord around her neck. At least she had a decent helmet now, apparently her first, so that showed just how much of a Mandalorian her father had been—or how little she'd seen of him.

Maybe Mando *fathers have been disappointing her all her life.*

"One last thing," Fett said. "I'm going to be away from base for a few days. Uncontactable."

"How will we notice?" someone muttered.

It was a fair point. "So I'm not the governing kind. But I haven't let you down yet. While I'm away, Goran Beviin stands in for me."

There was no dissent. Beviin was solid and trustworthy, and he didn't want to be Mandalore. He was also a complete savage with a *beskad,* an ancient Mandalorian iron saber, as many Yuuzhan Vong had discovered the hard way. Any argument about the isolationist policy in Fett's absence wouldn't last long.

"We're done here," said Carid. "You give me the inventory of all the farmland lying fallow, and my clan will make sure it gets allocated to whoever returns to farm it." He hung back for a moment and made an exaggerated job of replacing his helmet. "I'm glad you brought Jango home, *Mand'alor*. It was the right thing to do."

Was it? Home for his father was Concord Dawn. It was right for Mandalore, maybe. They liked their figureheads where they could see them, even their dead ones.

"Nobody has to listen to me if they don't feel like it."

"Never known you to stay out of a fight. You've got your reasons. That's why we're listening." Carid paused. "I'm sorry about your daughter."

"Yeah." So everyone knew about Ailyn. Fett didn't remember telling anyone that she was dead, let alone that Jacen Solo had killed her. Mandalore wasn't her home, either; she wouldn't have appreciated ending up buried here. "And I bet you're all wondering why that Jedi isn't a pile of smoking charcoal by now."

"Like I said, you have your reasons. Anything we can do—just say the word."

"His time will come. Leave him to me." *But not now,* Fett thought. He had to get back to the hunt for a clone with gray gloves and his best chance of a cure for his terminal illness.

As the hall cleared, Mirta was left standing alone, arms folded, leaning against the wall. "I wonder if Cal Omas has such an easy time in the Senate," she said.

"You can't rule Mandalorians. You just make sensible suggestions they want to follow." Fett walked outside and swung his leg over the seat of the speeder that Beviin had lent him, wincing behind his visor. He was close to giving in to daily painkillers. "And since when have Mandalorians needed to be told what makes sense?"

"Since they got in the habit of *ba'slan shev'la* when situations didn't look winnable."

Fett remembered that phrase. Beviin had used it a lot in the Yuuzhan Vong war. It translated as "strategic disappearance"— scattering and going to ground in uncertain times. It was hard to wipe out a people that fragmented like mercury droplets and waited for the right time to coalesce again. It wasn't retreat. It was lying in wait.

"Come on," he said. "I've got some leads to follow up on the clone."

Mirta scrambled onto the pillion seat. Her armor clanked against his. She had the full set now, even a jet pack, courtesy of Beviin. "Has it ever taken you this long to track somebody? It's been months."

Don't push it. "I make it about sixty-five days."

"You believe he exists, then."

"You wouldn't lie to me again, and you wouldn't make up the name *Skirata*."

"No. You want me to come with you?"

"You think I need a nurse?"

"I said I wouldn't lie to you again."

Fett almost wished he hadn't told her. He really should have told Beviin first. That was a man he could *trust*. As the speeder swooped over Keldabe and out into the countryside beyond, the scale of the Yuuzhan Vong's retribution became all too clear again. The course of the winding Kelita River was visible for kilometers now because most of the woodland surrounding it had been flattened. Keldabe stood on a bend in the river, a defiant flat-topped hill glittering with granite, and MandalMotors's hundred-meter tower had somehow survived the war despite the damage it had sustained. The shattered stone and scorch marks were still there as a reminder that Mandalore could be battered, bruised, and temporarily subdued, but never completely conquered.

The small settlements of tree-homes in the branches of the slow-growing, ancient veshok forest had been wiped off the face of the map. Beneath the speeder there were no longer patches of crops in clearings. There was blackened soil and charcoal stumps of trees, and still nothing grew, not even the seedlings that usually emerged after fires.

"Scum," Fett cursed. He banked the speeder sharply and heard Mirta hold her breath. "They didn't even try to plant their Vong weeds here. They just poisoned the soil."

It was a high price to pay for double-crossing the invaders. But the alternative would have been much, much worse.

"No help from the New Republic *or* the GA?" Mirta said. "No reconstruction funding like everyone else?"

"We didn't expect anything. And we didn't get it."

Fett gunned the speeder's drives and headed out over the countryside, mindful of the fact that he'd have taken on the Yuuzhan Vong even if they'd been the New Republic's best buddies. The Beviin-Vasur farm appeared in the distance almost on cue as a kind of reassurance that the devastation wasn't global.

And there was *Slave I*, sitting on a makeshift landing pad. *That* was home. His ship, his father's ship, the cockpit where he had spent literally years of his life.

"So am I coming with you or not?"

Mirta was more trouble left to her own devices. Besides, he didn't want to let that heart-of-fire necklace stray too far. It was the one link he had to finding out how Sintas had died.

"Okay," he said. She was his grandchild, even if she had tried to kill him. He didn't care about that, but he struggled to find that protective devotion he'd seen in his own father. Something just didn't click. So he acted it out, because that was how he'd learned everything that became second nature to him—he went through the motions until it was part of him. He could learn to be a good grandfather, too. He could *excel* at it. "What's the best way to find another bounty hunter?"

"Think like him?"

Fett shook his head and set the speeder down with a thud. He'd have to tell Beviin where he was going. If anything happened to him, Goran Beviin was his chosen successor.

Fett hadn't told him yet, but Beviin took that kind of news in his stride.

"No," Fett said. "You *hire* him."

chapter two

If you can't beat them, divide them.

—*Cal Omas, Chief of State, Galactic Alliance.*

OFFICE OF THE CHIEF OF STATE, SENATE BUILDING, CORUSCANT

"NOT EXACTLY OUR FINEST HOUR, ADMIRAL."

Chief of State Cal Omas looked a much older man than he'd been just a few months earlier. Cha Niathal prided herself on a decent understanding of human facial expressions and the telltale little signs of fatigue and stress. Omas had them all: fluid-filled bulges under his watery blue eyes, a peppering of reddish spots on his chin, and a sour smell of caf when she got too close to him.

But mainly it was the eyes. Human eyes told her everything she needed to know. When she glanced at Jacen Solo, he was a model of confidence and composure—except for his eyes. There were no signs of poor health, but he was far from the glacially calm façade he presented. She could see the changes in the pupils of his dark eyes. Small, almost imperceptible: but his pupils flickered, showing that some things got to him.

That was useful to know.

"We didn't lose the battle at Gilatter Eight," she said. "Whatever the Confederation claims."

"We didn't win it, either," said Omas. He'd developed a habit of moving sheets of flimsi around his desk. He didn't need hard-copy records, but it seemed to give him some comfort to handle them, as if they were the last tangible grip he had on his own government. "Consider this a wash-up."

"We've *had* our wash-up," Jacen said. "We know what went wrong and why we fell for a trap."

"Poor intel," said Omas. "As a Jedi, do you not sense these ambushes?"

Niathal noted Jacen's three rapid blinks. There was little love lost between the two men now. That remark really stung Jacen for some reason, even though he was far too smart to delude himself with ideas of omniscience.

"We're neither invincible nor infallible," he said softly. That was when he was at his most lethal, when he sounded quietly reasonable. "I had unreliable intelligence, and that's an occupational hazard. The fact that we got out in one piece is largely due to Jedi skills. Ironically, my parents' and my uncle's skills . . ."

Don't mind me, Jacen. Or the fleet. "You're too modest, Colonel Solo," she said. "I hear you fought quite remarkably."

Jacen let the comment pass without reply or a self-effacing half smile, which was his usual response. Omas flicked the controls of the holoscreen set in his office wall. A fly-through image of a planet resolved into a cityscape; hololinks showed inset three-D images of explosions and smoking skylines. "Now we have reports of fighting breaking out on Ripoblus."

"Why?" Jacen asked. "Nobody in the Sepan system has any interest in the Confederation. I've had no intelligence—"

"They don't need any love for either cause," said Niathal. "We've reached the free-for-all stage. What better time than during a civil war

to resurrect their dispute with Dimok? Like a cantina brawl. One fight breaks out and everyone suddenly remembers they have a score to settle."

"There'll be plenty more me-too conflicts." Omas sighed. "And we have to ask where we draw the line."

Jacen looked as if he was studying the schematic of Ripoblus's capital. Niathal judged that he was actually fretting about the limited scope of his intelligence.

"Chief of State, even the Empire never managed to stop the Sepan wars, and it was prepared to take far more extreme measures than we are," she said. "We should resist any pressure to get involved. We're getting perilously close to overstretch."

Omas changed the holoimage to a tote board of the Senate composition. The names of most of the member planets were listed in red, but some were in blue; there were more blue names than she remembered from the last time she'd seen this list.

"Two more members seceded last night," Omas said. "Las Lagon and Beris. Minor worlds, but let's do the arithmetic. The more planets that secede from the GA, the fewer military assets I have to call on, and the more assets there are that are potentially available to the Confederation."

Jacen was a master of expressionless contempt. "I think I can work that out, yes."

"And you still believe in responding with maximum force—within the boundaries of ethical treaties."

"Yes."

"Then we're on the downward spiral." Omas walked into the center of the room and gave Niathal a glance that verged on pleading: *Come on, you're the military, you know this is true.* "Sooner or later, secessions reach a point where the GA becomes the rump—where the Confederation equals and then outnumbers us." Omas held up two fingers and counted off theatrically. "Problem one: We would be outgunned. Problem two: Where's our legitimacy? What peace would we be enforcing?"

Niathal decided to let Jacen respond and keep her powder dry. Omas had an excellent point, but it was a politician's point, not a chief of staff's. Her job at that moment was to decide how to use force to achieve Omas's objectives, not to define what those objectives should be.

That was a battle for Jacen Solo. She watched.

"In that case," Jacen said, so softly that it was almost a whisper, "they can defeat us without a shot being fired. They can break us with a sheet of flimsi. I'd call that surrender."

"I'd call it war-gaming the worst scenario." Omas looked to Niathal again. "And you, Admiral, will know when we reach the military tipping point."

Niathal had two strategies—one with all the GA pieces she had in play at the current time, and one with Coruscant-based forces alone. It made sense to work on the basis of the latter if support was falling away. She glanced at the list of red names and the growing tally of blue ones while keeping an eye on Jacen—humans always had a hard time working out where Mon Calamari were looking—and realized that the graph wouldn't be a straight line. If there was to be an erosion of the Alliance, it wouldn't be a tidy progression; it would be a sudden collapse.

"That point hasn't come," she said at last. "I'll let you know as soon as I start getting nervous. But I can tell you that we're already overstretched because of the geography. Multiple fronts. Not good."

"And if we withdraw support from allies, then we magnify the problem," Omas said. "They'll switch."

Jacen inhaled audibly. "This is why I advocated going in very hard and very fast in the first place."

Omas smiled, but without humor. "Ah. *I told you so.* I wondered how long it would be before we reached that stage."

"Chief Omas, I know hindsight gets us nowhere now, but we might as well be honest with each other, and recognize what we can each contribute."

Niathal was working through her phases of Jacen. First he'd been a useful ally; then an instrument for getting the tougher decisions past Omas. He was still good for the Alliance, she thought, but he was far more the politician than the soldier lately. His language had changed—less direct, more circumspect. She longed for plain talking.

But she wasn't doing any in front of Jacen now.

"My sources tell me the Corellians failed to recruit the Mandalori-

ans fairly early on," she said. "For some obscure reason, they appear to be staying neutral. Unless they've had some collective lobotomy, I call that interesting."

Omas looked at Jacen pointedly, hands in pockets. "Have we approached them? Have any of your shadowy little operatives signed some of them up? They were pretty handy during the last war, as I recall."

Jacen looked serene—except for his pupils. "No, and I suspect we wouldn't receive a positive response."

"Why? Don't tell me they've discovered pacifism after millennia of pillaging and destroying. They're congenital thugs. Any excuse for a fight that they can get paid for."

You think I don't know what you did, Jacen. Niathal feigned mild interest. *But word gets around. Let's see if you play this straight.*

Jacen was completely still except for the fact that he meshed his fingers in his lap. It looked like a meditation pose, utterly at odds with his black Galactic Alliance Guard coveralls.

"There's the small matter of the fact that I . . . lost Boba Fett's daughter during an interrogation," he said.

Aha.

"Lost." Omas blinked a few times. "What exactly is *lost?*"

"She died while I was interrogating her. I had no idea who she was at the time."

Omas looked stunned for a moment but then let out a small involuntary "Hah!" of oddly horrified amusement. "And Fett *knows* this?"

Jacen's face was as calm and impenetrable as a statue's. "He does now."

"Then I imagine you'll be looking over your shoulder for the rest of your life, Colonel."

Jacen looked as if he hadn't thought about that. His composure wobbled for a second as he rearranged his clasped hands. "Asking him for a favor wouldn't be the smartest thing to do, no."

Niathal wondered if Jacen had finally bitten off more than he could chew. Gossip reached her ears, and gossip from Jacen's secret police was a wholly different and much more reliable source than the murmurings in the pleekwood-paneled Senate corridors.

But it didn't suit her plans to have Jacen crash and burn. And she didn't have to like people to work with them.

"I've arranged to meet the ambassadors from Las Lagon and Beris with the diplomatic corps later today," said Omas. "Let's see if we can talk them back inside the fold. I don't want to start a stampede."

"What's their problem?" asked Niathal.

"Unwilling to commit troops."

"Give them a waiver."

"And what kind of message does that send to Corellia? That's backpedaling." Omas seemed indignant. "That's why we went to war in the first place—the principle of pooled defensive capability for the Alliance."

"Las Lagon and Beris between them contribute twenty thousand troops, tops. The diplomatic benefit strikes me as outweighing both the principle and any use they might be." The worst thing in the world, Niathal decided, was a politician who discovered scrupulous principle halfway through the game. "They're badly trained and poorly equipped, so I don't think I'll miss their military input to the GA."

Jacen eased himself out of his chair and stood up, making it clear he was heading for the door. "Well, at least there's some positive news on the counterterrorism front. It's the second month running that arms seizures are up. We're shutting down their supply routes."

"Are you certain they're all politically motivated, and not just criminals?" Omas asked.

"If you were shot by one of them," Jacen said, "would you care about that fine distinction? Ordinary crime and terror tend to become bedfellows sooner or later. And ask Coruscant Security Force for their latest violent-crime statistics. It's becoming a lot quieter all around."

He gave them both a polite nod and left. Omas watched the doors close behind him and then wandered over to the main window overlooking the plaza to stare out in calculated silence.

"What have we come to, Admiral, that my first thought on hearing that Colonel Solo kills a prisoner is that he might now have enemies big enough to keep him off my back?"

It was a blisteringly frank admission. "You're only human," she said.

Omas didn't see the other side of that verbal coin. "It's an indict-ment of what we've all become that my inner circle of advisers isn't the security or justice secretary, or even diplomats, but the chief of staff and the head of the secret police." Omas began his ritual amble around the office, leaving faint and short-lived footprints in the pale blue pile of the carpet. "I think about that, you know. I wonder how a colonel rises to be so influential, and I really don't know if I let it hap-pen because he's a Jedi, or because he's GAG."

Niathal thought it was smart of Omas to keep the real discussions to a handful of people who could be trusted not to shift allegiance to Corellia. There was no telling with some Senators. "In these uncertain times, it's necessary. We can convene all the emergency committees we like, but the conduct of the war is a matter for very few. The war be-yond our boundaries, and the war within them."

"Do you think we still have a war within?"

"Enough Coruscanti think we do. There's no such thing as 'only' thousands dying in terror attacks. Lose a ship with thousands of crew, and civilians say that's too bad, that's what they signed up for. Lose a few civilians, and it's a planetary tragedy." The GAG had smashed most of the terror networks in a matter of months: they were very ef-ficient at tracking down funding and establishing links. But they were still active, and kicking down different doors now—Bothan, Confed-eration sympathizers, and a few people who just "breached the peace" while emergency powers were in force. "It's as valid to deal with the fear of terrorism as with the reality."

Omas paused to try to look her in the eye. "Admiral, you strike me as an officer raised in the traditions of decency. Honor. The rule of law. That goes out the window all too often in trying times."

"I stick to what I'm tasked to do, and I'm grateful I don't have to get involved in GAG business."

Omas appeared to note the ambivalence. "Nominally, the GAG is under your command."

Nominally . . . "You feel Colonel Solo is exceeding his boundaries and that I should apply them a little more emphatically."

"I'm concerned about his operating procedures with suspects, I'll admit that."

"What do you want—for me to admit I'm concerned, too?"

"Are you?"

"Sometimes."

Omas's brows lifted in a split second of hope. "I appreciate that it's not easy to curb an officer who does so much to reassure the public."

"We all need heroes in difficult times, even if we don't need their protection as much as we think."

"Indeed. And for all their muttering, I do believe the Jedi Council secretly relishes seeing one of their own kind adored for his two-fisted and muscular approach to keeping the peace. It dispels the image of their being passive mystics out of touch with grim reality."

"Success is everyone's child. Failure is an orphan."

Omas smiled ruefully. "Well, he'll either win the war for us . . . or bring us down." He went back to his polished plain of a desk, looking somewhat shrunken when he sat behind it now. The small bronzium vase holding a single purple kibo bloom made the desk look all the more vast and empty. "Heroes have a habit of doing that."

Us. Bring us *down.*

And politicians had a habit of sowing doubts and ideas that wormed into the subconscious. Niathal noted Omas's subtle warning and almost began to explain that she already had the required degree of paranoia for a more political career, but he probably knew that by now. If he didn't, she was slipping.

"I'll bear that in mind," she said.

Omas was a consummate statesbeing who'd survived attempts on his life and his career several times. He'd understand the entire conversation that was packed into that one line: that she knew Jacen was a loose cannon, that she knew he was massively, overwhelmingly ambitious, and that she knew she might find herself sidelined by him if she didn't keep on her toes. And that she knew Omas was aware that her eyes were on *his* job, and that he might make that accession easier for her one day if she worked with him rather than with Jacen Solo.

Us. Political code was a very economical way of imparting delicate information without actually using incriminating words. It saved a lot of time and trouble.

Niathal took the silence as a cue that the meeting was over. As the doors closed behind her, she glanced back at Omas; her last glimpse

was one of a man who shut his eyes for a second as if completely exhausted.

He'll strut back into the Senate in a couple of hours as if everything's under control. Do I really want a job like that?

She still thought she did.

She had lunch in one of the Senate's many eateries. There was always at least one tapcaf or restaurant open at any time of the day or night, some of them relaxed, some of them formal, all of them hotbeds of gossip, debate, and deal making. More government business went on in these places than ever transpired in the Senate chamber. They were also relatively safe places to talk to beings who might attract attention if she met them at the officers' club. Hiding in plain sight worked remarkably well now, and nobody took much notice of the fact that she happened to be grabbing a snack at the same table as a Gossam called Gefal Keb, a senior civil servant in the public protection department. Their voices were drowned in the general chatter. They referred to Jacen as the New Boy, the GAG as the Club; Omas became, inevitably, the Boss. It was unoriginal, but for ears attuned to picking out names from across the room, it seized no attention.

"Is the New Boy under any threat from our boisterous friends in Keldabe?" she asked.

"Not a word coming out of there." Keb had a way of slowly taking in everything around him, 360 degrees. "But if they were planning anything, they wouldn't tell CSF. Word is that Shevu is seriously hacked off with his way of doing business, too."

"Shevu's very old-fashioned about losing prisoners. Anyone else in the Club unhappy with the management?"

"Oddly, no. The New Boy's willingness to lead from the front does breed loyalty, I admit."

"Who's he spying on now?"

"Not you, as far as I can tell. I'd be very surprised if he wasn't keeping an unauthorized eye on the Boss, but I don't have any hard evidence yet. The Club's good at covering its tracks, as you'd expect."

"Anything else I ought to be aware of?"

"Minor procurement issues, but that's nothing to do with the New Boy."

"How minor?"

"Griping in the mess about substandard kit and difficult shortages at the moment. You might want to kick a few data pushers before it turns into a problem."

"I'll have someone look at it." It would keep Jacen occupied. He cared about troop welfare. "Matters like kit seem to hit morale hardest."

It was a brief conversation, two GA personnel who had every reason to be exchanging a few words. Nobody took any notice. The Supreme Commander and senior domestic security staff talked all the time.

Nobody knew that the three individuals who were running the war dared not turn their backs on one another.

That was politics. Admiral Cha Niathal was determined to get used to it.

STAR SYSTEM M2X32905, NEAR BIMMIEL

There was a presence following her, and Lumiya could pick it out like a beacon even at this range. So could the meditation sphere. *Broken,* said the ship.

In the back of her mind, the presence manifested as a jagged, shattered mass of black and white glass. If she concentrated on it long enough, it resolved into a whole vessel again, but the cracks were still visible.

"It's broken, all right," Lumiya said. "What shall we do, allow it to catch up? Or shall we see how good a hunter it is?"

The meditation sphere felt elated. The smoldering red flame that seemed embedded in its bulkheads grew brighter and more golden, and Lumiya felt a conspiratorial sense of humor flood her. *The ship was enjoying itself.* Of course: it had been dormant on Ziost for untold years, a conscious thing waiting for purpose and interaction.

Nothing in the galaxy enjoyed being alone, be it flesh or metal.

Lumiya rocked back on her heels, still a little disoriented by a cockpit that didn't wrap around her. It didn't feel like an extension of her body as a starfighter did. Instead of neatly arranged screens and controls within her reach, there was nothing except stark, grainy, stone-like surfaces in which images appeared and then vanished again.

The ship's bulkhead showed her a pattern of lights. A small craft matched their course at a range of five thousand kilometers. The asteroid belt where her base was hidden appeared as a sprinkling of stars on a dark blue ground as if a hole had been punched in the bulkhead, and she almost expected to feel air rushing past as the vacuum beyond claimed her.

"Time to jump," she said.

The meditation sphere felt as if it took a deep breath and lunged forward. There was no inertia, no sensation of movement whatsoever, and yet Lumiya was sure her stomach leapt and her head spun with the acceleration. The tracking screen was gone. She was looking at the streaming lights of stars and then velvet blackness, unlit except for random pinprick flares. She could see beyond the ship. It was as if it weren't there. She knew where she was. She could feel the pursuing vessel dwindling to nothing behind her, and the transparisteel shattering into broken chaos again.

For a moment, she felt panic.

For a moment, she was in a stricken TIE fighter, struggling for life—broken, fired upon by Luke Skywalker, certain she'd die.

Instantly the bulkheads became red-hot pumice again. She jerked back to the present.

You're safe, the ship said.

It felt almost guilty for alarming her. She wanted to reassure it: *Just a memory,* she thought, *nothing to concern you.* And it seemed reassured. Nobody—nothing—had cared about her welfare for a very long time, not since she'd been in Imperial training. Luke Skywalker's brief affection didn't count.

The broken pursuer has jumped, too, said the ship.

"Try not to outrun it too far." Lumiya searched herself for regret and loneliness, and found none. It was still good to find a sense of kinship with another intelligence. "We don't want it to lose us."

It is still following us, said the ship.

"What did you think of your last pilot?" Lumiya asked.

Not like us.

"Not Sith material, then."

No. The ship knew Ben wasn't fit to be Jacen's apprentice. *Less like us than the one who follows.*

The meditation sphere dropped out of hyperspace and made convincing speed for the asteroid. Lumiya gave it a mental image of marking time until the pilot on their tail had located them again, and then showed it her habitat on the asteroid.

They prepared to dock, Lumiya and the ship, somehow one mind for brief moments. Ben had proven he wasn't the right apprentice for Jacen. For all his fierce courage on Ziost, the boy had still succumbed to a sentimental Jedi urge and risked his life to rescue that child. He lacked the ruthless edge a Sith needed. But at least he had done something right: without him, she wouldn't have this rare vessel. It would be instrumental in Jacen's future. She could see it in the Force. Somehow her own future wasn't linked with it, but she'd look after it until the time came to relinquish control.

Ben. She bore the boy no ill will, but he was simply surplus to requirements now.

Is it him, though? Is this who Jacen has to kill?

Perhaps the Force had spared Ben from her plot for a reason. Perhaps it was his destiny to help his Master by sacrificing his life, and so it wasn't Lumiya's to take.

I don't know what Jacen has to do. I just don't know. I can't see the bridge he has to cross to become the Sith Lord he's destined to be.

Did Jacen believe that she had no more answers to that question than he did?

She doubted it.

He had to immortalize his love—to kill it, to destroy what he loved most.

As the meditation sphere slipped into the docking bay of her habitat, Lumiya pondered on what Jacen Solo loved and couldn't bear to lose, the sacrifice that would take him beyond the mundane world and into greatness. His sister, Jaina? No, he'd already tried to have her court-martialed. His parents? He'd ordered their arrest. But punishment was one thing, and killing was another.

Home, said the ship. *I can defend you against the one who follows.*

"Thank you." Lumiya was taken aback. "It's not necessary. Let the other ship land."

Would it be Ben Skywalker? The boy was the nearest Lumiya had

seen to someone Jacen loved. He wanted Ben to succeed. He ignored the weakness in the boy.

Luke Skywalker? No, Jacen cared nothing for Luke, and perhaps even despised him. Mara? She might have been the last person to stand by Jacen, but he had less feeling for her than for his own parents.

Ben, then. It was almost certainly Ben.

Or . . . maybe it wasn't a person. Maybe he had to kill an organization, or something abstract. Perhaps he didn't have to kill anything at all. Lumiya fought impatience; whatever Jacen's destiny might be, whatever pivotal act he had to perform, it would be soon. She could almost feel the fabric of the Force anticipating it.

And perhaps . . . it's going to be me *he kills.*

But she was Sith, and any Sith would expect that of her pupil. It was a price she had to be ready to pay.

Very broken, said the ship, snapping her out of her thoughts.

Lumiya got to her feet and stood in front of the bulkhead. The glowing pumice thinned to transparency, but it wasn't a visual illusion; the bulkhead opened to the atmosphere and a ramp formed from the ship's casing. When Lumiya walked down it into the hangar area, an old Conqueror assault vessel was edging through the air locks. She hadn't seen one of the figure-eight-shaped ships in a long time.

The hatch popped and someone emerged, partly swathed in a cloak but with a distinctive limping gait.

"You take your risks, dancer." Lumiya was beginning to find Alema Rar a liability. "I might have fired on you."

The Twi'lek threw the cloak back from her face and tilted her head. It was the practiced pose of a woman who had spent so much of her life being coquettish that it had become unconscious habit. She had been used to male attention and still behaved as if she deserved it, even if there were no males around, and even if her looks had been ruined by lightsaber wounds. The severed stump of her lekku gave her a grotesquely comic look.

But Alema wasn't a laughing matter at all. She was, as the ship put it, broken. This was a damaged, vengeful creature that wanted to lash out, and Lumiya had no patience with lack of discipline. Alema was also insane, and a Dark Jedi with those problems was a very dangerous complication.

"But you didn't." The Twi'lek's eyes were on the meditation sphere. "We find this ship interesting."

"I thought you might." Lumiya indicated the doors leading to her chambers. *Home* wasn't the word. "Seeing as you're here, you might as well come in."

Alema prowled around the ship, gazing at it from all angles, clearly fascinated.

"It thinks," she said. "This ship *thinks*."

"Thinking's useful. Try it sometime." Lumiya knew she ought to handle a madwoman more carefully, but she was short on tolerance today. She strained to sense what the ship might be saying, but all she could detect was its watchfulness, its sensors taking a wary interest in Alema. It could probably taste her darkness. "What brings you here?"

"We have been tracking the *Anakin Solo*. We have considered Jacen Solo's attitude to his parents, and we think we might gain access to Han and Leia Solo by working *with* Jacen."

Alema put a caressing hand on the meditation sphere, and Lumiya felt it flinch, then somehow soften. It knew Alema was damaged. Its duty was to aid, to take care of its pilot. That tendency seemed to make it oddly sympathetic to those in need of assistance.

Lumiya sighed to herself. That was the last thing she needed: a Sith vessel that felt sorry for a crazy Twi'lek trollop. She sent the ship a sharp image of Alema, face twisted with psychotic rage, crashing the sphere into a jagged mountain. The ship got the idea right away. Alema pulled back as if burned.

"It would be helpful for all of us," Lumiya said carefully, "if you avoided crossing Jacen Solo's path at the moment. There's a war on, you know . . ."

"We have our task, and you have yours. Ours is to have Balance for what the Solos did to us. Leia will still be trying to bring her precious son back to the light, and that means he remains good *bait* for our purposes."

"Let me put it another way," Lumiya said kindly, steering her toward the doors. "Get in my way, and I'll kill you."

Alema gave her a curious lopsided smile but allowed herself to be ushered into the living quarters.

"Do you know who you're dealing with?" Alema asked.

Lumiya probed Alema's presence again. It felt like shards of broken glass in her mouth, as alien as any being she'd ever encountered. She'd been in the minds of the insane before, but never a Jedi, and never one this deluded. It was almost frightening. It was the sense of *us* that was most disturbing. She found it hard to pick her way between the hive-mind elements and the fragmented personality of one being.

"Yes, I do," Lumiya said. "And I'll still kill you if you let this feud ruin bigger strategies. There'll be time for you to have your revenge later. Interfere with my plans and I'll kill the Solos myself, and then you'll never have your Balance." Lumiya lowered her voice to a soothing whisper. "And you know I can do that, don't you?"

Seemingly unperturbed, Alema gazed around Lumiya's quarters. They were sparsely furnished now because she'd taken most of her necessary possessions back to the safe house on Coruscant—or the latest address, anyway—except for duplicates of the equipment she kept to maintain her cybernetic prosthetics, and basic essentials for a brief stay. Alema had the look of someone sizing up an apartment and deciding whether to buy it.

"No, you can't stay here," said Lumiya. Telepathy was beyond her, but she knew a proprietorial look when she saw it. It made sense to keep an eye on Alema: she was so fixated and reckless that she might—just might—put a hydrospanner in the works, and that wasn't something Lumiya was prepared to risk. The stakes were too high, the moment too close.

If I had any sense, I'd kill her now before she becomes too much trouble. But . . .

Alema still had her uses, until her madness became too unmanageable.

"You understand revenge," said Alema. She settled on a sofa, one arm conspicuously limp, and a petulant frown creased her brow for a moment. "Luke Skywalker destroyed your life. He left you scarred, too."

"Oh, much more than scarred." Lumiya pulled her veil from her face and let Alema see the damage to her jaw. Then she placed one boot on a chair, took out a vibroblade, and rammed it into her thigh. There was a metallic scrape. Alema's expression was suitably surprised.

"I'm actually more machine than organic," Lumiya went on. "There's a point, I think, at which a woman ceases to be a human with cybernetic implants and becomes a machine with organic parts. I believe I've passed that threshold. And you know what? I'm not unhappy with that."

"You want to punish Luke, as we want to punish Leia."

Lumiya leaned over Alema and caught her by her collar, jerking her face close to hers so she couldn't look away.

"Luke seems to think that, too, which I find staggeringly arrogant." Was that a little fear in Alema's eyes? Sometimes it was interesting to play the madwoman herself. "The galaxy revolves around him, he thinks, but then many men think that way. No, I don't miss my beauty, you fool, because it would have vanished by now anyway. Once I understood that my injuries freed me from worrying about such trivia, I realized I had a task that only I could fulfill." She tightened her grip on the flimsy fabric at Alema's throat. "And that task is close to completion, so if you thwart me in any way, I'll become very focused on *you*. Do you understand?"

For a moment, Alema lost that oddly demented expression and looked like a normal sane person in fear of her life. Lumiya wasn't sure what she looked like herself at that moment, but it seemed to work.

"We will . . . respect your wishes," Alema said imperiously.

Lumiya decided not to backhand her, but it took an effort. She didn't have time for this nonsense.

"Do yourself a favor," she said, and let Alema's collar slide out of her grasp with a hiss of sheer fabric over her gloves. "Ask yourself what you have against Leia Solo other than the fact that she made you ugly. If there's nothing beyond that, then your quest for Balance is a waste of time."

Alema blinked as if she'd been slapped. Maybe it was the first time anyone had used the word *ugly* to her. She wasn't; she wasn't *anything*. In a galaxy of vastly diverse life-forms, Lumiya had ceased to be able to judge appeal, or even want to. It was fascinating how the once beautiful fared so much worse than lesser mortals when age and disfigurement overtook them. It was all illusion. The millions of species in the galaxy couldn't agree on what constituted beauty anyway.

But Alema looked as if she was thinking it over.

"We still wish to help you achieve your objective."

"Good," said Lumiya. The way Alema used *we* gnawed away at her patience for some reason. She knew it was a hive-mind remnant of her Joiner days, but it irked her. "Because if hurting Leia is what you want most, letting Jacen get on with what he has to do is going to hurt her most of all."

"Do you want to hurt Leia?"

"She's done nothing to me. I have no feelings either way. There might be something you can do to help me, something you do better than anyone." *Appeal to her vanity. It's big enough.* "Keep tabs on Jacen for me. Covert observation."

"We will, but can you not locate him anytime you want?"

"Not closely enough." Lumiya didn't have the complete Sith ability to see all the pieces in the game, every element in the battle. That was for a full Sith Master. But she didn't need to let on that she had fewer powers than Alema might think. "I don't have time to log his movements, but for his own safety, I need to know exactly where he is at all times, especially when he leaves Coruscant. Do you think you can do that? It's tedious work, but necessary."

"We can."

"And lose the Conqueror. I'll find you a less conspicuous ship."

"The orange sphere?"

"No." Alema seemed to have taken a fancy to the Sith vessel. Perhaps it was because she could communicate with it: once Lumiya penetrated the jagged chaos in her mind, there was a sense of isolation in the Twi'lek that made her recoil. "Something more suitable. And cover your tracks when you leave—don't lead anyone back to this asteroid."

"Our expertise is surveillance and assassination," Alema said stiffly. "We aren't an amateur."

Lumiya took her through the winding passages that honeycombed the asteroid and brought her to the emergency access—even in space, she thought of it as the backdoor—where a few small ships were standing idle. Once she'd had a battle fleet, but it was long gone in the Yuuzhan Vong war. Her needs were different now anyway. She needed stealth, not firepower.

"There." She pointed Alema to a decidedly scruffy shuttle, the kind that priority couriers used to ferry urgent consignments between worlds. It was fifteen meters long, and a third of that was now given over to a hyperdrive and discreet armaments. A courier shuttle needed to be fast and able to defend itself against piracy, but this one had considerably more than the standard specifications. Lumiya waited for Alema to complain about it.

"We won't be noticed in this," the Twi'lek said, appearing satisfied.

"You can change the identification transponder and the livery panel to any of a hundred courier companies." That configuration was actually standard, but Lumiya had added a few bogus and untraceable companies for good measure. "It's not luxurious, but it does the job."

Alema lifted the hatch. It sprung away from the casing to form an awning. She peered inside.

"She took everything from us." Her voice was muffled by the hatchway. Then she pulled out again. "We're alone. She's made us solitary."

Oh, give me strength, she's rambling again. "Who did?"

"Leia Solo. She took our lekku, and so we can't communicate fully with others. She caused the destruction of our nest, too. And she took what attracted others to us, our beauty." Alema had been thinking, then: she'd chewed over Lumiya's challenge and worked out what really drove her. "We're lonely, and we can never touch the world properly again."

Lumiya had been trained never to drop her guard, and pity wasn't something she was accustomed to feeling. She didn't quite feel pity for Alema, but she did get a sudden and painful glimpse of her loss, and it must have been a particularly agonizing one for a Twi'lek; without both lekku intact, she would have difficulty communicating with others of her kind, feeling pleasure—even loving someone. The head-tails were part of her nervous system. And how much more in need of intimacy was she now, after becoming part of a close-knit Killik nest?

Alema did have her reasons for wanting retribution, then. Lumiya was careful not to let that brief flood of pity start her thinking about what normality she, too, had lost.

"I'm sorry," Lumiya said, and meant it. "Now use that to remain focused, and to bide your time."

Alema looked at the courier shuttle and seemed to be somewhere else entirely. Then she gazed down at the deck of the hangar and began swaying a little as if listening to music. She raised one arm—the other hung limp, paralyzed by Luke Skywalker's lightsaber—and seemed to be going through the motions of a dance, turning slowly and with difficulty on her crippled foot.

For a moment Lumiya thought it was one of her affectations. Then she realized that it was quite genuine: Alema was remembering her past, and what she could no longer do.

"We were a dancer," she said wistfully, but she was talking to herself. "We loved to dance."

Lumiya tried to think of all the things she had once loved to do, in the days before she entered Imperial service, and remembered none of them. "Get a move on, dancer," she said. "You can start by tracking the *Anakin Solo.*"

The past didn't matter, any of it. There was only the future.

SANVIA VITAJUICE BAR, CORUSCANT

Mara swirled the sediment of groundapple and dewflower juice around her glass and drank reluctantly as Kyp Durron watched. He clearly had something to say that he didn't want to bring up in the Jedi Council Chamber—or in front of Luke.

And Ben still hadn't called in. The *Anakin Solo* had arrived back at Corsucant two days earlier and there was no sign of Ben. Somehow she'd hoped he would have made his way to Jacen even if he wasn't feeling communicative. Just feeling that he was alive and unharmed wasn't enough.

He was her little boy. She didn't care how many Centerpoints he could take out. This was her kid, and she couldn't stand it. Sometimes, when she looked at their lives through the eyes of a normal mother for a brief moment, she was horrified.

"If I didn't know better," Kyp said, "I'd think you were avoiding me. The whole Jedi Council, in fact."

"Just busy. But you called me here for a reason, and it wasn't to boost my antioxidant levels."

"Well, maybe I'm just observant, but we have an out-of-control Jedi on the loose. Maybe the Council can help you with that. Y'know, combined efforts of the most experienced Jedi in the galaxy?"

"What if I say Luke and I can handle it on our own?"

"Oh, family business . . ."

"That. And the fact that not all the Council is on the same side, so we don't want to open a rift," Mara said.

"Been there—"

"—done that. Put yourself in Corran's position. Would you feel comfortable helping the chief of the GA's bullyboy police after what he's been doing to Corellians and even his own parents? Better we clear up our own family mess."

"I'm surprised that Luke's tolerated Jacen this long," Kyp commented. "I wasn't entirely joking when I said we should make Jacen a Master. People tend to stop throwing rocks when they're inside the tent."

"I think now might not be the best time."

"Is Luke embarrassed he's got problems within his own family?"

Mara almost blurted out that she'd stopped Luke from acting more than once and now she bitterly regretted it, but that wasn't wholly true. "If I tell you that I've identified the root cause and I'm going to deal with it, will you back off?"

"I note the pronoun."

"Luke knows what I'm doing."

"Which is?"

"I'm going to kill Lumiya."

"That removes the threat to Ben, but how does it deal with Jacen?"

"She's infiltrated the GAG. I don't know who her insiders are, but we have to assume she can get at Jacen, too. She might even influence him. She's got to go."

"What took you so long? The old cyborg must be running low on lube oil by now. You could take her anytime."

"Luke tends to favor taking people alive and trying to talk them around." She couldn't bring herself to tell Kyp that Luke had had a civilized chat with Lumiya on the resort satellite. *Touched* her—even when she had her lightwhip in the other hand. He said her intentions

felt *peaceful.* What was he thinking? "But she's not so decrepit, believe me. I won't have an easy time of it."

"I'll help you if you want backup."

"I don't think I'll need it, but thanks." Mara couldn't avoid the next question. "What are the rest of the Council members saying?"

"That you need to get a grip on this. We talk, you know."

"So we have a Jedi Council with the Skywalkers, and a shadow Council meeting without them . . . sounds like a fault line's forming."

"Well, you decided to go whack a Sith without consulting us . . ."

Mara tried to see the double standard, spotted it easily, and ignored it. "If I'd stood up in Council and said, *Hey, this lunatic is threatening my kid and keeps coming after my husband, so I'm going to take her head off*—you really think the other members would have nodded politely and voted on it? There are folks who think like Luke does, that the Council doesn't condone assassinations, and that would make that fault line into a big rift faster than a greased Podracer."

Kyp inspected the depths of his juice. He'd ordered something thick and opaquely orange that he didn't seem to be enjoying. "So you're saving us from the moral dilemma."

"If that's the way you want to see it."

The vitajuice bar was quiet and smelled unappetizingly of wet raw greenery like a flower shop. Maybe that was why it was so quiet; it made it a good place to meet. Nobody knew them here. Most of the customers seemed to be Ementes, probably because they could guarantee getting totally fruit-based nourishment here, prepared right in front of their six eyes. Ementes weren't big on trust, least of all in Coruscant's catering industry.

How much do I expect everyone to trust me?

Mara struggled with not telling her husband the entire truth while she confided in a friend. That was the problem: they were all friends, the whole Jedi Council. The Galactic Alliance Senate could tear chunks out of itself and not feel it, because it was thousands of rivals and enemies and even strangers, but the Council—they'd grown up together in many cases. They'd fought together. They were family, and not just because they were Jedi.

Cilghal often cited the ancient rule of no attachments, but the Council was one big attachment in its own right.

Mara realized she didn't like dewflower, mused on ways to get around a lightwhip, and then flinched as her comlink chirped. She pulled it from her belt and raised it to see Ben's face.

"Mom, I just landed," he said. "I—"

"Ben? Are you at the military port?"

"No, the civilian one. Galactic City. Look, I'm sorry that—"

"Stay right where you are. Don't move, okay? I'll meet you at Arrivals Seven-B, okay?"

"Mom—"

"No arguing this time. Be there." Mara snapped the comlink closed and grabbed her jacket. "If you're thinking of telling Luke, Kyp, give me a head start."

"Wouldn't dream of getting involved," he said, shrugging. "I'm glad Ben's okay. Just remember that kids like clear limits. He's still too young to set his own."

"Tried that," Mara said, and strode for the doors. "And he set his own just fine."

She worked her way through the crowds at the spaceport, sensing Ben's location. There were black-suited GAG personnel operating openly now, on foot patrol in the arrivals hall with blue-uniformed CSF officers. They were pretty conspicuous for secret police. Jacen was adept at hearts-and-minds operations; he seemed to like to have his deterrents visible. It certainly seemed to reassure the public, despite the black visors that gave the GAG troopers the facelessly dispassionate air of battle droids.

And suddenly there was Ben, sitting on the white marble pedestal of the ten-meter abstract statue of *Prosperity* that formed one of the supports for the central dome of the roof of the arrivals hall. *Prosperity, Progress, Culture,* and *Peace.*

Peace. Fat chance.

Ben looked like any other fourteen-year-old kid, drumming his heels idly against the marble, staring intently at his datapad and keying in something one-handed. A GAG trooper passed him. Ben looked up, nodded in acknowledgment, and got a respectful nod back.

If Mara needed a reminder that Ben was anything but a normal teenager, that was it. He was a junior lieutenant. He commanded troopers like that. *Her son helped run the secret police.*

But she'd learned the most silent and efficient ways to kill the Emperor's enemies by Ben's age, and Luke had been just five years older when he joined the Rebellion.

What did we expect to give birth to, a librarian?

"Hi, Mom." Ben slid the datapad into his jacket pocket. He had that tight-lipped look that went with bracing for a dressing-down. "You're mad at me, right?"

Mara paused, wanting at the same time to yell at him for terrifying her and to grab him in a ferocious hug. She settled for swallowing both reactions and ruffling his hair. He'd never live it down back at the barracks otherwise.

"You couldn't call us?" she said. "You couldn't even tell Jacen where you were?"

Ben frowned slightly. "I'm sorry. I was on a mission and I didn't want to give away my location."

"We can talk about it later. Let's have lunch." She gestured toward the exit. "It's okay. Your dad will be happy just to see you back safe. No yelling. I promise."

Ben slid off the pedestal in uncharacteristic silence, and they walked to the speeder platforms. Mara kept a careful eye on the crowd, not entirely sure if she'd recognize or even sense Lumiya if she was around. Lumiya might even send one of her minions, and she had people within the GAG. The biggest threat might be one of Ben's own troopers.

"What are you frightened of, Mom?" Ben asked.

Mara didn't take her eyes off the crowds around them. She scanned constantly, as she had been trained to do. "Okay, you might as well know. Lumiya is trying to kill you."

Ben gave a little grunt that might have been disbelief and seemed to mull over the idea rather than show alarm. "Because she's still got this vendetta with Dad?"

"Mainly because you killed her daughter."

"Uh . . . okay, I'll take her word for it."

Mara shielded Ben as he got into the speeder. It was always a vulnerable moment: she'd taken a few targets as they ducked into vehicles, caught off-balance for a moment. The hatches closed with a sigh of air, and she turned to look at him closely.

"I mean it, Ben. She's dangerous and she's subtle, so until we neutralize her, you have to be on your guard. She's got connections within the GAG. It could be anyone."

"If she was going to have this spy of hers in the Guard kill me, she'd have done it by now." He slouched in the passenger's seat. "But I'll be careful. Wow, this is getting messy. What with Jacen on Fett's list for killing his daughter, and me killing Lumiya's . . . I suppose that's what the job's about, isn't it? You collect enemies. Hey, the boys have got a bet going on when and how Fett's going to come after Jacen."

Mara wasn't sure if Ben was making light of the threat for her sake or just indulging in normal teenage dismissal. Fett was the least of her worries. "And . . . have you placed your bet?"

"Oh, Jacen can take him. But it's kind of weird that Fett hasn't made a move. The longer he waits, the more people get freaked, I suppose."

"If Fett comes for Jacen," she said, "let *him* handle it. Okay?"

The speeder climbed into one of the automated skylanes and headed for the Rotunda Zone. Ben gazed out of the side screen in silence.

"So can you tell me what this mission was?" Mara asked.

Ben did that three-second pause that meant he was framing his words carefully. "I had to bring back a prototype vessel. I wasn't in any more danger than I could comfortably handle."

That was a relief. It was just an errand, although why Jacen hadn't known about it baffled her. "And you missed your birthday celebration."

"You know how folks say that you get to a point in life when birthdays don't matter? That's how it felt."

"Sweetheart, that's only when you get a lot older. Not fourteen." If anything could break Mara's heart, it was that: Ben's childhood had passed him by. "Next year, I promise, we'll have a family get-together. Really mark the day."

"You think the war will be over by then?"

"If it's not, we'll still have a party. All of us."

"Uncle Han and Aunt Leia, too? Even after I tried to arrest Uncle Han?"

And that was the bizarre reality of a civil war: a teenage boy sent to

detain his aunt and uncle, and then fretting over whether they'd attend his next birthday party. Mara sometimes tried to add up the days she'd lived that weren't about killing and warfare, and there were so very, very few. She wanted a different future for Ben.

"Yes, even after that," she said. "Ben, does Jacen know you're back?"

"Yeah." He didn't volunteer any more. "It's okay. I report back for duty at oh-eight-hundred tomorrow. I haven't gone AWOL."

"I'll have one last try, then. Ben, I worry about you. Your dad and I would really sleep a lot better if you left the GAG and came on missions with us."

Mara braced for incoming. But Ben thought visibly for a while, and when he spoke his tone was soft and unsettlingly adult—unsettlingly *old*.

"Mom, have you ever had to do something you didn't want to do, but knew you had to?"

Mara certainly had, so many times that she took it for granted. And at any given time, whether working for the Empire or for the New Republic, or whatever the stang her paymaster called itself, she'd always thought it was *right*.

"Yes, sweetheart, I have," she said, and knew she now had no moral high ground from which to look down upon her son, or anyone else for that matter. "And the problem was that when I looked back, I found I'd done the wrong thing sometimes. But it'll be years before I'll know if what I'm doing now is right."

"You have to go with the best data you have at the time."

It was a weary man's statement, not a boy's. Ben was a soldier. He was what she and Luke had made him. She'd wanted a Jedi son, and now she had one.

"Next year," she said. "Next year, we'll have that party, come what may."

chapter three

Mishuk gotal'u meshuroke, pako kyore.
(Pressure makes gems, ease makes decay.)

—*Mandalorian proverb*

MIRTA GEV HAD SETTLED FOR BEING TOLERATED BY HER GRAND-father, and although she made an effort to love him, it was hard.

Part of her still wanted to make him pay for the life her mother—and grandmother—had endured. And part saw a man who had every form of regard shown him except love, and pitied him. Overall, she saw a man who put up duracrete barriers and defied anyone to breach them. As he took the Firespray out of Mandalore's orbit and prepared to jump to hyperspace, his expression was set in apparent blank disdain for the everyday world. She decided his helmet presented the softer face of the two.

At least she got to sit in the copilot's seat. That seemed to be the nearest that Boba Fett could ever get to approving of her as his own flesh and blood.

"Your clone's not an active bounty hunter," said Fett. There was never any preamble in his conversations, no small talk, no intimacy. He was all business. "I checked every bounty hunter and wannabe on the books, but none is called *Skirata*. Plenty of people on Mandalore knew Kal Skirata, and then—gone. Vanished."

"But he *was* on a hunt, I know that. He told me to get out of his way." Did Fett believe her? She'd stitched him up and tried to lure him to his death, so she could hardly blame him if he was having second thoughts about the clone. The man was real, all right. "So we're retracing his steps?"

"Yours."

"How are you going to pass yourself off as a client looking to hire a bounty hunter?"

"I'm not. You are."

Mirta suddenly realized why he'd agreed to let her ride along. "My, I do come in handy, don't I?"

"Earn your keep. Rules of any partnership."

Mirta thought that sounded remarkably like her dead mother. Ailyn Vel was more a chip from the granite block of Fett than she'd ever admit, but that was impossible. She'd been a baby when Fett had left her grandmother, too young to pick up his callous ways.

"How do you cope?" Mirta asked.

"What?"

"How do you cope with being alone?"

"Are you going to yap all the way to Kuat?"

"You can't bring yourself to tell me to shut up, can you?"

"I cope because I like it that way," Fett said.

"Well, Mama was all I had and I *don't* like it that way."

Fett paused, and there was the faintest movement of his lips—as if he was stopping himself from saying something he'd regret. He *ought* to have understood, she thought. He'd lost his father at the hands of a Jedi, too.

"Yeah," he said. "What about your dad?"

"He died in a hull breach. Not even in combat."

"Why'd Ailyn marry a *Mando*? Sintas must have warned her we're bad news."

Mirta found she was clutching the heart-of-fire pendant tight in her fist. It was just half of the original stone. The other slice, split from it with a blow from the butt of Fett's blaster, was buried with Ailyn Vel in a modest grave outside Keldabe, in an ancient wood that the *vongese* hadn't managed to destroy.

I can't feel anything from this stone. It ought to tell *me something. I'm Kiffar. Part Kiffar, anyway.*

"She hung around *Mando'ade* to get a better idea of how to hunt you. Then she met Papa. It didn't last."

"Romantic."

"She *cared* about him."

"And she let him make a *Mando* of you."

"I spent two summers with Papa on Null, after he and Mama split up. He taught me everything he could. And then he got killed."

She didn't say it to shut Fett up. He was hardly a talkative man anyway, but there was quiet, and then there was breath-holding silence. That was what she heard now.

"That's too bad," he said.

"Don't try to out-orphan me, *Ba'buir*. I know what it's like."

She struggled between the hatred she'd been taught to feel for him and the evidence of her own eyes that he wasn't a monster—at least not the monster painted by her mother. The very thought felt disloyal to the dead. After almost two months, she'd reached the stage where she had days when her mother wasn't her first waking thought, and didn't haunt her dreams. That felt like betrayal, too.

But life had to go on. She had to make sense of this, and not let Ailyn Vel's death be for nothing.

"No need to discuss it, then." He inhaled. He looked like he'd been holding his breath all that time. "Are you okay living where you are?"

"Yeah."

"I could buy you a house of your own. Anywhere."

Mirta never knew when he was going to flip over into awkward generosity. Beviin said he had his moments. He might, of course, have been trying to get rid of her with the lure of a place on a far planet.

"I'm okay where I am, thanks." No, that sounded dismissive. "I meant that I like living with Vevut's family."

Fett said nothing. She knew what he was thinking now.

"Yes, I *do* like Orade," she said. "He's a good man."

"You're a grown woman. None of my business."

But everyone knew she was a Fett now, and that carried with it some burdens. It took a brave man to risk a *Mand'alor* for a grandfather-in-law, especially one with Boba Fett's reputation. Mirta shut her eyes and tried to listen for whispered messages from the heart-of-fire.

"Why can't you get information from *that?*" Fett asked suddenly.

"I'm only part Kiffar. I don't have the full ability to sense things from objects." She opened her eyes again. Fett was still an implacable statue of detachment. She studied his profile to see what of him might be in her. "It's called psychometry. They say some Jedi can do it, too."

Mentioning Jedi might not have been a good idea, but Fett didn't show any reaction. "The stone absorbs memories from the giver and receiver," he said. "Sintas said so." *Ah.* Under the veneer there might have been a man who wanted to either relive happier times or hide the ones he preferred to forget. The stone held a little bit of Sintas Vel's spirit, and a little bit of his. There was more veneer to him now than core, Mirta suspected, but she'd seen him cry, and nobody else had ever seen the adult Boba Fett weaken, she was sure of that. Maybe he hadn't even cried as a kid.

"I'm trying hard, *Ba'buir.*"

"Worst thing you did was tell me you knew what happened to Sintas."

It was a slap in the face. When she'd said it, she hadn't even known if it would do the trick and lead him into her mother's ambush. Now she regretted hurting a dying man, even if she had been raised to loathe him.

"We'll find out how Grandmama died, I promise."

"After I get that clone," Fett said, all gravel and calculation, "I'll find a full-blooded Kiffar to read the stone."

Mirta took it as a cue to shut up. Playing happy families wasn't the Fett way. She wondered how many other families had the record of violent death and attempted murder that theirs did. *I hope what's in me is more like Papa.* Then she recalled Leia Solo deflecting her blaster shot at Fett, and knew that it was *Ba'buir's* blood in her veins after all—Grandpapa's.

"Stand by," said Fett.

He didn't deploy full dampers when *Slave I* jumped. He never did. The acceleration to lightspeed and beyond felt like being punched in the chest and then sat on by a Hutt. She made a point of biting her lip discreetly as the stars streaked to lines of blue-white fire and the crushing sensation passed.

That had to hurt him, too. He was a sick man. Mirta fumbled in her pocket, pulled out some painkiller capsules, and held them out to him. He took them without a word. His fingertips were cold.

It felt like a long, silent lifetime to Kuati space. Mirta filled it with planning how she would disembowel Jacen Solo if and when she got the chance. There was already a line forming for the privilege. *Ba'buir* wouldn't say what he had in mind for him; all she was certain of was that Boba Fett never turned his back on a score that required settling.

"Decelerating in half a standard hour," he said.

She wanted very badly to love him, but couldn't. If she had found out what happened between him and her grandmother, she might have found it easier, but she knew it might also have confirmed her legacy of revenge. One thing she'd learned fast was that it was a subject to avoid. It wasn't that she was afraid of asking; she just couldn't get past the silent routine. He could make the world outside vanish if he wanted to.

Bador was a striking contrast to Mandalore. *Slave I* swept on a descent path past orbiters and over cities studded with straight roads and open plazas. Mirta checked her datapad to orient herself.

"What was your dad's name?" Fett asked.

"Makin Marec."

Fett always had a reason for asking questions. Perhaps he was wondering who else he might be related to. They landed at one of the massive public ports in Bunar and Fett went through his ritual of setting all the alarms, trip-beams, and other lethal traps that would greet anyone stupid enough to try breaking into *Slave I*. He'd brought a small

speeder bike in the hold, and he swung onto the seat a lot more easily than he had last time. The painkillers were strong enough to anesthetize a bantha.

"You're navigating," he said. He bounced a little on the leather saddle as if testing whether he could feel any pain. "Get on."

Mirta patched her datapad into her helmet's system. "Head down that speeder lane and go south for five kilometers."

She was getting used to wearing a *buy'ce*. At first, it had seemed suffocating and disorienting, but weeks of being surrounded by people who relied on theirs had made her feel a misfit without one. The streaming data on the HUD now got her attention without distracting her. She hadn't fallen over anything for a while.

And—it made her feel *Mando*. Her father would have approved, but she tried not to think what Mama would have said. *I miss you, Mama. I miss you so much, and I never even said good-bye.* Fett's tattered cape slapped against her visor in the slipstream, jerking her out of her memories, and Mirta wondered if she'd eventually become like her grandfather—or like her mother. Bitter resentment about being robbed of a parent seemed to run in the family.

Fett steered the speeder through increasingly seedy neighborhoods and canyons of high-rise warehouses and apartment houses. Bounty hunters tended not to ply their trade in the better parts of town. The number of shabby family homes decreased and the scattering of unsavory characters loitering on corners and in speeders increased.

"So what were you after *here*?" Fett asked.

"Recovering stolen data."

"You mean people around here can read?"

"No, I have clients who can. The locals steal anything, even if they don't know what it is. I go and persuade them to hand it back."

"And your clone with the gray gloves was definitely here."

"Yes."

After a couple of wrong turns, the cantina appeared right on cue. In daylight, it looked even worse than it had when she'd last visited. A peppering of blaster burns had left blisters in the paint on the doors, and the masonry was pocked with holes from ballistic rounds that hadn't been there last time—as far as she could tell. A trail of blood drops from the door ended in a larger pool, dried to a dull tarry blackness. Street cleaning wasn't frequent here.

A sign above the door said WELCOME TO THE PARADISE CANTINA. It also said NO HELMETS.

"I'm offended that they don't respect cultural diversity," Fett muttered.

"That's how I know what the clone in gray looked like. He took his helmet off."

"Fine." A couple of low-life males—a human and a Rodian—ambled to within ten meters of the speeder and stared at it. Then they seemed to notice Fett, and then his blaster and rocket-loaded backpack, and suddenly they appeared to remember pressing business elsewhere. Fett locked the speeder and set the anti-theft device with a thermal detonator. The two males broke into a run in the opposite direction and vanished. "They don't seem to know me here, anyway. Fame's fleeting."

Mirta took off her helmet. Fett ignored the request above the doors. The bar smelled as bad as it ever had, a mix of vomit, stale ale, and oil that could have been from machines or very old fried food. The clientele matched their environment, possibly because they'd spent their disposable income on state-of-the-art weaponry. The Kuati barkeeper was filling small dishes on the countertop with pickles that bore an unappetizing resemblance to eyeballs, so they stood at the bar trying to look normal—normal for the Paradise, anyway.

The barkeep caught sight of Mirta first. She must have been staring at the pickles too carefully.

"You got to buy a drink," he said. "No snacks without—" Then his gaze swiveled. The helmet got his attention the way a chest plate alone didn't. "*Ohhh,* you got the nerve to come in here, have you, you *Mando* slag?"

He ducked below the counter for a split second, and that meant only one thing. Mirta wasn't sure if she had her blaster level before *Ba'buir* did, but when the man straightened up with a highly illegal short-barreled Tenloss disruptor that could have reduced them both to ground nerf, he was looking down the muzzles of Fett's sawn-off EE-3 and her BlasTech 515.

It startled the barkeep long enough for Fett to land a left hook

straight in his face. He fell back against the glasses stacked behind him, and a couple smashed on the tiles. Fett caught the disruptor as it clattered onto the counter; Mirta instinctively covered his back, but none of the customers moved. She was starting to feel comfortable doing this double act. The sense of camaraderie—a long way short of family bond—had crept up on her.

Fett examined the disruptor and jammed the safety catch on hard, one-handed. "Remember—no disintegrations."

The bartender staggered upright, cupping one hand under his nose to catch the dripping blood. "The last *Mando* who came in here wrecked this place. You're all the kriffing same, and I don't want you in here, so why don't you—"

Mirta realized she must have missed some fun and games after she'd left the gray clone to his hunting. "That was a long-lost relative," she said. "We're looking for him."

"Well, when you have your family reunion, I want him to pay for the damage from last time."

The man didn't seem to recognize *Ba'buir,* but then Fett wouldn't have taken a contract from this low down the food chain. Senators, crime lords, and the wealthy who could afford him knew his armor. Barkeeps tended not to.

"Time we shared some reminiscences about my wayward kin," said Fett, tapping his forefinger impatiently against the trigger guard of his blaster. "I'm not as careful as him. My name's Fett."

The barkeeper's face drained of what blood there was left in it. Mirta actually watched his color change to a pasty gray. She'd never seen physical fear like that before. The man's eyes scanned Fett's visor, and the revelation was almost comic.

"It was awhile ago . . ."

"Mandalorian in gray armor with gray gloves. Called Skirata." If the bartender was expecting some credits to be slapped on the counter to jog his memory, Fett wasn't playing. "What do you know?"

"Okay, he killed a guy here. *Lot* of damage. Lot of attention from security, too." The barkeeper stared at Mirta now, and he was evidently piecing things together. "Yeah, you were with him, weren't you?"

"Not for long," said Mirta. She'd moved out of the clone's way fast—into a different cantina, in fact. "Who did he kill?"

"Gang boss called Cherit. It made the local holonews, even."

Obviously most shoot-outs here didn't warrant a headline. Mirta made a mental note to check the archives. "What do you know about Cherit that *didn't* make the news?"

"Nothing."

"I realize a blow to the face can affect your memory." Fett still hadn't lowered his blaster. "Try again."

"Okay, Cherit's outfit supplied rak, lxetallic, and Twi'lek girls to some minor Kuati nobs. He was doing his deals here for a while. Maybe he was muscling in on your relative's turf."

"Doesn't sound like our line of work."

Fett stood facing the man for a long, long time. The barkeeper looked like he was grasping for something else to say to fill the silence. Eventually Fett leaned his blaster against his shoulder, muzzle up in the safety position, and seemed appeased.

"If you see him again, tell him little Boba wants to see him about a job."

"How's he going to get in touch with you?"

"Mandalore. Right turn off the Hydian Way. Can't miss it."

"Okay . . ."

"And where does Cherit's gang hang out now?"

The barkeeper turned to the shelves behind him and fumbled frantically in a pile of flimsi sheets. "Don't tell Fraig I gave you this." It was a napkin embossed with a logo that said THE TEKSHAR FALLS CASINO. "You'll find Fraig there most afternoons at the sabacc tables. Kuat City. Fraig took over from Cherit."

Fett pocketed the napkin and strode out. Mirta followed him, backing through the doors more from habit than fear of attack.

"You reckon Fraig paid the clone for a change of management?" she said, scrambling astride the speeder behind him. "That's what I'm thinking."

"If he did, he'll know how to find him."

The speeder bike swooped over the rougher parts of Bunar and headed back to *Slave I*. "Do you play sabacc?" Fett asked.

Mirta knew without asking that her grandfather wasn't a recreational gambler. "No."

"Plan B, then."

"What Plan B?"

"I'll tell you when I've worked it out."

"What was Plan A?"

"Dress you up nice, send you in to play a hand or two, and wheedle something out of Fraig."

"Thanks."

"It'd never have worked anyway. You're not the wheedling type."

It might have been an insult or a compliment, but she had no way of knowing with Fett.

I want to like him. He's not likable, but he's not what you told me he was, either, Mama. How could you even know?

Mirta found herself arguing with a dead woman, hating herself for it, and finding that nothing she thought she knew was solid any longer. She took one hand off the speeder's grab bar and eased the heart-of-fire from under her chest plate to grasp it. Maybe it would tell her something sooner or later.

"Great painkillers," said Fett. She could see the dried blood on the knuckles of his left glove as he flexed his fist. The stain was bothering him. "Thanks."

There was the faintest tinge of warmth in his voice. It was a start.

JACEN SOLO'S OFFICE, GAG HQ, CORUSCANT

There was a voice in Jacen's head, and he never knew whose it was. At times it was clearly Vergere, clearly a memory, but at others he wasn't sure if it was his own thoughts, or Lumiya's suggestions surfacing from his subconscious, or something else altogether. There were times when he even thought it was his conscience.

It was his conscience now, he was sure of it. All he could see was his daughter, Allana.

So you're not thinking about Tenel Ka, then . . .

Whatever act he had to perform to become a full Sith Lord, it would be extreme. It had to be harder than killing a fellow Jedi; harder even than herding Corellians into camps, or turning on his own parents and sister, or subverting democracy.

It had to be the most painful decision he'd ever taken.

I just can't kill my little girl.

Who says I have to? What would that prove?

That you'd do anything to acquire the powers to bring peace and order to the galaxy.

It was Allana's future that had made him start down this path. Now it would be a secure future for everyone's kid except his own.

That's what it's about, Jacen. Service, painful service. Embrace that pain.

No, it wasn't service. It was *insane*. He wouldn't do it. But was it any different from sending your own children to war, making the same sacrifice as millions of other parents? Wasn't it always harder to give a loved one's life than your own?

No. The only sacrifice worth making is your own life.

But Lumiya said he'd know. She said he'd *know* what he had to do when the time came, and she couldn't tell him. He'd been with Tenel Ka and Allana since then. He'd felt nothing, no hint from the Force that this was the final step, that these were the people he had to kill.

Maybe this is denial. Delusion.

It's not Allana. It's not even Tenel Ka.

"It's not them," he said. "It has to be Ben."

And then he was back in his office, horribly aware, looking up at a bewildered Corporal Lekauf. There was a cup of caf on the desk in front of him and he hadn't seen anyone put it there.

He'd never been that distracted before. It scared him. He couldn't afford another lapse like that.

"Lieutenant Skywalker hasn't reported for duty yet, sir." Lekauf—grandson of the officer who had faithfully served Lord Vader—had a scrubbed freckled cheerfulness that prevented him from looking menacing even in black GAG armor with a BT25 blaster. "Can I help?"

Jacen felt his face burn. "Apologies, Corporal. I was thinking aloud."

"That's okay, sir. I thought you were doing some of that Jedi stuff. Communing."

Jacen had to think for a moment. "Melding?"

"That's the stuff."

"I think I need more caf before I try that today. Thank you."

"Did you get Admiral Niathal's message about kit, sir?"

"What's that?" Jacen checked his datapad and assorted comlinks. Bureaucracy didn't come easily to him. He'd make sure he had the best administrators when he—

When I what?

When I rule as a Sith Lord.

The idea was 90 percent sobering, 9 percent inappropriately exciting, and 1 percent repellent. If he could have identified the source of the revulsion—a distaste for power, an old Jedi taboo, plain ignorance—he would have listened to it. But the voice wasn't loud enough. It was his small fears, his reluctance to accept responsibility, and that was something he had to ignore.

"She says some of the front-line units are having problems getting the kit they need," Lekauf said. "Annoying stuff. Specialist ordnance, comm parts, but some seriously non-negotiable items like medical supplies, too. They're also complaining that the cannon maintenance packs aren't up to standard and they've had some malfunctions." Lekauf raised his eyebrows. "We're starting to find problems acquiring what we need, too, sir."

That got Jacen's attention. "This is the richest and most technically advanced planet in the galaxy, and we can't keep our forces adequately supplied in a war?"

Lekauf gave Jacen a significant nod that directed him to his holoscreen. "I think the admiral put it a little more emphatically, but that's her general reaction as well."

"Is there a reason for this?"

"Procurement and Supply seem to be dragging their feet, sir."

"Time I *un*dragged them," Jacen said. He hit the comm key and opened the line to Procurement. "I'm sure it's fixable."

"If you'd like me to talk to them, sir . . ."

"I think they need a full colonel to motivate them, Lekauf, but I'm grateful for your offer." Jacen suddenly felt it was the most pressing task on his list. He and Niathal expected a lot from the armed forces, and it wasn't too much to expect the military bureaucracy to back them up. "I'll get things moving. Find Captain Shevu for me, will you?"

"He's out on surveillance, sir. Intercepted some nasty ordnance, so he's out with Sergeant Wirut watching a drop-off point."

Shevu was hands-on. He didn't seem to be as enthusiastic about the GAG's role as he had been a few weeks earlier, but he did his job and led from the front. There was nothing more Jacen could ask of an officer.

"Okay, I'll catch up with him when he's relieved."

Procurement frustrated Jacen from the start. When he got an answer from the comm, his status as commander of the GAG didn't seem to open as many doors as it did in the rest of the Alliance. By the time he was put through to a senior civil servant in Fleet Supply—a woman called Gellus—he wasn't impressed, and his caf was cold.

"We can't bypass the supply system, sir," said Gellus. "All requests are dealt with in sequence."

"Shouldn't they be dealt with by urgency, as in *front line?*"

"I don't have the power to do that under the procurement regulations, sir."

"Who do I talk to about quality of supplies?"

"Which supplies? You see, we have four item departments—"

"Cannon maintenance packs. We're getting complaints about poor-quality replacement parts."

"That would be Engineering Support. They have their own system. You'll have to—"

Jacen had learned patience and a dozen ways to calm his mind in crisis from as many esoteric Force-using schools. He didn't want to use any of them. He wanted to lose his temper. He wanted *action.*

"There's a war on," he said quietly. "All I want is for the right kit to get to the people fighting. What's the fastest way to do that?"

"You're not Fleet, are you, sir? GAG is domestic."

"Meaning?"

"This isn't your chain of command. We'd need authorization from a senior officer from Fleet to pursue this request. It's the regulations, sir."

But I'm commander of the Galactic Alliance Guard. I don't even

have this much trouble getting to see Chief Omas. The apparently limited scope of his authority galled him. He could call on Star Destroyers and entire armies, but getting past a bureaucrat was impossible.

"Would the Supreme Commander's word do?"

Gellus swallowed audibly. "Yes, sir."

"Then I'll come back with that."

Jacen closed the link, furious. *Rules.* He wasn't used to these arbitrary limits. If he couldn't get simple supply issues ironed out, then his future as a Sith Lord looked limited.

His rational mind told him this was an annoyance that could be solved with a message to Niathal and a little delegation to a junior officer, but another sense entirely told him he had to stick with this.

Good for morale, he thought.

No, it was something else. He couldn't put his finger on it.

Rules and regulations. He scrolled through the comm codes for the Alliance defense departments and found Legal and Legislative. He tapped the sequence, and a human voice answered.

"Can I borrow a legal-analyst droid?" he asked the assistant. Jacen preferred his legal advice from the most dispassionate and unimaginatively honest sources. A droid could grind through the small print in the statutes for him.

"Right away, sir."

That was more like it. Jacen's mood improved.

In the meantime, he still needed that simple authorization from Admiral Niathal to get the kit moving.

Good officer. Good tactician. Hidebound attitudes.

But he needed her as much as she needed him.

Lekauf returned with fresh caf. He should have been off-duty, according to the roster. "You're too busy to do routine administration, sir," he said. "Are you sure I can't take it off your hands?"

"I'm sure," said Jacen. "Procurement and I need to get a few things straight between us."

Lekauf grinned. "You show 'em, sir."

Something told Jacen that it was more important to "show 'em" than he could ever imagine.

And *that* voice—he listened to it.

THE SKYWALKERS' APARTMENT, CORUSCANT

Luke looked at his hands, right then left. One was prosthetic, and one was flesh, and had been touched by someone he was beginning to think of as his nemesis.

Lumiya.

In the middle of a battle, he'd had the chance to kill her, and they'd ended up touching hands in a gesture that between normal people might have been considered reconciliation.

I said I didn't want to kill her.

Luke Skywalker had never wanted to kill anyone. Sometimes it happened, though. He stood up and took the shoto out of his belt, the short lightsaber that he felt he needed to deal with Lumiya and her lightwhip.

What's happening? What does she want?

She'd never been one to play mind games like Vergere. She was a soldier: a pilot, an intelligence agent, a fighter. He'd yet to put the pieces together, but she was connected to Jacen's slide into darkness in some way.

Luke made a few idle practice passes with the shoto and tried to visualize what might happen if he ran into Lumiya again. Then he wondered what he'd have done at nineteen, and he knew he wouldn't have thought about it too much. He wanted things to be that clear again.

The doors to the apartment opened, and he heard Mara and Ben talking. Relief flooded him. He laid the shoto on the table and every rehearsed line of warning and disapproval vanished, replaced by a simple need to grab his only son and crush him in a hug.

Ben stood rooted to the spot and submitted to it. Mara gave Luke a warning with a raised eyebrow, but he wasn't planning to scold Ben.

"I'm glad you're safe," Luke said. "But if anything I did made you go off like that, we need to talk about it."

Ben looked at Mara as if seeking a cue to explain. "I was working. I was on a mission, that's all."

Jacen, you liar. You said he resented the fact that I stopped him being your apprentice.

Only Jacen would—could—send him on a mission.

Luke considered casually asking Ben who'd sent him, but he knew anyway, and he didn't want to descend to tricking his own son into giving him information or putting him on the spot about Jacen. He didn't need any more proof that his nephew wasn't going to turn back to the light without some substantial help. It was help that Han and Leia couldn't give. It was beyond the Jedi Council, too.

This was family trouble. He'd sort it out, with or without Mara.

"Comlink silence?" he asked.

"Yes, Dad. Sorry." Ben might have been surprised by the hug, but he hadn't recoiled, either. "I can't discuss it. You understand, don't you?"

"Of course I do, son." *And I bet I know who told you not to.* "I really hoped you weren't going to stay in the GAG."

"I'm good at that kind of work."

"I know."

"I can't ever be a good little academy Jedi now, Dad. I have to see this through. We've had this argument before, haven't we?" Ben's tone was regretful, not a whiny teenager's protest about his parents' unfairness. It was sobering to see him growing up so fast. Growing up? No, *aging*. "There's a war going on, and once you've served, you know you can't walk away from it and sit it out while your . . . while your friends risk their lives."

"Luke . . ." Mara's tone was reproachful, with that slightly nasal edge that said she wanted Luke to stop. "Is this really the time for all that?"

He ignored her. "I understand, Ben. I do. But the GAG isn't the place you should be."

"Isn't it?"

"It's not the way the government should deal with dissent."

"Then that's why I should stay in," Ben said quietly. "If it's a bad organization, then it needs good people to stay in it and change it from the inside, and not abandon it to the bad guys. And if it's a good organization, then all you're really upset about is my safety, and I can handle that better than you think. You wanted me to be a Jedi. I'm *being* a Jedi."

Ben's logic and moral reasoning were impeccable. "You have a point."

"So am I a good person, Dad? Or do you think I've gone bad like you think the GAG has?"

It was a question Luke had never wanted to consider. What was a bad person? Most people who did evil things were neither good nor bad, just fallible mortals; the only truly irredeemable being he'd ever known was Palpatine. And presumably even Palpatine had once been a little boy, never dreaming he would be responsible for the deaths of billions and savoring his power.

Luke realized he wasn't sure he knew what a good person was when he saw one, or at which point they turned bad. He was painfully aware of Mara's gaze boring into him, green and icy like a river frozen in its flood.

"You're a good person, Ben." *Is he doing anything I didn't?* "You think about what you do."

"Thanks. And I'm not leaving the GAG, Dad. You'll have to make me, either physically or through the courts, and none of us wants that. Leave me where I can do some good."

Fights could be had without raised voices or angry words. Ben had fought and given his parents an ultimatum. Luke knew he would have to tackle this another way.

And blast it, Ben was actually right. The GAG couldn't be abandoned to the bullyboys.

"Just look out for Lumiya," Luke said. "You told him, Mara?"

"I told him."

"So are you going to stay for something to eat, son?" he asked, feeling Mara's gaze thaw a little.

"I'd like that," said Ben, fourteen going on forty.

It was hard to have a family conversation over a meal without mentioning the war. Ben wanted to know how Han and Leia were doing. Mara shunted vegetables around her plate as if trying to sweep them under a carpet.

"Things aren't too good between Jacen and your aunt and uncle at the moment, sweetheart," she said. "But whatever he tells you, they still care about him and want him to be okay."

"It's not personal," Ben said. "Hey, I tried to arrest Uncle Han because it was my job. I didn't mean him any harm."

Luke thought about Jacen's haste to abandon his parents during the attack on the resort satellite. He couldn't see Ben doing the same thing. If he could, he didn't *want* to see it.

"Dad, was the Empire really a reign of terror?"

"Just a bit . . ."

"I know you and Uncle Han and Aunt Leia had a rough time of it, but what about ordinary people?"

Mara chewed with slow deliberation, her gaze in slight defocus on a point in the mid-distance. "You might want to ask Alderaan. No, wait—it's gone, isn't it? Oops. That's what happened to ordinary people, and I know better than most."

Because you did some of it. Luke faced up to the fact that he couldn't expect Ben to believe a word either of them said to him. They'd both done things that they were telling him he couldn't do now.

"But most people didn't really notice, did they?" Ben seemed to be fixed on course. "Their lives went on as before. Maybe a few people who were political got a midnight visit from a few stormies, but most folks got on with their lives, right?"

"Right," Mara conceded. "But living in fear isn't living at all."

"It's better than dead."

"You think the Empire was okay, Ben?" Luke asked.

"I don't know. It just seems that a handful of people can think they have the duty—the right—to change things for everybody else. It's a big decision, rebellion, isn't it? But most decisions that affect trillions of beings get made by a few people."

Luke and Mara looked at each other discreetly and then at Ben. He'd acquired political curiosity somewhere along the line. Whatever mission Jacen had sent him on—and he had, Luke was certain—it had made the boy think.

Or maybe Luke was just losing touch with the fact that his kid was a young man now, and changing fast. When he left, though, Mara still helped him on with his jacket. Luke almost expected her to ask him if he was brushing his teeth every day. But, being Mara, she did her maternal fretting in more pragmatic ways and pressed a matte-gray object into Ben's hand.

"Humor me," she said, and kissed his forehead. "Carry this. You never know."

Ben stared into his palm. "Wow."

"That," she said, "was the best vibroblade the Empire could buy. It saved me more than once. A lightsaber is great, but a lightsaber and a vibroblade is even better."

"Plus a blaster," Ben said. He grinned. "That's better still. The triple whammy."

"That's my boy."

After Ben had left, Mara cleared the plates. "When did we produce a communally minded political analyst?"

"Too many Gorog buddies, maybe."

"Does that look like an out-of-control, screwed-up boy to you?"

"No," Luke said, "but it's not Jacen's influence that's making a man of him, even if he's the only one who seems to be able to handle Ben."

"Luke, we still have to do something."

"Oh, *now* we have to do something? What happened to 'Leave him with Jacen, he's good for the boy . . .'?" Luke almost had to bite his lip to avoid saying that he'd told her so, which he'd always thought was the mark of someone who wasn't looking for a solution to the problem, just points to score. "Besides, he doesn't seem to be getting corrupted by what's happening. Maybe he *is* that good man on the inside. Maybe you were right to make me let our kid join the secret police—"

"I meant about *Lumiya.*" Mara had a way of bracing her shoulders that said she knew she'd made a big mistake but he didn't have to rub her nose in it. "Okay, I've changed my mind. Jacen's gone bad. My fault we've wasted a few months placating Ben. Satisfied? Now what about the root cause of this?"

"We haven't picked up her trail again."

"And then what happens when we do?" Mara smacked the plates down on the counter so hard they rattled. "What are you going to do, hold her hand again?" He should never have told her that Lumiya had offered him her hand when they were fighting. It was eating away at her. "Because the poor old girl doesn't mean any harm? *Lumiya?* Queen of the stanging *Sith?*"

"There really was no ill intent in her."

Mara rolled her eyes. "Of course there wasn't. She doesn't want to kill *you*. She wants to kill our son." She grabbed Luke's face in both hands and made him look into her eyes. "Luke, you could have killed her. Cut her in two. Finished the job. But you didn't."

Luke felt inexplicably ashamed. "I couldn't."

"I know. We come from different schools of justice, don't we?"

"Sweetheart—"

"She's not your father, Luke. There's nothing good left in her to redeem. She's a threat that needs to be taken out, and that's what I'm trained to do, and you're *not*. Forget this *take her alive if possible* garbage. The only way anyone's taking her is *dead*."

Luke had had a feeling Mara might say that. He knew when she was building up to something. She might have thought she could keep things from him, but he knew her well enough by now to see the cogs grinding and the plan forming.

He'd missed his chance with Lumiya. He wouldn't get another.

"You're telling me you're going after her."

"You might tag along if you could be trusted not to go soft on her." Mara let him go and looked embarrassed. Her cheeks were flushed. "You can have Alema. She needs a serious attitude readjustment with a lightsaber, too. It's not as if we haven't got enough kill-crazy stalkers to go around."

No matter what happened, Luke knew he didn't have that assassin's ability to kill someone who wasn't trying to kill him right there and then. If he had . . .

So Ben wasn't the only one navigating a moral maze. Luke had been doing it for decades, but the maze was only acquiring more twists and turns each year.

"Let's see how much Jacen perks up with Lumiya gone," he said. *Wait, did I just bless an assassination?* "And with Alema out of the way, then Leia and Han can come back into the fold, and we can face this war as a family again."

Mara patted his cheek with a regretful smile and set a droid on cleaning the dishes. She spent the rest of the afternoon assembling and checking an array of weapons that definitely didn't come from a civilized age.

"I never knew you had one of *those*," he said, pointing to a blaster that had the widemouthed muzzle of a grenade launcher. "How are you planning to use it?"

"With a flechette cartridge. Let's see her try a lightwhip on *that*."

"Do you want to take my shoto?"

"You offering?"

"Good-luck token, maybe."

"Under-the-rib-cage token, more like. Unless that's all durasteel, too."

This was his wife. Sometimes he caught a glimpse of the woman she once had been, and she was a stranger for a second or two.

"How are you going to track her? She hides *very* well."

"I can *hunt* very well." Mara took the shoto hilt and spun it like a blade. "A little bait, a little investigation, and a little Force help." She ignited the energy beam. "Plus, if Alema is trailing after her, as seems to be the case, then one of them is going to slip up and show herself."

"Lumiya doesn't slip up."

"Well, she's not running the galaxy right now, so I guess she does sometimes . . ." Mara spun the shoto into the air and caught it by the hilt as it fell. "And she keeps showing up lately, so I'll be ready."

"Just keep me informed where you are, okay?"

"You'll know." Mara gave him her best *I-know-what-I'm-doing* grin. "And who better to go after a former Emperor's Hand than another one?"

"You did that before . . ."

"And that was before I had a son to worry about." The grin faded. "I'm much more dangerous now I have a cub to protect."

Luke had no doubt about that. But it was the first time in his life that he regretted not killing someone when he'd had the chance.

chapter four

To: *Chief of Defense Logistics*
From: *Supreme Commander, Galactic Alliance Defense Force*
CC: *Chief of State; OC GAG; Head of Defense Procurement*
Re: *Fleet supply and procurement concerns*

The shortfall in supplies in theater and the failure of equipment to meet standards are intolerable. You are to give Colonel Solo, OC GAG, every cooperation in resolving this situation as rapidly as possible. This is to be your top priority, and Colonel Solo is authorized to use any means necessary to achieve it.

Admiral Cha Niathal, SC GADF

DEFENSE PROCUREMENT AND SUPPLY AGENCY, CORUSCANT

"ARE YOU SURE?"

Jacen had no reason to disbelieve a legal-analyst droid. Metal lawyers were even more meticulous than flesh-and-blood ones. HM-3 clunked along beside him as they ambled up the apparently interminable corridor to the offices of the head of procurement, explaining the hurriedly assembled data as they went. Jacen believed in understanding the enemy, and that meant grinding through the tedium of small print. He was set on taking a lightsaber to a planet-sized ball of red tape.

"Yes, sir, this is routine." HM-3 reminded him a little of C-3PO—humanoid in shape, with a necessarily pedantic personality—but he was a sober dark gray and had a reassuring air of solid professional authority. "A piece of legislation that's overdue for reform. Would you like the full explanation, or a simplified lay-being's version?"

"Consider me as lay as they come."

"As the legislation stands, it takes the agreement of the Defense Council to change the regulations on procurement. It's designed to stop civil servants from bending the rules to line their pockets. Or to stop anyone from commissioning an entire army and its accompanying fleet and weapons without the Senate's knowledge, which I do believe happened not so long ago . . . you *might* want to look back at the final years of the Republic, sir."

Jacen mulled that over and tried to strip it down to basics. "So Senators have to vote on what flimsi to purchase and what flavor dry rations to serve to the troops. Monumental waste of time and expense, if you ask me."

"I admit it involves top-level decision makers in *very* low-level decisions, sir. But it's the law. Every time you want to change something about supplies, or any other minor administrative issue, you need Chief Omas or Admiral Niathal or someone else equally senior to rubber-stamp it. It's the same for other departments—health, education, *all* of them."

HM-3 seemed apologetic. Jacen had little patience with people who found comfort in impenetrable rules and ritual: He wanted things *done*.

"I don't want to take every complaint about hydrospanners and fuel inductors through committees." *How did I ever become the procurement go-to guy? Is Niathal sidelining me? Never mind. I'll learn a lot.* "Is there a way around this?"

"Actually, there is."

"Go on."

"It's a simple matter of giving *appropriate* officers of the GA—in the most general sense—the power to change regulations. To remove the requirement for every cough and spit to be dealt with by Senators."

"How do we do that?"

"By removing the requirement for approval by Defense Council members. Shall I draft an amendment, sir?"

"How does that work?"

"I draft a request for a change in the existing law to relieve regulatory burdens, so that order-making powers can be devolved to appropriate persons such as senior military officers and ministers of state without the need to refer the issue to committees, councils, or even the full Senate." HM-3 shuddered. It was a very human touch. "Give them something to debate, and the more trivial it is, the more hours they'll spend on it, because they can grasp the *small* concepts better, you see."

"Yes, but what happens to the amendment? And how long is that going to take?"

"If I table it today, then it goes before the weekly Policy and Resources Council in two days' time, and, as an appropriate person who already has the Chief of State's sanction, you can start changing what you need the next day."

Jacen clasped his hands behind his back and thought about it. This was making a new law to allow him to change laws.

Bizarre.

"I wonder how much the Defense Department spends on carpeting," HM-3 said peevishly, scanning the floor. Droids preferred smooth surfaces. "Here's *one* area where they could economize."

As he walked, Jacen was calculating how many simple decisions were mired in approvals, but he had the sensation of someone trying to get his attention. It was wholly in his head: he wondered if it was the voice again, and then realized it was his common sense screaming to be heard.

You're changing laws about changing laws. Think about that.

Jacen only had a vague idea about what use he might make of that beyond getting supplies moving, but it struck him as a promising area to address.

"What would I be limited to?" he asked.

"Well, there has to be a fail-safe in the wording or you'll never get P and R to agree to it, but if I were to cap the scope of this, say that the existing budget can't be exceeded, then that would satisfy them."

Legislation was terminally boring. No, it *should* have been. But something in it was forming a hard ball of an idea in Jacen's mind. "Would it be possible to word it so that if I come across any more stupid red tape in the process, I can change that, too? Even if I don't know where I'm likely to find it? I don't want some jobsworth holding up vital supplies because I didn't specify the right subsection of some obscure regulation."

"That would make it somewhat . . . open-ended."

"But it's just administration. It's not the constitution or a common charter."

HM-3 ground his gears quietly. "I'll word it generically so that you can change any administrative procedure you need to. The other fail-safe is that only *authorized* individuals can make use of this, and that can be limited to whomever the Chief of State decides. So there'll be no spending sprees on secret armies, and only a few very *visible*, accountable people can make use of it. That will reassure the P and R members." HM-3 went silent for a moment, consulting his agenda link. "I do believe the day after tomorrow is a very, very busy day for P and R, sir. I think the amendment will get through rather more quickly than usual."

It was a good day to bury the Legislative and Regulations Statute Amendment. Jacen smiled.

"You'll have to tell me more about how this fits in with the emergency measures legislation that Chief Omas already enacted."

"Full explanation, or—"

"—the lay-being's executive summary, please."

"The three of you can do anything you need to for the duration of the war. With Admiral Niathal, you are effectively a triumvirate. I have yet to hear Senator G'vli G'Sil take note of that, despite his position as head of the Security Council. The Defense Council is simply nodding everything through—when it actually meets, of course."

The thought took Jacen aback. He had his own plans for upending the galaxy, but they were large-scale, strategic, and focused on order, justice, and the benign application of military might. The petty minutiae of bureaucracy had never crossed his mind as a weapon in the battle for order.

He'd spent five years learning the most arcane Force techniques in the galaxy, but—again—he didn't have to use a single Force skill to gain power this time. It was simply a matter of using psychology to manipulate people around him.

This is what makes Jedi weaker and lazier. They instantly resort to Force techniques, without thinking.

HM-3 didn't have to remind him to look at the fall of the Republic. In his desire to understand the environment that had turned his grandfather from Anakin Skywalker into Darth Vader, he'd examined that final decade. Palpatine seemed to have grabbed most of his power by brilliant manipulation and understanding of people's weaknesses, not simply by channeling the power of the dark side.

Jacen and the droid reached the mighty carved doors of the procurement center. They were almost as fine as the doors to Chief Omas's office. No—they were actually *more* opulent. Jacen turned to his infallible legal adviser.

"Do you think it's *wrong* that we're effectively a triumvirate, Aitch-Em?" Jacen asked. "Undemocratic?"

"I'm not programmed for right and wrong, sir." HM-3 sounded a little disappointed, as if Jacen hadn't fully understood the complexity of his art. "I can tell you only what's legal and illegal, because they have definitions. *Right* has no parameters. *Justice* doesn't, either, nor *good*. Flesh has to make those decisions."

"Flesh makes a different decision on those every day, my friend." Jacen put his hand on the controls, and the splendid relief of an ancient Coruscanti cityscape split into two to admit him into the procurement offices.

I can change a law to let me change laws.

But can I use the law that lets me change laws to change that law itself?

He thought for a moment that he was enjoying a few childish seconds of playing at circular logic. Then it struck him he'd just had an insight of significant proportions.

"Colonel Solo," said the head of the procurement agency. Tav Vello was an edgy human male who looked in need of a good meal. "I've tasked one of my assistants to investigate the shortages. It might simply be a case of delays in the process."

"Is there anyone ahead of the fleet or the GAG in this line?" Jacen asked.

"Our suppliers do have other clients."

"I hope they're on our side."

"We source our equipment from allies."

"Are your people moving as fast as they can?"

"Of course they are, Colonel Solo. We're also looking for ways to streamline the process."

Jacen smiled. "So am I." He looked around the office. It wasn't gold-plated, but he was expecting to see some evidence of lack of frugality. "Now, about the cannon service packs. The parts that need swapping out frequently. I asked for an explanation of why there have been so many misfires."

Vello consulted his datapad with the air of a man with a very good defense, or at least a robust excuse. "We ran random sampling on those packs yesterday for all the main cannon specs, and the service packs we buy are adequate."

"But we don't want *adequate*. We want *best*."

"We do have budget constraints, sir."

"Is this decision made by a department?"

"There's a senior purchasing officer, yes."

Jacen knew there was only one way to focus people who didn't quite understand what *adequate* meant in the field. He turned to the droid. "Aitch, under the current powers, is there a mechanism by which I can co-opt civilian staff to carry out research?"

HM-3 hummed on the threshold of Jacen's normal hearing for a few seconds. "Yes, sir."

"Is there any restriction on location and conditions?"

"No, sir."

"That's what I like to hear." Jacen was starting to enjoy the rich

scope for inventiveness that regulations gave him. They didn't limit his options at all: they created new ones. He started to see the joy of the letter of the law. "I'd like to meet the chief purchasing officer who signed off on the cannon packs."

Vello looked slightly bemused. "I take responsibility for what my staff do, sir."

"That's very commendable, but I really want to understand the process, and that means getting to know the people. Understanding of the other person's situation is the key to this, I think."

Vello, still looking bewildered, went to summon the purchasing officer via his desk comm.

"No, that's quite all right," Jacen said. "I'll go to his office."

HM-3 made an inscrutable clicking sound as the three of them took the turbolift to the purchasing floor. They stepped out of the cab into an open-plan office that could have accommodated wandering herds without trouble. *Good.* Jacen wanted an audience. *Hearts and minds.*

"Let me introduce you to Biris Te Gaf," said Vello. "He's our senior purchasing officer for engineering support."

Te Gaf was visibly nervous, and his staff and co-workers—mainly humans, but Nimbanese, Gossams, and Sy Myrthian, too—feigned work while watching discreetly. Jacen could feel the pervading anxiety throughout the floor. Gaf offered a damp hand for shaking, and Jacen turned on his full charm. Te Gaf had a lot of data about why the cannon pack was fit for the job. It was a *very* good price, he told Jacen.

"But we have misfires and various problems to iron out," said Jacen. He checked that everyone could hear him, judging their attention by the close-range ripples in the Force and their body language. "I'd really like your help on this. I'm asking you to do some evaluation of the cannon pack."

"Of course, Colonel Solo. Anything I can do to help."

HM-3 leaned in close and whispered to Jacen. "Article five, subsection C-twenty-seven."

"I'm glad to hear that." Jacen smiled at the purchasing officer. "That's why, under article five, subsection C-twenty-seven of the Emergency Measures Act, I'm assigning you to the front-line ship that's had the most cannon misfires in the fleet, because there's no better place to gather facts than from the people who have to use this kit, and in the place where they have to use it." Jacen glanced around. Even with Force-enhanced hearing, he could detect very little breathing and no swallowing. "I'm more than happy to extend this field deployment to anyone who wants to better understand the end users' experience of procurement. Just say the word. We're always happy to accommodate you. In fact, I can guarantee you a ringside seat for the action."

Jacen smiled with all the diplomatic sweetness he'd learned from his mother and looked around the room, knowing he wouldn't be mown down by volunteers. Te Gef looked stricken. Jacen felt he'd focused everyone on the significance of their job more effectively, and that they now knew what would happen if they thought *adequate* was good enough.

If you think it's good enough, then it's good enough for you to use personally—on the front line.

HM-3 followed Jacen out of the building, and they took an air taxi back to the GAG headquarters. It took a little while because the traffic was heavier than usual, and by the time Jacen got back to his office, the arrangements to transfer one civilian—Te Gaf, Biris J.—to the *Ocean* were already being discussed by GAG personnel. Corporal Lekauf and two of the other 967 Commando troopers greeted him like a hero in the briefing room.

"That was a good clean thing you did there, sir," said one trooper, grinning. "My rifle parts feel more efficient already."

Lekauf gave him a thumbs-up. "Your grandfather would have done the same, sir. Nice move."

In these barracks, that was an honest compliment and not a warning of the temptations of the dark side. Jacen preferred the judgment of ordinary soldiers to the arcane philosophical debate of the Jedi Council.

It's all going to change.

No more wars flaring up in each generation.

No more career politicians wringing what they can out of the system.

No more talk of freedom *that just means a handful can do as they please while the rest struggle for survival.*

No wonder the old guard feared the Sith, if that was what they threatened—the end of chaos that served only the few.

Jacen returned the thumbs-up to Lekauf. "You ain't seen *nothing* yet."

HM-3 plucked out a datapad. "I'll keep you apprised of the progress of the amendment, Colonel Solo. Is that all for today?"

"I may consult you again. You make all this easier to understand."

"That's my job."

Jacen just wanted to check. He had the germ of an idea. "Funny thing, laws and regulations, aren't they? That amendment gives me— and others, of course—the ability to change the amended law itself, doesn't it? It's quite circular."

HM-3 didn't care about right and wrong: just legal and illegal. If Jacen had designs on manipulating the amendment for uses beyond speeding up the dispatch of medical supplies, then the droid didn't re- gard it as part of his remit.

"Yes," HM-3 said. "It is."

Jacen tackled the pile of intelligence reports that had stacked up on his desk with renewed enthusiasm. The air was alive with immi- nence, of things about to happen. The endless thoughts of whom he would have to kill to achieve his sacrifice had gone away for a while, but they'd be back. In the meantime, he had a new tool with which to effect change.

I can change the law that lets me change laws.

If I use that wisely, I can bypass the Senate when I need to.

The power of simple human reason was as effective as the Force some days.

TEKSHAR FALLS CASINO, KUAT CITY, KUAT

"What happened to the clones?" Mirta asked.

Kuat City stank of credits. Fett had never been able to un- derstand how an industrial society whose wealth was built on heavy engineering still had an ancient aristocracy. *Funny place. Anachronis- tic.* Ahead of him, the smarter part of Kuat City glittered, elegant towers and spires that seemed a refined echo of the industrial skyline of cranes in the orbital shipyards.

He knew Kuat well. He'd once saved its shipyards from an attempt to destroy them. He hoped the place was going to show him some gratitude.

"Cannon fodder," he said, answering Mirta at last. He brought the speeder bike to a halt by an arcade of smart shops. "They died."

"Not the one I saw. He said some left the army."

"The only way out," said Fett, "was death or desertion."

"None of them retired?"

"Depends what you mean by *retired*. I heard a few ended up in care homes run by well-meaning peace campaigners, though."

Mirta seemed to be working out what *retire* meant for men who were trained to kill, who'd been kept apart from regular society, and who had an artificially shortened life span. The slight jut of her chin— a sure sign she was annoyed—communicated itself through the helmet. There was only so much she could hide.

"Did you ever hunt deserters?"

"No." He'd seen plenty, though. "Didn't pay enough."

"Did you care about them, *Ba'buir?*"

Okay, she finds comfort in playing Mando. *But I'll never get used to that name.* "Not really."

"They were your brothers."

"No, they weren't." He motioned her to get off the speeder. "Blood isn't everything. You know that's the *Mando* way."

"But I bet you'll be shooting that clone a different line," she said. "How else are you going to get him to help you? Beat it out of him? He looks as tough as you are."

"Maybe I'll just ask nicely," said Fett. "Right now I need to walk into the Tekshar and have a chat with Fraig. That might be a little inconvenient for him."

The Tekshar Falls was one of those feats of architectural near impossibility at which the Kuati excelled. Other establishments in the galaxy had impressive water features, but the Tekshar was a waterfall, a raging, hammering torrent from a river diverted at vast expense into the entertainment center of the city. It provided its own hydroelectric

power, which was just as well given the ferocious array of lights that pierced the curtains of water. The casino was set within the waterfall it-self, part construction, part natural stone, with turrets jutting through the water like tree fungi. To get to the entrance, gamblers had to walk through water plummeting five hundred meters.

"Pity, I've just had my hair done," Mirta said, solidly encased in armor from head to toe. "Is this how they stop the riffraff from com-ing in?"

"We *are* the riffraff," said Fett. "And we're going in."

He paused to hack into the Kuat police database from his HUD system. They wouldn't mind. He was just contributing to law and order around here. Images of scumbags, petty villains, and serious bad boys—and girls—scrolled down the display inside his helmet. He waited, and shortly FRAIG, L., appeared. For gangland vermin, Fraig looked remarkably respectable: fresh-faced and framed with gold curls that would have made a mother weep. Fett suspected that if Fraig still had a mother, he'd have sold her to a Hutt by now.

"So you're just going to stroll in," said Mirta.

"I only want to ask him a question."

"It's never that easy, is it?"

"We'll see." Fett strode down the tree-lined boulevard that led to the foot of the falls and forked around it. Only the stupidly wealthy had the time to gamble this early. It said a lot for Fraig's business acu-men. "There's no reason for him to get upset. Just check that your jet pack's primed."

"We might be leaving rapidly, then . . . ," Mirta said, keeping up with him without apparent effort, a reminder that he was slowing down. "Will they make a fuss about letting us in dressed like this?"

"It's all about making an entrance." Fett wiped the windborne spray from his visor. "People usually find my dress acceptable. Sooner or later."

He walked straight across the bridge at the wall of roaring water and churning white foam. The falls parted like a curtain to create a wide portal. Behind, the casino was a vividly lit—and completely dry—haven.

"Very impressive," said Mirta.

It was a nice trick played by automated force fields triggered by a motion sensor. But it was, as he often thought, all about presentation. A little theater. It always helped.

"Keep up," he said.

The lobby of the casino was a study in opulence, as if someone had taken a bet on how many credits they could spend on each square meter. It was everything Fett didn't care for: flocked wall coverings, gilding, mirrors, and low-level lighting, all the trappings of illusion, and hard to clean, too. The lobby parted into two sections, one leading to the restaurant and the other to the gaming tables. Fett consulted his investment portfolio via his HUD. He noted TIRUAL CONSTRUCTION HOLDINGS.

"Let's not do too much damage," he said. "I think I have shares in this place."

There was a steward at the front desk and a few very large assistants—humans, Trandoshans, and Gran—walking in slow, considered circles around the thick purple carpet that dragged at Fett's boots like tar. He'd never seen a Trandoshan in a formal suit before, and wondered what poor old Bossk would have made of that. It was also unusual to see a Gran in this line of work. It was clear none of them was there to help diners make informed choices from the wine list.

The steward was scanning a screen in his desk, probably matching Fett's image to the database of guests he needed to recognize for one reason or another. Judging by his sudden flinch, he'd found FETT.

"Do you have proof of identity, sir?"

Fett touched his blaster. "This used to do nicely."

The steward—human, male, utterly ugly—was doing a very good job of not wetting his pants. Fett had to hand it to him. "Ah . . . haven't seen you here in a long time, sir."

"I've come to visit someone." Fett indicated Mirta with a thumb gesture. "With my associate."

"Will that *seeing* require repairs afterward?"

Fett flicked a very large-denomination credit chip onto the desk. "Keep the change in case it does. Where's Fraig?"

Credits talked. Blasters talked, too, but credits could whisper menacingly every bit as well.

"He's hosting a private sabacc game in his suite on the thirtieth floor, sir." The steward smiled valiantly and snapped his fingers at the hired help. "I'll let him know you're on the way up."

The nattily attired Trandoshan rushed to his summons, looking like he'd picked the wrong outfit for a costume party.

"Take . . . the . . . er . . . President of Mandalore up to Master Fraig's suite. All drinks on the house."

So they didn't quite grasp what being Mandalore meant. That was okay, because Fett didn't, either. Mirta stifled laughter, but only Fett heard it. He switched to the helmet comlink with a blink.

"So you *do* have shares here, *Ba'buir*," she said.

"Depending on how many guests Fraig's got, I might need your help. Try not to kill them unless they ask for it."

"*Yessir*, Mister President!"

"I liked you better without a sense of humor."

He didn't dislike Mirta. She'd tried to kill him, but that was a couple of months ago, and things had moved on. She worked hard and she wasn't mired in fluffy trivia like fashion and holovids. She was strong in every sense. Beviin—and Fett *listened* to Beviin—said she was a real *Mando'ad,* a solid Mandalorian woman, because she could shoot straight, cook passably well, and had the shoulders of an armorsmith. *Mando'ade* valued the frontier kind of female, not decorative trophies who couldn't even dig a defensive entrenchment.

She's just like Sintas. Not as pretty, but she's so much like her.

He hadn't known Ailyn long enough to tell if Mirta took after her mother. *Sin. I used to call her Sin, and she called me Bo.* Did Mirta have a nickname? What had Sintas told Ailyn about him, and what had Ailyn told Mirta, to breed such hatred toward him?

Fett pulled his attention back to the present and followed the Trandoshan, aware of a full 360-degree vista around him, the dulled pain in his guts, and the fact that the closer he got to death, the more he thought about people who hadn't been on his mind in a long, long time.

The turbolift doors opened onto a floor of the same thick purple carpet as the lobby, with small salons leading off it. Gaming tables rattled, clicked, and flashed with lives ruined and fortunes lost. Even through his helmet's filter, he could smell the cloying amalgam of a hundred different perfumes distilled from plants facing extinction and parts of animals he didn't even want to think about.

The Trandoshan led them along a corridor to an imposing set of gilded doors, then beat a lumbering retreat. The doors parted and Fett found himself visor-to-nose with a Hamadryas who didn't seem to know how to blink. Behind him, a group of six splendidly dressed gamblers—three human males, two females, and a Weequay—sat around a gilt-framed sabacc table with Fraig. There were two more heavies standing by the kitchen doors, probably on drinks patrol.

"Master Fett," said Fraig, not looking up from the table. "How good to meet you."

Fraig had a great hand. Fett could see it embedded in the table's display as he loomed over him. It was a pity to interrupt. His guests were trying to concentrate on the sabacc game, but it was hard to give the cards full attention when there were two bounty hunters paying an unexpected visit. They all found reasons to go to the kitchen to top up their drinks while the Hamadryas watched silently, one hand now on his holster.

"Got a few questions for you," Fett said. "About your predecessor."

"Depends on what you want to know." Fraig was as well spoken as his hair was coiffed. His gangster dad must have sent him to a very exclusive school. But he hadn't been tutored in the subtle art of putting his hand under the table to check his hold-out blaster discreetly. Fett hoped he didn't have to shoot the man before he got some answers. "I do hope you haven't been sent by Cherit's associates to express their displeasure."

"I'm not going to kill you," Fett said. "If I did that, then you wouldn't be able to tell me things. And I *want* you to tell me things. I'm a curious man."

The Hamadryas on the door already had his blaster visible on his belt, but Mirta had him covered. Fett could see from their HUD comlink connection that she was watching him, the helmet sensors responding to her eye movements.

Fraig shrugged. "What exactly do you want me to tell you?"

"The Mandalorian who killed Cherit. I need to find him."

Fraig had the kind of smile that spread like a crack in ice. "I've been asked some subtle questions, but that's a good one. I assure you I didn't order Cherit's death."

"I don't care if you sent a wreath and took care of his widow. Do you know where I can find the man who killed him?"

"Shall we step outside onto the balcony?" Fraig gestured and picked up his drink. "It's a sensitive matter to discuss in front of my guests."

"Suit yourself," said Fett, and decided instantly where he was prepared to be maneuvered. *Step outside. Right.* Mirta stood guard at the open doors, but the Hamadryas bodyguard tried to move her out of the way. He made the mistake of putting his hand on her back, and a little too low at that. She simply raised her clenched fist to shoulder height and ejected her gauntlet vibroblade.

"Touch me again, *chakaar*, and I'll ram this into your carotid artery."

"I haven't got one."

"Then I'll have to keep stabbing you until I find somewhere else that bleeds copiously."

Fraig intervened. "Serku, let's not upset the lady, shall we? Let her wait wherever she wishes."

Fraig was making a lot of mistakes tonight for a crime boss. It was just as well Fett always assumed the worst. Fraig might have thought that a balcony reduced Fett's options, but it didn't represent much of a problem for a man with a jet pack. Fraig didn't have one. He also lacked a fibercord line.

This wouldn't take long.

Amateurs.

Fett had to fight an urge to explain to Fraig how to do it right. Out on the balcony, Kuat City's lights shimmered through a veil of rushing water in the dusk. An overhang diverted the water a couple of meters from the face of the building.

Fett leaned one hand on the rail, feigning casual disinterest but actually testing the strength of the metal. He cast an eye over Fraig to estimate his weight. "Let me repeat that simple question. Tell me anything you know about the Mandalorian who whacked your predecessor."

"I had nothing to do with it. Cherit upset a lot of folks. Occupational hazard."

"Question still stands. I'll bet your organization was keen to find out, too."

"We didn't know who he was. All we knew was that he had a grudge about a certain Twi'lek clan. We do business with Twi'leks in the *entertainment* industry."

"I'll bet." Fraig meant Twi'lek girls. "What kind of grudge?"

"He didn't think we were treating them properly. We lost a couple of very popular entertainers thanks to him."

Fraig was lying scum. And the clone in Mandalorian armor was settling a score for some Twi'leks, but he wasn't a bounty hunter. Another link, then: personal, not professional.

Time. He didn't have *time* for this.

"Seen him since?"

"No."

"Want to tell me who the Twi'leks were?"

"Why do you want this man so badly? It has to be something big for you to be hunting him." Fraig examined his manicured nails. "Or perhaps some of my associates regret Cherit's passing, so they've hired you to come after me."

"Not for hire right now." Fett could never understand why they didn't listen. They never heard what he said. He played it straight, and they always looked for a second meaning. "I want the *Mando* in one piece. I need him to do something for me."

Fraig had missed his chance. Fett switched to the helmet comlink and got Mirta's attention, which was fixed on him—and the Hamadryas—anyway. "I'm just going to help our friend remember a few things."

Useful stuff, fibercord.

Fett shot out the line in a loop from his backpack and whipped it around Fraig, jammed the grappling hook between the bars, and shoved him over the railing. It took two seconds. Fraig screamed, clinging to the top rail, but a good hard whack on the knuckles with the butt of the blaster made the scumbag let go. Fraig plummeted and Fett braced for the inevitable thump into the rail when the rope ran out. It nearly winded him. Fraig bounced and twisted in the line's

strangling grip, still shrieking. Fett kept a few meters of line secured in reserve in the winch assembly.

Mirta was taking good care of the Hamadryas. She'd half closed the transparisteel doors on him, but the bodyguard wedged his body in the gap and tried to get a blaster shot through the opening. His arm was trapped. Fett watched, impressed, as Mirta head-butted the guard a second time, shoved the vibroblade into his thigh, and forced him— shrieking in pain, nice touch—back through the doors so that they crashed shut. Then she fired a few rounds into the controls.

"Make it quick, *Ba'buir*." She flexed her shoulders as if easing torn neck muscles. "The doors might be blasterproof, but they'll get them open sooner or later."

Fett peered over the side. Fraig was twisting helplessly like a devee hooked on a fishing line, making gasping sounds. The line was tight around his waist and chest. He was dangling fifteen meters below the rail.

"Don't struggle, and think calm thoughts," Fett called. "It helps you remember. And it'll stop you from slipping out of the loop."

"You're crazy—I'll have your throat cut for this—"

"You're on the end of a line. I'm on solid ground. Think about it."

"You're a dead man."

"Perceptive to the last. Give me names, vermin."

"I tell you I didn't pay the Mando. I'm glad he whacked Cherit, but I never paid him to do it—"

"Try again."

Fraig's voice was almost drowned out by the roar of the waterfall behind him. "The Twi'leks were from some family called Himar."

"Good start." Fett paid out another meter of line with a jolt. Fraig shrieked as he slipped farther toward the permacrete, stone, and raging water a hundred meters below. "Is that helping? Memory often needs a trigger."

Himar. Any *Mando* who pitched in hard to play the hero for a couple of dancers would be known in the Twi'lek community. It didn't happen that often; nobody else cared what happened to Twi'lek girls. Fett had his lead. He'd have a contact somewhere—and if he didn't, Beviin would. Beviin wouldn't press him to find out why.

"Anything else you want to get off your chest?"

"I don't know the guy, Fett. But I know you're going to regret this."

Fett could hear the dull rhythmic thuds of Fraig's bodyguards trying to smash the doors apart. "If I find you've given me a load of garbage, I'll be back to finish the job."

He braced his boot on the bottom rail and began winching in the gangster. Mirta stood next to him with her blaster trained on the doors.

"You're going soft. Why are you reeling him back in?"

"I want the fibercord back. It's my favorite Ultra-fine."

"When you get him on the balcony, I'll tranquilize him . . ."

"Then back to *Slave I*. Scenic route."

"You're lucky we've got jets."

"I wouldn't have come up here if I hadn't." Fett felt the sweat breaking out and running down his spine. This would have been an easier task a few years ago. "And I wouldn't have gone much above thirty floors anyway."

"Why?"

"Hundred-meter line. In case I had to rappel down."

Fraig's face was two meters away now. He'd stopped yelling and settled for labored breathing.

"I haven't got a hundred-meter line," Mirta said.

"Lucky you've got jets, then." He heaved Fraig over the rail in a tangled heap, and Mirta delivered a roundhouse punch that laid the man out. If that was her tranquilizer treatment, she was a born medic. "Time to go."

Mirta shot off at an awkward angle and crashed through the sheet of water ahead of him; there was no force field up here to part the falls. When Fett looked down, he could see speeders crisscrossing the plaza on either side of the boulevard. He needed to land and find the speeder bike: jets were great for fast exits, but the flame made both of them conspicuous targets in the night sky.

The speeder was still where he'd left it, primed with a detonator and hidden in bushes on the edge of a park. Both the painkiller and the adrenaline were wearing off at the same time, and Fett had never been

more conscious of the reason for his search. He set off for the landing strip at top speed down freight lanes that had the lightest traffic, noting that Mirta was happily fixing a grenade launcher attachment to her blaster with both hands and gripping the saddle of the speeder with her knees. She looked like she was used to fast getaways.

"You're doing okay for a dead man, *Ba'buir*."

"Your dad trained you well, too."

"Most of that I learned from Mama."

"Well . . . she did a good job of it."

Fett took one hand off the bars and activated *Slave I*'s remote controls. Her drives would be primed: he could drop the speeder into the cargo hold and get off this planet inside a minute. In his HUD display, he was already scanning databases for that Twi'lek family name.

This was the one time he felt truly, thrillingly alive: when he was winning, being the best, surviving. *Is that it? Is that all I can do?* He almost envied the Beviins and Carids of this world, who delighted in simple things like good food and family. But there was a clean, uncomplicated satisfaction in danger. It erased worries and fears and memories. There was only the moment, and surviving it.

Fett concentrated on feeling good and ignoring the pain right up to the time his rearview caught speeder headlights closing fast and Mirta turned to level her blaster.

"They must be calling in our course," she said. "You think it's Fraig's grunts, or security?"

"We won't get the police's attention until you fire that blaster." His motion sensors showed two speeders in pursuit, and two coming at them from the right on the crossroads ahead. Another single speeder was approaching from the left. They might have been ordinary citizens unlucky enough to be on the same route, or they might have been rushing to intercept him. If he timed it right, he could slip between them and give Mirta a clean shot at the speeders behind. He gunned the drive.

Fett counted down the seconds. He was almost at the crossroads, but he wasn't going to make it. From the right, one shot in front of him, and he raised his arm to give it a burst of flamethrower, but the rider suddenly fell sideways and crashed to the ground without a shot being fired. Two speeders heading the other way soared to avoid it.

Fett watched the speeder approaching from the left cut across him without even slowing down.

He heard a loud crash, but no *ba-dapp* of a discharging blaster: had they collided? Had they hit someone who happened to be on the wrong road at the wrong time?

Mirta fired a grenade. "Gotcha!" A ball of flame lit up the night. "One down, one to go. Reloading."

"Can't see the third speeder."

"Maybe they crashed."

"We've got a couple of minutes before the police join in," Fett said.

"Hey, where did he—"

There was a massive *whoomp* of a white-hot explosion behind them. Fett saw the debris falling hot and red in the rearview of his HUD. "Good shot."

"Not me. Didn't fire."

"What is this, a crash epidemic?"

"I think we have help."

"I hate help I didn't ask for."

But help it was, so he took the breathing space with grudgingly grateful caution. Maybe their invisible benefactor was saving them for himself. *Slave I* was standing between two battered freighters, looking nothing special to anyone who didn't know the ship, just an old Firespray idling her drives.

Fett grounded the speeder bike and ran for the ship. Who would pick off Fraig's morons for him? Generosity like that came with a price. Fett left Mirta to dock the speeder in the hold and climbed up into the cockpit.

"Come on, girl, what's keeping you?" He tapped the console switches and *Slave I* whined up to full power, a faint tremor passing through her airframe. It said *safe*. It said *home*. It was the most reassuring sound he knew. "You've got twenty seconds before I close the cargo hatch."

There was no answer, and just as that fact registered, *Slave I*'s entry warning light flashed. There was someone else on board. The systems didn't recognize them.

"Mirta? *Mirta!*"

The internal security cams showed nothing but the speeder. Fett grabbed his blaster and went aft to check. Even through the helmet filter, he could smell a strong, oily stench that he hadn't smelled in years.

He couldn't quite place it, but he knew it.

The speeder was stowed. The hatch was open. He raised the blaster and wondered whether to just seal the hatch and launch *Slave I,* and hate himself for the rest of his life, what was left of it.

Dad wouldn't have left you stranded. He'd have risked anything for you.

Fett had abandoned quite a few people over the years. He'd even left Sintas wounded the last time he'd seen her—the very last time. It had seemed the right decision then.

And you wonder why your daughter and granddaughter tried to kill you.

Fett stood to one side of the hatch. His sensors showed him two shapes on the ramp, one humanoid and one animal whose form wasn't clearly defined. He counted to three and came out, blaster and flamethrower aimed.

Mirta, minus helmet, was in the tight headlock of a Mandalorian in gray armor, and a large gold-furred animal had its huge jaws locked around her leg, trailing a curtain of drool. It wasn't attacking: it was frozen, pinning her down—and *stinking.*

And she didn't look scared. Just embarrassed.

Fett stared down the barrel of a custom Verpine rifle aimed one-handed, and understood why he'd heard no blasterfire when the speeder bikes dropped from the air. Verpines were silent.

"Well, well . . . ," said the Mandalorian in gray armor. He really *did* have a very fine pair of gray leather gloves. "It's little *Bob'ika.* Last time we met, my brother was shoving your head down the 'freshers to teach you some manners. What do you want me for, *ner vod?*"

GALACTIC ALLIANCE GUARD BRIEFING ROOM,
GAG HQ, CORUSCANT

Ben was glad to be back among people he trusted.

The sea of black uniforms might have been a sinister sight to some people, but to him they felt like a brotherhood—like family. He was in that rare position of being young enough to be treated like one of the troopers despite his officer status, and he liked that. The sense of camaraderie and the knowledge that everyone watched everyone else's back was both comforting and thrilling.

He settled into a seat on the end of a row in the briefing room. A trooper called Almak nudged him.

"Nice vacation? Glad you could fit us into your busy schedule, sir."

"Couldn't wait to get back."

"You didn't miss much," Almak said. "Been a bit quieter. I think we've broken the back of the Corellian networks."

"I always miss the good stuff."

A couple of the other troopers in the row in front turned in their seats and joined in. "We'll find some excitement for you."

"Or some filing . . ."

" 'Freshers need a good clean. Here's a toothbrush."

Ben grinned and lobbed a pellet of flimsi at them. It was good to be part of a team. It was good to have friends. They didn't see him as Son of Skywalker, Jedi to be feared. He was just Ben, and they looked out for him as they always seemed to for young officers they liked.

And they never asked him where he'd been. Everything was on a need-to-know basis.

But the spate of bombings seemed to be over for the time being. It was just a case of working out who to keep an eye on and round up next. Corellians, Bothans . . . and now Fondorians.

Captain Lon Shevu strode onto the dais at the front of the room, looking as committed as ever, but Ben felt the reluctance and misgivings in him. He could sense it in a few of the other troopers, too, generally the ones who'd been in the CSF. Jacen followed Shevu and got instant undivided attention. Jacen could do that: Ben wasn't sure if he envied him or not. It was interesting that he seemed to enjoy being the focus for ordinary beings but chose to hide himself from Force-sensitives. It was as if he only wanted to be seen by the mundane world.

I have to learn how to do that. Mom says I did it as a little kid, but that was by instinct, like babies swimming. I want to learn how to do it like Jacen does.

"Brief for the next forty-eight hours, ladies and gentlemen," said Jacen. "We're moving into a different phase. The priority now is to look for professionals—Confederation intelligence agents. Now, normally we'd leave that to our colleagues in Alliance Intel, but seeing as we've got all their best operatives—" Applause and laughter interrupted him. He paused with a big grin and picked up again. "—seeing as we got the pick of the litter, we'll be helping them out. We'll also be providing close protection for Chief Omas and key ministers, to relieve CSF, and monitoring for them. Results of interrogation suggest we might be looking at more targeted and professional assassination attempts—as in government agents, not just disgruntled amateurs and bounty hunters."

A hand was raised at the front. Ben couldn't see who it was. "What's *monitoring* in this context, sir?"

Jacen flashed a holoimage onto the screen behind him. It showed a diagram of the various routes by which GA ministers could be reached, physically or virtually: offices, home addresses, private clubs, routes to the Senate, comlinks. "Like this," he said.

"Are we *allowed* to tap Senators' comlinks, sir?" asked Shevu.

"Under the Emergency Measures Act, we're authorized to carry out any surveillance to prevent acts of violence against ministers of state and visiting allies."

Shevu's face was unreadable, but Ben felt the sharp unhappiness in him. Now, *there* was a guy who knew how to conceal what he was thinking. Ben wondered if that was a more useful skill than hiding in the Force.

Tapping Senators' comlinks didn't seem to bother anyone else at the briefing. Ben couldn't see the problem, either. It made sense, for their own protection. Jacen tasked squads to their roles, and there was discussion about supplies.

"Draw up a wish list," Jacen said, beaming. "I think we've eased the supply situation. Or we will have, by the end of this week."

There was a ripple of laughter. "Did you persuade them to see things your way, sir?"

"Oh, I just made sure the flimsi was in order . . ."

There was more laughter and a ripple of applause. For a moment, Ben felt a conspiratorial closeness between Jacen and the troopers. It was genuine: Jacen wasn't doing his charisma act to persuade people to do what he wanted, although he was very good at that. He enjoyed the company of his troops, and they enjoyed his. There was a sense of shared danger and that the rest of the world wasn't part of all this. Ben took mental notes about the art of effortless leadership.

The briefing broke up. Ben hung back to talk to Jacen, getting a few joking comments about his recent absence as the troopers filed out, and giving as good as he got. He felt a sudden pressure at the back of his head, and when he looked around, Jacen was watching him from the side of the dais, smiling slightly.

"They like you," he said. "That's good for an officer, as long as you're liked for the right reasons."

"Isn't it important to be respected instead?"

"What's respect, Ben?"

Ben pondered the question, hearing a subtle test in it. "Thinking that a person does something right, and that they do it better than you, and so you feel positive toward them."

"Excellent."

"That's not the same as being liked, though, is it?"

"Not at all. We can respect those we dislike," Jacen said. "The way to be liked by your men is this—that they believe that you would never spend their lives cheaply, that their welfare comes first, and that you wouldn't ask them to do anything that you wouldn't do yourself. To share their trials and triumphs without being one of them, and they know that's how it has to be—because they know an officer has to make decisions that cost lives, and that's something you can only do if you remain sufficiently separate."

Ben hadn't lost a trooper from 967 Commando yet. In fact, they'd had no fatalities or even serious injuries. They led charmed lives as far as the rest of the military were concerned. He had no idea how he'd feel if he had to put them in a position where deaths were inevitable.

Jacen seemed to read his mind again. "Until you can make those decisions, you're not safe to lead."

"But it's easier if you're prepared to die yourself, right?" Ben suddenly felt much better about Lumiya's attempt on his life. He knew it was her now, piecing together what had happened on Ziost and what Mom had told him. But it was okay. He could look all the 967 in the

eye now. "Because if you're willing to make the same sacrifice, that's the one thing that matters."

Jacen leaned close to him. "It *inspires*. It's the ultimate act of honesty with your troops."

Ben knew that was how Jacen led, and why everyone was so loyal to him. He led from the front, and he loved being in the thick of the fighting. The fact that as a Jedi he had survival advantages they didn't have rarely seemed to cross their minds.

"I don't know which way I'll jump when the time comes," Ben said. "Nobody does. But I'll try to do what's right for the majority."

Jacen's smile was utterly luminous for a moment, but then it faded as if he'd recalled something awful. His Force presence vanished for a few seconds and then returned. That was weird, Ben thought: Jacen was standing right next to him, so what was he hiding from?

"Can you teach me to do that?" Ben asked. "Hide in the Force?"

Jacen seemed shaken. "Why?"

"Because Lumiya is trying to kill me. I thought it might come in handy." *And for avoiding Mom and Dad sometimes. Yes, it would be handy.* "Mom says she's got evidence that I killed—that Lumiya *thinks* I killed her daughter. I don't remember a thing about what happened on that asteroid, Jacen, but maybe it doesn't matter, because Lumiya believes it, and I bet she was behind what happened on Ziost."

Jacen's face was carefully blank. Ben couldn't tell what he was thinking now, not even from the Force.

"Yes, why not?" Jacen said. His voice was softer, almost hesitant. "Don't you worry about Lumiya. She's not up to killing you."

"When can we start?"

"It's very simple."

"Yeah," Ben said dubiously.

"No, it is. The *principle* is simple—it's the practice that's hard. It might take you years to master it." Jacen motioned him to sit down on the floor. "Come on. Meditation position."

Ben sat down cross-legged and closed his eyes automatically, taking deeper and slower breaths until he reached the stage where the world beyond him seemed distant and he was hyperaware of his own body, even the movement of blood in his veins.

Jacen's voice seemed to be coming from another time and place. "You're contained. The world can't touch you."

"Yes."

"Now break the shell. Break the container." Jacen's tone was even and soothing. "See the world in its component atoms. See yourself as atoms, too. Find the line where you end and the world begins."

Ben visualized the room around him and the air in it. It became a frozen snowfall of varying density, some particles clustered, some scattered; then he looked into himself, and saw the microscopic unevenness of the surface of his skin, and the overlapping plates of keratin in his hair, and then beyond that to where he was just like the room around him—a snowstorm of molecules. Some of the room was within him as oxygen and dust, and some of him was in the room as fragments of skin and droplets of water.

There was no line. There was no edge that divided Ben Skywalker from the room, or from Coruscant, or from the galaxy. He merged with it all, and it merged with him. There was nothing solid: just a warm, drifting sea of molecules, some of which assembled loosely and long enough to be Ben Skywalker.

"So you *can* do it . . ."

Jacen's voice drifted from a long way away. Ben suddenly felt as if he were dissolving and would never be whole again. Panic gripped him. He jerked his eyes open with a massive effort like tearing open rock with his bare hands, an effort so immense that he found himself gasping for air.

"Oh . . . wow . . ."

"Now," Jacen said softly, "you see why practice is necessary. But full marks for technique."

"How does that hide me?"

"You blend with the universe. Think of it as Force camouflage. The trick is to become so comfortable with it that you can slip into this state of being . . . *dissolved,* yet still carry on functioning, fully aware."

Ben couldn't even manage another *wow.* He was absolutely determined to master the technique, and at the same time scared by it because it felt like a seductive, comfortable death. He was afraid he might sink so deeply into it that he'd never get out again.

It was as close as he'd ever come to both knowing *and* feeling what the Force was. He felt he'd never be the same again, or see the world in quite the same way.

Wow.

If only all his Force knowledge had manifested itself that fast and that vividly.

"You need to practice regularly," said Jacen.

Ben nodded, worried about looking too enthusiastic. It was more than just a useful way to evade his father now. It was worth pursuing in its own right, for the sheer sensation of it.

"I will," he said. The moment of ecstatic revelation had passed, and he felt oddly chilled. "Any orders for me? Or am I just going to be listening to comlinks now?"

"Oh, I have a mission for you."

"Like the Amulet?" Maybe he shouldn't have said it, but he felt bad about the whole thing, as if it had been not only a waste of a man's life but also nowhere near as important as he'd been led to believe. He hated being humored. "I can handle the truth, Jacen. You'd be surprised."

Jacen was all serene composure. "I've got a job that only you can do, and it's critical. You might not want to accept the mission."

"If it's an order, it's an order."

"Better hear it first." Jacen reached into his jacket and pulled out a datapad. "Read this. It's the original sources of the intelligence I received, so you can judge for yourself."

Ben took the datapad and studied the screen. There were transcripts of comlink conversations, and even grainy images of a meeting taken from such an odd angle that it must have been captured by a spy droid in a very awkward location, probably on the top of a cupboard. Men in expensive suits and tunics, sipping caf and talking in hushed tones: a man with well-cut dark hair, younger than Jacen. Ben recognized him as Dur Gejjen.

"That's the Corellian Prime Minister," he said.

"That's all intel gathered from our contacts inside the Corellian government offices. Read on."

There was discussion of *driving a wedge* between Hapes and the

Galactic Alliance. It sounded like the usual political maneuvering that always bored Ben until he started to read recurring phrases, like *Queen Mother* and *seeing the disadvantages* of siding with the Alliance.

And then there were references to *removing obstacles*. It all fell into place when he flicked to the next holoimage and saw discussion of *appropriate bounty hunters* and who might be willing to operate in the Hapan royal house.

Ben might have been bored by politics, but he understood better than he imagined, and he knew he *had* to if he wanted to survive.

"This is about Tenel Ka."

"Correct."

"Gejjen really *did* plan the attack on her, then."

"Correct. We finally have hard evidence, and so we can act."

Ben should have felt outrage, he knew, but what filled him then was despair that people found it so easy and so necessary to plot to kill each other. It was happening to his own family, and to him, and it was happening between heads of state.

They were all crazy. They'd lost all reason. Or was this the way the adult world really worked, doing all the stupid, cruel, destructive, impulsive things that they swore they'd grown out of?

"What do you want me to do?" Ben asked, pretty sure what the answer would be.

"Assassinate Gejjen." Jacen rubbed his forehead wearily. "He's a piece of work, and he'll destabilize our allies. There's no negotiating with a man who routinely resorts to state-sponsored assassination like that. The Corellians need to know we can reach out and take them, too. Sober them up a bit. *Way* too cocky."

"Isn't that what we're doing, though? How is our assassination different from theirs? Won't it just lead to more killings?"

"You want to do this by the book? Okay, call Corellian Security and report Gejjen for conspiracy to murder. Oh, and for having Thrackan Sal-Solo assassinated, too, even if we can't call my father in court to testify to that. Let's see how fast they arrest him."

"I know . . ."

"You don't have to do it." Jacen had that slightly wounded tone that said quite the opposite. "But you proved you were competent at

covert ops when we hit Centerpoint, and you can get close to Gejjen a lot more easily than some big hairy commando like Duvil. You can look like a harmless teenager."

I am a teenager . . . and I'm usually pretty harmless. But Ben had a point. If anyone was going to do it—and the fact that Jacen had mentioned it meant he'd already made up his mind—then Ben had the best chance of getting close enough to Gejjen without being spotted.

Jacen stared at him, head slightly on one side, with that almost-smile that said he was sure Ben was going to say yes.

"I can't exactly ask Boba Fett to do this, can I?" Jacen said quietly.

"They're taking bets on how and when he's going to try to kill you." *An officer shouldn't ask his troops to do anything he wouldn't do himself. I can't leave this to one of the 967.* "Okay. I agree Gejjen's rotten to the core. And once we can go public on this stuff . . . then the warrant on Uncle Han and Aunt Leia is dropped, right?"

"I can't, Ben." Jacen sighed. "Everyone knows they had nothing to do with the attack. But they're still working for Corellia, and I can't suspend arrest warrants just because they're family. That's how corruption starts. Besides, what example does that set the troops? Will they ever trust us again if officers bend the rules for family?"

Ben was reminded once more that he didn't take after his father, who would have insisted on arresting Gejjen.

It was dirty work, but he should have realized that by now. He couldn't hand it on to someone else if he wanted to think of himself as a man—or an officer.

"I'll send you with good backup," Jacen said. "Shevu and Lekauf. Our contacts on Corellia are working out a time and place. You'll have to be ready to go at a moment's notice."

Ben wondered how he was meant to kill Gejjen. It seemed a sacrilege to use a lightsaber. He concentrated on the practicalities and logistics, pondering briefly on where the hit would take place, how close he could get, and what would work best—blaster, projectile, or something more exotic.

There was his mother's vibroblade, but Ben wasn't sure he had the stomach to use it in cold blood. He only knew how to defend himself and others, not how to hunt for the sole purpose of killing.

"You can do it," said Jacen, who always seemed to know his

thoughts. "Same techniques you use already—just a different mind-set. Go talk to the sniper team."

The best person he could have consulted on the finer points of assassination was his mother, once the Emperor's Hands, the best assassin of her day. *Hey, Mom, is a head shot best? Double tap or triple? Do you think a silenced blaster is a better option than a lightsaber?*

Ben knew that was a conversation he could never have.

Jacen watched Ben leave the briefing room and took a deep breath. It was all he could do to keep the breath steady and not let it become a sob.

I can't do this.

I can't kill him.

If the Force had made things clearer, explained explicitly what he had to do—go here, kill this, recite that—then it might have been easier. It was *not knowing* that was unbearable; not knowing if he was reading too much into the uncertain interpretations of knotted tassels, into Lumiya's vague pronouncements, into parallels with his grandfather that might not even have been there. He knew his destiny was to be a Sith Lord more surely than he knew anything, but it was this final test that left him in agonized turmoil.

What if I'm wrong? What if Lumiya's wrong? What if I don't have to kill anyone at all, and I kill Ben because I couldn't translate a stupid prophecy straight?

The prophecy said: *He will immortalize his love.*

It said a lot of other things, too, like he'd make a pet. He still didn't have anything fluffy, scaly, or feathered to his name, and it was stretching it to apply that to the faithful Corporal Lekauf who served him as selflessly as his grandfather had served Vader.

Immortalize doesn't have to mean kill.

But he had no idea what else it might mean. This—*this* was the worst thing about Sith teaching. There weren't just two possible interpretations of anything, but three, four, five . . .

So only the Sith deal in absolutes, do they, Obi-Wan? You told Vader that, or so Lumiya says. You liar. The Sith deal in anything but absolutes, because—

Because life itself was like that. A million choices to be freely made, all of them to be lived with, and requiring the courage of conviction.

Just a clue. How will I know? What will the sign be?

Lumiya didn't know, either, or if she did—he wasn't going to listen. Enough games; enough guessing. This all rested on his judgment.

I'm looking for signs and portents like a Ryn fortune-teller. It has to be more rational than this.

It was.

Ben's comment from the conversation they'd only just finished leapt into his mind.

An officer has to make decisions that cost lives.

It was for the good of the majority, he said. And if Ben could think it, then Jacen had to, as well.

He thought it, activated the security locks on the briefing room doors, sat down in a corner with his head resting on his knees.

When he put his hand to his face, he found it wet with tears.

chapter five

The main barrier to getting the Galactic Alliance to talk sense is Jacen Solo. He leads Chief Omas by the nose and he makes Admiral Niathal worse by encouraging her short-sharp-shock tendencies. Get him out of the way, and things would calm down enough for us to maneuver around Omas. I think I'll have a statesman-to-statesman chat with him . . . privately.

—*Dur Gejjen, Corellian Prime Minister, in private discussion*

GALACTIC ALLIANCE XJ7, IN NEUTRAL SPACE
BETWEEN CORELLIA AND CORUSCANT

MARA WONDERED IF SHE'D BOTHER TO SPIN JACEN A LINE ABOUT why she needed to take an XJ7.

Look, Jacen, it's like this. You've turned into a thug since Lumiya came on the scene, and the witch is trying to kill my son, so how's about I do what I do best, and kill her for all our sakes?

She would have loved to tell him that. But she still didn't know

who Lumiya's accomplices were inside the GAG, and Jacen didn't take kindly to doubts about his precious secret police. He wasn't being helpful. He didn't even seem to believe that Mara and Luke had found convincing evidence of Lumiya's GAG connections.

Jacen might have been a gifted Jedi, but he could also be a very human idiot, too. Or at least she'd thought in those more benign terms before the debacle of Gilatter VIII. She'd never imagined that Jacen would leave his parents to die.

Mara tried Leia's comlink again, hopping from frequency to frequency in case she was being tracked. Old habits died hard, and she didn't want Crazy Woman Two, Alema, to get a fix on her—or Leia.

Or . . . maybe she *did*.

"We can't go on meeting like this," said Leia's voice. She laughed, and that was pretty remarkable under the circumstances. She didn't have much to laugh about. "Do I have to give you a password?"

"I'll trust you." Mara checked her cockpit display, watching the frequency shift on the monitor in multicolored bars of light. "You okay?"

"For a woman on the run, I'm doing great."

"I don't know where to start."

"Try, *Hey, did your son really abandon you to suck vacuum?* Because that'd be *my* first question . . ."

"I'm so sorry, Leia, I really am. But I'm going to put a stop to this. Take Lumiya out of the equation, and I think you'll see a major improvement in Jacen's attitude."

"Is that where you are now?"

"I'm trying to work out how Lumiya moves around. Forget all this lightwhip garbage. I'm going to find her ship and finish what Luke started. They're always vulnerable in transit."

Leia's end of the link went quiet for a few moments. "Want me to play bait?"

"Don't you think you've been through enough lately?"

"I can guarantee that Alema would show up if I asked nicely," Leia said. "And maybe Lumiya wouldn't be far behind."

"Tell you what, why don't I lob in Ben and make certain of it?"

"Mara . . ."

"Sorry. I don't want to expose you to any more risk. But if I can devise a safer way of exploiting the fact that neither of those crazies can keep away from us, I'll do it."

"We're going to need to break this link soon," Leia said.

"Okay. Look, I have to see Jacen sooner or later. Do you want me to put it to him straight? Ask him why he ran when you'd come to save him?"

Mara couldn't think of a single thing Jacen might say that would sound plausible, but she didn't want to make Leia feel any worse than she did. *My fault anyway. I defended him when Luke was telling me he was going dark. If I'd seen what was in front of me and acted then, things might be different now.*

She had thought that about Palpatine, too. She was spending too much time looking back, and not enough getting on with the here and now. The past couldn't be changed, just the future.

"What if he tells you," said Leia, "and it's a reason I won't enjoy hearing?"

"Your call." *How much worse has it got to get before you accept he's treating you worse than dirt?* Mara tried to imagine how she'd feel if Ben issued a warrant for her arrest or left her on a space station venting atmosphere. It would devastate her—but she'd take him back in a heartbeat. No, there was no advice she could give Leia about her wayward son. "But I want to know anyway, seeing as Luke and I were there to help him, too, and wasted our time."

"All I can say is do whatever you feel you must to get Lumiya. Then we'll see about bringing Jacen back into the fold."

"If I find Alema, I'll save her for you."

"I'd like that."

"Thought you might."

"You take care, Mara."

Leia's link went dead. Mara had to assume she and Han were on Corellia, and that meant Alema couldn't get at her so easily.

Take care. Oh, I will. I've got one advantage you haven't, Leia, and that's darkness. I've been that dark. I was trained by a Sith Lord. I can think like them.

At least Leia hadn't made any cracks about Luke not taking the opportunity to finish off Lumiya. Sometimes, when she considered her sister-in-law, Mara regretted her own temper and wished she could learn a little of that steely diplomacy.

Mara turned the XJ7 and checked Ben's transponder again. *Still on Coruscant.* That didn't guarantee his safety, but at least she could pinpoint him. She zoomed her screen in on the trace, and the coordinates resolved into a grid, and then into neighborhoods and skylanes. Ben was at GAG HQ. She could locate him accurately to within three meters.

He liked the vibroblade she'd given him. She felt bad not telling him it housed a long-range passive transponder, and that it had saved her more than once because she'd used it as a homing beacon, but that was just detail. It was a superb weapon, so it wasn't a lie.

The tagged vibroblade ensured she knew exactly where Ben was at all times now.

He'd never spot it. The GAG thought they had all the best kit, but she had a few devices that could get past them, using older technology, frequencies, and relays they'd never spot. A surveillance system using the most sophisticated technology wasn't looking for devices almost as basic as a code flashed with a piece of broken mirror. Tech could be blind. If they scanned Ben, they'd only find his comlink code, not the signal hiding within it, because they didn't have the active end of the transponder link. She did.

She had one more transponder left, and she was saving that for a rainy day.

Sorry, sweetheart. Had to do it.

She turned her attention back to Lumiya. Now Lumiya was showing up at confrontations with the Confederation. Perhaps everyone was looking in the wrong direction, and Lumiya was working for Corellia.

The last time she'd seen her on the resort satellite, Ben wasn't even around—but Jacen was. Who was Lumiya going after, Ben or Jacen? If Lumiya's presence was making Jacen forget what being a Jedi was all about, then maybe Mara needed to keep tabs on Jacen, too.

That was easier said than done. She needed to try a more direct approach there, maybe talk to him for once. Nobody else had managed to. It was hard to get Jacen to listen, and even harder to get hold of him these days. He took the *secret* in *secret police* literally.

Then something vanished from the Force.

Ben—

It was like a shape flashing past her peripheral vision, and a famil-iar background noise stopping abruptly, leaving a dead, soundless ringing in the ears.

Ben's gone—

Ben had disappeared from the Force.

Mara's hand was on the controls to jump to hyperspace and head back to Coruscant at top speed when the sense of her son flooded back as if the sound had been turned on again. Her stomach rolled.

Maybe it's me.

He'd done it before as a little boy, scared by the last war, the one against the Yuuzhan Vong. It was uncontrolled and instinctive. But what Mara had just experienced felt like something more deliberate. When she concentrated on him, he felt fine—no, more than fine. He felt *elated.*

It still bothered her. She set a course for home and before she jumped, she felt him vanish and return again.

He seemed . . . *delighted.* She could feel the profound wonder in him. So he *was* doing it deliberately. No son of hers was going to pull that stunt on her: she'd had enough of Jacen doing it without Ben learning to hide in the Force as well. She'd go back and check on him, but pick her time to confront him about his new skill.

Maybe he won't get any farther than short bursts.

But he was Ben, and Ben had proved capable of astounding feats. He'd master it, all right. She just knew it.

Suddenly she didn't feel quite so guilty about giving him a tagged vibroblade. A mother had to keep ahead of the game somehow.

SOUTH SIDE LANDING STRIP, KUAT CITY

"So," said the clone. He hauled Mirta to her feet and dusted her down, and she tolerated it. His animal watched her with red-rimmed yellow eyes, and she grabbed her helmet from where he'd dropped it, expecting the creature to spring at her. "What part of *stay out of my way* didn't you understand?"

Mirta opened her mouth to give him a piece of her mind but Fett cut in. "Nice of you to drop in, but can we continue this discussion elsewhere?"

"Ah, the almighty *Mand'alor*. Hanging a gang boss over a balcony in the center of town. Yeah, that's subtle." The clone motioned the animal into the cargo bay, where it lay rumbling ominously like a distant storm. It was the ugliest thing Mirta had ever seen: loose gold fur that made it look like its skin was several sizes too big for it, six legs, and a truly ghastly mouthful of fangs. "Thanks for getting everyone's attention."

"I was looking for you," Fett said. He closed the hatch. "We have to go. Shut up and secure yourself for takeoff."

"You abducting me?"

"Would you rather have a chat and a cup of caf while we wait for the Kuat police and all of Fraig's scumbags to show up?"

"Okay, I borrowed the speeder anyway. Sort of. Tell you what, drop us off on Coruscant and we'll be on our way." The clone grabbed his helmet with both hands and lifted it off. He didn't look any less intimidating, but after a couple of seconds he broke into an unexpected grin that completely transformed him. He looked more like Fett's brother than his twin, not identical at all. "They say there's some family resemblance, but I don't see it myself . . ."

Fett paused for a telling moment and then stalked off to the cockpit. Mirta wasn't certain whether to land a punch on the clone or thank him for showing up.

"What's your name?" she asked.

"Jaing Skirata. You?"

"Mirta Gev." Then she realized it didn't have the required impact. "Fett's granddaughter."

Jaing raised his eyebrows and burst out laughing. The animal lifted its head and whined. Mirta went forward to the cockpit to strap herself in for takeoff, unhappy at the laughter still ringing behind her.

"You let him ambush you," said Fett.

Mirta seethed. "I didn't pick him up on my sensors and I didn't even see him coming at me. He flattened me before I could *kalik* him."

"Stab?"

"You're learning."

"And you're *not*." Fett punched the controls, and Kuat dwindled to a disk beneath them. "You didn't check visually. Don't rely on the helmet tech all the time."

"Hey, you didn't spot him, either. That's got to be stealth armor."

"He's a Null." There was some history there, she could see that. "They were black ops clones. The Kaminoans' attempt to improve on my dad's genome for cloning. You can see it didn't work."

"He says his name's Jaing. And did they really shove your head down—"

Fett just turned his head. He still had his helmet on, and even though few things scared Mirta these days, he had a way of being glacially slow and silent that was unsettling. She was just trying to get him to talk, looking for the long-buried man within. It was a forlorn hope. She gripped the console in front of her as Fett tapped in the co-ordinates for Coruscant, 000—and *Slave I* jumped to hyperspace.

"Jaing's not as bad as I thought," Mirta said.

"They were all psychiatric cases." Considering he probably hadn't seen them since he was a kid, Fett's recollection seemed painfully vivid. "They say Jaing tracked Grievous in the war. Master assassin, sniper, general pain in the backside. Don't underestimate him."

"The war before last, you mean."

"It's all one long war to me."

It was time to shut up, she decided. Fett was braced against the pilot's seat, looking uncomfortable; it could be folded down so the pilot could stand at the controls, or raised to form a ledge. He usually opted for the latter. She had a feeling that he was in too much pain to sit down.

"Course laid in," he said. "Let's go talk to him."

Mirta pulled out another painkiller, grabbed his hand, and slapped the capsule into his palm. "And when we drop him off on Coruscant, you see Doctor Beluine. Okay?"

Fett grunted. That was as near as she'd get to agreement. She could see his dread of mortal weakness.

"I'm not relying completely on drugs yet," he said. "All the time I hurt, I know how far it's progressed."

Jaing was sitting cross-legged on the deck of the cargo bay, face-

to-face with the animal, which was gazing into his eyes and making lit-tle whining, grumbling sounds as if trying to get him to understand something. He seemed oblivious to its smell. They both looked around when Fett and Mirta came through the hatch.

"What is he?" Mirta asked.

"You asking me or Lord Mirdalan?" Jaing held his gloved fingers up in front of the animal's face, some kind of signal that produced in-stant attention and made it lie flat on the deck. Jaing got to his feet. "He's an *it*. Strills are hermaphrodites. I promised Mird's last owner I'd look after it when he passed to the *manda*. Strills live a lot longer than we do."

"Heard of them, but never seen one."

"They're nearly extinct on Mandalore. Mird—well, you might say it's a black ops strill. Saw a lot of commando action in a few wars."

Fett shoved his thumbs into his belt in that I'm-fed-up-with-waiting pose. "When you two finish the nature lesson . . ."

Jaing had more lines, fewer gray hairs, and a heavier build than Fett. Mirta could see the cords of muscle in his neck. And he had no scars. He looked like a man who'd spent a lot of time in the sun with-out a helmet, and who'd laughed a lot. Genetically, this *was* Fett, but they couldn't have been more different.

"Ain't I gorgeous?" He grinned, and she realized she was staring at him.

"A vision," Fett said sourly, and removed his helmet.

"I think I aged better, *Bob'ika*."

"It's the fact that you reached this age at all that interests me."

"So why do you want me? Need a loan? You've been looking for me for *weeks*, 'cos I've been hearing all kinds of people putting out the word for me—"

"I'm dying," Fett said.

Jaing chewed over the news, head slightly to one side. "Sorry to hear that. You're not the only clone who met a premature end."

Fett usually cut to the chase. Now he stood silent for a while, jaw muscles twitching. Mirta wondered if he was hurt by the rebuff. She guessed that he was working up to the hardest thing he ever had to say.

He was. "I want your help, Jaing."

Jaing just stared at him. The staring went on for a long time. Mirta wondered who would give in first. Then it went on a little *too* long.

"Oh, for fierfek's sake," she sighed. "It's the cloning. His tissues are breaking down and he's got tumors. He needs to know what stopped you aging at double the rate, because his doctor can't help him and neither can the Kaminoans, not even Taun We."

Fett pursed his lips slightly. "What she said."

"So Taun We's still going strong, too, the old aiwha bait. Well, well." Jaing looked Fett up and down. "You had trouble with your leg, I heard. Had to have a transplant. Yes?"

"You're *very* well informed."

"I'm still a Tipoca boy at heart. I stay in touch with events in the old country."

"What have I got to pay you to quit gloating and give me what I need?"

"No offense, but you can shove your credits where your armor don't reach, *Mand'alor.*"

"You don't know what I need yet."

"I can guess."

"Ko Sai's research." Fett gave Jaing's gloves a pointed glance. "Because I know you found it. You certainly found her."

"You get more with honey than with sour-sap, Boba. Didn't getting your head shoved down the 'freshers teach you anything?"

Fett had no idea how to ask for help. Mirta wasn't sure if it was some male bravado thing or just that he'd never learned, but he wasn't getting far with Jaing, who seemed equally hard and obstinate.

"Can you help him?" she said. "*Gedet'ye?* Mandalore needs him alive, and so do I."

The clone was still staring into Fett's face. "Remember leading an Imperial force against clone troops on Kamino?"

Fett nodded, utterly impassive. "Yes."

"You didn't feel that we were family then."

"Didn't see any of *you* defending your brothers, either."

"And you deposed Shysa, you *hut'uun.* The man who put us back on our feet as a people. Where were *you* when the Empire was bleeding us dry?"

Hut'uun was the worst insult any Mando could throw at another, but Fett didn't seem to notice or care. Mirta found out more about her grandfather's murky past every day. So there was no reason to feel her mother and grandmother had been singled out for his total disregard, then: he didn't give a stuff about *anyone,* except his father, who seemed to have been elevated to an icon of perfection since his death. So *Ba'buir* fought against his own brothers. Maybe he hadn't seen the irony. If he had, she suspected he'd made a point of looking the other way.

"I'm not proud of anything I've done," Fett said, no hint of emotion in his voice. "But I'm not ashamed of anything, either. I just do what I have to. You don't know what went on between me and Shysa, and maybe you never will."

"He was there when we needed him," said Jaing. "And you weren't. That's all I need to know."

Fett didn't so much as blink. "I take it you won't be handing over Ko Sai's data, then."

Jaing glanced at Mirta as if he felt sorry for her. She wondered how different her life might have been if Jaing had met Sintas Vel instead of Boba Fett.

"There isn't any data," he said at last. He was still looking at her, not Fett. "Sorry, kid."

Fett didn't even blink. "You must have taken all your vitamins, then, because you *should* be dead by now."

"I didn't say the research didn't exist. I'm saying that we destroyed it after we took what we needed."

Fett aborbed that slowly. Mirta's heart sank in that conflicting way it had now, part of her desperate to find a reason to love her *ba'buir,* and half of her wishing Leia Solo hadn't blocked her shot when she'd tried to kill him.

Do something to make me forgive you. Please. Anything.

"You could have made a fortune from it," Fett said.

"We didn't want it used again. Ever."

"You can't stop cloning. You never will."

"No, but we put a dent in the Kaminoans. That's better than nothing. I don't like Kaminoans."

"I can tell." Fett glanced at Jaing's fine gray gloves. "But I've worked for worse."

"They *paid* you. They bred us like animals." Jaing looked as if he'd remembered something satisfying. "So Taun We's still alive. I always wondered."

"Leave her alone, Jaing. She's old now."

"So am I, no thanks to her. So how long have you got to live?"

"A year. Maybe two, if my luck holds."

"How long before you have to hand over command?"

"I don't know."

"The last thing Mandalore needs at the moment is a power vacuum."

Mirta saw a glimmer of hope. "So help him, Jaing."

"Best I can do is a blood sample," he said. "But I think you'll hand it over to the Kaminoans, Boba, or your doctors will, and we really wouldn't be very happy about that. Not at all."

"We?" Mirta felt she was getting on better with Jaing. She'd use her advantage as the harmless, tragic granddaughter. If Jaing wouldn't cooperate, she might find one of his brothers who would. "How many of you are there left?"

"You don't need to know that. Look, I've got grandchildren, too, Boba, and great-grandchildren. I've got family on Mandalore. So I care what happens when you're gone." As soon as he said it, it took on a terrible reality for her, and she wondered if it had the same impact on her grandfather. *The great Boba Fett's on the way out.* "Much as it pains me, your *bu'ad* here is right—Mandalore needs you for the foreseeable future."

Fett made a very good job of looking bored. Maybe he was. Mirta doubted it. He was negotiating for his life, and if Fett was anything, he was a survivor. He didn't know how to die gracefully like everyone else.

"So I get the blood if I keep the Kaminoans out of it."

"Not that simple," said Jaing.

"It never is."

"You give me blood and tissue samples, and I'll get something made up for you. If I can."

"And I'm supposed to trust you."

"As much as I'm supposed to trust you. And don't even think about taking a sample from me the hard way."

"Okay." Fett's jaw twitched again. "Thank you."

He made it sound like a foreign language, awkward and unfamiliar in his mouth. Mirta resisted the urge to react. *Well done*, Ba'buir. *Was that so hard?*

Jaing wasn't done, though. "There's a condition, of course."

"There always is." Fett crossed his arms. "What?"

"Get your *shebs* back to Mandalore, listen to Kad'ika's advice, and build a strong, united, *stable* state. Prove you're even half the man that Jaster Mereel and Fenn Shysa were. All you want to do is emulate your old man, Boba. But you're too scared to *exceed* him, aren't you? You can't be *better* than Jango. That would never do."

Mirta flinched. Mentioning his father without due reverence seemed to be the one thing that really got Fett riled. His voice didn't change, but he unfolded his arms with slow care.

"My father," said Fett, "finally destroyed the Death Watch. That's his legacy to Mandalore."

"Sectarian feud. *Irrelevant* to most *Mando'ade*'s lives. Now, are you going to give me a sample?"

"What kind of scientists have you got access to that I haven't?"

"Some things," Jaing said softly, "can't be bought. I have my resources, believe me. Got a medpac with a sharp in it?"

"Yes."

"Draw some blood, then."

"I'll do it," said Mirta.

With Fett, it wasn't a case of simply rolling up sleeves. He had so much equipment on his forearms that Jaing ended up holding the flamethrower attachment, whip assembly, and assorted projectiles. Fett was an armory on legs. Mirta didn't expect him to flinch when she finally found a vein, and he didn't. The few moments while she applied pressure to the blood vessel with her thumb to stop the bleeding afterward were the longest of her life, because he wouldn't meet her eyes, and it reminded her that she could touch him and *still* not reach him.

Jaing held the vial of red-black blood up to the light and admired it. "That'll do nicely. Give him some candy for being a brave boy, Mirta."

"What now?" Fett asked, unmoved.

"You drop me off, and I'll let you know what we get."

"How?"

"I'll deliver it personally to Keldabe."

"Better make it snappy, then. Or you might be in time for my funeral."

"Oh, I'll be back, and so will plenty of other *Mando'ade*. You asked us, remember? You asked us to come home." He turned to Mirta. "When the old *chakaar* dies and they divvy up his armor, make sure you get the flamethrower. Because his plates are *duse*. Not even proper *beskar*."

So Jaing wasn't out of touch with events on Mandalore, and he thought Fett's durasteel armor was garbage. The strill padded closer to Jaing and yawned extravagantly with an expression that said it was totally underwhelmed by the discussion. Mirta could smell its breath, which—oddly—wasn't unpleasant at all.

"How does that thing hunt if it's got such a strong scent?" Fett asked.

Jaing bent and ruffled Mird's neck folds. "Only humanoids can smell it. And don't be too hard on Mirta for getting ambushed, *Bob'ika*. Few people can deal with a full-grown strill swooping down on them. These things fly, you know."

"I don't keep pets." Fett seemed on the edge of a concession. "If you want something to eat, the galley's through that hatch."

Jaing opened a pouch on his belt and took out something dried and dark that looked like leather straps. He threw a strip to Mird and chewed on one himself. "We're fine, thanks."

It took a few seconds for Mirta to work out what was going on. *He doesn't want to leave any DNA. He's even more cunning than you,* Ba'buir.

Fett turned and swung back through the hatch. Mirta had hoped the two men would find something else to talk about, but the fact they shared a genome clearly meant nothing. Still . . . this was a relative. This was *her* relative, a great-uncle, even if Mandos didn't care about bloodline half as much as most species. The Kiffar half of her cared about it a lot.

"I feel bad for you, kid," Jaing said. "I feel bad for him, too, I suppose. But apart from some admiration for his skills, I think he's the worst excuse for a *Mando'ad* this side of the Core. On the other hand,

he *wins,* and we need winners. And my dad would have expected me
to help him, no questions asked."

Jaing spoke as if he came from a totally different family, not a vat
that contained the duplicated chromosomes of Jango Fett. He slipped
a three-sided knife from his forearm plate and trimmed the dried meat
into smaller chunks, utterly at ease.

"Jango's not who you mean by 'dad,' is he?" Mirta said.

"No." Jaing smiled wistfully to himself for a moment. "Genes
don't count. You ought to know that by now. The man who adopted
me was my training sergeant. Finest man who ever lived."

Jaing sounded like he'd come from a far happier family, a strange
thing for a clone soldier. "I seem to be bucking the trend of devoted
kids," Mirta said. "I tried to kill my grandfather."

"So did your mother, I hear. Boba's obviously got this magic
touch with the ladies."

"You seem to know everything about me, but I don't know much
about you."

Jaing just grinned. "That's my job, sweetheart."

"So why did you get involved with Cherit's gang over the Twi'leks?"

"Another promise I made a long time ago." He chewed, looking
slightly past her in recollection. "I tend to keep them."

He went on chewing, occasionally throwing chunks to Mird. And
that was it. Silence descended. She thought he might talk about his
family on Mandalore, all the undiscovered relatives she now found she
had, but he didn't.

Mirta realized she wasn't going to get anything more out of him,
and she didn't want to look needy. She returned to the cockpit, settled
into the copilot's seat, and clutched the heart-of-fire against her chest
plate. Even if it told her nothing, it was still a connection to her
mother and grandmother.

"You fed up with him already?" Fett asked.

She wanted to think Jaing had given Fett some hope and raised his
spirits, but it was hard to tell. "Is your armor really rubbish? Why
don't you use proper Mandalorian iron, like Beviin says—"

"Don't push your luck. I let you stick a needle in me. That's your
fun for the day."

It *had* cheered him up. Mirta could tell. She hoped that not only would Jaing's unspecified "resources" come through, but that Boba Fett would redeem himself so that her only kin wasn't someone that she wished were someone else.

GAG HQ, CORUSCANT

Jacen didn't want to look too interested in the Policy and Resources Council proceedings. If he showed up for the meeting and sat in the gallery reserved for those hardy citizens who actually cared about the minutiae of government, he might cause questions to be asked.

On the other hand, he might just have been seen as a micromanaging, interfering colonel who put his troops' welfare above schools, health, and transport.

That was fine by him. He did.

But a low profile was called for, so he stayed at GAG HQ and switched to the HoloNet channel that broadcast Senate proceedings. Lumiya should have been there by now. He waited for the holocam to pan to the public gallery and saw, as he expected, a woman in a sober business suit and veiled headdress. She wasn't the only one, either. Veils were considered very chic this year. She drew no attention at all.

HM-3's amendment to the procurement regulations was Item 357 on an agenda of 563 mind-bogglingly boring tweaks and changes to laws Jacen didn't even know were on the statute books.

I'm going to have to do a lot of delegating when I'm . . . in charge. A handpicked team of administrators. Led by HM-3, I think.

The session had already started, and Senators who were happy to do the small routine work—and not be noticed—were on Item 24, having a particularly arcane piece of hazardous waste legislation explained to them. Jacen turned off the audio feed and set the monitor to alert him when Item 357 was up. Then he got on with reading more intelligence reports, with the doors to his office wide open.

He almost always kept the doors open. It reassured the troops. It told them that he was an accessible officer, always willing to listen.

But Jori Lekauf peered in, boots still firmly on the corridor side of the doors as if there were a barrier marked OFFICER TERRITORY—DO NOT PASS.

"Lady at the security gate asking to see you, sir."

Jacen, distracted, felt in the Force to see who it might be. "Mara Skywalker."

Lekauf grinned. "It's great the way you can do that, sir."

"I don't get many women coming to see me, so I could have guessed . . ." Jaina wouldn't be visiting, not without him feeling her resentment and mistrust marching ahead of her like a vanguard. And it wouldn't have been Tenel Ka. He missed her, and he missed Allana even more. *I don't have to kill them. I'd know if I had to, wouldn't I?* "Bring her in."

"Yes, sir." Lekauf turned to go.

"Lekauf . . ."

"Sir?"

"Have you ever considered a commission?"

"Not sure if I'm officer material, sir."

"I think you could be. I'm not forcing you, but we need good officers coming through the ranks, because we'll have a challenging role in the years to come."

Lekauf seemed dubious. "I'm willing to give it a go, sir."

"Excellent. I'll get the adjutant to fix the paperwork. We'll probably have to delay staff college until the security situation is more stable, but I'm sure Shevu or Girdun will be happy to guide you. And you'll be able to keep an eye on Ben. He really trusts you."

Lekauf blinked, but there was no expression on his face. "Captain Shevu looks after me very well. I'll learn a lot from him."

Non sequiturs said a lot. Lekauf wasn't naïve, for all his cheerful schoolboy appearance. His careful avoidance of Captain Girdun's name confirmed Jacen's observations that the ex-Intel man wasn't a popular officer with troops from the military and CSF side. Spies had that effect. Shevu had come from the CSF—familiar, visible, reliable folks you were happy to see in a crisis.

Jacen couldn't afford divisions. "You might do Captain Girdun good, too. It's interesting how a good apprentice creates a better teacher."

"Thank you, sir." Lekauf showed not a flicker of reaction. "I'll show your guest in."

Jacen kept one eye on the silent holoscreen while he looked through the reports, one of which he forwarded for Niathal's immediate attention—the Bothans had a new class of frigate coming into service in a matter of days. The P&R meeting had reached Item 102. A busy day: a lot of rubber-stamping was going on. He opened his comlink and switched the signal to the small bead deep in his ear. Lumiya had a concealed receiver in her cybernetic implants and would hear it in the depths of her skull, silent as a thought.

He used her cover name, the one he'd used in front of Ben. It was common enough. It also helped avoid accidental slips. "Are you helping them make decisions, Shira?"

"Giving them a sense of urgency, that's all. Not that they don't have fancy lunches on their minds anyway."

"Does it look as if anyone troublesome has read the agenda sheets in advance?"

"Not as far as I can see. But don't worry. I can deal with that."

Jacen felt Mara approaching down the corridor, a little tornado of determination. Unlike Lekauf, she walked straight in. Jacen projected a veneer of weary good humor in the Force and smiled at her.

She glanced at the holoscreen. "That looks thrilling."

"Just making sure we get our supply issues worked out." Hiding in plain sight was always the best option, Jacen found. "An amendment so that we can cut the red tape and get our people the right kit. It's been an issue with the troops."

"I'm all for that." Mara sat down in the rickety chair across from his desk—Jacen believed in being seen *not* to spend budget on himself—and crossed her legs. She'd taken to wearing a gray jacket that looked more like battledress, an indication of her state of mind lately. "I've come about Ben."

"He's doing well. He's doing very well, in fact."

"You've certainly focused him. Quite the responsible young man now." Mara glanced at the open doors as if they troubled her. "Let's get to the point. I know Lumiya's trying to kill him. Whatever he did or didn't do, Lumiya thinks he killed her daughter. Now, seeing as we also found evidence that Lumiya has a mole in the GAG, that concerns me somewhat. A *lot* of somewhat. If anything happened to my boy from inside the GAG, I'd take it pretty badly, I think."

Ah. Has she worked it out? Has Mara actually seen what's coming? Jacen felt a moment of sinking dismay as he wondered if this last mystery about his path was transparent to everyone. *She was Palpatine's Hand. If anyone on the Jedi Council can see it, she will.*

Jacen managed to project genuine concern. His link was still open: Lumiya could hear all this. "I've investigated that, and I can assure you I found nothing to support it."

"Is Ben around? I don't see much of him these days."

Ben was out on patrol, on routine weapons searches. Mara didn't need to know that. "He's doing some research for me."

"Okay," Mara said. "Just asking you to bear in mind that it's not the Confederation that's most likely to threaten his life, and even if *you* don't think Lumiya has an insider in your ranks, then *I'm* assuming she has until I'm convinced otherwise." She stood up slowly, and Jacen was on the edge of believing that she could see what was happening. "Just ask yourself which member of the GAG would ally with Lumiya. I'm not sure you'd see it, being so close to it."

Jacen expected to hear some sigh or other reaction from Lumiya, but either she was more concerned with the passage of the amendment or she couldn't hear after all.

"I'll certainly ask that question, Aunt Mara," he said. "Just bear in mind that Ben's learning to take care of himself."

"And are you?"

"What do you mean?"

"Well, if nobody else is going to say it to your face, I will. What's happening to you, Jacen? Why did you run out on your parents like that? Okay, there's a warrant out on them, but—"

Jacen wondered why it had taken so long for anyone to confront him. He'd expected Jaina to be the first, given her perpetual sulk with him, but Mara probably felt her defense of him had now made her look stupid.

"My fault," he said. "I assumed they were okay and could get to safety, so I decided to get to where I could make a difference to the battle—my ship."

"Right," said Mara. "Just a lapse in judgment."

"I'm human."

"We all have times when our judgment lets us down. I certainly do." Mara gave him an unconvincing smile, turning for the doors. "Thanks for your time."

She knows.

She knows because it's inevitable, and that proves it has to be Ben.

It wasn't his parents, or Tenel Ka, or Allana. It was Ben. He wondered how long he could go on facing the boy, knowing that. How would it happen? Would he have to kill him in cold blood? Or would they end up in some violent confrontation, where death was so much easier to deal out?

Lumiya's voice was a breath in his ear. If anyone overheard her, she sounded like any bureaucrat having a discreet comlink conversation, not a Sith planning the greatest coup of all time. "I think my former colleague will be looking for me now, with maximum disapproval."

Jacen closed the doors with his remote control. "It *was* you who engineered the attack on Ben on Ziost, wasn't it?"

"He'll never be your successor. He hasn't got what it takes to be your apprentice. It's my duty to retire the unsuitable."

"Stay away from him from now on. You've gone too far, and I think Mara suspects what's happening."

"My former colleague can't touch you if—wait, they're taking your amendment out of sequence. Someone has asked to speak on it."

"Who?"

"Someone in the public gallery—they've invoked the right to address the council, and they've identified themselves as Citizen Watch."

It was interesting to note how fast things could come unraveled. The civil rights lobby was largely drowned out by events, but he still didn't want them to point out what nobody seemed to have spotted hidden in his amendment. "You know what you have to do."

"Indeed." Lumiya went very quiet, her voice almost inaudible. "I think . . . that they're going to decide . . . that they wish to ask if this is going to be retroactive legislation . . . yes, they have. How *vigilant*."

If she thought she'd redeemed herself in his eyes, she was wrong. She was becoming a risk. But that was always the Sith way; always this struggle between two.

He turned the audio back on while the amendment was discussed.

HM-3 was right. Senators chewed over the sums involved and satisfied themselves that the budget wouldn't be exceeded without authorization from the Treasury. Nobody seemed to see that the finely tuned wording by HM-3 would enable Jacen to change other legislation, too.

He'd think of things that needed changing.

Once I kill Ben Skywalker, once Mara and Luke find out that it's me—and that day will have to come—then they'll hunt me down. I'll bring down the whole Jedi order on my head.

Who would be his apprentice then?

It'll finish the Jedi.

He just wanted things to become clear when the time came. He had to trust his destiny. He was too far along the path to stop now.

"Item three fifty-seven, carried. Next item, variance of regulations regarding the licensing of air taxis . . ."

And that was it.

The amendment had been passed, and when the revised statute came into effect at midnight, Colonel Jacen Solo—and Admiral Cha Niathal, because it applied equally to her—would be able to order whatever the defense forces needed, and get it fast.

And change any other administrative legislation within existing budgets, without recourse to the Senate.

They'd handed him an extraordinary power, and one that he'd use to change the way the galaxy was governed. He'd use it to take down Chief of State Omas: he wasn't sure of the details yet, but he could do it, and soon. The Galactic Alliance would fall, not with a clash of lightsaber blades, or ion cannons fired, or troops surrounding the Senate, but with a sheet of flimsi and a nod of heads.

"Well done," he said softly. "Nicely influenced."

"Not me," Lumiya said. He could hear the smile in her voice. "They reached the decision themselves, without any help from me. I just redirected a little opposition from the gallery."

The irony was too delicious sometimes. Jacen didn't know whether to be satisfied at the outcome, or angry that Senators were so stupid that they let him get away with this.

They *deserved* to be ruled by the Sith.

They *needed* to be.

chapter six

Reports are coming in of a major battle between Sikan forces and invading Chekut troops on the Sika homeworld. The Sikan administration has called for Galactic Alliance forces to intervene in what it calls "an act of opportunist aggression," and share prices have tumbled over fears that the invasion will draw more planets in the Expansion Region into the conflict.

—*HNE newsflash*

GALACTIC ALLIANCE WARSHIP <u>BOUNTY,</u>
ON STATION WITH ALLIANCE FRIGATE <u>DARING,</u>
BOTHAN SECTOR

IT WAS A TIDY-LOOKING VESSEL, SHE HAD TO ADMIT THAT.
The new Bothan frigate wasn't even in their database. Admiral Niathal watched it on *Bounty*'s bridge screen, curving out of Bothawui orbit trailed by five small unarmed tenders. The profile and signature were immediately logged in the ship's recognition systems.

"Looks like the Bothans have been shopping after all," she said. "At least the intel was right on that."

"Seems they're still doing work-ups, too," said Captain Piris. The warship was being assisted by the tenders, or maybe it was simply feigning helplessness: Niathal never took Bothans at face value. "Let's see what specs we can collate on them before we scratch the paint-work. I hope they kept their receipts . . ."

"KDY construction, do you think?"

"Tallaan," Piris said. "We'd *know* if Kuat was building them."

"Well, they're not going to level Coruscant with those, but they certainly will spread us thin if they've got as many as Intelligence estimates."

Admiral Niathal shared a number of military philosophies with Jacen Solo, and being seen on the front line was one of them. She also liked to see things for herself, especially if Galactic Alliance Intelligence was involved. The current overstretch gave her cause to wonder what Cal Omas was playing at—an anxiety that might have been visible to the bridge crew as she paced up and down, glancing over shoulders to check screens and readouts.

"We need every hull we can hang on to, Admiral." *Bounty*'s commanding officer, Piris, had been on the bridge far too long. He was a Quarren, evolved for an amphibious existence, and the atmosphere on board was too dry to keep pulling double watches; his uniform was sealed tightly at the cuffs and neck, but he kept wiping his face with a moist cloth. He needed a rest in his humid cabin. "If the Bothan fleet is growing as fast now as Intelligence suggests, then I fail to see how we're going to contain it if we have to support Sika and every other local skirmish, too."

"Looks like the Kem Stor Ai dispute will be the next to boil over." Niathal had a brief moment of wishing that she could target one world, reduce its surface to slag from orbit just to make her point, and then ask who else wanted some of the same. But it passed. It always did. "Every backworld with a grievance is resurrecting old fights in the guise of Alliance loyalty and asking us to help out. And Omas thinks he can hold the Alliance together by placating every call for a backup fleet across the galaxy."

"When is he going to admit he can't?"

"When I give him no other option, I think."

Maybe the Bothans were ahead of the curve. Instead of commissioning more capital ships—juicy, high-value targets in battle—they'd opted for a big fleet of smaller, more agile warships that could be stockpiled without anyone panicking about the escalation in arms.

"It's a different kind of war. Flexibility and rapid response, that's the name of the game now." Piris put his hand on the ship's comm control. "Let's see what they're made of. Mothma Squadron, launch when ready. Qaresi Squadron, remain on alert five. Confine them to their own space, but attack if fired upon."

Niathal still wondered who'd assassinated the Bothans and kicked off this escalation. *Could have been our assets, if we'd played the Bothans right.* Some Intel moron, she decided. She'd get to the bottom of that sooner or later. If she was going to be Chief of State one day, she'd weed out the loose cannons first.

"If you can get our furry friends to give us a ship's tour, in one piece . . . ," she suggested. But intercepting and boarding the new frigate in these circumstances was next to impossible. The best break they'd get would be to retrieve debris for inspection. "I'd love to know their top speed."

Niathal quite liked Bothans, even if she didn't trust them as far as she could spit, which was a lot farther than anyone might have believed.

She didn't dislike Quarren, either, even if it was almost expected of Mon Calamari. Quarren were a rare sight on ships; she knew Mon Cal officers who made every effort to avoid being assigned Quarren crew, and few Quarren wanted to serve alongside Mon Cals even now. But when they were good, they were very, *very* good. Piris was outstanding. If she caught any Mon Cal referring to him as *Squid Head*, they'd answer to her, and she didn't care how many whispered that she was an apologist.

Did we have the right to take their kids for some social engineering experiment—for our benefit?

She asked herself that question more often these days, and the answer always came up negative. Jacen Solo would think she was a hopeless wet liberal.

She wondered how she was going to wipe him off her boots when the time came. It wouldn't be easy.

"*Bounty, Daring,* stand by."

Twelve fighters shot out of the *Bounty*'s hangar bay, spiraling away from the warship and streaking off in pursuit of the Bothan frigate. Then the three flights separated. Observation cams in each cockpit gave *Bounty*'s combined bridge and combat information center a composite view of the engagement. *Daring* sat off *Bounty*'s starboard bow, ready to divert any Bothan retaliation from her larger charge.

"Did you ever train as a pilot, ma'am?" Piris asked.

"No. You?"

"Indeed I did. At times like this, I miss it."

"If we get any busier, Captain, there'll be a droid running this ship and you'll be flying sorties. Where that leaves me I have no idea."

"You'll be Chief of State, ma'am," said Piris.

The worst thing about Quarren was that their amusement wasn't as easy to spot as a human's. With a human, all those teeth on display made life easier. Quarren face-tentacles could hide a multitude of emotions.

"That'll be the day," she said, hoping to avoid more gossip about her ambitions. Right then being Chief of State didn't matter at all. She had a battle, and all her training and instinct kicked in to say this was where she wanted to be, not behind a desk.

The first flight to come within range of the Bothan frigate shadowed it, cutting back and forth across its path at a thousand meters. The second flight trailed aft of it, scanning the hull and sending back data.

It took a few seconds for the Bothans to react; perhaps some of their systems were still offline. The ship picked up speed and began to move out of the Bothawui limits, its accompanying tenders trailing like escort fish.

So the Bothans thought they had a nice new asset to surprise the Alliance, but the Alliance had spotted it. Niathal waited for the reaction while the third flight of Mothma Squadron monitored the situation, weapons trained but not locked. There was no point blowing it to pieces before they'd taken the measure of the new class.

"Very heavy hull plating for a frigate," said Niathal, looking at the recce scans coming back from the starfighters. Piris pored over the images and penetrating scans, too. "At least a dozen turbolasers and twenty cannons."

"Not exceptional."

"Depends how many hulls they have."

They didn't have long to wait to find out how many vessels were out there. The weapons officer shouted at the same time as the sensor warning Klaxon sounded.

"Sir, enemy contact at—correction, *multiple* contacts in range. We've got trade."

"*Bounty, Daring,* close up at battle stations, synchronize command information. Helm, all ahead. Qaresi Squadron, *launch*—Bronzium and remainder of air group, launch when ready."

Nobody said *ambush.* The cockpit chatter from the pilots broke in. "Copy that . . . five, six . . . correction, *ten*—detecting cannons charging, will engage—"

"Targeting source."

"I make that nineteen—"

"He's got a lock on me."

"Got your six. Deploying chaff."

Piris's face-tentacles were completely still. It gave him a commendable look of calm. "Cannons, engage all Bothan vessels in range, in your own time, go on . . ."

One moment they'd been watching a single fresh-out-of-the-box frigate, and the next more were dropping out of hyperspace at regular five-second intervals. Mothma Squadron picked up images on their cockpit cams: all in the same Bothan livery, all brand spanking new and unmarked by debris pocks and scrapes.

A flare of red laser blazed on the screens as one XJ cam view winked out and the fighter broke up into spinning, red-hot debris. Pilots' voices were still audible in the background, but the focus on the bridge was on "fighting the ship"—attacking the enemy. *Daring* moved between *Bounty* and the Bothan flotilla. Her cannons and lasers showed up on the synchronized command information screen as blinking icons, fully charged and acquiring firing solutions.

"Eight contacts not firing, sir, and no sign of charging cannons." *Bounty* shuddered from deflected pulsed laserfire. Niathal moved to supervise damage control, which was already under a competent commander, but there was nothing worse than an idle visiting admiral on a ship at battle stations. She needed to be occupied.

"Take them out anyway." Piris turned to Niathal. "If they cripple us, at least we transmitted the data we have. If they don't—that's a whole Bothan flotilla that never leaves home."

"I don't expect a tactical withdrawal, Captain." Three more XJs were hit: Niathal noted it as lost assets, not knowing the pilots personally, and disliked her detachment for a moment. She always did. "We're here. Let's do as much damage as we can."

The Bothans, of course, had the same goal.

Two Bothan frigates were on a ramming course with *Bounty*. Of the remaining flotilla, five were firing on the XJs. *Daring* opened fire. The bridge crew watched as a frigate's aft section rippled with a sequence of explosions before debris blew away from it and smashed into an XJ. Five minutes into the engagement, *Bounty*'s air group was taking a pounding, not all of it from direct hits. The second frigate veered away from the stream of fire from the XJ, a red-hot rip in its hull.

"Their targeting's not affected by chaff measures, sir." The pilot's voice was breathless with effort. "They're using narrow-range heat seekers. In future we'll need to—"

And he was gone, his cockpit cam blank and flickering.

"Air group, pull out," Piris barked. "Cannons, solutions on all targets, *now*."

Species perceived time differently in battle. For humans, it slowed because their brains took in far more detailed information about the threat, but that also meant they didn't notice low-priority things. But Mon Cals—and Quarren—saw it all, and factored in every cough and spit. That was what made them good commanders. Niathal's instinct was to fight back, and for a moment she couldn't imagine why she'd ever had designs on high office. She saw the tactical displays and heard the comm chatter, and the real-time three-dimensional image in her mind showed her the whole battlefield—and she wanted to hit hard.

Nine Bothan frigates were now disabled, either drifting with no sign of power, reduced to cold debris, or venting brief bursts of flame into the vacuum as they broke up. Some of the remaining ten returned fire for a further thirty seconds, then powered down their cannons.

"Surrendering?" asked the officer of the watch.

"They're preparing to jump," said Piris. *"Take take take—"*

Seven frigates jumped in a tight sequence: three weren't so quick off the mark, and took a furious barrage of laser and cannons.

Piris gave Niathal a nod of relief and leaned over the command console. "Air group, anyone too damaged to make an RV point?"

"Mothma Five-zero, sir. Slow hull breach."

"Qarisa Eight, sir."

The bridge crew waited for a few seconds, utterly silent, cannons still trained while XJs streaked back to the hangar and recovery units passed them outbound to haul in damaged craft.

"Secure hatches when ready and prepare to jump," Piris said. "Any sign of the Bothan cavalry arriving on long-range scans? No? Good." He looked at the chrono hanging from a fob on his jacket. "Not quite twenty minutes, Admiral. Now, was that a planned ambush we walked into, or are the Bothans making the best of an unfortunately timed arrival? The score's twelve–nil to us, not counting starfighters lost. But did we win or lose?"

"I'll let you know when our public information colleagues tell me," Niathal said. "But this confirms my position yet again. If we're stuck with the resources we've got, then we *have* to focus everything on Corellia, Commenor, and now Bothawui. If the Chief of State wants to extend to every bushfire that's starting, he has to give us at least another fleet, and even if the Alliance had the credits—where would we get the personnel?"

Piris shrugged. "All empires become too big and collapse under their own weight."

"Maybe that's what we're seeing."

Her body was telling her that it was all over now. She felt hot as her biochemical defenses rushed around looking for damage to repair, and found none. The aftermath of battle was always a restless hour or two for her, so she occupied herself wandering around the bridge, patting crew members on the back, and telling them what a fine job they'd done. One young human male was wiping tears away with the back of his hand, his attention fixed unnaturally on the sensor screen in front of him; he'd lost a friend today, maybe more than one. There was nothing to say. She simply put her hand on his shoulder and stood there in silence for a while until the helm crew began their checks before hyperjumping.

"I'll be in my day cabin," she said, pausing to shake Piris's hand. "Well done, Captain."

She knew what they'd be saying as soon as the bridge hatches closed behind her. They'd be expressing surprise that old Iceberg Face could go around patting backs and showing sympathy. Combat did that to her: she had a brief period of dropping her guard, and then she was back to normal, a politician who used to be a competent naval officer and still missed fleet action.

The hyperspace vista from her cabin viewport was soothing. Sometimes she picked a streak of starlight that was stretched into a line, and tried to think of it as a star with orbiting planets full of life, and picture what was happening there. She did it now to clear her mind before deciding what to say to Cal Omas.

She knew she had to give him an ultimatum. And to make it stick, she needed Jacen Solo to stand by her.

GAG HEADQUARTERS, CORUSCANT

Captain Heol Girdun smiled and beckoned Ben into a dark office. Somehow the two elements combined into Ben's least favorite way to spend an afternoon.

"Behold," he said, and Ben's eyes adjusted to the low light. There were no windows. The only illumination was from banks of holoscreens and monitors. Ben realized there were GAG troopers sitting at consoles, with that glaze of defocused concentration that looked like blank boredom. "The eyes and ears of the Guard. Welcome to the monitoring center. The ultimate in scrutiny."

"Sir," whispered one of the lieutenants, "keep the noise down, will you?"

Girdun's grin was picked out in blue by the light from a frequency analyzer. "They're all such artists." He steered Ben by his shoulder, taking him to an alcove away from the active consoles. Girdun probably didn't realize how well a Jedi could navigate in darkness, but Ben humored him. "This is where we keep an eye on Senators and other social misfits for their own good."

"Whose calls do you tap?" Ben felt uneasy about it. "I bet it's not even exciting."

"All government staff, our special list of probable and proven scumbags, and politicians," said Girdun. "And given the number of Senators and the volume of hot air they emit, we get automated voice recognition systems to do it, or we'd be here for the next thousand years. If the droid picks up any keywords of interest, it tags the conversation and alerts us. Then we have to sit and actually listen to it."

One of the troopers—Zavirk—was ladling sweetener into a cup of caf. He sipped it gingerly, looking slightly comical with an audio buffer lead dangling from his ear. "I joined the army to see the galaxy," he whispered, "but all I got was eight-hour watches of listening to weird politicians making appointments to—"

"Ben's *fourteen*," Girdun said.

"Well, if you want him to do monitoring, he's going to hear stuff that'll make his hair curl, sir."

Ben had never considered what tapping comlinks of suspects and people in sensitive posts actually entailed. "I won't faint," he said. "And if I'm old enough to get shot at, I'm old enough to hear . . . stuff."

"Can't argue with that logic." Girdun sat him down at a console and gave him an earpiece. "Okay, the screen here shows you the sound files the droid's lined up as worth listening to, as well as holocam footage. You just work through it and make notes if anything seems worth following up. You're looking for anyone who might be contacting Senators and seems a bit odd, any conversations about Senators or government staff . . . look, you're a Jedi. You've probably got a sixth sense about this stuff just like you have about hidden explosives."

"So do nek battle dogs," said Zavirk, "but Lieutenant Skywalker smells better, and he can do tricks."

Ben decided he might like it here for a while. It didn't feel like spy HQ at all: just a bunch of troopers he knew well, doing a routine wartime surveillance job. Ben realized he'd partitioned his feelings so that he didn't have to think about Dur Gejjen as a person. The man had a wife and child. Tenel Ka had a child, too, though, and Gejjen had been happy to hire someone to assassinate her. Ben had been

weighing the morality of his mission and wasn't sure if he was only telling himself what he wanted to hear.

And there was nobody he could talk it over with.

He settled in his seat to begin checking recordings, and tried not to think about Gejjen. The conversations—mostly boring, some bizarre, a few incomprehensible—almost lulled him into meditation. It was an effort not to try hiding in the Force again, something he now practiced whenever he could.

The monitoring center smelled strongly of caf. Ben felt in need of some, too, after a few hours, and he lost himself in a conversation between two government staff about the regular route that a certain Senator took from the Senate to her apartment. But he was jerked out of his concentration by a rustle of fabric and quiet, intense activity at another console. Zavirk had summoned Girdun, and they both looked grim. Ben paused to listen.

"You sure?" Girdun asked.

"Run a voice profile if you don't believe me," Zavirk said. "That's the Corellian PM."

There were ten people in the room, and they'd all stopped to listen. Gejjen's soothingly persuasive voice with its faint accent was telling someone that there was no point doing this through the usual channels, because nobody else was in a negotiating mood.

". . . you and I know that this could be solved by the removal of a few hotheads . . . some of our military need slapping down, and so do some of yours. I'd call an immediate cease-fire if I could be assured of a few things."

"Such as?" said the unmistakable voice of Chief of State Omas. They were tapping the Chief of State's secure comm line. Ben wasn't sure they had authorization to do that.

"We'll agree that Corellia pools its military assets with the GA as long as we have an opt-out clause that says we have the right to withdraw it if our own needs are more urgent. Niathal has to go. Jacen Solo has to go. Once that's out of the way, we're back to normal and you've got what you want."

"Centerpoint."

"Well, we're having problems repairing it anyway."

"Centerpoint has to be made inoperative."

A pause: too brief even for most people to notice, but Ben did. *"It already is. But if you want a multiplanetary force or observers there, fine."*

"What about the Bothans, and the other planets fighting their own wars?"

"I can bring the Commenorians into line, and the Bothans . . . well, once we're all back in the GA then Bothawui's got to toe the line. The little people—if the fighting gets out of hand, we'll commit troops to put a stop to that."

"The Senate won't agree to this."

"Take Niathal and Solo out of the equation first and they'll calm down. What's left of the Senate, anyway . . ."

"Take out . . . they won't go quietly . . . they might split the Senate. G'Sil's totally in their camp, and he's got weight."

"Well, there's take out, and take out."

Omas swallowed but didn't respond.

Gejjen filled the silence. *"You know we have a job to do before this draws in the whole galaxy."*

"Okay. Okay."

"We need to meet. Can you get to Vulpter?"

Long pause. *"I'll find an excuse. Send me the details . . ."*

Girdun stood looking at the screen as if he could get some sense out of it if he stared long enough. Zavirk sat with his chin propped on his hand, gazing up at the captain for orders.

"Get a transcription of that to Colonel Solo right away."

Ben still wasn't clear what was happening, even though he thought Omas should have mentioned the approach to the Security Council. "Can't the Chief of State talk to the Corellian Prime Minister?"

"Depends what he's talking about," said Girdun. "And what he has in mind for Colonel Solo and Admiral Niathal."

If Gejjen could plot the assassination of the Queen Mother of Hapes and have Thrackan Sal-Solo killed, then making Jacen and Niathal disappear was just another routine job for him. Ben knew he had his answer about the necessity of his mission.

Girdun leaned over Zavirk and tapped the console. "That conversation was four hours ago. Better check on the Chief of State's travel arrangements, because he hasn't informed us he's going offworld and needs a close protection squad."

"You think he needs one?" asked Ben.

"With Gejjen? He needs *two*."

Ben didn't know if he could mention Tenel Ka. It was always hard knowing who knew what inside the GAG. "Would he really try something with Chief Omas?"

"I think he does it out of habit, just like I chew nervesticks."

Ben now had no idea if Cal Omas was bypassing the Senate illicitly to do a personal deal with the enemy, or walking into a trap like the one Gejjen had set for Tenel Ka—and Uncle Han's late, unlamented cousin Thrackan.

Jacen was right, as ever. Gejjen had to be stopped.

SUPREME COMMANDER'S OFFICE, SENATE BUILDING, CORUSCANT

Jacen read the transcript a third time and laid his datapad down on Niathal's desk.

She had a hologram of Mon Cal on the wall behind her, all shimmering blue ocean and sinuous buildings emerging from the waves in floating cities. He wondered if she was homesick. Right now she was fresh back from a battle that hadn't gone as planned, and impatient to see Cal Omas about it.

That meant she was receptive to ideas. He made a conscious effort not to influence her, because she wasn't the kind to fall for Jedi tricks. And it would only provoke her.

"Nothing like a united front in wartime." He leaned back in the chair, fingers meshed behind his head. "So we're not the flavor of the month. Our glorious leader didn't exactly spring to our defense."

Niathal's white uniform didn't look crumpled, even though she'd just disembarked from a warship fresh from a battle. "Smacks of ingratitude, I'd say."

She wasn't one for humor. Jacen knew enough about Mon Cal body language now to know she was angry. She kept rolling her head slightly, as if she was getting hot and her collar was pinching her neck.

Her nostrils flared. That meant she was ripe for a few radical suggestions about Omas.

He laid the bait. "You realize that when Gejjen says someone has to go, he doesn't mean a golden handshake and a framed certificate thanking them for loyal service."

"Spit it out, Jacen."

"He was behind Sal-Solo's premature death—"

She narrowed her eyes, heavy with sarcasm. "I'm shocked, I tell you. *Shocked.*"

"—and the attempt on the Hapan Queen Mother's life." *My lover. Mother of my daughter, my little darling. I wish I could see them.* "We're next."

Niathal's nostrils closed tight for a second. It was a giveaway with Mon Cals, a little sign that said they were surprised, and not in a good way.

"He wouldn't be stupid enough to try that."

"Right now I don't know what he'd try."

"Omas isn't a fool," she said. "He must have a good idea of what he's dealing with."

"What do you think he's he up to?"

"All he wants to do is hold the Alliance together. He always thinks a few raps over the knuckles can bring naughty governments into line. Well, it didn't work with Corellia, and now he's watching the Alliance shrink a planet at a time." She kept looking at the chrono on her desk. "My rules say we should notify the chair of the Security Council about the meeting. He's beginning to feel sidelined as it is. I'm not sure what outcome that will have, though."

Jacen kept G'Sil sweet by delivering results on terrorism and not telling him anything he would have to deny knowing later. If he had serious designs on Omas's job, he hadn't shown any sign of it—yet.

"Senator G'Sil would simply task me to take care of it," Jacen said. "I'm saving him the trouble of knowing. Plausible deniability."

"Do you enjoy the irony?"

"What?"

"Bypassing the Senate about our head of state bypassing the Senate. Nice job with the procurement amendment, by the way. Slipped through like an oiled eel." Niathal got up and wandered around her office, long, webbed, bony fingers clasped behind her back. She had that upright bearing all the GA military had, regardless of species or spinal arrangement. "Now that we both have the ability to vary statutes—any statutes—within budgetary limits, I imagine you've given its potential plenty of thought."

Jacen wanted her to stand still and look at him, but she continued her slow amble around the office.

She plays these games beautifully. I'll have to be careful not to cross her.

"It's an emergency kit," he said. "If we need to, we can change any minor law, and we can also change any big one if we play this smart." *We. Not I.* He thought it important to emphasize that they were partners. "For example, if Aitch-Em-Three were to amend the Emergency Measures Act to include in its scope the GAG's powers to detain heads of state, politicians, and any other individuals believed to be presenting a genuine risk to the security of the Galactic Alliance, and to seize their assets via the Treasury Orders Act, then I suspect people would look at Prime Minister Gejjen and nod approvingly."

"You even *talk* like a legislator now . . ."

"But am I right?"

Niathal turned. She couldn't smile like a human, but the amusement was written all over her face in a slight compression of the lips. Jacen felt her shift from her perpetual wariness and impatience to a satisfied warmth—even triumph—for a brief moment.

"That nobody will think of asking if the Chief of State of the GA is covered by that amendment? Yes, Jacen, you're right." She made a gesture, holding her hand like a blade and weaving it through imaginary water. "That eel of yours will slip through again."

"If I feel we have to . . . act to restore stability and security, will you be standing with me?"

Will you stage a coup with me? Did I really say that?

Niathal did pause. But it wasn't the taken-aback pause of someone shocked by an outrageous proposal; just a moment of sizing up Jacen Solo.

"You might have the GAG behind you, Jacen, but you need the fleet, too, don't you? And the rest of the army."

"Is that a yes?"

"It's an 'If things get worse, I put my allegiance to the GA before my allegiance to an individual.' "

"I'm . . . interested to see that the military will cross the line from carrying out the government's will into deciding policy."

"In case you forget," said Niathal softly, "the office of Supreme Commander effectively combines the role of defense secretary and the chair of the Joint Chiefs of Staff. I *am* a politician. I also happen to be the most senior military officer."

She was his equal in maneuvering, but she didn't have Force powers. He hoped he would never have to point that out to her.

"It's time we had a chat with Omas, then." Jacen stood up and brushed down his black GAG fatigues with his hands. "Just to be certain. For all we know, he might be meeting Gejjen to whip out a blaster himself and effect another Corellian regime change."

Niathal followed him into the corridor that led to the Chief of State's suite, elegant blue and gold marble and niche-studded walls with fine statues from across the galaxy. Jacen found his heart pounding. Although he could control it, he let it race because it made him feel alive and human. These were momentous times, and if he cut himself off completely from normality he might forget the magnitude of his task—and the stakes.

How can I forget Ben has to die?

When Jacen thought in words, when he heard himself in his mind, he realized how his language was shifting. He was distancing himself from the reality. *Ben has to die.* It felt very different from *I have to kill him.* Perhaps the Force was telling him it wouldn't be a simple betrayal of Ben's trust delivered with a lightsaber, but death by another route.

If it has to happen . . . perhaps not by my hand.

The doors to the Chief of State's suite slid open, and he walked into the quiet, thickly carpeted reception room with Niathal at his side; not behind, not ahead, but exactly level with him. Omas was leaning over his aide's desk, talking in hushed tones.

"I'm sorry to have kept you waiting," he said, looking up. "Do come in."

Jacen moved his chair so he wasn't forced to squint at Omas

against the light from the window. So did Niathal. It was an eloquent, silent statement of who would have the upper hand, and they hadn't rehearsed it. Omas, a man finely attuned to the subtleties of body language and psychological advantage, radiated wariness in the Force. He knew he was dealing with a united front.

"You've seen the battle report, I take it," Niathal said.

"Yes." Omas reached for a datapad as if to reassure her that he had. "Whether it was lucky timing on the Bothans' part or a smart trap, the real issue now is how we deal with a Bothawui that's becoming even better armed and aggressive."

"Actually, it does matter if it was lucky or not," said Jacen. "Because it goes to the heart of the quality of our intelligence. I'm not happy with the quality of GA Intel, which, if you recall, is why I wanted to form the GAG from selected personnel. Intel isn't up to the task we face now."

Omas looked weary. "Okay, you've both got a complaint. Who's first?"

Niathal inclined her head politely, but Jacen could feel her resolution forming a box around her almost like durasteel. It was tangible. "I'll keep it brief," she said. "We can't get involved in every little skirmish to keep obscure Senators and tin-pot heads of state in the Alliance. We're at overstretch. We couldn't maintain the Corellian blockade, and now we have the Bothans ramping up. Pick your battles, Chief of State. I can't fight them all."

Omas did his displacement act and poured himself a cup of caf from the jug on his desk. There was just one cup, and he didn't offer more.

"If we fail to show support to Alliance member worlds, then we lose them," he said. "This is basic numbers. We've been through all this. If more secede, then we've lost. The issue of how we maintain a joint defense force for the Alliance—which is what started this, in case we forget—then becomes academic."

"If we don't concentrate our forces on the worlds that present the most immediate and serious threat, then we'll be ground down a ship at a time, and we might not even be able to defend Coruscant if it comes to the worst."

"You think it might come to that?" Omas didn't appear convinced. He glanced at Jacen, but Jacen kept his counsel. "Is this about Coruscant in the end?"

"Of course it is," Niathal said. "It *always* is. The Alliance and Coruscant are indivisible, and that's half the problem for all the other worlds."

Omas turned to Jacen. "Your turn, Colonel."

"I share the admiral's fears about overstretch." Now Jacen slipped in his challenge, subtle and multilayered, to give Omas a chance to come clean. He found himself hoping Omas didn't take it. "Corellia is still the heart of this. I say we devote all our resources in the immediate term to an all-out assault on Corellia—invasion, in fact. Destroy their industrial base, and remove Gejjen and his cronies. The man's already had his predecessor killed and made an attempt on the Hapan Queen Mother." Jacen paused a beat, because timing was everything. "I've no doubt you'll be next."

Jacen felt Niathal's reaction although her expression was set in neutral: amusement, plus a little anxious excitement like preparing for battle. Omas felt suddenly more wary—but Jacen couldn't tell if that was aimed at him, or at the idea that Gejjen might be setting Omas up.

"You have intelligence to suggest that?" Omas asked.

Jacen shook his head. "No, and I don't need it or help from the Force to work it out. It's how Gejjen does business."

"If we launch that kind of assault on Corellia, it's something I should take to the Security Council. And even if they agree to it—"

"We're at war. You have all the legal powers to determine the conduct of the war with Admiral Niathal, as you see fit."

"Until it costs more credits," said Omas. "And once we're conspicuously focused on Corellia, what are Bothawui and Commenor going to do? Answers on a small piece of flimsi, please . . ."

Omas had the perfect excuse now to admit to the meeting with Gejjen. He could have said that he was going to give peace talks one last try. He could have said anything to indicate that he was going to talk terms with a state that showed no signs of understanding the words *common good,* and whose quietly lethal leader could have scared a Hutt gang lord.

And, Jacen thought, any smart politician might have suspected that his Intelligence Service spied on him, just as they spied on all the other Senators. A little game of words: Omas could have made the suggestion and watched Jacen's reaction, brazening it out to test if his clandestine call had been picked up.

But he didn't. And his future—and his fate—were sealed.

"So where are we going with this?" Niathal asked. "Same strategy? Keep dividing up the fleet until we have one ship per theater?"

"I think a full assault on Corellia is madness," said Omas. "We might well have to consider it—but much later. In the meantime, my priority is to stop secessions from the Alliance from reaching the tipping point."

Jacen sat feigning suppressed anger and disappointment. It had to be subtle, because Omas knew Jacen's capacity for smiling self-control. But Omas needed to pick up the faintest whiff of dissent and savor it for a few moments; his suspicions would be aroused if Jacen caved in too readily.

Jacen placed his hands squarely on the arms of the apocia wood chair and eased himself to his feet.

"For the record, I think this is a big mistake, sir," he said. "And I would be happier if GAG could support our intelligence community in their efforts beyond Coruscant."

"I note your views, Colonel Solo, and I'm grateful for your strategic input so far." Omas meshed his fingers and leaned on the desk, a gesture that said *defensive* more than it said *resolute*. "The GAG's remit is domestic, though. I appreciate your concern for the quality of our intelligence."

Jacen didn't catch Niathal's eye. He walked out, followed closely by her, and said nothing until they were back in her office.

"Well?"

"Not good," she said. She wandered up to the window to watch the traffic streaming in orderly lines in the skylanes around the Senate District. "Not exactly open with us, is he?"

"I never told him we have GAG personnel operating on Corellia, so we're even."

"We can't sustain the current strategy. Perhaps I should talk to Senator G'Sil and get it referred to the Security Council."

"And then we divert our energies into an internal power struggle with Omas while we have a war to fight. I'm sure I don't have to tell you that if you take a shot at someone, you keep firing until they can no longer return fire. Wound them, and you have an angry enemy who knows your position."

"I know where you're heading with this, Jacen."

"You know I'm right."

"That doesn't make it any easier."

"If he does a deal with Gejjen, we're not just back to square one: the Alliance is in a worse position than when it started."

"And we'll be out of the game."

"That's academic." Jacen almost asked Niathal if she had children, and then realized he had almost done the most stupid thing imaginable: reveal his constant fears for the future of his own daughter, a child whose paternity had to stay hidden. He recovered fast, astonished at his weakness. "Because the game will be recurring wars."

"Or Omas might end up with a vibroblade in his throat."

"He's insane to meet Gejjen face-to-face without close protection anyway. He hasn't asked for it from us. He hasn't asked CSF, either—"

"GA Intel?"

"No. We tap their comms, too."

"You're a source of constant revelation, Jacen Solo . . ."

"Are you in?"

"Say it."

Jacen looked around the room, trying to look as if he was simply thinking, but suspicious that someone else might be doing to him what he did to them—eavesdrop electronically. Was Niathal setting him up? No, he was sure he could sense bugs in a room. There were none. "You know what I'm proposing."

"I don't, actually. Not in detail. Say it."

"Regime change." Too late. But he couldn't sense any risk. His logical brain was the paranoid, whispering voice, not his Force-senses. He realized he'd become less instinct-driven and more rational, and that was the problem. *Thinking too much, feeling too little, just like Lumiya says.* "We remove him from office long enough to get this war won, and then hand it back to Senator G'Sil when the situation is stable so that new elections can take place."

His words emerged like uninvited strangers, and he didn't even

believe himself. Niathal made a little splutter that could have been laughter.

"I get the removal. It's the gap in the middle between *remove* and *elections* that fascinates me."

"We run the GA during the interim as a duumvirate. No dictatorship. Joint control."

Niathal indicated her uniform and then reached out to jab a bony finger into the rank tab on his shoulder. "*Military coup*. That's what it's called. Let's not prevaricate."

"Okay, I remove him and *you* take over, alone."

"I don't think so. Duumvirate sounds best to me."

Jacen liked two; two was the Sith way. Knowing Niathal's ambition for the Chief's office, he'd have the same circling, edgy power struggle with her as a Sith Master with an apprentice who was expected and encouraged to plot to overthrow him.

But he would rule as Sith Lord in due course, when the GA and elections were academic, and she would administer the state. That would satisfy her.

"I'll take care of Gejjen, by the way," he said. "He's a massively destabilizing influence, and removing him will throw Corellia into disarray."

"How will you take care of Omas?"

"I'll remove him by house arrest."

"Deposed heads of state tend to become martyrs and hostages."

"We can't be seen to kill our own, and framing Gejjen for it did occur to me, but it's not necessary. We need to show ourselves as civilized people working within the law."

"With a coup."

"Under the law, as the law will stand, it won't be."

"Ahhhh. I forgot." No, she hadn't, he knew that. "Your amendment to the law."

"I'm tabling it for next week, through Aitch-Em-Three."

"And in the meantime?"

"Leave that to me. I'll have someone there when Omas meets Gejjen." Jacen checked his datapad. "He needs only a day to do his business with Gejjen, no more, so—my people have him under surveillance, ready to move. Then we have evidence to present to G'Sil."

"And then you arrest him."

"I was thinking I might arrest him at the same time you present the evidence to G'Sil. When we move, we have to move fast. No room to be outmaneuvered."

Niathal let out a long breath. Jacen waited.

"I'll be ready to move on your signal. Make sure you keep me up to speed with all this, won't you?"

It was done. Jacen's takeover was in place. He had the GAG at his back, and Niathal would deliver the fleet as well as the army. With the right presentation of Omas selling out to the Corellians, it would be a very orderly coup.

There was no need for unnecessary bloodshed. That was what this was all about: an end to violence, chaos, and instability.

That was worth everything he was risking.

Jacen took an air taxi back to a plaza a few minutes' walk from the GAG HQ: just another citizen, no sleek black GA transport, no privilege. Either the driver didn't recognize the uniform, or he hesitated to say, *Here, you're the chief of the secret police, aren't you?* It was a silent, contemplative journey.

It was time to make sure nothing went wrong, if manifest destiny *could* go wrong. He opened his comlink and called Lumiya.

"Shira," he said, aware of the pilot up front. "I need you to do a job for me."

chapter seven

Goran, in Fett's absence, I think you really ought to see this. I don't think it can wait. Sometimes the *vongese* do you a favor.

—Site foreman Herik Vorad, *on examination of excavated rock from land north of Enceri, Mandalore*

SAFE HOUSE, CORUSCANT

"SO YOU'RE GOING TO DO IT BEFORE YOU ACHIEVE YOUR FULL SITH powers," said Lumiya. She lit the candles and closed the blinds. Jacen needed to shut out the world and *feel* what was happening; he was running increasingly on a mundane agenda, the agenda of the lesser beings he worked with. "Why?"

"If I do it afterward, when might *afterward* be?" Jacen watched the flames shimmering and settled down cross-legged on a floor cushion, but his eyes kept wandering away from the focus of concentration, and Lumiya felt obliged to rap him sharply on the top of his head and point at the candle. "Omas is doing a deal with Gejjen. The deal excludes me, and Niathal, possibly in a rather *terminal* way."

Working in the world of those who couldn't use the Force, Jacen was falling into conniving and manipulating just like them, and while Lumiya didn't think that was a bad thing—all tools were valid to achieve the outcome—he was letting himself be bound by their rules. He was talking about *timing*. He had full mastery of the Force, but he seemed to enjoy using the limited tricks of ordinary people.

The admiral was irrelevant in the long term. He had to be aware of that. "Niathal is afraid of you, Jacen. Or at least wary."

"Don't you think I know that? She'd be an idiot if she trusted anyone at this level of government."

"You waste too much energy playing mundanes' games instead of using the Force."

"I'll use it when I need to. Most of the time now, it's overkill."

Jacen always seemed to want to prove how much smarter, how much more skilled he was than his adversaries, how he could beat them on their own terms. Vanity wasn't always a bad thing in a Sith— as long as it didn't control him. It was just a matter of getting him to pause and refocus.

"Meditate," said Lumiya.

Jacen stared through her for a moment, and then stared unblinking at the candle until he eventually closed his eyes. He opened one eye slowly, looking as if he might be about to make a joke. Lumiya didn't feel in a humorous mood.

"Actually, I called you for a reason," he said.

"I know. But I'd like to approach this like Force-users, not like some tedious little committee in the Senate." It was time to remind him he still had one more step to take before he could begin to teach her anything. "Calm yourself and put the world to one side."

Jacen shut his eyes again, and—for once—seemed to relax enough to allow a little of his state of mind to filter through the barrier that he now kept in place most of the time. Lumiya sensed the solid confidence and focus that typified him. But there was still the faintest hint of the old Jacen, wounded by bereavement and pain, scared of doing necessary things. *That* was the last tinge of doubt and reluctance that

his final step would erase. It would enable him to cross the line into his full Sith legacy.

She didn't know when *afterward* might be, either, or even *who*. She only knew it was *soon*.

"You don't need to play their games, Jacen," she said softly. "Even now your powers put you far beyond their reach. Omas can't touch you. Neither can Gejjen. When you achieve your destiny, they'll be less than irrelevant."

"Powers or not, I can't control a galaxy on my own. I need to persuade, to carry people with me. The Force can't affect the minds of millions."

Ah, you enjoy the power you can wield with simple mind games. Don't make Palpatine's mistakes. That's an indulgence. It's not worthy of you.

"Jacen," she said. "I want you to take stock and feel. Stop overanalyzing. It won't reveal any truths to you. Just facts. Facts only show you what you want to see."

Jacen opened his eyes again. "But it's so *fleeting*. The line between a crazy impulse and guidance from the Force is getting harder to draw."

"Because you *think* about it too much."

The impenetrable wall went up again. Lumiya felt it as he lapsed into silence.

"It's Ben," he said at last. "It has to be Ben."

Now she understood. "You're fond of the boy. Perhaps he's the child you don't have. This will be hard, and that's probably why it has to be him."

For a moment, Jacen's gaze flickered—too brief, too insignificant for any ordinary observer to spot—and she knew she'd hit a nerve. That was it: conscious of his own mortality, he wanted a son, and there was a little subconscious desire to possess what was Luke's as part of the overthrow of the Jedi dynasty. Now that he had it, and Ben looked to him as a heroic father figure, he had to throw away that prize.

It was an odd sort of love, but if it was powerful enough, it would do fine.

"That's probably it," Jacen said, and looked down at his clasped hands. "And it's hard to kill someone who doesn't deserve it."

"But you don't know how it'll happen."

"Exactly."

"You can't see yourself taking a lightsaber to a fourteen-year-old boy."

"Maybe it won't be so literal. I'm sending him to assassinate Dur Gejjen when he meets Omas to do his deal. It's a job that needs doing, it tests Ben's skills and commitment, it's far easier for a teenage boy to get past Gejjen's security, and . . . perhaps it will put him in real mortal danger." Jacen reached out to the low table nearby, leaning on one hand to stretch and pick up one of the candles in its transparent blue holder. "Now, is that a consequence of the task, or is that why I'm sending him? Am I sending him to his death?"

"Let it play out," Lumiya said. "Stop rationalizing and let it happen."

She stood up to take the candle from him. She could see he wanted to play that brinkmanship game again of how long he could hold his hand in the flame. Some men would do it out of bravado after too many drinks, but Jacen was testing himself, a private struggle rooted in his experience of pain at Vergere's hands and his lingering doubts that he could stay the course and make himself do something he wanted to run from.

"I need your help," he said. "I need you to distract Mara for a while."

"Whatever you wish."

"She's taken the Brisha story to heart. Nothing like killing someone's child to guarantee a blood feud, is there?"

"I thought that story might tie her up and explain my presence. In an ideal world, I would have avoided all contact with the Skywalkers."

"So . . . why *did* you offer your hand to Luke instead of taking his head off?"

Lumiya was still considering that. She might not have meant Luke any harm, but she didn't have to hate someone to kill him in the line of duty. Did it matter that he still thought all her actions were dictated by an old romance, and by a trauma that had been her destiny anyway? Why did she feel the need to show him they weren't?

"It certainly had its shock value in the fight," she said. "And killing him would have changed the course of events for all of us."

"And you wanted to put him in his place. Show him he had no leverage . . . that you were over him?"

Jacen sometimes seemed to understand and then he'd say something banal like that, which made her think he had missed the point of passing through powerful emotions to become stronger.

"The Skywalkers are too mired in their domesticity to be effective Jedi, Jacen," she said. "It's a warning to us all. Luke can't see what's in front of him because he thinks my motive is lost love and revenge, because that's the level *he* thinks at—family and friends. It would never occur to him that I want to see a Sith-controlled galaxy and that the personal issues we had are trivial by comparison."

"You taught me that anger and passion are what make Sith strong."

"There's anger, and then there's being controlled by it—not seeing the forest for the trees." Lumiya had a moment of self-doubt and decided to meditate on it later. "So what about Mara?"

"She's hanging on to that GAG connection she found to track you. Keep her occupied elsewhere."

"I'll let her find me. That should do the trick. Can you give me a possession of Ben's, something that would prove to Mara that I could get at him easily, without being traceable to you?"

"I'll get you a pair of his boots. He keeps several pairs in his locker, and Mara already suspects a GAG connection." He gave her a little frown of concern, but she felt nothing emanating from him. "What if she actually catches you?"

"I might win, and anyway—it'll buy you time." Lumiya was still testing herself to see if she resented Jacen for leaving her to die, too. "I'm expendable, as you've proven. My life's purpose is to enable you to become a Sith Lord, because that secures the stability of the galaxy. The ambition of most beings is just to stay alive, overeat, spend too much, and avoid hard work. I'm happy that I can achieve much more than that . . . and we all die sooner or later. A death in service of a great ideal is a fine thing."

Jacen gave her a long, blank stare, and she wondered if the idea of an eternal principle being more important than the short confines of his own mortal life was alien to him. He had to pass beyond that. He *would*.

"When you think of Ben's fate," she said, "think of the legacy you'll leave in years to come, and ask who'll be able to name the Skywalkers, or even the Solos. This is about the fate of trillions upon trillions for millennia to come—not one small family over a few decades."

Jacen got to his feet, but Lumiya could tell he was looking at her without seeing her now.

"I'll keep telling myself that," he said. "The boots will get Mara's attention, for sure."

"I think I'll play up the maternal grief and do something emotional, too. What are you going to do when Mara and Luke come after you—when they find out about Ben in due course?"

"I'll deal with that when I have to."

"It might be sooner than you think. I suggest you make sure you're *properly* armed."

"I have quite an armory," said Jacen. "And I'll be ready when the time comes."

"Think laterally," Lumiya said gently. "Luke can still take you in a lightsaber fight."

"I'm already a few steps ahead of him. Trust me."

She had to. The future of the galaxy depended on Jacen. He was the end of chaos and the beginning of order, and—like all forces of change—he would *not* be hailed by everyone as a savior. Some wouldn't see how necessary he was. Some would try to stop him.

She would do whatever it took to clear his path—even if the price was her own life.

SURVEILLANCE CENTER, GAG HQ, CORUSCANT

Captain Girdun loomed in the doorway, backlit by the light from the corridor. "Showtime," he said. "Niathal's just been designated as acting Chief of State as of midnight."

The troopers on duty in the listening post looked up. Ben detached the bead amplifier in his ear and tried to make sense of that news. "What's happened to Omas?"

"He's going to be out of the office for a day."

"Oh, I thought—"

"He has to give a little notice to hand over the reins of state to Niathal when he's out of contact—you know, command codes, that kind of stuff. So we have a window for his trip to Vulpter. Tomorrow."

It was all moving too fast. Ben could recall feeling excited by the turmoil of events, but now that he was part of them, they were too fast for his comfort. They brought him closer to his mission. He wasn't relishing the prospect; he knew how he'd felt after killing a suspect he thought was armed, so he could work out that he wouldn't be any happier after dispatching Gejjen.

I'm an assassin. And everyone else my age who isn't a Jedi is in school.

"What cover story has he given?" Ben asked.

"Private medical matter."

"Yeah, saving his backside," said Zavirk.

"I think this is the opportunity you've been waiting for, Ben." Girdun beckoned to him. "Come on. Briefing room." He turned to Zavirk. "I want to know his itinerary to Vulpter. He won't be taking us along, but he'll still need transport, a minder, and a pilot, so let's keep an eye on the logistics."

"Bet he takes an Intel zombie or two with him for company."

"Well, we're keeping an eye on them, too, so that'll help us triangulate, won't it? Get to it, Trooper."

The captain strode off down the corridor whistling, which was unlike him. Ben hadn't realized Girdun disliked Omas so much. Maybe he just enjoyed a really major hunt. It couldn't get much bigger than tailing the Chief of State to an illicit meeting with the enemy. There was no hate in Girdun, just a wonderful sense of focus and excitement. Ben wondered if darkness was as easy to spot as Jedi seemed to think.

But what's darkness? Killing Gejjen?

The worst thing about growing up was that there were fewer right-or-wrong answers every day. It wasn't a math test.

When they reached the briefing room, Shevu and Lekauf were already there, poring over a wall full of illuminated holodisplays. Lekauf, looking far from comfortable in his brand-new lieutenant's rank insignia, gave Ben a nervous grin.

"Our source in Coronet confirms that Gejjen's rescheduled all his engagements for tomorrow," said Shevu. "It's on for sure."

"Timetable?"

"No outbound timings, but he expects to be back in time for a meeting by oh-eight-hundred the next day."

The displays on the walls showed two sets of charts and data: one was Coruscant, the other Corellia. Ben checked off the list of surveillance points—Omas's private residence, the security cams from the Senate offices, the handful of private landing pads nearest to both, and a tally of flight plans filed for Vulpter. The Corellian status board also showed recent flight plans logged with that planet as a destination.

"What if Omas breaks his journey somewhere, and doesn't fly straight to Vulpter?" Ben asked.

"That's where marrying it up with arrivals and flight plans for Vulpter helps." Lekauf pointed to a datapad on the table. "Check that out. Even if the flight doesn't originate from Coruscant, we can run checks to see what's arriving with Coruscant as its point of departure within that time window."

"The boring number-crunching stuff," said Girdun. "Don't worry, a computer's narrowing down the choices. Once we spot Omas moving—or even Gejjen—then we put a tail on them. Easier to tail Omas, but we might get a break from Gejjen."

"How?"

"We have an informant in the Corellian government building. This is the thing about information, Ben. It's not a case of finding a big *X* on a chart labeled *the secret meeting is here*. It's actually about assembling a lot of apparently routine stuff that's not secret at all and looking for the patterns."

Ben watched the flight plans from Coronet appearing on the screen. Any neutral pilot entering Corellian airspace could get access to this. Anybody could get information from ATC on Vulpter. And Coruscant ATC was an open book, available from any dataport. There was a daunting amount of data, but a computer or a droid could sift through it just as they sifted through the thousands of comlink calls to flag those that were worth the scrutiny of flesh and blood. It was just a matter of setting the parameters right.

Ben wasn't sure why he was here other than to learn the tedious and painstaking side of the job. Shevu and Lekauf seemed to be planning an interception.

"They're just working out how we get you close enough to Gej-

jen." Girdun seemed to assume Ben knew what he was talking about. "And that has to be *after* he's finished his meeting with Omas, because the boss wants the evidence of the meeting for the Security Council."

Revelation dawned. Ben had hoped he'd have more preparation time, but this was it. "We're doing the hit at the same time as the meeting? Not when he's on the way back, or—"

"We might not get another chance to take a crack at Gejjen away from his home turf."

Lekauf beckoned to Ben and made him look inside a fabric holdall leaning against the wall. "Like it?"

Ben couldn't work out what it was at first, but when he took it from the bag, it turned out to be a rifle with a folding stock. He unfolded it and snapped the stock into place, staring at it in numb realization.

"It's a modified Karpaki Fifty," Lekauf said, totally misreading Ben's reaction to the weapon. "Can't leave lightsaber marks all over Gejjen, can we? Bit of a giveaway. You're now going to make a *very* fast acquaint of a ballistic sniper rifle. Y'know—projectiles."

"If you're trying to get me close to Gejjen, why do I need a sniper weapon?"

"In case we can't. Come on, let's get in a few hours on the indoor range."

Ben wondered if it was his last chance to refuse, but he knew he couldn't. If Shevu was taking part in this—and Shevu was dead straight, a man the other officers described as an old-fashioned kind of cop—then it had to be the right thing to do.

Girdun responded to his chirping comlink. It was Zavirk, judging by the side of the conversation that Ben could hear. Girdun slid the comlink back in his pocket, a big grin on his face.

"Intelligence is sending a couple of handlers with Omas," he said. "Just overheard their arrangements. Oh-five-hundred start, leaving from his private landing pad and transferring to an unmarked Intelligence cutter in Coruscant orbit. Sneaky, eh? But it helps when you know their code names for various VIPs." He checked his chrono. "If I ever end up back in Intelligence, remind me to make them *better*. Got to go."

Shevu raised an eyebrow. "He loves his work."

"Are you okay with this?" Ben asked.

"Okay with what?"

"Gejjen."

"I'm not a spook," Shevu said. "Never was. But if Gejjen has Omas killed, it'll destabilize the whole GA. So I'm okay with it."

"Do you think he will?"

"I'd want proof that he *wouldn't*. Personally, I think we should blow our cover and stop Omas from going, but that just compromises our whole operation. So we're riding along with you to make sure Omas gets home in one piece."

Shevu never made any comments on whether he thought Omas was a traitor betraying the GA, or a visionary taking a massive risk for peace. He didn't get involved with politics and opinions. He just stuck to the law as best he could. And that wasn't easy in the GAG.

"What are you waiting for?" Shevu asked.

"I just wondered if you think I'm right to do this."

"That's not my call." Shevu busied himself with holocharts of Vulpter, opening three-D images of the spaceports and public buildings. "You've got your orders."

Lekauf gave Ben a nudge in the back. "Come on, I've got to turn you into a passable sniper by tomorrow morning."

The indoor range had that ozonic discharged-blaster smell with a tinge of burned plastoid. Something in the air made Ben's eyes sting. It was an expensive facility that Lekauf said had been cobbled together from equipment originally intended for Intelligence: hologram simulations, regular targets, and even something he called "dead meat."

"I'm not sure I'm going to be much use with a rifle," Ben said.

"Aw, come on." Lekauf was unconvinced. "You're a Jedi. You're not like the rest of us. You've got this visuospatial ability we haven't— my granddad used to tell my dad amazing things about Lord Vader. Really uncanny accuracy in three dimensions, whether he was flying a ship or using a weapon. I used to think Dad was making it up until I saw real Jedi doing that stuff."

"Why not a blaster?"

"Loads of reasons. We need overkill. We need something that

doesn't light the place up like fireworks. And we want something that can be silenced. Believe it or not, that thing is quite discreet."

Ben steadied the Karpaki against his shoulder, sighted up a few times, and took his firing position. He was quite pleased to get that far without making a fool of himself. "You seem to have a good opinion of Vader."

"My granddad thought the world of him. When he got badly burned on a mission and had to be discharged from the Imperial Army, Lord Vader made sure he was taken care of for the rest of his life. Whatever some people say about Vader, monsters don't look out for lieutenants."

"That's good to know," said Ben. He liked the idea of his grandfather having his kind moments, and that some people still thought well of him. Not everyone had been sympathetic to the Rebellion. Ben imagined Vader doing the difficult things that Jacen was facing now.

And that I'm facing.

At the end of the range, a shadowy man walked quickly across Ben's field of view and vanished. Ben's instinctive reaction was that this person was real, and breaking safety regulations, so he lowered his weapon and called a warning. Lekauf burst out laughing.

"Ben, that's your *target*."

"That wasn't a hologram. It was *solid*."

"Uh, yeah . . ." Lekauf put his hand on the control console and the "man" walked back into view again to sit on a chair in the target zone. "It's a gel-form. It's an adjustable droid made of gel and plastoid to mimic flesh and bone. So you . . . well, so you get used to a target moving like a real person. That one's been adjusted to match Gejjen's build and gait based on holonews footage, so you get used to what he'll look like and how he'll probably fall."

Ben was transfixed. It was just a dummy, just a clever piece of training technology. He checked it in the Force—yes, it was just a machine—but he still felt awful about it.

"That's pretty yucky."

"You know how much those things *cost*?"

"What happens when I shoot . . . it?"

"It gets up and repairs itself."

"Okay." Ben found it disturbing to watch the figure walking around in the small bay at the end of the range. Through the rifle's optics, it was clearly a featureless, translucent gel figure with the shadowy framework of artificial bone within. "You sure it doesn't feel anything?"

"It just moves, Ben. It doesn't think. It's not even a proper droid. More like a puppet." He looked at the chrono display on the wall. "You've got less than nineteen hours to get up to speed."

"No pressure, then . . ."

"In your own time, fire when ready."

Ben recalled his recent training. "Why not center mass?"

"That's the army way—kill or wound, you've still put the target out of action. Police snipers have to worry about hostages and stuff, so they're trained to incapacitate instantly—head shot. Assassination doesn't have to be as instant, just *dead*. But a head shot's still best." Lekauf crooked his forefingers and thumbs five centimeters apart and made a gesture as if he were putting on a blindfold. "That's the zone you're aiming at. A five-centimeter band around the head at eye level. Put one in there and you've got a kill. But with the kind of frangible round you'll be using, as long as you hit the head or neck at all, the result's the same."

"What if I can only get a shot at center mass?"

"He won't respond to cardiopulmonary resuscitation after a round hits him, believe me." When Lekauf was getting technical, Ben knew he was enjoying his subject. "Optimum is still the head shot, though."

"But there's wind speed and everything."

"This Karpaki has smart sensor optics. Senses the windage and allows for it. They've improved a bit in recent years."

"If it's that clever, then why do I have to train?"

"To get used to shooting someone who's not trying to kill you. Who doesn't even know you're there. Not the Jedi way, is it?"

It was just a dummy. But it moved like Gejjen.

Ben aimed.

It was just like using a lightsaber, really. Letting the Force guide the hand, the eye . . .

He squeezed the trigger as the gel-form sat down on the chair, and the round caught the point of its right temple. Gel and fragments plumed in the air, and the dummy slumped forward.

Lekauf, arms folded, considered the inert form with the eye of a connoisseur. Ben was taken aback by how uncomfortable it made him feel, especially when the gel-form suddenly sat upright, then stood.

He was sure he couldn't shoot it a second time.

"And again," said Lekauf.

Ben spent the next hour getting used to anticipating movement, waiting for the gel-form to settle for just long enough to take the shot. It was harder than he thought: the dummy made no impression in the Force, which limited Ben's senses. And it kept getting up and walking around each time, a distressing gel ghost of a man he was going to kill.

There was no emotion in it. That made it hard. But he was getting good single shots. He tried to see it as a technical exercise, like lightsaber drill, an action totally separate from the nasty business of taking off heads, and imagined the gel-form with the short dark hair of Dur Gejjen.

"Ben," Lekauf said quietly, "I'll be there and so will Shevu. You've got backup if anything goes wrong. If you can't get at him, or you don't get a clean shot, we'll make sure he drops and stays down. Don't sweat it."

"But that'll expose you two."

"Like I said, it's just in case things don't go according to plan. Makes sense to build in some contingency in case we don't get another chance—because it'll be easier than hitting him on Corellia."

Ben pondered. "We don't even know the location. I could be doing this in the middle of a field or a crowded restaurant."

"You sabotaged Centerpoint. This is going to be a lot easier."

"When I did that, I still thought it was fun."

"Come on, you can do it."

There was something about Lekauf's faith and admiration that galvanized Ben. He concentrated on the dummy and tried to see himself not as shooting a helpless automaton or even a corrupt politician, but as *solving a problem*. A couple of hours later, he was hitting the five-centimeter zone 95 percent of the time.

"Better have a break now," Lekauf said.

Ben checked to make sure the adjacent lanes were clear and walked up the range to look at the gel-form. The more times he'd hit it, the slower the self-repair became. Its internal power supply needed recharging. It was struggling to get up, and Ben found himself increasingly disturbed as he watched the pathetic, anonymous figure scrambling to roll onto its chest and get on all fours. He forced himself to stop looking at it.

It was all the worse for there being none of the real aftermath of injury that he'd seen once too often.

"Lunch," Lekauf called, more insistently this time.

Ben wasn't certain he was that hungry.

BEVIIN-VASUR FARM, TEN KILOMETERS OUTSIDE KELDABE, MANDALORE

Goran Beviin looked up from the trench, a pitchfork in one hand and a muddy grin on his face. It was beginning to rain and he was up to his ankles in animal dung, but it seemed to make him perfectly happy.

"And they said being acting Mandalore would go to my head," he said, rubbing his nose on his sleeve. "So you came home fast, then."

Fett kept his distance. "Found what I was looking for. You didn't expect me back."

"*I* did. Some of the clan chieftains didn't. You have a habit of wandering off for a few years at a time." Beviin heaved himself out of the trench and wiped his palms on the seat of his pants. He looked very, very pleased with himself. "If you'd been away any longer, I'd have called you, but since you're back . . . Want to see something amazing?"

Fett wondered if now was a good time to tell Beviin the truth about his illness. The man had to know sooner or later. He could have formally declared himself Mandalore while Fett was gone, and probably found a lot of support among the clans, but he hadn't; he'd gone on shoveling dung and running his farm. He was happy with his life as it was. The galaxy would have worked better with a few more Beviins around.

"Okay," Fett said. "Amaze me."

Beviin beckoned and trudged through the mud toward the farm buildings. The fine drizzle was turning into rain, and the land looked bare—not in the ruined sense of the postwar devastation that blighted so much of the planet, but as if it had settled down to sleep for the coming winter. Despite the derivation of the *Fett* surname—derived from the word for "farmer"—and his father's childhood on his parents' Concord Dawn farm, Fett knew nothing about agriculture. He wished he could learn, sometimes, to better understand who his father had once been.

"Mirta behaving herself?" Beviin didn't look back over his shoulder. "Well, at least she hasn't tried to kill you again. It's a good sign. Kids can be such a handful."

Fett felt the mud suck at his boots. "She's a useful pair of fists in a fight."

"She'll produce wonderfully ferocious great-grandchildren for you, *Bob'ika*." Beviin paused a few beats. Fett tried to take in the phrase *great-grandchildren,* and it left him stranded. "So whatever it was you went to do ended in a fight, did it?"

"Just had to ask questions *emphatically.*"

"You going to tell me about it?"

It seemed as good a time as any, and Fett didn't see the point of sugarcoating it. "I'm terminally ill. Two years, tops. Eight, nine months if I carry on like this."

Beviin still didn't turn around. He walked on for a few more meters, head lowered against the rain, and then stopped in his tracks and finally faced Fett. He looked genuinely upset. Fett couldn't recall anyone being upset for him before, except his father. Lack of caring worked both ways.

Maybe Sintas had felt for him. He hadn't noticed.

"You're not going to sit back and let it happen, are you, *Bob'ika*? We can do *something,* surely."

Using the way-too-familiar form of his name didn't bother Fett at all now. "I found a clone who survived."

"So they *did* get a little more out of Ko Sai than revenge and a few souvenirs, then."

"There's no research data. Just the clone, Jaing Skirata. He wouldn't give me a blood sample, but he says he's got good medical resources." Now that Fett was back on Mandalore and Jaing was light-years away, though, the whole premise struck him as flimsy. The man hadn't even accepted a meal from him, which would have at least left useful traces of his genetic material on the utensils. Fett had nothing except time counting down and a suspicion that his judgment was failing just like his health. "I'll explain later."

"Why didn't you *tell* me? I could have tracked some clones for you. Enough of them deserted and ended up here."

"Ones who'd had the accelerated aging stopped?"

"I don't know, but I could have worked from those leads. *Shab, Bob'ika,* couldn't you have squeezed a little sample out of him anyway?"

"It's done now. And there was never a guarantee that Taun We or Beluine could make anything from it anyway."

Beviin looked disappointed for a moment, as if Fett had let the side down by not simply grabbing what he needed. But Jaing had been right. Fett needed Taun We to decode whatever it was in that clone's cells that stopped the degeneration, and Taun We would have turned that research over to her new bosses at Arkanian Micro. That was a bad deal for the clone, and a bad deal for Fett, because if anyone was going to make credits out of that data, it was him, and Mandalore needed those—

Well, there's a funny thing. Now I'm thinking long-term.

Beviin turned around and started walking again in silence. Fett's news had certainly taken the shine off whatever had made him so happy a little earlier.

The farm was a rambling collection of buildings scattered around a stone farmhouse with impressive dirtworks and defensive walls. The other structures—including the outbuilding that Fett was staying in—weren't so well defended, just variations on the traditional circular *vheh'yaime* set in deep pits and so thickly thatched that they were camouflaged. But the farmhouse was the last bastion in the event of an attack.

At the back of the building, and connected to it by an underground tunnel, stood a workshop with a smithy. Fett could hear the rhythmic hammering of metal across the clearing. There was no smoke curling from the roof. It vented many meters away to hide the loca-

tion, and Fett was sure there was a network of tunnels extending a long way into the hills to the west of the farm. It was one of the ways the Mandalorians had fought—and beaten—the Yuuzhan Vong.

Beviin walked down the steps cut into the hard-packed soil and leading down to the front door. It opened and Dinua, his adopted daughter, stood with hands on hips.

"*Boots,*" she said ominously, pointing at the clods of dung and mud. Two small children clung to her legs. "You too, *Mand'alor*. And you can take those coveralls off as well, *Buir*."

"Okay, okay." Beviin—spy, fixer, veteran commando—was driven back by a resolute woman. But Dinua had fought and killed Yuuzhan Vong from the age of fourteen, so making a mess on her clean floor wasn't to be attempted rashly. "We'll go the long way around."

They tramped around the perimeter of the farmhouse, following the sound of ringing metal.

"She's a good girl," Beviin said. "Just a bit irritable now that Jintar's away fighting. She's not one for staying at home. But the little ones are too young for both parents to be away."

So some had already taken mercenary work. Fett didn't think Beviin's farm was doing that badly, but maybe Jintar was too proud to accept his father-in-law's support.

"But you and Medrit are good with kids."

"Yeah, but this way, one parent stays alive . . ."

That was the harsh reality Fett had grown up with. It bred hard people.

As the door to the workshop swung open, a blast of warm air registered on his sensors. The interior was bathed in a red glow; sparks flew in arcing showers. How Beviin stood the noise, Fett would never know. His helmet controls had decided the volume was above danger level, and buffered the sound.

A mountain of a man in a singlet, burn-scarred leather apron, and ear defenders was hammering a strip of red-hot metal. Every time he raised his arm, sweat flew from him and hissed into steam on the hot surfaces. He folded the strip with tongs as he hammered, layering the metal with a steady rhythm that said he was a master armorsmith. After a while, he realized Fett and Beviin were standing watching; he gestured with an impatient jab of his finger to show he was going to finish working the metal before he'd stop to talk.

It was actually fascinating. Fett could see from the length and emerging form of the metal bar that he was making a *beskad*, the traditional saber of the ancient Mandalorians. Beviin had one, an antique blade fashioned from Mandalore's unique iron—*beskar*. Fett had watched him swing the weapon so hard into a Yuuzhan Vong officer that he'd had to stand on him to pull it free.

"There." Medrit Vasur cooled the rough form of the saber in a tub of hissing liquid and turned it this way and that to check the line. He took off his ear defenders, and his face cracked into a beatific smile of satisfaction as he wiped the sweat from his brow with his forearm. "Now, that's going to be a thing of beauty."

"*Med'ika*, I haven't told him yet," said Beviin.

"Shall I blurt it out, then?"

"You're the metallurgist . . ."

"*Mand'alor*," Medrit said stiffly, "you're looking at a test forging from a new lode of *beskar*."

It took Fett a slow second to grasp the importance of what Medrit had said. "But the Empire strip-mined Mandalore. They took all the iron."

"They missed a bit. A *big* bit."

"How? And how big?"

"This is a big planet with a tiny population, and even the Imperials didn't survey all of it. They stripped the shallow veins. This is a deeper lode, and we'd never have found it if the *vongese* hadn't left craters you could sink a small moon in." Medrit picked up a cloth and wiped his face. Fett couldn't feel the full impact of the temperature in the workshop, but Beviin had started sweating visibly; he left a mucky smear across his forehead as he wiped it. "There's a crew a hundred klicks north of Enceri still doing test drills, but it looks like a big, *big* lode that was exposed."

Enceri was remote even by Mandalore's standards; no wonder it had taken years to stumble across it. The Yuuzhan Vong had used singularity ordnance indiscriminately, smashing huge craters across the planet because they wanted to annihilate Mandalore, not conquer it.

Fett enjoyed a rare moment of pleasure imagining the look on their vile, arrogant, disfigured faces if they'd known they were helping Mandalore find a new source of the metal that had once made it mighty.

Beskar was the toughest metal known to science. Even lightsabers had trouble with it. There had been a time when every army in the galaxy wanted a supply.

It was still the most valuable metal on the market, and there was a war raging around them.

"I feel a new economic era coming on," said Fett.

Beviin winked. *"Oya manda."*

"And it's not on anyone's land." Fett realized the reason he'd never quite got a handle on what Mandalorian government actually meant was because it was so nebulous. "This is a resource for Mandalore as a whole."

"If you say it is, then it is. That's the Mandalore's prerogative."

"Okay, I say it is. Time to gather the chieftains and do a little forward planning."

"Shab," said Medrit, underwhelmed by the *Mand'alor*'s power to requisition resources. "You're sounding just like a proper head of state."

Fett would normally have found a family meal and a long explanation of the finer points of metallurgy worse than a spell in the Sarlacc. It was hard enough getting used to having a granddaughter without being besieged by Beviin's noisy, messy, demonstrative family. But that evening, he tolerated it.

"It's not just the ore," Medrit said, drawing an imaginary graph in midair with a nuna drumstick. "It's the *processing*. Part of the strength of the metal is in what's added during smelting and how it's worked. What you saw was just a test batch."

"Have we got the facilities to do that anymore?" Fett wasn't used to eating in front of anyone else. Dinua's son and daughter, Shalk and Briila—seven and five, he estimated—stared at him, unimpressed, across the table. The scrutiny of small children was unnerving. "Do we have a windfall we can't exploit?"

"On a small scale—we can do it," Beviin said. "I've done a few rough calculations. If the lode produces the yield we think it will, we're going to need some help from mining right through to processing. MandalMotors could process some of it, if they're willing to shift resources from combat craft. But the rest . . . we need droids."

"But what are you going to do with it?" Dinua asked.

"What?"

"Sell it for foreign currency, or use it to arm ourselves?"

Dinua, orphaned on the battlefield like Fett, was a savagely smart woman. Beviin had adopted her the moment her mother was killed, but Fett found that ability to turn strangers into family—that central part of Mandalorian culture—was beyond him. Even Medrit— impatient, critical, short-tempered—had accepted the unexpected addition to their household without a murmur. Adoption was what Mandalorians did, and always had.

If he can do it, why can't I? With my own flesh and blood, too.

"We do *both*," said Fett, trying to stay on the subject. "Some manufactured goods for export, some for our own rearmament."

"You'll find a lot of support for that," Beviin said. "Satisfies both camps."

What else can I do with the time I have left to me, except leave Mandalore in decent shape? "If we've got it, someone will want to take it."

"You think anyone's stupid enough to try invading like the Empire did?" Beviin said. "After we kicked Vong *shebs* like that?"

"*Ba'buir's* cussing," said Shalk gravely. "Can I say *shebs,* too?"

"No, you can't." Dinua clicked her teeth in annoyance. "*Buir,* please, not in front of the kids. *Mand'alor,* how are you going to announce the find? Other than the old-fashioned *Mando* way, by showing up at the border with an invading army?"

"Do we have to announce it?"

"If we want foreign revenue."

"We don't have a finance minister, but the job's yours."

"I'm serious."

"Commission a few starfighters and see who notices," Fett said. "Maybe this Kad'ika has a point—that we don't have to be on one side or the other. There's a third side, as . . . Goran says." It was only courtesy to address him by his first name in his own house. Fett had so little nonhostile interaction with anyone that basic etiquette felt like a minefield. "Our own."

"I could make sure the *aruetiise* notice," said Beviin. "But maybe a surprise is better."

"What kind of surprise?"

"The kind that makes you look up and run for a bomb shelter," Beviin said. "With a MandalMotors logo on the fuselage."

"We've got no territorial ambitions beyond the sector. We've got at least a dozen planets here to worry about."

"I know. But take a planet in postwar recovery, an ongoing civil war, and a new find of *beskar*, and we might have visitors. If not armed, then at least trying to do deals."

"Whatever. I don't lose sleep over what . . ."

Beviin filled the gap. *"Aruetiise."*

". . . *aruetiise* think of us. I'll talk to Yomaget in the morning. See what MandalMotors can commit."

Medrit chewed thoughtfully, staring at Fett. "You could have a decent set of *beskar'gam* to replace that durasteel *osik* you're wearing, too. It'll last several lifetimes."

"It only has to last a year, then."

Medrit stared at Fett, got no response, and turned to Beviin. He shook his head: *Later.* Dinua took the hint, too. Her kids gazed from face to face, looking for an explanation of what had plunged the grown-ups into silence. Fett was past caring whether anyone knew he was dying. Most wouldn't believe it anyway. It was hard to imagine the mortality of someone whose face you couldn't see.

"Plenty more nuna," Beviin said suddenly, pushing the serving plate of glistening, spice-crusted meat in front of him. "Home-raised, too."

It was never going to be a relaxed family dinner anyway. Just being Fett made sure of that. The food was spicier than he was used to and the portions were too big, but he cleared his plate because these were generous people who gave him a refuge here and who refused payment, even though he could have bought the entire planet twice over. It was what *Mando'ade* did for one another when someone was in trouble. The fact that he was *Mand'alor* was irrelevant.

He could almost hear Medrit telling Beviin later what a surly *shabuir* Fett was, and asking if Beviin really had to invite him around so often.

"You didn't tell me how the lode was found," Fett said. It was his best shot at small talk, given that they didn't seem to want to talk about his death. "After ten years? In the middle of nowhere?"

"From orbit." Medrit paused in midslice as he carved a sticky pile of nut-studded, glistening pastry into six portions and licked his fingers. Little burn scars peppered his hands. Fett wondered if he'd find metal filings in the cake. "Some *Mando'ade* coming home after a few generations in the Outer Rim. A minerals engineer and a geologist ran a few scans, compared them with the old geological charts, and decided to take a look on close approach. Result—*wayii!*"

"Good timing," Fett said.

"We're getting a lot of skilled people coming home, *Bob'ika*," Beviin said. "You said you wanted *Mando'ade* to come back, and some already have."

"Impressive." Fett was surprised at the willingness of people to abandon all they'd ever known simply at his suggestion. "Let's hope they're all that lucky."

"More resourcefulness than luck."

Fett thought of the last thing that Fenn Shysa had said to him. *If you only look after your own hide, then you're not a man.* No, Jaing didn't have any idea what went on between them in those final moments. People generally believed what they wanted to.

"Makes me wonder what else is still lying undiscovered on this planet," said Fett.

That night, lying awake far too long on the rickety trestle bed in the outbuilding, Fett reflected on the fact that Mirta hadn't been in touch since they'd returned, and wondered what his father would have done had he been Mandalore now.

Exhaustion was the best sleeping pill he knew. Before he let it engulf him, his last thought was that the *beskar* changed everything, except his own mortality.

chapter eight

Once Omas pulls his troops back, we'll talk the Bothans into behaving. Give it a month or two, let everyone calm down and get used to a cease-fire, and we'll use that lull to regroup with Commenor, Fondor, and Bothuwai to give Coruscant a pounding it'll never forget.

—*Corellian Prime Minister Dur Gejjen, discussing longer-term plans with Confederation defense staff*

GAG HQ LOCKER ROOMS, CORUSCANT: 2100 HOURS

SHEVU TOOK A LONG LOOK AT BEN AND HANDED HIM A SMALL CONtainer. It was filled with a dark brown fluid.

"You look dead beat," said Shevu. "But before you turn in for the night, there's a few loose ends to tie up."

Ben, slumped on a bench with his back resting on his locker door, was ready to drop. He had to be up at 0300 to prep for the flight to

Vulpter, and he still didn't know his final destination, or the location for the hit.

That wasn't unusual, apparently. It was just as well he was used to improvising.

"I'm scoring ninety-seven percent, sir."

Shevu sounded as if he'd stifled a laugh. He exuded a sense of pity. "It's hard to know what to say."

"I'm ready. Really I am."

"I meant that it's amazing that we can pretty well train a sniper in a day. If he's a Jedi, of course." Shevu put the bottle in Ben's hand. There was the slow and steady drip of water somewhere in the locker rooms, and the scent of faintly herbal soap. "You're being inserted ahead of time with Lekauf, and I'll be shadowing Omas's flight. We'll RV on Vulpter at Charbi City Spaceport, because he's meeting Gejjen in one of the conference rooms there that they hire out for business meetings by the hour. Personally, I think GA Intel is insane to let him do that. No sterile area, no screening, no security except for two guys with him for close protection. But it's anonymous, there's no advance booking to trace, Charbi is a slum—and we can stroll in."

"Won't someone recognize him?"

Shevu pointed to the bottle of brown liquid. "I don't think it'll even take some of this to let him get through a spaceport unrecognized. How many checks does a business passenger go through, landing in a private vessel? *One,* at the Customs and Immigration desk. And this is Vulpter, for goodness' sake—their security isn't exactly a ring of durasteel. He could even use the rooms on the other side of that control, and he never has to be seen at all. Effectively, it all happens on the landing strip side."

Ben thought it through, seeing the spaceport in his mind's eye, adding permacrete and passengers to the holochart image of red and blue lines. He was getting used to thinking like this, and part of him relished solving the puzzle while the other half wondered what was happening to him.

"In a way, it's better for us if he meets Gejjen in the conference rooms on the public side of Customs," Ben said. "A bigger crowd out there for us to disappear into."

"I agree. In the end, we'll grab what chance we get."

Ben held the bottle up to the light. "So what's this?"

"Hair dye. Most species tend to recall redheaded humans a bit too well. You're still a genetic minority. And Omas knows you well enough to look twice if he spots you."

"Tell me I don't have to wear makeup to cover my freckles . . ." Ben's mind was a couple of hours ahead, thinking of the few hours' sleep he could get on the flight. He could study the layout of the spaceport on his datapad. It was all going to go fine, he told himself. "So the second vessel's for backup in case he diverts?"

"Partly. And partly so we have something incriminating to abandon on Vulpter. Read the label, dye your hair, and report to the landing strip at twenty-two thirty. I'll see you there."

Shevu started to walk away. Ben jumped to his feet.

"Sir, what's going to be *incriminating*?"

The captain always seemed old to Ben, but he was younger than Jacen; twenty-eight, maybe. He looked at Ben with that mix of sadness and patience that Ben had seen on his dad's face too often.

"I think anyone would believe Corellians had neutralized Gejjen, given the right vessel abandoned at the port. You now . . . Corellian-registered, Corellian trace for forensics . . . you can do a Corellian accent, can't you? If push comes to shove and you need to speak, that is. There have to be plenty of Corellians with a grudge against him, knowing their politics."

Ben thought of Uncle Han's accent, or what was left of it. He sounded more Coruscanti these days. "Can do. But how do we know we won't fall over *real* Corellians trying to stop Gejjen doing a deal with the enemy?"

"That," said Shevu, "would be unbelievably hilarious for all the wrong reasons. Assuming he has a deal to put on the table anyway."

I'm going to kill someone, and in twenty-four hours I'll be back here as if nothing's happened.

"Any reason why I can't take my vibroblade?" Ben fished it from his pocket and held it out to Shevu. "My mom gave it to me and . . . well, you know."

"You can take whatever works for you, as long as you don't leave or carry evidence that links the hit to us." Shevu examined the blade.

"Yeah, I understand." He pulled down the neck of his shirt a little to reveal a gold chain. "No ID, of course, but my girlfriend gave it to me, and I never go on patrol without it."

It helped to know everyone got edgy before a mission and needed a little reminder of their loved ones. Shevu got halfway to the doors before he turned around and seemed to be working up to saying something.

"I realize your father might find it hard to accept what you do, Ben, but I'm proud of you," he said. "Still, if I had a son, I wouldn't be letting him do this kind of thing until he was an adult. It's not as if we haven't got enough trained men to do it. But . . . well, Colonel Solo has his reasons, I'm sure."

Ben sat thinking over that statement for a while, and realized that Shevu had said *father*—not *parents*. Maybe he thought that his mother would understand a job like this. Ben felt he was hanging on to the relationship with his family by his fingertips, but there had been no more fights, and he didn't feel quite so angry about having to compromise. Maybe that was really what growing up was about—an increasing distance from parents, knowing that there would always be tomorrow and that he didn't have to get what he wanted right *now*, and starting to understand the things they'd been through when they were younger.

I wouldn't be letting him do this kind of thing until he was an adult.

But his father *had* done this kind of thing, more or less. He'd just been a little older, that was all. This was no different from blowing up the Death Star, and plenty of ordinary people just doing their jobs had died when Luke Skywalker had done that. Ben was removing a single man—no bystanders.

He'd remind Dad of that if it ever came out and he had to defend his decision. Dad would probably say Jacen made him do it.

Ben stood in the refresher with the dye worked into lather on his head, and caught sight of himself in a mirror. He felt ridiculous. The foam looked mauve, and he wondered if something had gone horribly wrong. When he rinsed it off, though, his hair was brown, just brown, and he was looking at a stranger.

Good.

He needed to be someone else for all kinds of reasons.

When his hair had dried, he took out the civilian clothes Lekauf had left for him—all Corellian style, all Corellian labels. *This is in case I get caught.* The thought chilled Ben, but it was standard procedure. Nobody had spoken to him about what would happen if he did get caught, and what interrogation might be like, but he could guess. They probably didn't know what advice to give a Jedi about resisting interrogation anyway.

Maybe they thought he could just nudge a mind here and a thought there, and walk out of the cell.

Maybe he could.

Ben checked himself in the mirror a few times, trying to see himself as a stranger might, and was satisfied that he looked unlike Ben Skywalker, and disturbingly like a Corellian boy a little older than he was, but blond—Barit Saiy.

He hadn't seen Saiy since they'd rounded him up with the other Corellians. After that, Ben had stopped asking what happened, but he still wondered silently.

He squatted down and placed his boots in the locker. Then he counted the various pieces of kit. Daily pair, battered raid pair for good luck—but no parade-best pair.

He couldn't imagine where they'd gone. No, actually, he *could:* Lekauf. Ben would find them full of something unmentionable just before kit inspection. Or painted bright pink.

"Jori, I'm going to think up something special for you," he said aloud, and grinned, wanting the diversion.

It was nice to be one of the boys. Ben slipped his datapad into his pocket, wondered where he was going to leave it for safekeeping, and went to pick up the Karpaki and some ammo packs from the armory.

It was just a job, and he had to do it.

THE SKYWALKERS' APARTMENT, CORUSCANT

Luke woke in a heart-pounding panic and reached out toward a hooded shape at the foot of the bed, knowing he was dreaming but unable to stop himself from reacting to the specter that dissolved as he became fully awake.

He hadn't had the dream of the menacing figure in the hooded cloak for a while. Now it was back. It was four in the morning, and Mara still hadn't come home.

Usually, the Force dream vanished and just left him with that sick jolt in his gut as if he'd seen a speeder crash. But this was different; as he swung his legs over the side of the bed, he had a sense of someone still being in the room, and he was sure he wasn't asleep. He checked the chrono to make certain he wasn't still mired in the nightmare.

0410 hours.

He wasn't.

Luke reached for his lightsaber, which he'd been keeping on the nightstand lately, and made a cautious inspection of all the rooms. He couldn't sense flesh and blood anywhere, but he could detect something. The presence was so close now that he could almost feel breath on the back on his neck.

And then he sensed . . . *amusement.*

The presence—now at the door to the apartment, he was sure—was like a cloud of billowing smoke in his mind. He could almost see it. As he felt it becoming more solid, more real, more *here*, it suddenly lit up as if a silent explosion had lifted it in a ball of soaring flame.

Lumiya.

Lumiya.

Luke rushed to the front doors, at the same time concentrating hard on using the Force to jam the two sets of doors in the corridor outside that stood between the apartment and the lifts. He'd trap her. She'd *lied*. Mara was right. All that nonsense on the resort satellite, all that I-mean-you-no-harm was just a feint, mocking his indecision—

The doors parted with a gasp of air and Luke sprang into the corridor with his lightsaber raised. One set of doors was wedged open with something, trying repeatedly to close and making little mechanical groans each time the inner edges hit the obstruction and bounced back a few centimeters. There was no sign of Lumiya.

But she'd been here seconds before. Luke could almost taste her on the air. It was as if she'd sprayed perfume too liberally and was leaving a cloud wafting behind her, except it was a scent of darkness, not rare oils. Frustrated and furious, he strode down the corridor to see what had jammed the doors apart.

It was a pair of black boots, army boots with segmented durasteel plates around the ankle, the kind that Ben wore. He parted the doors with a Force push and squatted to recover the boots.

They *were* Ben's. Not only did Luke recognize them, but he also felt Ben in them when he picked them up. Luke rarely jumped to conclusions. But he was certain who'd left them there, and what the message was: *If I can take personal items from your son, I can take him, too.*

The thought hit Luke like a hard slap in the face. *Maybe she's abducted Ben.* He felt for his son in the Force, and sensed no crisis; in fact, Ben seemed to be leaving a trace in the Force of someone soundly and safely asleep. How long he'd stay that way, though, Luke wasn't ready to bet.

He went back into the apartment to grab his jacket, opening his comlink to Jacen as he went. He didn't care what time it was. Jacen answered immediately. It seemed he didn't sleep much, either.

"Where's Ben?" Luke demanded.

"Asleep, Luke." Jacen had that calm, mock-soothing tone that did anything but soothe him. *Patronizing little jerk.* "Is there a problem?"

"Have you had any intruders in GAG HQ tonight?"

Jacen gave a quiet little laugh. "We're the ones who do the forced entry, Luke."

"Someone's left Ben's boots here as a calling card."

"I don't understand. Did he leave them behind?"

"He doesn't keep any of his uniform at our place. Someone's taken them from your headquarters, and as juvenile a prank as it seems—" Luke almost stopped short of mentioning Lumiya, because he had no idea yet how deep her inroads into the GAG had become, or even if Jacen was consciously aware of them. But he was angry and scared for his boy, and that always colored his judgment. "It's Lumiya. She's taunting me. Showing me she can get at Ben anytime she pleases."

Jacen was silent. Luke waited.

"I can't give you an explanation for that, I really can't," Jacen said eventually.

"Well, Lumiya's jerking my chain, as she probably was at Gilatter, too." *Stupid, stupid, stupid. How could I ever have been fooled like that?*

"And she has someone inside your organization, so I suggest you get that sorted out *fast*."

"We've had one investigation already, and found nothing. We'll have another, if it makes you happier." Jacen's voice sounded both offended and irritated, but Luke couldn't even take that at face value any longer. "But I can assure you Ben is safe—he's even got pretty good protection right next to him. Lieutenant Lekauf."

"Nice to see the guy get promoted. He strikes me as being very *loyal* to you."

"As his grandfather was to Vader, Luke. You can't buy loyalty like that. Ben's in good hands. Let's talk again in the morning."

Luke shut the link dead. No, the morning *wouldn't* do, and there was no point talking to Jacen, who was clearly trussed and tied as far as Lumiya's influence was concerned. She was right under his nose. So much for what he'd learned about arcane Force techniques during his five-year sabbatical.

Luke jogged to the landing pad and tore off in the speeder, maybe a little faster than was safe. Lumiya had left a very clear trail, beckoning Luke to follow. Well, he wasn't falling for that. It had to be a diversion—or an ambush.

I've never been afraid of an ambush, Lumiya. I'll walk into one happily, knowing my enemies are there. Nice try. I'm coming, don't you worry.

He resisted the impulse to drop everything and charge after her trail. She was still near, or at least still on Coruscant; he could feel it. But he had to talk to Mara first, and she was at Starfighter Command. He opened the comlink.

How could I have let this go on for so long? I don't care if I'm expected to be the elder statesman. This stops; this stops now.

"Mara, we have a problem," he said. "Lumiya."

"I'm with Jaina, sweetheart. Do you want me to—"

"She's been outside our apartment." Luke picked his words a little more carefully now. Mara would go ballistic as soon as he mentioned Ben's boots. It was a sinister, silent threat. "Stay where you are. I'll be there in a few minutes."

"When there's a trail going cold?"

"Or a diversion."

"Or a trail she wants you to *think* is a diversion."

Yes, Mara and Lumiya both had that layer-upon-layer way of thinking, just as Palpatine had taught them. "I know what she wants," he said, and shut the link.

Luke broke the traffic regulations a dozen times. He skipped out of the regulated skylanes—always busy on Coruscant—and got a discordant blast of horns from vessels whose noses he nearly clipped. In the way of automatic actions, his mind slipped into deep contemplation as he took the familiar route to Starfighter Command.

I know what my problem is.

He thought back forty years, when he'd been ready to rush to the aid of a total stranger on the basis of a message in an intercepted hologram. The plea for rescue hadn't even been aimed at him, but he'd responded to it anyway, without thinking, without questioning, because it had felt like something he had to do.

And now I act sensibly and soberly, because I'm leader of the Jedi Council, and I'm not nineteen anymore.

But it wasn't his nature. It wasn't what he *did best*. Just because he had whatever gifts the Force had given him more generously than other Jedi, it didn't mean he was cut out for . . . *management*. Yes, management: that was it. He thought of the nagging frustration he always felt when he sent other Jedi on missions, and how he thought that was just reluctance to admit it was the turn of the young Jedi to take on the physical derring-do while he made wise judgments in the Chamber.

Sitting on my backside.

What he did best was right wrongs, and if he couldn't put *this* right for his only child, then what was he?

I forgot who I am.

He was an uncomplicated man who cared enough about his friends and family to die for them, if that was what it took to save them. He was, as Mara told him at least once a day, a farmboy.

He was Luke Skywalker. And if he could take on the Empire without a second thought, he could certainly finish off one of the last pitiful remnants of its rule—Lumiya.

GA STARFIGHTER COMMAND, CORUSCANT

"Y' know, this always works on the crime holovids . . ."

Mara added another illuminated marker to the holochart of the galaxy and stepped back to see if a pattern of Lumiya's movements emerged. It was a big galaxy, and Lumiya seemed to cover a lot of space, which now included Mara's own front doors.

Keep it up, cyborg girl. You're just focusing me better.

"Might as well use the time productively." Jaina leaned over the desk and tapped in more coordinates. Now that she was a civilian again, she was here in her capacity as a Jedi working for Luke Skywalker and the Council, but she slipped back into fleet ways fast. "So let's add in Alema's known whereabouts . . ."

"Well, there's no pattern there, either . . . Do you think it's a case of Alema stalking Lumiya, looking for scraps from her table? Why do those two seem to hang out together?"

"They both need a lot of spare parts?"

Mara stifled a laugh. "That's not nice, Jaina . . ."

"Seriously. They haven't got enough functioning parts to make one decent humanoid between them."

"They're both good at hiding, whether by disguising their presence or erasing the memory of being seen." Mara was feeling around her in the Force, just waiting for Lumiya to spring from nowhere. She could sense her, but not near. "Lumiya's broken her cover, and she's not stupid, so she wants to be seen."

Jaina kept checking the chrono on the wall and then looking at her own timepiece. "Did you go to see Jacen?"

"Yes."

"And?"

"You want the truth, Jaina?"

"Don't I always?"

"Lumiya's bending him somehow. Okay, no need to tell me I was the last person to notice that."

"I wasn't going to. Did you . . . mention that?"

"Yes. I thought it was time someone dropped a hint that we'd no-

ticed our Jacen had turned into a monster." Mara was getting angry, and her honest inner voice told her that the only person who deserved that anger was herself, for defending Jacen while the fact that things were going disastrously wrong was staring her in the face. But Mara was human, and scared for Ben, and it boiled over onto Jaina. "Forgive me for asking, but being his twin, have *you* never had this out with him?"

"I tried. He responded with a court-martial charge, remember?"

"I can't help thinking that you might have tried slugging him."

"Suddenly he's my responsibility? I'm the one who said he was going dark, way back."

"Okay, okay, I'm sorry." Mara put her hands up in mock submission. She could apologize, but she couldn't retract her acid tone, and she regretted that. "I just—okay, none of my business."

"Spit it out, Mara."

"I just don't get how you can be so caught up in worrying whether you want Jag or Zekk when your own brother's going to pieces and taking others with him."

"Whoa . . ."

"Sorry. I said it was none of my business."

"Well, you said it, so—yes, I *want* to be distracted by personal issues, because otherwise I'd go nuts trying to understand why Jacen's doing what he's doing to our parents."

"Maybe it's time we all faced that. Together."

There was an awkward silence. Mara wanted to tell Jaina that she was a grown woman now and it was time to stop messing around like a teenager, and that Ben was more adult at fourteen than she was at thirty-one. It was spiteful, partly true, and partly fueled by Mara's incomprehension of anyone who wasn't as totally focused on the mission as she was, to the exclusion of all else.

She kept her thoughts to herself. It was a sign of weary middle age, along with gray hairs and fading stretch marks.

I spent my whole youth on duty for the Emperor. I never had the freedom that Jaina's always had. And a little bit of me . . . resents that now.

It wasn't Jaina's fault. She was headstrong and passionate like her father, but she hadn't quite found the silent, hidden durasteel of her mother yet.

She'll rise to the challenge when it comes. But if this isn't it, I don't know what is.

Jaina had her head down, hair forming a dark curtain as she leaned over the desk, pretending to be absorbed in the chart, but Mara could feel she was hurt. It wasn't the first time in recent weeks.

Mara would make it up to her when she calmed down. Families had spats all the time. The storms blew over.

"Change of plan," said Luke, stepping out of the turbolift with his hair disheveled and a bag in one hand. Sometimes he had that Don't-stop-me look, and he had it now. It always made Mara want to stop him. "I'm going after Lumiya. Enough."

"No, you're not," Mara said. "You're too close to this. She's baiting you."

Luke dumped the bag on the desk, disrupting the holochart. Jaina stepped back.

"Ben's boots," said Luke.

"And the point is . . . ?"

"Deposited at our apartment by Lumiya."

Mara put her hand on the boots and felt the remnants of dark energy. *Now* she was mad: cold, clear, *icy* mad. "She's been into GAG HQ. Or Jacen's apartment. I don't know which idea I like less."

"*I* need to settle this with her."

"It is, as some admiral once said, a trap—"

"For *her.* Biting off more than she can chew."

Jaina glanced at them both, still looking a little wounded. "Uncle Luke, I'll stick my nose in here and say it's better if *we* go after Lumiya now, because she's clearly playing a game, and . . . I've never seen you angry like this before."

"Luke, the question to ask yourself is this," Mara said, pulling on her jacket and checking her personal weapons. "What will you do when you catch her?"

Luke swallowed hard. "I know what I have to do."

"And what was that conversation we had the other day, about being fit for the role? Me trained killer, you honest guardian of right?" *Lightsaber, vibroblades, hold-out blaster, flechette launcher, and the last of my transponders. Check.* "Here's the plan. You keep an eye on Jacen while I go after her."

"I'm coming, too," Jaina said. "I'd hate to miss Alema if she shows up."

Things were getting back to normal, then. Mara would apologize when they were on their way and Luke was making sure that he knew what Jacen was up to—in case Lumiya was staging an elaborate diversion to draw them all away from Coruscant.

Luke looked at his hands. "I know you're right. It doesn't *feel* right, but I know I shouldn't be going after her bent on vengeance, and I don't know what it's going to take to make me kill her. And nothing short of that makes sense now."

Mara nodded and hit the comm to the hangar ground crew. "Stand by an X-wing, please." She pulled on her gloves, the fingerless ones that gave her a good grip but still let her feel the weapon. "I'm going back, starting from the apartment, and tracking her from there. She wants to leave a nice trail? She's found just the right person to follow it."

I'll sort this out, because it's my fault it got this far.

"I should have gone straight after her, and then you wouldn't have talked me out of this," said Luke.

"Jaina's dead right. You have too much history with Lumiya, and you're too stoked up. You have to kill *cold*."

Luke looked heartbroken for a moment. It wasn't disappointment that he was losing the argument to her, because there was no argument. It was common sense. Just because they were family didn't mean that military best practice went out the window. But something had struck him that he didn't like, something more than Lumiya's constant threats to Ben.

"I hate it when you're right," he said, and managed a smile. "Jacen says Ben's asleep, and it seems that way. So he's okay."

"There you go," said Mara. She still hadn't told Luke that Ben could shut down in the Force. She'd have a little chat with her son about that first. "We're off now. Keep tabs on Jacen. Go and have a concerned avuncular chat with him over caf if you have to. But be around in case that's where your ex is heading." She patted Luke's cheek and winked, wanting to make light of it so he didn't see how much Lumiya was getting to her. "I might be going gray, farmboy, and

I don't have her dramatic dress sense, but at least what I've got is all flesh and blood . . ."

Luke almost laughed. Mara tapped her forefinger to her brow in a mock salute and walked off with Jaina. When she got in the turbo-lift, she checked her datapad to see where Ben's transponder had gotten to.

If you've left that blade in your locker, Ben . . .

A little earlier, it had shown up on the datapad's small screen as a static blip in Galactic City, in GAG HQ. Now—it didn't.

Mara never panicked, but she reserved the right to professional apprehension. She switched the scale of the chart.

"What's wrong?" Jaina asked.

"Nothing." *Where are you?* "Nothing at all."

Mara flicked through ever-larger scales of screen until she picked up the transponder blip again, and the coordinates didn't make sense.

Ben appeared to be on Vulpter.

What takes you there, Ben? Vulpter's not in the war.

If she told Luke, with the head of steam he'd built up, she knew he'd go in with all cannons blazing.

So she simply smiled at Jaina, ready to let Lumiya play her game of tag before Mara finally separated her smug head from her metal body, ending her feud with the Skywalkers once and for all.

I'm coming, cyborg. It's time.

chapter nine

I don't want to worry, you, sir, but I've just heard something on the metal commodities market that might concern us. Someone's talking about offering futures in Mandalorian iron. And MandalMotors shares are being snapped up for the first time in years.

—*Investment analyst, Galactic Alliance Treasury*

MANDALMOTORS RESEARCH WING,
KELDABE, MANDALORE

"WHAT DO YOU THINK, THEN, FETT?"

Jir Yomaget was the kind of man who probably had to be anesthetized to get him into a business suit. He stood with his arms folded, gazing rapt at an airframe that Fett hadn't seen before, an incongruously scruffy and disturbingly young man in dark green coveralls and partial armor.

"Prototype?"

Yomaget nodded. "Started life as the *Kyr'galaar*. Up to three crew, or two with extra payload, atmosphere-capable, configurable for anything from planet pounding to hunter-killer roles, and fast. Now tell me it's not gorgeous."

Research wing was a flattering term for the collection of scruffy sheds and hangars. But the ramshackle appearance of the exterior belied the technology within. MandalMotors had struggled to get back on its feet under a Galactic Alliance that wasn't handing out reconstruction grants to Mandalore. Now it had an edge it could exploit.

"How fast?" asked Fett.

Yomaget probably didn't look at his wife and kids with as much adoration as he was lavishing on the assault fighter. "Point four hyperdrive. The ultimate shock weapon."

"And you never offered me the chance to purchase." Fett had modified *Slave I* to a point-seven. "That beats an X-wing."

"Unfinished prototype."

It was about fifteen meters nose-to-tail with an eight-meter span, a faceted charcoal-gray wedge of a ship that had none of the insectoid lines of the StarViper. Fett walked around it, noting empty racks and housings, and took a guess that it would pack four laser cannons and maybe a couple of other weapons. The tail ended in a flat section with grilles and vents that looked like the ports on a datapad.

The skin was totally plain, its angled surfaces unbroken except for the mythosaur logo picked out in a lighter gray on the side hatches: no brightwork, no sharp-edged recesses, and the tinted transparisteel canopy seemed to merge into the superstructure. Fett would have ducked underneath it to take a look at the blaster pods and store pylons, but the fighter sat too low for him to do it comfortably. He couldn't face being gripped by pain and having to crawl out like an idiot.

"So it's fast. And pretty."

"Deflective stealth hull, cooled vents, scanner-absorbent coating." Yomaget flourished a forearm plate attachment, tapped it, and the canopy popped. It parted into two top-hinged hatches, and he swung himself into the cockpit. "Also hinges from the lower edge, in case the pilot has to bang out. Now, the avionics . . . synthetic vision, panoramic cockpit display, eye-controlled switch selection, aiming, the works."

"Sounds like you had a contest to see how many gizmos you could cram into one fighter."

"All we've been able to do since the Vong war ended is reestablish our basic production models and work up some better ideas." Yomaget leaned over the side of the fighter. "They all ended up in here."

"So . . ."

"Well, you wanted to know what we might manufacture with the new *beskar*. Personally, I'd be inclined to incorporate it into the airframe. Micronized *beskar* skin, or laminate *beskar* armor."

"Beviin would call that over-egging the cake."

"Think of this as the demonstrator."

"That would make it the fastest, least vulnerable fighter on the market. The weapons load might be a compromise." Fett wasn't sure if he had the power or right to tell MandalMotors what to do with their product. This wasn't Coruscant, where national security overrode commercial concerns by law. "Add the top-end armaments, though, and I wouldn't want that sold to anyone else."

"Don't worry, we'll de-enrich the spec for export. We live here, remember. We all lost family to the Vong." Yomaget jumped down from the cockpit with an agility Fett envied. Then he pressed the forearm plate attachment, and the fighter made a faint grinding sound before tilting back on its tail section and lifting through a full ninety degrees to sit upright, a mechanism not dissimilar to *Slave I*'s. "It can land vertically in a footprint of a little over thirty-two square meters."

Fett walked a few meters away to get a better idea of the shape. It didn't look like any other vessel he'd seen. "I bet it does tricks, too."

"Our shares have rocketed and we haven't even unveiled this."

"I bought a few. Someone had to make sure the majority shareholding stayed in Mandalorian hands."

"Just as well we don't have a law against insider dealing."

"I don't intend to sell. Might sign them over to someone on the condition they never sell on to . . . *aruetiise*."

"Is that a go-ahead for production?"

"Full spec for us, de-enriched for them." Fett walked away briskly, feeling his unconnected acts of prudence falling together into a policy of sorts. "Make sure the export hyperdrive spec is a fraction better than an X-wing, no more."

Yomaget trailed after him. This was defense policy on the fly, and the clans didn't get consulted. And they wouldn't care, Fett knew.

"We're going to arm the Confederation, then," said Yomaget.

"We'll arm anybody, including the GA, if they can pay." Fett hadn't even thought about the next move: it just happened. "Provided Colonel Jacen Solo comes here in person to negotiate the deal."

"You're a subtle man, Fett."

"I've never been called that before."

"Fifty percent of production for our own defense?"

Defense. That was one word for it. "Agreed."

Mandalorians liked a sensible compromise. The best deals were where both sides were happy, or where one was happy and the other dead. Fett stopped short of asking to fly the first *beskar* fighter off the production line. He wanted that privilege to go to Beviin, the nearest he would ever have to a friend.

He looked forward to seeing the reaction when MandalMotors opened their order book. Jacen Solo would have the choice between letting the GA's enemy buy better fighters than his, and showing up here. Fett had no doubt which he'd choose, but it would be fun seeing him have to handle the messy presentational issues in public. That could be arranged.

"It'll be called the *Bes'uliik*," Yomaget called after him. "The Basilisk. I always had a soft spot for the ancient battle droids. Good old *Mando* name and old-fashioned *Mando* iron in a state-of-the-art package."

Fett nodded to himself. *Bes'uliik.* It had a nice ring to it. A name from the past, a name that wouldn't go away, however hard the rest of the galaxy tried to make it—ever.

Bes'uliik.

It was the kind of news that made other men walk away whistling.

CHARBI SPACEPORT, VULPTER, DEEP CORE

Ben pressed as close to the viewport as he could to peer at the permacrete below. It was hazy daylight outside, but his body said it was still last night and he needed more sleep.

As far as the rest of the spaceport was concerned, the well-maintained but very old Incom tourer was *not* a Galactic Alliance Guard ship carefully contaminated with Corellian dust, Corellian food waste, Corellian fabric, and any number of other touches designed to show a forensics team that the vessel definitely came from Corellia. And the battered intersystem delivery cutter tailing Cal Omas's shuttle wasn't a spy vessel with top-of-the-line comms, spoofing devices, and an overpowered hyperdrive.

Jori Lekauf wasn't a GAG assassin, either. He was just a nice ordinary young Corellian on an adventure with his younger cousin in an elderly ship he'd saved every spare credit for a couple of years to buy. The trouble was that Ben could believe that all too easily, even though he'd seen the range of weapons Lekauf carried under his jacket.

"If I'd kept my hair red, the family resemblance would have looked more convincing," Ben said. He wanted another caf to keep him alert, but he had a vision of being desperate to visit the refreshers at a critical point in the operation if he drank any more. "Your hair's reddish, really."

"More sandy blond," Lekauf said. "One redheaded human is noticeable, but two is asking to be remembered by witnesses. If we have any, that is."

"Could have dressed as Ubese . . . with masks."

"I think that's been done before."

"I'm just worrying."

"I know."

It was a long wait. Shevu would make contact with them when he landed. His last transmission said he was a few minutes behind Omas's shuttle, which wouldn't attract suspicion; Charbi was a busy port freighting cheap and shoddy goods, and ships landed almost too close together for safety and comfort. Nobody cared who you were as long as port fees and taxes were paid.

They said Vulpter had once been a lovely planet. It didn't look lovely now: the skies had that polluted smoky haze that meant there were wonderful red sunsets here, and not much else to be grateful for. And this was *after* they'd tried to clean up the environment. The vast landing strip—landing field, more like—was scattered with dozens upon dozens of craft in varying stages of disrepair, some taking on board supplies and fuel, some berthing next to freight warehouses where conveyor belts disgorged crates into their holds. Their outlines shimmered in the heat haze from idling drives. And there were all kinds of species wandering around on foot between the vessels, stretching their legs—anywhere between one pair and four of them, it seemed. The only concession to landing field safety was a tracery of red and white painted lines across the permacrete bearing the warnings PEDES-TRIANS DO NOT CROSS THIS LINE and BEWARE GROUND TRAFFIC.

But everyone was crossing the lines as they pleased, and battered speeders with Charbi Port Authority livery swerved around them, honking in annoyance.

Ben decided it *was* the last place anyone would expect two heads of state to conduct a top-level meeting.

"Stand by," Lekauf said quietly, pressing his fingertip to his ear. "It's the captain . . . yes, sir . . . copy that." He looked up. "About twelve minutes before Omas lands. Shevu's right behind him in the landing queue."

Ben perked up. The Karpaki was folded in two inside his jacket, right on the limit of what he could hide, and the vibroblade was tucked in his hip pocket. He'd rehearsed it all in his mind on a continuous loop of what-ifs and if-onlys: rifle to drop Gejjen, preferably at very long range, and vibroblade to escape if seized.

It would have been better to get Gejjen as the man disembarked, while he was exposed on the landing field for a few moments without bystanders milling around. But Jacen wanted the meeting recorded. It was a case of following Gejjen—or Omas—to the room they'd hired by the hour, then slipping a strip-cam through a gap under the doors. The building blueprints showed plenty of places to insert the flimsi-thin device. Each room's doors were set in a recess, so—for once—it was a simple matter of squatting down as if picking up a piece of litter and shoving the strip-cam into the gap.

"Should have put a hidden bug in Omas's coat or folio or something," Lekauf muttered. "Then we sit here, pinpoint Gejjen's ship, and slot him on the ramp as he leaves."

Ben fidgeted with the vibroblade, wondering how his mother would have tackled a job like this. "You can't stick bugs on people without them finding out sooner or later."

"Yeah, with our luck he'd have changed his jacket. They used to have this stuff called tracking dust, you know. Just like powder. If the target inhaled it, you could pick up signals from it for ages afterward."

"Makes you wonder how much all this stuff costs," said Ben. "I mean, we're dirt-cheap, but we have to abandon this ship."

"It's an old crate. Saves the Defense Department the cost of disposal."

And leaving it behind would add weight to the setup that Corellian dissidents had killed their own Prime Minister for giving in to the GA. That was the plan, anyway.

Ben switched seats in the cramped interior to look out from the starboard side. Gejjen's ship should have landed by now, according to its flight plan: one pilot, three passengers, maximum five-hour stopover. That was what it said on the CPA information database that his datapad—scrubbed of all identity, in case of capture—showed him.

Ben avoided looking at the chrono on the bulkhead. He just waited for the word from Lekauf.

"So how do you feel being an officer now?" Ben asked.

"Weird. But my granddad would have been so proud. I wish he'd been alive to see it."

Lekauf never mentioned his parents. It was always his grandfather. It struck Ben that almost everyone he'd grown up with or worked with either had no family or had key members missing or totally absent. It wasn't normal. He thought about how *routine* killing was for his whole family, and knew that most of the beings in the galaxy got through their entire lives without ever killing anyone, deliberately or accidentally.

It was strange that families like his got to make the really big decisions for worlds of normal, ordinary, nonlethal people.

Ben concentrated on centering himself, edging a little toward that state where he vanished from the Force. He pulled himself back just as he felt a drifting sensation that could have been disappearance, or nodding off.

"Plug yourself in," Lekauf whispered. "It's a go."

Ben activated his comlink and earpiece, and shut down the environmental controls to leave the tourer.

When Lekauf opened the hatch, the air and noise hit Ben like a solid wall. It smelled of factories and sulfur. They ambled down the ramp, working hard at looking ordinary, and made their way toward the terminal buildings as if they were killing time, not politicians.

Lekauf scratched his ear, repositioning the earpiece. "Got you, sir. Position?"

Ben picked up Shevu's voice clearly. "He'll pass thirty meters to the left of you unless he deviates. Heading for Building G. You pick him up and I'll follow you in."

"No visual on the target yet."

"He must be inside already."

Oh, this is real. This is happening.

It was a throwback of a thought, back to the time when Ben first started taking crazy risks, but this mission had an extra dose of risk: Omas knew him by sight, and had even met Shevu, too. They couldn't afford to be spotted. Ben slouched and meandered as fourteen-year-old boys were prone to do, turning around from time to time to chat to Lekauf about safe and meaningless trivia—baka rock, speeders, anything—while he took a cautious look across the permacrete in Omas's direction. And there he was: flanked by two men in working clothes, a carefully scruffy figure himself. His confident bearing gave him away as a man used to being obeyed, but only to someone who knew what he was looking for. And Ben did.

"Going okay," Lekauf whispered, not looking toward the three men.

One of the GA Intelligence agents walked through the doors of Building G in front of Omas. The other followed close enough to tread on his heels. They almost vanished in the crowds inside the terminal building, but Ben kept them in sight even though he lost Lekauf for a few moments. One of them appeared to be checking the numbers on various doors and exits as he walked, and eventually he stopped at one marked 53-L and inserted a credit chip in the slot to one side. The doors parted and Ben got a glimpse of a small, brightly lit room almost filled by a white duraplast table ringed by chairs. There was already someone in there.

The doors closed again. A steady two-way river of passengers, port workers, flight crew, and the general temporary population of a space-port stood between Ben and the doors.

"You can do this," Lekauf said. "How many in there? I can't place the strip-cam under the doors if someone else is going to come along and open them again."

Ben closed his eyes and concentrated on the ebb and flow of the Force, the patterns of density that he could both feel at the roof of his mouth and see as speckled color behind his eyelids.

"Six," he said. That made sense: two close protection agents each, even numbers, two statesmen who didn't trust each other. "Yes, six. They're all inside now."

"Can you see lottery numbers, too?" Lekauf made his way casually through the shoals of people and squatted down to adjust his boot. Ben saw him take out what looked like a small flimsi strip, then slide the thing under the hairline gap with quick ease.

Strip-cams were very small these days, the size of a coat-check stub. They really *were* flimsi, and just as disposable once they'd finished transmitting.

"Lovely," said Shevu's voice in Ben's ear. "I can see right up Gejjen's nose. Good clear sound. Nice job, Jori."

Eventually, Ben glanced around and spotted Shevu leaning against a drinks dispenser on the other side of the concourse. He was recording the output from the strip-cam and transmitting it back to GAG HQ. As soon as he had confirmation that it had been received and stored, he'd erase his datapad and send a code to the strip-cam to shred its data. It'd be just a scrap of garbage the cleaners would sweep up, if they ever came this way. It looked as if they wouldn't.

Ben and Lekauf could hear the conversation in their earpieces, both of them monitoring it so they knew when to vanish, wait for Gejjen to emerge, and follow him.

It was a fascinating conversation. Ben had started to get the hang of the code and insinuation that beings in power used to say unpleasant things, a different language that let them deny later that they'd meant any harm. Jacen was good at it. Ben hoped he never would be, because it got to be a habit and Jacen seemed to enjoy playing that game for its own sake.

He recognized Omas's voice. Gejjen sounded softer than he did on the HNE bulletins.

It was very weird to listen to a man you were about to kill. Ben was hearing the last words Dur Gejjen would ever speak.

"So . . . can we agree as gentlebeings to cease hostilities while we sort out a compromise?"

"Before or after I take this to the Senate?" Omas asked.

"I'm not referring this to my assembly—yet. You might not need to refer it to yours," Gejjen replied. "We'll stand down if you agree to that form of revised wording in the commitment of planetary defense assets to the GA."

"You might be able to deliver that with Corellian forces, but can you pull back the Bothans?"

"Are you sure Niathal will do as you tell her?"

"She's a career officer. She will."

"The Bothans are pragmatists. *They* will."

"As a show of goodwill, you'll commit forces to helping us restore order in places like the Sepan system."

"Of course. And you need us to come back into the GA fold to stop the membership hemorrhaging away."

"I won't ask for any statement that causes loss of face. I know how . . . proud Corellians are. Just something along the lines of differences being bridgeable."

"That's very gracious, Chief Omas. Now, those differences will only be bridged if Admiral Niathal and Colonel Solo no longer carry the military weight that they do now."

"You want me to fire them."

"I think you might need to do more than fire them now that they've become used to getting their own way."

"I think I know what you mean, and I don't care for that solution."

"Niathal—ambitious. Dangerous. Solo—ambitious, dangerous, and Jedi, too. We can solve the problem for you permanently."

"If you do, I don't need to know about it."

"If we do, I'd like your security services to look the other way. Solo has ambitious minions who'd be temporarily blind and deaf in exchange for promotion, I think."

"I see you know of Captain Girdun, then . . ."

And they laughed. The two of them actually *laughed*. Ben heard a faint sound as if Shevu was clearing his throat. When Ben turned his head, Lekauf was looking at him, for once not the permanently cheerful man who looked so much younger than he was. He looked old and angry.

"That's how much we're worth," he said quietly. "I bet our Intel guys in there love the idea of having their man back in command."

Ben's gut turned suddenly heavy and cold. It was a dirty game all the way to the top. While he was preparing to assassinate Gejjen, Gejjen was doing a deal to strike at Jacen and Niathal, with Omas turning a blind eye.

Everyone could be bought if the price was high enough. Omas obviously put peace above individual lives. It might not have been any different in the long run from any general risking combat casualties, but it didn't feel anywhere near as clean.

Ben switched his attention. He began to visualize the exterior of the terminal buildings. A walkway ran along the roof, a little-used observation deck where anyone could sit and watch vessels taking off and landing. It wasn't a popular spot, but it was perfect for a sniper. As soon as the meeting sounded as if it was coming to an end, Ben had a minute or two to get up on that roof and wait for Gejjen to exit.

There were three sets of doors Gejjen could leave through to walk back onto the landing field and rejoin his ship. To cover that span—a couple of hundred meters—Ben would have to be ready to sprint along that platform in either direction from a central point.

I'm ready.

He pressed his arm against his side and felt the Karpaki. It would be almost completely silent. He'd also be standing on top of a stark permacrete platform with no cover.

I'll just have to be fast, then . . .

The conversation between Omas and Gejjen slowed, and there were longer pauses and more restless grunts and sighs. Business was drawing to a close. At a nudge from Lekauf, Ben began walking to the roof turbolift without even looking back. He stood in the turbolift cab with a family of Trianii looking for a tapcaf, wondering if they could smell his intentions.

One of the GAG troopers liked free-falling. He'd told Ben that to jump off a five-thousand-meter building, there was a point where a free-faller had to simply stop working up to it and step off into the void. Ben was at that point now as he walked along the rooftop terrace and took up position. He stepped back into the shadow of a single lonely air-conditioning outflow and unfolded the Karpaki. If he held it against the leg of his baggy, creased pants, it didn't present such an obvious profile.

There was nobody around anyway. The observation platform was cracked, and weeds were thriving in the crevices. He settled down to wait for Shevu and Lekauf to do the spotting for him.

Jacen's going to go crazy when he hears what Omas has in mind for him.

"Ben, heads up." It was Shevu. "Gejjen's on the move. He's exiting via the south doors. Go right."

Ben checked around him and jogged to the far end of the platform, keeping close to the rear wall. He hoped he'd recognize Gejjen. He'd studied the man's face and walk intently before the mission, but now he might be looking at the back of his head, depending on the exact path he took back to the ship. It was a silly, petty doubt. He hadn't thought it through enough before he embarked.

But when he looked down on the permacrete, and the chaos of ships, freight droids, and species of all kinds wandering around as if it were a theme park, that neat military haircut—jet black, glossy, not a strand out of place—drew his eye like a beacon.

He lay prone and sighted up. The optics brought him instantly a hundred meters closer to Dur Gejjen, and then there was no doubt that he had the right man in his cross wires. As Gejjen walked, two security guards in discreet casual clothes weaved in and out of Ben's shot.

As soon as Gejjen dropped, at least one of them would be looking for where the shot had originated. Ben would have to stay low and melt back into the crowds in the airside terminal, then rendezvous with Lekauf at Shevu's transport.

I can do it. I got in and out of Centerpoint, didn't I?

Ben held his breath, let the Karpaki's smart optics adjust for wind and angle, and felt his finger tighten on the trigger. One second Gejjen's neat dark head was filling the scope, and the next Ben was staring

at empty permacrete as the rifle kicked back against his shoulder. The muffled report seemed to come from a long way away. Nothing seemed to have gone down in the order he expected—shot, recoil, drop. He lay flat.

What happened?

Did I kill him?

He could hear shouts carried on the air from three stories below. His body made the decisions for him and he found himself scrambling backward to the rear wall while Shevu's voice in his ear kept saying, "Get out of there, Ben."

He ran at a crouch to the turbolift, found that it was on a lower floor, and took the fire-escape stairway. It was going to plan. He could merge into the crowd.

Back on the ground floor, he slipped through the fire doors and made a conscious effort not to look panicked. Maybe professional assassins could take this in their stride, but he couldn't. He'd put aside the fact that he'd just killed a man and found he was totally caught up in the simple act of getting away.

When Shevu put his hand on his shoulder from behind, Ben thought he was going to have a heart attack.

"Keep walking," Shevu whispered. Curious crowds were gathering at the transparisteel doors to gawp at the unfolding drama on the landing strip, and security staff were struggling to get through the crowd. "Just keep on walking."

If they sealed the doors . . .

It was chaos. Nobody seemed to know what had happened yet. That bought Ben, Shevu, and Lekauf a few more minutes. Charbi seemed the kind of place where passengers and freighter captains would walk right past a dead body if it meant their flight left on time.

They were counting on it.

"I'm right behind you," said Lekauf's voice in his earpiece. "If we walk down to the south doors, we can just go around the perimeter to Shevu's shuttle."

Ben was scared. He was happy to admit it. He hadn't been afraid at all on Centerpoint, but now he knew better. He kept a little distance between him and Shevu, remembering to pause every so often and look at the commotion as if he were genuinely curious about what was happening, but he carried on walking.

Above him, the holoscreen that usually showed arrivals and departures was turned over to the traffic-control tower's view of the landing strip.

Yes, he'd killed Gejjen, a textbook head shot.

I can't feel my face. My lips feel numb.

Now Ben was seconds away from those doors, walking with the steady but thinning stream of droids, repulsorlifts, and passengers heading out to the vessels.

Nearly there.

He was a few meters away from the transparisteel doors when he saw a man in familiar casual clothes running at full tilt toward them. The doors parted, and Ben was staring down the muzzle of a blaster.

"Armed officer, CSA!" the man barked. "Everybody—*stay where you are—*"

Ben balanced on a blade's edge between surrender and making a run for it.

chapter ten

Verpine negotiator Sass Sikili, speaking today at the opening of BastEx, has warned Murkhana that the Roche government will respond with "appropriate measures" if it continues to breach trade agreements on technology exports. Murkhana is keen to move into the growing market for secure small-unit comlink networking, a field dominated by Verpine products.

—*HNE business news, noted with interest by Boba Fett, Mandalore*

SPEEDER PARK, ROTUNDA ZONE, CORUSCANT

LUMIYA HAD LEFT A MAGNIFIED WAKE IN THE FORCE LIKE A WATER speeder on a lake. While it was generous of her, Mara wasn't amused.

"I didn't get stupid overnight," she muttered. "Don't insult me, tin-can."

"And what were you saying about Luke being too close to all this?" Jaina asked. "Deep breaths, Aunt Mara. Deep breaths."

"I'm psyching up. I find it helps. You use the Force your way, and I'll use it mine."

"Wow, am I calming *you* down now? That's a headline to save for the grandchildren."

Mara paced a ten-meter square of the area, feeling dark energies pulsing like shock waves. Jaina stood back and watched.

"She's taken off from here," Mara stated.

"Has she led us here to divert us from somewhere else on Coruscant?"

"She's got a narrow range of targets, Jaina. Ben or Jacen—or even Han and Leia, if she's teamed up with Alema. Your parents aren't on Coruscant, and if she's after Jacen, she must have had her chance to take him when she got into GAG HQ to grab Ben's boots." Mara squatted down to touch the permacrete. She expected to get a jolt of some kind, a taste of Lumiya mocking her, but there was something disconcertingly benign about the impression the Sith had left behind. *Yes, like she managed to convince Luke she meant him no harm.* Lumiya seemed to have discovered a rare talent for Force-acting. "If she's after Luke, she's passed up two chances now."

"So it's Ben."

"Ben's . . . away. He's not on Coruscant."

Jaina looked at Mara with an expression that said she couldn't work out why Mara was stalling her. But Mara wouldn't budge. The less the family knew about Ben's situation, the better. Sooner or later, it'd slip out that she'd put a trace on him, and however old he was when that finally happened she'd lose his trust forever. It would hurt him.

"GAG business," Mara said, answering the unasked question. She cast around in the Force, groping for anything that said Lumiya was heading for Vulpter, but she had no sense of that at all. What she picked up was Ben, nervous for a moment, then disappearing as Jacen must have taught him. She'd have to tackle that when the current emergency was under control. "Okay, if she wants me to follow her, I'll follow."

"Let's call in Zekk and Jag, because I'm betting Alema's in town again, and—"

"No offense, Jaina, but I think it's me she wants. You go find Bug Girl."

Jaina's pursed lips looked like she'd decided to swallow an argument. "Okay," she said at last.

"It's just an old dark side feud." Mara didn't want Jaina to feel that she was snubbing her. Relations were edgy enough at the moment. "Let's not allow her to divert both of us."

So Lumiya was taunting her. *I can get at your husband. I can get at your son.* If she was so set on killing Ben for the death of her daughter, she still seemed to be missing chances. So what did Lumiya want from her?

Mara returned to base to find one of the ground crew waiting patiently by her allocated XJ7. She climbed into the cockpit and started her instrument check.

"Is Lumiya really a Sith?" the technician asked.

"The very last of her kind," said Mara, not asking what he'd heard and how he knew the name anyway. She felt a pang of guilt at her sloppiness for arguing loudly and forgetting there were other personnel around. She sealed the XJ7's hatches. "I'll make sure of that."

Mara ignored military air traffic regulations and circled over the area where she'd last picked up Lumiya's powerful wake. If she concentrated, it was relatively easy to follow, and she found herself leaving Coruscant orbit on a bearing for one of the moons, Hesperidium.

"Oh, yes, Palpatine loved that place," she said aloud. "You heading there for old times' sake?"

Lumiya was definitely playing a game. But she wasn't stupid enough to think she could offer Mara her hand and find it still intact like she had with Luke.

The wake led to Hesperidium's main resort, which wasn't quite as splendid as Mara recalled. She wondered if it was feeling the pinch of postwar recovery, and if there still weren't enough tastelessly wealthy folk to go around. Port traffic control was surprised—to say the least—to find a military vessel on its scanners.

"I need to put down for a while," Mara said, knowing they had no choice about the matter. They could hardly stop her landing. "Getting weird readings on my instruments. I have to check it out."

"Let us know if you need help," the ATC controller said. "We pride ourselves on doing anything and everything for all our visitors."

"Classified," Mara said, and ended the conversation in the way that only she could.

When she landed and saw the selection of vessels standing on the private strips of the hotels, she realized that a XJ7 probably looked like an eccentric billionaire's toy, and a small one at that. Some of the craft here were staggering in their size and opulence; she wondered how they even managed to land. There was clearly a thriving class of the ultrawealthy that had come through the last decade pretty well un-scathed, and life was going on uninterrupted for them now, regardless of another war. Credits seemed to operate like deflector shields: if you had enough of either, nothing could touch you.

She checked around her—in the Force, and visually—before slid-ing out of the cockpit and jumping to the ground. At least she'd man-aged to dress like eccentric wealth, and few would look at her.

Yes, there were definitely some bizarre-looking flying palaces here . . .

And then she felt darkness touch her shoulder in the brilliant morning sunshine.

It was so tangible, so dense, that she spun around with her hand on her lightsaber hilt expecting to find Lumiya ready to swing at her. But there was nobody.

You want to play games?

It was early. A couple of hotel guests in sports clothes jogged by and glanced at her, but ran on. She prowled between the vessels on the strip, feeling the darkness pressing on her sternum like a coronary. Something dark was here—and that meant Lumiya. The crushing sen-sation in her chest was getting so powerful that she ignited her lightsaber's blade, ready to fight when she rounded the next hull.

This is it, Lumiya. No more games.

She sprang into the gap, lightsaber humming.

Staring back at her wasn't a veiled figure with a lightwhip but a single, disembodied, flame-red eye ten meters wide. Her instinct said it was alive, an alien being, but it was clearly a ship of some kind, and that meant only one thing: Lumiya was inside.

It was a trap, Mara was sure of that.

Fine. But sometimes traps swallow prey that's way too big for them . . .

She looked over the hull for a hatch, but the roughly textured surface—was it stone?—was unbroken.

Come inside.

Mara wondered why she was thinking that and then realized that the thought was actually a voice inside her head, in the fabric of the Force itself. It was inanimate, yet sentient; and it wasn't a droid.

It was the *ship*.

Mara concentrated hard on sensing Lumiya, but she could detect nobody inside the vessel. Suddenly an aperture appeared in the hull and a ramp extruded. It was too tempting, and she was too old a hand at this kind of game to walk straight in, but she had to know what was going on. The wake ended here. Lumiya had used this ship. But—

I can take her. This is all mind games. I'm not falling for it.

If Lumiya was waiting within, hiding somehow, then Mara would kill her. If she wasn't, then Mara would sit in wait for her, and kill her then. It was all the same to Mara. She didn't have anything more urgent to do right then.

She placed her boot on the ramp and took a few cautious steps, lightsaber held two-handed. If the hotel had security cams and could see what was going on, it was just too bad.

Mara felt bewilderment that wasn't hers.

You're not who I expected.

It was the ship again.

"What d'you mean, I'm not who you expected?" No, she didn't need to speak: she realized she could *think* back at this thing.

You are . . . very similar.

"Thanks. Thanks a bunch." Maybe the ship had a high regard for Lumiya. Mara decided that it was as good a source as any of information. She thought her next question, not even in words, but in concepts and attitudes she thought she'd left behind a long time ago. The mental conversation left a taste in her like being a Hand again.

Where is she, Ship?

The other one? Close by.

You're a thing of the Sith, aren't you?

You know darkness well. Better than the other one that I expected to see return.

Mara didn't know what to make of that, but right then she was prepared to accept that her intent was far more malevolent than Lumiya knew how to be. She wanted destruction. She wanted *obliteration.*

Last of your kind, Lumiya. And about time.

Mara hesitated on the brow of the ramp. She thought for a minute that she might be pulled in, and the spherical ship would then trap her inside and make a run for it. She took the precaution of reaching inside with one hand to place the last of her tiny transponders—her only remaining gadget from her previous existence—just inside the hatch. It attached to the oddly stone-like coating she could feel within. At least if that happened, someone might trace her. And if Lumiya ever returned to the ship, the transponder would report her position every time Mara's emitter pinged it.

Mara took a cautious breath and lowered her head to look inside. The ship really was empty.

Not just devoid of crew—*empty.* There was nothing within the hull; no cockpit, no instruments, no systems indicators, nothing. It was hollow, lit by a red glow as if there were a fire burning steadily behind the bulkheads. She hadn't seen that light from the outside.

And that was as far as she got. She felt something coming, and she knew what that something was. She took a few steps back down the ramp and waited, lightsaber still extended.

A slim figure in a dark gray suit and veiled triangular headdress stepped into the space between the parked ships.

"Hello, little housewife . . . ," said Lumiya.

Mara's autopilot kicked in and she was the Emperor's Hand again, silent and focused. There was nothing worth saying anyway. Amateurs gave speeches; professionals got on with the job.

She Force-leapt five meters at Lumiya, slashing down right to left, two-handed. The stroke—all power, no finesse—clipped the Sith's headdress as she sprang back, slicing off a section. Lumiya's eyes widened, pupils dilated, but she was already whirling her lightwhip about her head. The tails crackled and hissed, missing Mara only because she threw all her energy into a Force push to slow them a fraction.

Mara didn't take that weapon lightly. It was the worst of both worlds, leather strips studded with impervious Mandalorian iron fragments and tendrils of sheer, raw, murderous dark energy. Mara drew her blaster and rolled under the hull of the ship next to her. The lightwhip gouged through the durasteel with a shriek of tearing metal, filling the air with the smell of hydraulic fluid, and the spurt of liquid turned into a torrent that began spreading in a thick pool. As Mara rolled clear on the other side of the ship, Lumiya landed heavily on both feet and brought the whip down so close to Mara's head that she felt the rush of air on her right cheek like a breath. The crack was deafening.

Mara wasn't even thinking when she aimed the blaster. Lumiya's whip hand was raised to throw as much weight as possible from the back stroke. A puff of white vapor burst from Lumiya's shoulder, and she staggered a few paces.

Metal. Maybe I hit metal.

Maybe she had, because Lumiya teetered for a second but came right back. Mara sprang horizontally from a crouch and cannoned into Lumiya's legs with all the power she could muster from the Force. She hit solid durasteel. Blood filled her mouth but she couldn't feel a thing—yet. Clinging to Lumiya's knees with one arm, denying her the space to swing the whip, she brought her down like a felled tree before smashing her head into the woman's face.

And that *hurt.* Oh yes, Mara felt that. She'd caught not Lumiya's nose but the cybernetic jaw, and it cut deep into her forehead. Fighting on pure reflex now, part stunned, she killed the lightsaber blade for a second and held the hilt like a dagger, stabbing it down into Lumiya's chest before flicking the energy back on. Lumiya pulled to the side as the blade punched through flesh. Mara smelled it. She flicked off the blade to pull back again, triumphant.

I've done it. Dead. Dead, you—

But Lumiya was screaming, and that wasn't right at all. The scream seared through Mara's spinning head. It was more than sound. It was—

Mara scrambled to her knees to look down at what should have been a dead woman, and stared into green eyes that were utterly devoid of any emotion, and then the world darkened like an eclipse.

Maybe I'm the one who's dead.

Something hit her square in the back, pitching her forward onto Lumiya. Mara struggled to turn over without letting go of either lightsaber or blaster, but something coiled around her neck and jerked her backward. The lightwhip was still in Lumiya's fist, she could see the thing, she could *see* it, so what was around her neck, choking her? She felt as if she was flying backward at high speed, and then she hit something so hard that it punched every bit of breath out of her lungs and left her gulping for air.

A second or two was all it took. Mara lay trying to suck in air in painful, straining gulps, eyes stinging, and saw Lumiya's boots run past her face at a stagger, missing her by centimeters.

What's in my eyes? What's stinging?

She raised her hand to rub them and her knuckles came away red and wet. It was blood. The last thing she saw as she looked up was the orange sphere, that impossible Sith ship, soaring vertically into the air and extending webbed vanes like living wings.

Mara managed to prop herself up on her elbows. She was suddenly aware of the two runners she'd seen earlier, all nice and neat in their crisp white sports gear, staring at her in horror. She summoned what focus she had and concentrated hard.

"You've just seen two stuntwomen performing for a holovid, shot by a hidden cam," she said. "You didn't see a fight at all."

"We didn't see a fight at all, dear," said the woman obediently.

The man gawped, and then grinned. "Wow, it's amazing how *real* that blood stuff looks!"

"Isn't it . . . ," said Mara, and somehow got to her feet, retrieved her lightsaber hilt and blaster, and walked off with as much grace as she could manage.

I was sure I'd finished her off. How did I miss?

She almost sobbed with frustration and struggled to get into the XJ7's cockpit, still trying to work out what had jumped her from behind. When she checked her injuries in the reflective surface of her datapad, her face was streaked with blood, her right eye was swelling and closing already, and there was something like a rope burn across her neck. She could see indentations in her skin that looked like a twisted wire cable.

Something like a droid jumped me. A machine, anyway. That's why I didn't sense it.

It was crazy to fly a fighter after a head injury, she knew, but there was no other way back to Coruscant. She fired up the drives, swearing and cursing. She'd had the cyborg witch right there, her lightsaber in her, and she still hadn't *killed* her.

And I didn't feel any malice from her, either, Luke. Just a busted head.

This was going to take plenty of bacta. Mara lifted the XJ7 clear and set it on automatic for the homeward leg.

Luke is going to go nuts when he sees me in this state.

Her adrenaline was ebbing, and the pain was making itself felt now. She settled into a shallow meditative trance to speed the healing process.

Why didn't she kill me? She had the chance. I brained myself on her kriffing metal jaw.

Then Mara remembered the transponder. She fumbled for the datapad again and activated the search emitter. A yellow blip—no, two yellow blips—showed.

One was still on Vulpter: Ben. The other was edging across the grid on her screen, moving away from the Core.

Lumiya.

Gotcha, she thought, smiling for a second before she remembered her split lip. *Gotcha.*

Lumiya and her bizarre Sith ship were on a bearing for the Hydian Way node. Either she wanted Mara to follow, or she didn't know about the transponder.

It was okay. Mara could take her anytime now. And two could play the Come-and-get-me game.

She leaned back in her seat and concentrated on reducing her ripening black eye.

JACEN SOLO'S OFFICE—DOORS CLOSED—GAG HQ,
CORUSCANT

Jacen played the recording four or five times before he was satisfied.
It was a distorted ground-up shot, the sort that endoscopic
strip-cams tended to capture, but the soundtrack was clear and the
participants in the meeting were clearly identifiable as the GA Chief of
State and the Corellian Prime Minister. There would be no argument
that the two men had met, thrown out the GA's entire defense policy,
agreed on private terms for a cease-fire without reference to the
Supreme Commander or the Senate, and discussed the removal by assassination of Colonel Jacen Solo and Admiral Niathal.

This was all he needed to justify the next step.

He leaned across his desk and tapped the internal comm. Droids
didn't mind how many times they were summoned to the office.

"Aitch," he said. "I need you right away."

"Certainly, sir," said HM-3.

The droid took ten minutes to show up. When he clunked in, his
arms were laden with datapads and even bound flimsi. He'd come prepared for one of Jacen's explain-the-law-to-me sessions. Sometimes it
was disturbing to meet a droid who could anticipate needs that well.
Jacen settled for being impressed.

"It's time to action the amendment," Jacen said.

If a droid could have registered disappointment on an immobile
face, then HM-3 did. His voice left no doubt. He enjoyed going
through the finer points of administrative law with Jacen, probably because nobody else wanted to hear. The fact that he carried the statutes
around with him rather than simply tapping into the GA networked
archive was a sign of his genuine . . . *affection* for the law. It was an en-
tity to him, not simply words.

"Let me recap, then, sir." HM-3 laid the armful of legal reference
sources on the desk and pulled out his working datapad. "*. . . amend
the Emergency Measures Act to include in its scope the GAG's powers to
detain heads of state, politicians, and any other individuals believed to be*

presenting a genuine risk to the security of the Galactic Alliance, and to seize their assets via the Treasury Orders Act."

"That's the one," Jacen said. "When might that be enacted?"

"I can circulate it right now, sir, and it becomes effective at midnight. You're very *regular* about these amendments."

"I've learned a lot about the importance of administrative discipline from you, Aitch."

"Thank you, sir. So many don't."

"And my apologies for dragging you in here for so little."

Even with a droid, humility and gratitude could go a very long way. HM-3 gathered up his source data and made for the doors.

"My pleasure, sir," he said.

Jacen waited for the doors to close and let out a breath. He steeled himself not to think of Tenel Ka and Allana, because that was a luxury he couldn't afford at this moment, but he missed them so much—especially Allana—that it hurt him to breathe sometimes when he thought of them. Lumiya was occupied elsewhere; there was little chance that she'd catch him reaching out in the Force to his family. But he was taking no risks, not now that so many things were coming within his grasp.

I've got you now, Cal Omas. I've got you, you fool.

At midnight, he would have the legal authority to arrest Chief of State Cal Omas for actions likely to present a risk to the security of the Galactic Alliance. He would notify the Supreme Commander, who was—until 0900 tomorrow—the acting Chief of State in Omas's absence, and who would step into his place if for any reason he couldn't discharge his duties.

Like when he's arrested for selling us down the river to the Corellians, and planning to assassinate me and Niathal. She's going to love that bit.

It was too late to pull back from the brink now. This had to happen. Niathal knew it was coming, and the promise of power had secured her silence. She needed to take the evidence to Senator G'vli G'Sil, chair of the Security Council, to "clear her bows" as she liked to put it. Once that nicety was out of the way, she could participate in the coup with a clear military conscience.

After that, the next stage would be to settle her in the titular role as Chief of State while consolidating his own power base quietly behind the scenes, because he wouldn't be part of that structure laughingly called *democracy*.

It was chaos, pure and simple. It was a glorious word to justify abdication of responsibility by those who could, if they were prepared to make the effort, create a better galaxy for the vast majority. It was a word for finding someone else to blame.

Democracy, freedom, and *peace.* They were all tricks, like words used to train veermoks to come to heel or attack. They were sounds with no real meaning, nothing definable, just triggers that everyone had been conditioned to think were desirable, tangible things. Peace— well, Jacen *could* define that. But democracy? Freedom? Whose freedom, and to do what? Freedom was a pretty nebulous concept when all most beings wanted was an absence of disorder, a full stomach, and some hope that their offspring would have a more comfortable life than they had.

Jacen rubbed his eyes, feeling the lack of sleep of the past week but determined not to doze even for a few minutes. Shevu hadn't called in. Half the job was done, but Jacen didn't yet know what had happened to Gejjen. Whatever had happened, Ben had either shot him or missed by now. Jacen switched on HNE, expecting a newsflash about the assassination, but it was still showing some nonsense about a holovid star with an embarrassing personal life. There was nothing to do but fill the waiting time with productive work. He opened the comm to Niathal.

"I'm sending you something on your secure datalink," he said. "At one minute past midnight, I'll be acting on it. Time your visit to G'Sil carefully."

"I think I can manage that, Jacen . . ."

"Wait until you see what I'm sending you," he said. "It's rather different *watching* them carve up our future."

"Let me know five minutes before you . . . pay your visit."

Jacen leaned back in his seat and waited for the call from Shevu.

And he could still feel that Ben was alive, if not well.

CHARBI SPACEPORT, VULPTER

It was a lockdown.

Ben, like everyone else in the crowd, stood still as the Corellian Security officer—ministerial protection branch, he guessed—trained his blaster on the crowd.

"Nobody's going anywhere," he said. "This port is being sealed by the Vulpter authorities and you're all going to be scanned for ballistic residue."

"Why?" a male voice called from the crowd.

"There's been a projectile shooting," the officer said. "A murder. I want you all to wait, nice and calm, and then we'll check you all out, and you'll be free to go."

"That's going to take hours," someone said.

"Then it'll *take* hours," said the officer, and flicked the charge test on his blaster so they could hear the whir and see the flash of an indicator bar that said he was ready to shoot. "I'd really like your cooperation, folks."

The hum of murmurs, gasps, clicks, and other varied expressions of horror and impatience swept across the gathering crowd. Ben's gut was knotted tight. He didn't dare look behind him to see where Shevu and Lekauf were. He could feel their presence and had a good idea of their positions, but that wasn't enough. He needed to see them.

Carefully, he turned around and caught Lekauf's eye. He ambled over to him, slowing down as he passed so it wasn't obvious they were together. He'd need to steer clear of Shevu, too. There was no point getting them all arrested.

Ben activated his earpiece and spoke barely moving his lips to contain the whisper.

"I'm going to find a weak point and get out," he said. He felt everyone could see the rifle folded under his jacket, even though they all seemed far more interested in what was happening beyond the transparisteel doors to the landing area. Red and blue lights were reflecting off the walls as security vehicles streamed onto the field. "I can jump anywhere, open any door, remember. I'll make my own way back home."

"You do that," said Lekauf's voice in his ear, "and they'll know it was a Jedi."

"No Force nonsense," said Shevu. "Relax. We'll get around this. Contingency plans, gentlemen."

"I'm covered in trace, sir."

"Jori," said Shevu. He never normally used Lekauf's first name. "Jori, I'm going to—"

"I don't think that's a good use of manpower, sir." Lekauf was moving toward Ben. He looked grim. "And you're too far from Ben to do anything about it."

Lekauf was right next to Ben now. In the crush of passengers and pilots milling around, getting in one another's way, he could press right up against him unnoticed. The lieutenant reached under Ben's coat and grasped the rifle. Ben clamped his arm tight against his side to stop him from taking it.

"What are you *doing?*"

"Contingency plan. Let go, Ben."

"You're going to dump it?"

"Yeah. Yeah, I'm going to get rid of it."

"What about the ballistic contamination? You can't dump *that.*"

"Announce it to everyone, why don't you . . ." Lekauf was suddenly Master Efficient again, like he'd been on the practice range, his slightly goofy good humor gone. He stood chest-to-chest with Ben, and after a two-second, almost immobile tussle that nobody else could see, he loosened Ben's clamped elbow and slid the folded Karpaki under his own jacket. "Now stick with the boss. Promise me you will."

"You're nuts, Jori."

"Yeah, like Granddad."

Ben felt utterly useless. Lekauf had to bail him out of this mess. He should have been able to do it by himself. *Some Jedi. Some supersoldier.* He wondered how he'd live this down, and also why he was more worried about that at this moment than about taking a life, even a rotten one like Gejjen's.

Lekauf moved back along the terminal hall to the central doors

that led onto the landing area. Ben went to follow him, but Shevu stepped into his path casually, as if being rude and careless to a stranger.

"Whatever happens," he said, almost inaudible, lips barely moving, "you're to stick with *me,* and follow me, unless I get grabbed—and in that case, get back to base any way you can."

They'd war-gamed a few scenarios in briefings, including getting split up or captured, but this all felt very different now.

Lekauf was at the main doors, looking as if he were trying to check where the tourer was. Then without warning, he grabbed a woman tight around her neck, drew his blaster, and held it to her temple.

"Open the doors!" he yelled. "Open them *now,* or I blow her head off!"

Pandemonium broke out. People scattered, leaving a clear area around Lekauf; security officers and the Corellian cop struggled against the tide of bodies trying to get clear, blasters held high. Lekauf was suddenly doing an amazing job of looking red-faced and dangerous.

How's he going to pull this off? We're surrounded. Locked in.

This hadn't been in the briefings. Lekauf was improvising. He had to be. Ben broke away from Shevu and pushed through the crowd.

"I said *open the kriffing doors,* or you'll be scraping her off the ceiling." Lekauf clicked the blaster and the woman hostage started shrieking, a thin little wail at first that rose into a full-blown panting sequence of screams and yelps. "You're going to let me board my ship and leave here, and she gets to live. Don't mess with me. Don't kriffing *mess* with me."

"Just let the lady go," said the officer. He pushed through and stood at the edge of the cleared floor area. "Just put the blaster down. Let her go."

"So you can spray my brains all over the terminal? Yeah. As if."

"Kid, this isn't going to do you any good. We can talk—"

"Yeah, like you'll have a nice chat with me about Gejjen. I killed the scumbag and I'm proud of it. He was caving in to the GA. Lining his own pockets. I'm a patriot. You hear? I love Corellia. They ought to give me a medal."

The officer gestured to the security guard at the exit, and the doors parted. Ben watched in horror, unable to move. Lekauf backed out of the doors, half dragging and half carrying the terrified hostage, and made his way laboriously to the tourer. It seemed to take forever. It was a long, long way to struggle with a woman in a headlock, edging backward, followed by a slowly moving knot of police and guards waiting for the first slip that would give them a clear shot at him. Ben wanted to run after him and help, but had no idea what to do; even if he created a diversion, they were all still trapped one way or another.

Lekauf activated the tourer's ramp and backed up it. The woman had stopped screaming and started sobbing.

"Okay, out, *now*." Shevu was right behind Ben, mouth right next to his ear, and he grabbed his collar in a slow, twisting grip to show he meant business. "Slow and calm. Don't waste this. He's bought us time."

Ben wanted to yell, *But what about him?* He didn't, though. He'd already abandoned too much of his training, and this wasn't the way soldiers did it. His legs were shaking under him. Lekauf reached the top of the ramp and shoved the woman down it; the hatch slammed behind him, leaving the hostage crying and screaming on the permacrete. Police rushed forward to grab her. Marksmen moved in to take up positions around the vessel.

Now everyone else in the terminal was forgotten, and the Corellian officer ran onto the field, met up with his buddy, and ran for the cordon.

"Ben, that's it, come on—" Shevu jerked on his collar, pulling him bodily toward the doors at the south end of the terminal. A little bit of Ben was calculating where they would be placing troops and what their tactics would be for stopping Lekauf from taking off. If Lekauf got a move on, he could be out of orbit and jumping to lightspeed before whatever excuse Vulpter had for a fleet could get airborne.

But the tourer sat on the permacrete, silent, no haze of heat exhaust venting from its jets. He could see it through the transparisteel walls as he moved toward escape, and couldn't feel relief.

It dawned on Ben that Lekauf wasn't going anywhere.

Maybe the thing had failed to start.

Oh no, no, no . . .

The drive hadn't stalled on him. Ben could feel Lekauf now—terrified, oddly triumphant, and with a strange sense of peace despite the dread. It was the strangest combination Ben had ever sensed in the Force.

"What's he doing, sir? How's he getting out?"

Shevu kept swallowing. Ben saw the lump in his throat bob up and down. "Has to be done."

"*What* has to be done?"

"A good cover story."

"I don't—"

"Ben, move it. *Now.*" Shevu grabbed his arm so hard that it hurt, and hauled him across the permacrete to the shuttle. The tourer was now surrounded by police and armed guards; lines of security droids were clearing an outer cordon and moving back vessels that were parked too close. "Don't blow this mission. The job's done."

"But Jori's going to be arrested. He can't sit there forever. We can't leave him, and what happens when they interrogate him, 'cos they're going to find—"

"Ben, *shut up.* And that's an order. There's nothing we can do."

Ben couldn't believe it of Shevu. He could have struggled free and gone to help Lekauf, and . . . and *what?* He couldn't use his Force powers in public. He couldn't take on a small army of police. He couldn't risk arrest and discovery.

He still wanted to go to Lekauf's aid. No comrade left behind, that was the rule, same for troopers as it was for Jedi, same for every tight-knit group who faced danger together.

"We can't leave him," Ben sobbed, and was about to change his mind, and let the GA and the Jedi Council sort out their own troubles if he was arrested and found to be Luke Skywalker's son, carrying out political assassinations. "We just *can't abandon him.*"

As he stared brokenhearted at the battered tourer, a massive explosion sent it flying into a thousand fragments, shooting a column of flame and roiling smoke high into the air, almost knocking Ben off his feet. Police scattered, those who could ran. Some were blown meters. It all seemed to take place in slow motion and silence, and then the sound rushed back in and time resumed normally.

The captain still had a grip on Ben's arm like a vise. Ben's lips moved but he couldn't hear himself.

"Yes," Shevu said softly, and dragged Ben as he craned his neck to stare back at the wreckage and flames, numb, shocked, and lost. "*Now we can.*"

chapter eleven

Breaking news . . . we're just getting reports that Corellian
Prime Minister Dur Gejjen has been shot dead at a spaceport
on Vulpter, Deep Core, by a Corellian terrorist. Early reports
indicate that an armed siege followed the shooting, but that
appears to have ended when the assassin blew himself up in his
ship on the landing strip. We'll have more on this story later.

—*HNE newsflash*

SLAVE I, LAID UP OUTSIDE KELDABE, MANDALORE

IT WAS A *VERY* INTERESTING NEWS DAY.

Fett had his cockpit monitor tuned to the news channel, watching the wheels come off the rest of the galaxy. He'd seen that happen
often enough to spot the signs of greater chaos to come.

Usually, it meant a time of good fees and rich pickings for bounty
hunters. Now his priorities had to be a little different, and he waited
for a call from the office of Sass Sikili, the Verpine whose job was to

communicate with outsiders on behalf of Roche. The Verpine were getting anxious. How any species that churned out that many high-quality ornaments could get anxious Fett didn't understand, but that was the Verpine for you. Insectoids could get jumpy, and when one got jumpy—the hive-mind made them *all* jittery.

Fett pondered the assassination while he waited. He couldn't say he was sorry to see the passing of Dur Gejjen, but at least the barve paid promptly. Fett had been betting on him staying in office for more than a few short months before getting the inevitable shot in the head, though. It was indecently premature even by the standards of Corellian politics. Who had really killed him? Not some Corellian hick waving the flag, that was for sure. Gejjen had a line of would-be killers that would have stretched from here to the Core.

"Mandalore Fett . . . ," said a voice on the comm. It was high-pitched, a little above tenor, and buzzed with a faint resonance. "We noted your return with delight."

"Need someone dragged screaming to your hive, Sikili?"

"Not today, thank you. But we have a business proposition for you."

"I'm all ears."

"Ah . . . we hear exciting things about iron deposits, which we assume to be true—"

"They are."

"—and many *highly* desirable things can be made with Mandalorian iron. We would like to acquire some."

"Happy to sell, when we have a surplus for export."

"We note the unstable nature of the galaxy these past months, which will be exacerbated, we expect, by the passing of Prime Minister Gejjen."

"Yeah. Good times for the arms trade."

"Indeed. But also *anxious* times for us, when Murkhana challenges our markets, and now Kem Stor Ai talks of war with Murkhana, which is too close for the hives' taste."

"You pack enough hardware to make Murkhana and Kem Stor Ai into their own asteroid field, Sikili. Half their kit comes from Roche. Spit it out."

"We are a literal people, Fett."

"I'm literal, too. Let's all be literal together."

Sikili went quiet for a moment. Fett could hear the faint clicking of his mouthparts. "Now that you have abundant *beskar*, you'll rearm. Roche may be outside of your sector, but the last time Mandalorians had plenty of *beskar*, the Mandalore sector became much, much bigger."

Verpine took a little time to explain where they were heading, grinding through each step of the sequence, but they got there in the end.

"You're worried we'll expand all over you," said Fett. "Invade you."

"Yes. It's the specialty of your species."

"We're homebodies now. We like to put our feet up and watch the holovids."

"When you make jokes, the hives become more worried, because you're not a joking man. Therefore—"

It was getting painful and he didn't want to hear Sikili's character analysis. Fett found it amusing that he hadn't threatened or hinted about the fate of Roche—or even thought much about it—but that had always been part of his armory, as it had been for the Mandalorians as a whole. They had a certain reputation that did the advance work for them.

"Sign a treaty with us, then," he offered.

"To do what, Fett?"

"Nonaggression pact. Neighborly mutual aid."

"You have nothing to fear from us, so you'll want something in exchange, because you're a mercenary and—"

"Bounty hunter, part-time. What I want is the mutual bit."

"What can we do for you to avoid being added to your collection?"

"Supply us with exclusive products in exchange for our exclusive metal. We give you our special skills—military strength—and you give us yours in defense technology and quality control. Maybe even joint work on new projects."

"Ah, you Mandalorians have always . . . adopted technology from others. You might forcibly *adopt* ours now."

"Deal's on the table. You made me notice you. Bad idea."

Sikili was silent again. Verpines had a way of communicating instantly with all hive members through some organ in their chests. Fett guessed that Sikili was consulting the hive.

"Deal accepted. We'll need details."

"I'll get my people to talk to your people." Fett could imagine the reaction on Coruscant—and Corellia. "We look forward to a long and productive alliance with Roche."

"We will announce this happy and reassuring news. Good day, Fett."

The good thing about literal-minded insectoids was that they were transparent in their business dealings: no games, no bluff, and—usually—no skipping out on deals. Fett wondered if he should have talked it through with the clans first, but it was his prerogative to choose Mandalore's allies, and teaming up with the best technologists in the galaxy wasn't going to upset anybody—not on Mandalore, anyway. It would certainly ruin everyone else's day.

So people think we're rearming. We are, but not for the reasons they think. This could be . . . interesting.

He secured *Slave I*, out of habit rather than mistrust of his own people, and took the speeder bike up to the woodland where he'd reburied his father's remains after exhuming them on Geonosis.

Ailyn was laid to rest there, too, but Mirta was clearly still uneasy about not returning her to Kiffu. She seemed to see the interment as a temporary stopover. He'd marked the graves with simple stones because it mattered to him to be able to find them again, although he had never been one for visiting graves.

Not even yours, Dad.

Now he was going to put that right. He had no excuse. He wasn't a galaxy away.

All the times I've traveled from world to world, all the light-years I've covered, and I never called in at Geonosis to pay my respects.

Fett grasped briefly at an excuse in his Mandalorian roots. Beviin had always told him it was the armor that mattered to Mandalorians, not the decayed shell abandoned by the spirit. *I did that, didn't I? I recovered my Dad's armor and left his body. I did that much, at least.*

Nomadic mercenaries couldn't have cemeteries, and they couldn't carry corpses with them. It was probably based on pragmatism, but Mandalorians—with few exceptions, like the Mandalores—still didn't have elaborate shrines and graves even here.

The clearing in the woods was a peaceful, unspoiled spot, somewhere the Yuuzhan Vong hadn't managed to destroy. Tall silver-leaved galek trees, centuries old, fringed an area of spongy moss and short yellow grass, giving the spot an air of permanent sunlit calm even on an overcast day. Even before Fett set down the speeder bike, he could see Mirta kneeling by her mother's grave, staring down at it, with Ghes Orade, Novoc Vevut's son, staring at her. Their helmets were placed to one side.

She had a funny idea of romance, that girl, but Orade seemed close to besotted, so maybe he didn't care where he had to follow her. They both looked around and watched Fett as he approached. He tried to avoid crushing clumps of fragile amber ferns.

"Tell me if I'm interrupting," Fett said. Orade looked up at him and got to his feet. "Here's the deal. You break her heart, I break your legs."

"Deal," said Orade. He had a sharp-featured pale face and a scrap of bright, blond beard. "See you later, Mirta."

Mirta looked past Fett to watch Orade leave, and then glared at him. "I suppose that's your idea of protective concern, *Ba'buir.*"

"Meant it," Fett said. "You're no use to me when you're emotional."

"So . . . what did you want me for?"

"Didn't. Just came to visit Dad's grave."

Her nerf-frying stare softened, probably from embarrassment. Weeping together over Ailyn just that one time hadn't opened the emotional floodgates and given them a blood-bound relationship cemented by shared grief. It was, and probably always would be, wary and restrained.

"I'll come back later," Fett said.

"No, I was just leaving anyway."

"Okay, let's both stand around in awkward silence for a while and I'll give you a ride back to town."

For some reason, the one thing that never embarrassed Fett was admitting his love for his father. He didn't care if that made him look soft. People said it didn't, especially if they wanted to carry on breathing. He hooked both thumbs in his belt and contemplated the slight depression in the soft mossy ground, realizing he should have filled the grave with more soil to allow for settling.

I'm not doing too bad, Dad. Did you ever have to make domestic policy when you were Mandalore, or did you just fight? I suppose you know I'm dying.

The last thought caught him unawares. Fett believed in decomposition and eternal oblivion: he'd dealt them out so many times, he knew what awaited him. It was Beviin and his talk of the *manda* that had him falling into those stupid thoughts about eternity.

"I knew you were basically okay when you split the heart-of-fire to bury half with Mama," Mirta said quietly.

"I'm not sentimental."

"A real scumbag would have kept the stone intact and sold it."

Fett resented the interruption of his one-sided conversation with his father. "Maybe if I'd left it whole, somebody could have read the information in it." He straightened up, arms at his side. "Are you done here?"

Mirta shrugged, collected her helmet, and began walking toward the speeder. It was an answer of sorts. They set off for Keldabe. There were no straight roads; it made ambushing and pinning down would-be invaders a lot easier.

"What does everyone else do with bodies?" Fett asked.

"Turn left when we get to the river and I'll show you."

Mirta seemed to have taken this born-again *Mando* thing seriously. Fett had expected her to kick over the traces and turn wholly Kiffar, like her mother, but she'd jumped to the other extreme. If he hadn't known she wasn't motivated by wealth, he'd have thought she was positioning herself to inherit his fortune. That would have been easier. Right now, he had no idea what her motive was.

"Gejjen's been assassinated, by the way," he said, banking the speeder to turn along the course of the Kelita River. "Heard it on the news."

"Good," she said. She was definitely his granddaughter. "Slimy *shabuir*."

"I put the full fee for Sal-Solo in a trust fund for you."

"Thanks. You didn't have to."

"No. I didn't."

"There it is."

"What?"

"The grave."

Fett couldn't see anything, just lush water meadows flanked by rich pasture, vibrantly green even after harvesttime. They said the area had beaten the Yuuzhan Vong's attempts at environmental destruction because the fast-flowing water in the meadow and the river carried the poisons away downstream. Even to Fett's urban and unagricultural eye, it looked like rich soil. "Where?"

"Try your terahertz GPR."

Fett blinked his ground-penetrating radar into life. When he looked at the land now, he saw the variations in density and the pockets of less compacted soil. He also saw clusters of lines and debris so tangled together that he couldn't make out what they were.

"It's a mass grave," Mirta said.

Fett stopped the speeder and they got off to look. His boots squelched in the sodden grass, and while it was far from the first time he'd walked on a carpet of the dead, this felt vaguely uncomfortable.

"Lost a lot of people," he said. *More than a million.* Nearly one in three Mandalorians had died defending the planet. Mirta seemed to be expecting some statesman-like behavior, so he tried. "And no memorial."

"This isn't a war grave," Mirta said. "*Mando'ade* usually bury in mass graves anyway. We all become part of the *manda.* We don't need a headstone."

The exceptional fertility of the soil suddenly made sense. There was no point wasting organic material.

"*Manda.*"

"Collective consciousness. Oversoul. We don't do heaven."

Fett winced. "I know what it is."

"And it gives back to the living. You'll get a marked grave, of course, being *Mand'alor.* Unless you choose not to."

"Probably just to make sure they know the old Mandalore won't show up again to reclaim the title."

"Maybe just to show *respect.*"

"Has it occurred to you," Fett asked, "that all this is a rationalization of the fact that Mandalorians were always on the move, couldn't maintain graves, and needed to dispose of lots of corpses? And that it's free fertilizer?"

Mirta took off her helmet, probably to let him see the full thundercloud of her disapproval. "There's nothing profound that you can't reduce to banality, is there?"

"I'm a practical man."

"We're a practical people." *We.* Kiffu had ceased to exist for her. "But there's nothing wrong with seeing the bigger picture."

"Can I opt out of the *manda*? I'm not spending eternity with Montross or Vizsla. Or do we take guests from other species? If we adopt them in life, makes sense we take them afterward, so what about the rest of the galaxy?"

Mirta seemed about to spit something vitriolic at him but instead sighed, jammed her helmet back in place, and went back to the speeder. Fett pondered how tedious it would be if there really were some existence after death, especially if it weren't ticket-only. The one person he wanted to see again was his father. The rest of the dead—loved and hated, but mostly just unloved and dismissed—could *stay* dead.

He resolved to keep his mouth shut in the future. It had always been the best policy in the past, and meaningful conversation was one of the few things he couldn't seem to master. He took her into the center of Keldabe following the twisting course of the Kelita, skimming above its meanders and river cliffs. The ancient river had gradually kinked back on itself as it ground away patiently at the banks, and it looked as if one good flood would break the narrow necks of land and straighten the course again. A quick inspection with his helmet GPR showed dried-up oxbow lakes pressed like hoofprints into the land on either side. Until the crab-boys had showed up, most of Mandalore had been as it had since before humans arrived: primeval, wild, and still full of the undiscovered. Fett hated the Yuuzhan Vong afresh for ruining that.

Novoc Vevut, Orade's father, built and repaired weapons. He was in the yard of the workshop that also served as his house, machining

blaster parts. Fett shut the speeder down at the entrance and Mirta slid off the saddle.

Vevut pushed his transparent protective visor back onto the top of his head and gave them both a big grin.

"Aw, nice to see you two doing stuff together," he said. "*Osi'kyr,* Fett, are we going to be related?"

Mirta looked at him with a warmth she didn't direct at her own grandfather. Fett hadn't picked up on how far the relationship with Vevut's son had progressed, then. "If *beskar* is such a good defense, how come you've got so many scars, *Buir?*" she teased. "Forgot to wear your helmet?"

She'd called him *Papa.* Vevut grinned. "I cut myself shaving."

"With a Trandoshan."

"Marry Ghes, and I'll make you a blaster that can take the head off a dozen Trandoshans with one shot."

"You know how to turn a girl's head," she said, and removed her helmet and boots before disappearing into the house.

Vevut brushed shiny coils of swarf from the grinding bench. His long woolly black braids were tied back with a piece of string while he worked, but the gold clips strung along them like trophies still rattled and chinked as he moved. Combined with the striking scars in his ebony skin, they made him look formidably battle-hardened. Beviin said the gold had come from his kills over the years, and that he'd melted it down to make the ornate clips. They made Fett's braided Wookiee scalps look low-key.

"When I adopted Ghes," Vevut said, not raising his eyes from the workbench, "we had a hard time accepting each other at first, too." He rasped glittering shavings from the metal he was shaping and held it up to check the edge. "And I'd known him all his life. His parents were my neighbors. Just because Mirta's your own blood doesn't mean it's automatic."

"I'll bear that in mind."

"Any objections to Orade?"

"Mirta's well over thirteen. She can make her own choices."

"He's a good lad."

"I know." Fett's own inability to cope with partners was no reason for him to have any opinion on his granddaughter's life. But he meant it about breaking Orade's legs. It was a paternal reflex that came out of nowhere. "I did a deal with the Verpine government today. We now have a nonaggression pact with Roche provided they share tech with us."

Vevut stopped rasping sharp edges. "Hey, I didn't even hear us fire any shots . . ."

"They heard the word *beskar*."

"I do believe good times are on their way again, *Mand'alor*."

"If you feel like sitting in when we talk weapons with them, your views would be useful."

"Okay. I'll leave my bug spray at home as a mark of respect."

"I'd better tell the clans. In case anyone's thinking of signing up for Kem Stor Ai. The Verpine would be upset about that."

It was a good relaxed way to run a nation. Fett sent word out via his datapad and waited for objections, not expecting any. Apart from questions like the discounts that might now be available on custom Verpine weapons, the chieftains took the news in their stride.

It was as if Mandalorians saved all their passions for two things: their families and their wars. Fett returned to Beviin's farm via the river and paused to look at the vast mass grave again.

Most species found the words *unmarked mass grave* the stuff of horror, the worst possible end to life. And yet Mandalorians *chose* it. Fett, on the cusp between *Mando* and *aruetii* despite his title, tried to see his people as the *aruetiise* saw them, to fully understand the fear just a few million of them could cause simply by existing. Detached, he saw an invading army wiping out whole species, fighting galactic wars, destroying everything in its path; and he saw mercenaries and bounty hunters, unemotional masked dealers in death. The image burned into the collective galactic psyche was one of violent savages, thieves, and looters, whose temporary loyalty to anyone but their own could be bought but never guaranteed.

It happened to be almost completely true—except the bit about loyalty. Most people didn't understand the nature of a contract.

And they never got close enough to see Mandalorians at peace. Come to that, not many Mandalorians did, either. It was a restless galaxy.

Fett resigned himself to existing in no-man's-land—too *Mando*

for the outsider but not *Mando* enough for some of the clans—and made his way back to *Slave I,* which was still the haven in which he preferred to sleep. He hoped Beviin wasn't offended. Worrying about someone else's feelings was a novelty, and Fett knew what Beviin would say about the psychology of sleeping in a spacecraft when a perfectly comfortable home—any number of homes—was available.

When Fett reached the ship and unlocked the hatch by remote, he found a message waiting for him. It could have been relayed straight to his HUD, but Jaing Skirata did things his own idiosyncratic way.

I SEE YOU DID RIGHT BY MANDALORE. I'LL DO RIGHT BY YOU.

Fett hadn't judged wrong, then. He dropped his dose of capsules into his palm and washed them down with a mix of water and the cocktail of liquid drugs that Beluine had prescribed. It was just slowing down his decline, not stopping it.

Jaing hadn't said he'd succeeded.

Death's a motivator, not a threat. You've still got things to achieve before you become fertilizer. You'll just have to do them sooner rather than later.

Fett switched on the monitor in his cramped quarters and sat back with a pack of dry rations to watch the news as Corellia went into meltdown, and the Verpine government of Roche announced talks with Mandalore to agree to a mutual aid and trade treaty.

Then he took out the black book his father had left him. He'd listened to every message recorded in it more than a hundred times, and studied his father's image in it. When he was afraid he was beginning to forget what Jango Fett once looked like, he'd take it out and run the messages again.

He hadn't forgotten: not a pore, not a hair, not a line. But he ran it again anyway, and decided tomorrow might be a very good day to go public on the *Bes'uliik.*

JEDI COUNCIL CHAMBER, CORUSCANT:
EMERGENCY MEETING

"This one," said Master Saba Sebatyne, "would like to be assured that the Alliance had nothing to do with Gejjen'z death. It was *unnezzzezary.*"

Luke couldn't blame her for jumping to conclusions. It was his first thought, too, and his second was that the GA's agents—or even Jacen—had a hand in it. But the assassin had, it seemed, sealed himself in his ship and blown it up, a Corellian-registered ship scattering solidly Corellian evidence. Luke had seen crazier things than that. It was a zealot's act, and all too common.

"There are plenty of Corellians with reasons to want Gejjen dead," he said. Where had Mara got to? He half expected her to stride through the doors of the chamber carrying Lumiya's head in triumph. "But I'll conduct my own investigations."

Corran Horn looked up from his clasped hands, which he'd been studying with unnatural concentration. It couldn't have been easy watching his homeworld plunge into recrimination and finger-pointing. "It's less about who actually did it than who the various factions *think* did it, and that won't be influenced by anything as irrelevant as hard facts."

"Well, I need to know, and I don't want HNE telling me," Luke said. "Kyp, can you monitor the headlines while we're meeting?"

"Time was," said Kyp Durron, "when the government of the day used to keep the Jedi Council informed, and we didn't have to rely on the media."

Yes, Luke had noticed that the Council was no longer kept in the loop. He returned to the main issue. "So what if it *is* us?" So far everyone had managed to avoid mentioning Jacen.

Kyle Katarn joined in. "Is assassinating heads of state legal?"

"In a war, I believe it is."

"Fine time for Omas to be away," said Katarn. "If I were the paranoid type, I'd say it was spooky that he was out of town, location

undisclosed, at the same time that Gejjen was shot. Better test him for ballistic residues when he gets back to the office."

"This isn't a joking matter," said Kyp.

"Okay, sorry. But it's lousy timing."

Luke thought Niathal had done a commendable job of looking calm and reassuring for the media. It had been a few hours since the news had broken, and the news channels had wheeled out every analyst, politician, and air taxi pilot who had ever held an opinion on Dur Gejjen. Niathal, quite splendid in her white uniform, was impressive. She looked as if being Chief of State was just another job she did when everyone else was too busy. She'd scored a lot of points.

And Luke hadn't had a chance to call Han or Leia. That was his next task, as soon as he got out of this meeting. They'd know what was really happening—if anyone did.

Come on, Mara. Where are you?

"So how does this change things?" Kyle asked. "Who's going to be leading the Confederation now? Is it going to stay a Corellian thing?"

"If it's the Bothans," said Corran, "Force preserve us."

Luke was still waiting for word from Niathal. The Jedi Council wasn't part of government, and while Omas was away it wasn't getting instant answers. Luke realized how fragile and informal the relationship between government and Council could be when different people were holding the reins.

"Just to spice up the mix, the Mandalorians are joining forces with the Verpine." Kyp seemed to be listening to the news via an earpiece, judging by the glazed and defocused look in his eyes. "What does that sound like to you?"

Luke thought of Fett's dead daughter, Jacen's guilt, and Fett's track record. He'd been awfully quiet; worryingly so.

"They're rearming," Luke said.

"They said they were staying neutral." Durron said.

Kyle shook his head slowly, brushing specks from his lap in a distracted way. "Oh, yeah, if my long-lost daughter was tortured to death by the GA's secret police, I'd be neutral. First thing I'd do. Walk away and be very, very *neutral*."

"You don't have to be on one of two sides to rearm, or even take part in a war," Luke said.

Still nobody had said the J-word. But Luke could hear the name at the back of every mind.

"Well, we know a few facts." Kyle counted off on his fingers. "One, Mandalorians aren't exactly heavily represented in social services and the caring professions. Two, they have a brand-new supply of that iron of theirs for their war machine. Three, allying with the Verpine makes them the single most powerful producer of advanced weapons technology. Four, I hear they're still sore about getting no help to rebuild postwar when they went out on a limb for the New Republic."

"It's not good, is it?" said Corran.

"I'm betting they'll step up for Corellia in the next few days."

"Fett's said to have killed Sal-Solo, or at least one of his *Mando* thugs did. Where does that leave them?"

Luke had heard the real story from Han. Never had he missed the good old clear-cut days of Rebellion versus Empire, good against demonstrable evil, as much as he had right then. The trouble with taking away the certainty of evil was that its vacuum was filled by all kinds of more nebulous threats, rivalries, and feuds. It became increasingly hard to judge where the threat was coming from.

If it hadn't been so ingrained in the nature of most species, Luke would have seen it as a Sith plot. It would have been so much simpler.

"I think we should offer Jedi mediation to both the GA and Corellia, as far as the assassination goes," he said. "I know it sounds bizarre in the middle of a war, but there's war with rules, and then there's war with no holds barred, and we need to—"

The doors opened and Mara walked in. "Sorry I'm late," she said. "Ran into a few problems."

She managed to stop the meeting dead. Luke stared in horror at her face. She had a black eye and split lip; she was holding herself as if her ribs hurt. She settled into her seat in the circle with slow care.

"Ran into an armored division, more like," said Kyp, staring. "What happened to you, and where shall we send the flowers for the other guy?"

"And this is *after* a healing trance." She smiled, and it was genuine, but there was definite anxiety. Luke could feel it. It was all he could do not to abandon the meeting there and then, and go to her. How had he not felt what was happening to her?

"Sorry to interrupt," she went on. "I assume we're worrying about the implications of Gejjen's death."

"And Mandalorian rearmament."

"Forget that for just a second," Luke said. "Mara, I need to know what happened to you."

"Why, darling, *thank you* for asking! I'm very well. Just a flesh wound." She shook her head in disbelief, but it seemed aimed at herself. "Look, I caught Lumiya. She's in a worse state than I am, believe me."

"And?"

"The situation's under control."

"Where *is* she?"

"I'm tracking her to her base."

All eleven Council members were waiting in complete silence for Mara's next words. She looked at the other Jedi around her, gently pushed Luke's unspoken inquiry and concern out of her mind with a firm *later,* and settled back in her chair. Luke couldn't pin it down, but she was in turmoil under that façade.

"It's no good looking at me like that," she said. "I'm not discussing it, I'm not sharing the mission, and I'm not going to take it easy, which I'll bet is going to be someone's suggestion. Yes?"

"Mara hath spoken," said Kyp. "But that doesn't stop me asking where Lumiya is, and what she's driving."

"Nice try, but go find your own deranged dark sider to play with, because Lumiya's mine."

Corran gave Luke a knowing smile. "She's fine."

Mara was certainly satisfied about something, but not so content about something else. Luke would find out later. He moved the meeting on.

"Can we actually do anything about the Gejjen situation here and now?" There was a chorus of a reluctant "no" around the circle. "Okay, then, all we can do is keep an eye on the situation, and I've got a request in with Omas's secretary to see him as soon as he gets back."

"You know what happens if heads of state are away when a crisis breaks," Kyp pointed out. "They take a pounding in the polls, and it's the beginning of the end. Let's make the most of Omas while we can."

"Who's friendly with Niathal?"

They all turned to look pointedly at Cilghal. She tilted her head slightly to fix Luke with one eye, always a disconcerting thing in a Mon Calamari. "Just because we're Mon Cals, Luke, it doesn't mean we have guaranteed harmony. We come from different schools of thought."

"You're Ackbar's niece, and I bet that counts for a lot with a Mon Cal admiral . . ."

"I'll do my best, then."

The meeting broke up, Mara remaining seated. Corran patted her on the head like an indulgent uncle as he passed, and then wagged a silent warning finger: *Get that black eye seen to.* Luke waited until everyone was well out of earshot and then walked over to squat in front of Mara and put his hands on her knees.

"You can't keep this from me."

"I head-butted her, that's all. Metal jaw, nonmetal head."

"If you got that close, how did she get away?" Oh, *bad* question: Luke braced for an onslaught about shaking hands again. "I mean . . ."

"I think she has a droid with her. Something jumped me from behind, and it wasn't organic." Mara showed him a discolored mark like a rope burn at the front of her neck. "Whatever it is, it can pay out a metal cable. And she has this weird spherical ship like a disembodied orange eye."

"Don't you think all that's a good case for *not* hunting her alone?"

"She wants me to catch up with her. I'll be extra-ready next time— and there *will* be a next time."

He'd promised her. If anyone could take Lumiya, Mara could, and he knew he had to put his own fixation with Lumiya out of his mind— stop it from clouding his judgment. He'd give Mara a little more time, but wondered how he'd feel if she came home battered and bruised like this again.

Chasing individual Dark Jedi was far more difficult and time consuming than he'd bargained for. Sometimes he wondered why Lumiya

and Alema had proved so much harder to hunt and deal with than a whole Empire, but that was the answer: the Empire, by its very size and pervasiveness, was everywhere. It was hard to avoid finding it, but two Jedi with concealment skills could vanish very effectively in an entire galaxy. It would always be a case of getting them to come to him—or Mara.

"But you'll be home for dinner tonight," Luke said. "Don't spend all night working again."

"Believe me, I'll be home," she said. "That's where I'm heading now."

"I'd better see what Han and Leia have to say about Gejjen, while I hang around the Senate and wait for Omas."

"If I'm still sitting at home with a congealing plate of nerf casserole at midnight . . ."

"Okay. Dinner at eight. Set in permacrete."

Luke walked down the corridor with her in silence and she gave him a conspiratorial grin as the turbolift doors closed. He opened his secure comlink and called Han.

"I'm not in mourning," Han said, utterly callous in that charming way he had. Luke knew he didn't care for Gejjen and never had: it was hard to weep for a man who approached you to kill your own cousin, even if that cousin was a grade-A scumbag. "No need to spare my feelings. He was a head shot waiting to happen."

"What's the public mood like over there?"

"There hasn't exactly been a run on mourning clothes, but folks are nervous."

"So who's at the helm in Coronet now?"

"They're slugging it out. For the while, it's going to be a committee job."

"Who do you think did it?"

"The biggest task CorSec has is to work out how to manage the lines of suspects. Not that they need to dig up any—two different terror groups here have already claimed responsibility for it. Yes, we have 'em, too."

"I never realized how divided you all were."

"We're never divided about Corellia. Just who's the best candidate to run it."

"Are you and Leia okay?"

"Yes, we're fine, and no, I'm not telling you what we're doing at the moment. Stop worrying."

Luke almost raised the topic of a GA smokescreen. It was fairly common to carry out a hit and set it up to look like another faction to achieve maximum discord. But he thought better of it, because it smacked of Jacen, and Han didn't need to hear that his best friend thought his son—stranger though he was—had a hand in it. Some things were best dealt with by friends, cleaned up, and smoothed over. When Lumiya was finally brought down, Luke would spend his time putting Jacen back on track. It was the least he could do for Han.

Omas couldn't have picked a worse day to visit his doctor, but it was unusual for him to be so reticent about routine arrangements. Luke hoped it wasn't something serious.

It was bad enough losing Gejjen, because at least he was a known quantity, and Luke had become used to his way of thinking. If Omas's future was in doubt, too—well, that was one unknown too many.

CORUSCANT MILITARY SPACEPORT

Ben sat in the cargo hold of the ship long after the ground crew had secured the landing dampers and the drives had cooled completely.

He was almost comfortable staring at the bulkhead opposite, in the sense that he feared taking his eyes off it. If he did that, the numbing meditation he'd slipped into would be broken, and he'd have to think.

Jori Lekauf was gone. It was one of those facts he couldn't take in even when he saw it happen. The guy had been alive and well the night before, even hours ago, and now he didn't exist. Ben simply couldn't *feel* death.

It was more than the biological facts, and he knew those all too well. The former CSF officers in the GAG had regaled him with fascinating stories from the police forensics labs, but knowing how to cause death and what it looked like, and being able to feel a life wink out of existence in the Force did nothing to hammer home the fact that his friend was gone forever, and that he wouldn't see him again, and all the things that made Jori Lekauf part of the fabric of the universe, someone who *mattered*, were so far beyond his reach.

And it was Ben's fault. Lekauf had died to protect him.

"Come on, Ben. The techs want to start stripping down this crate."

Captain Shevu stood in the hatch, fingers hooked over the top edge of the coaming. Ben felt that if he moved, the whole world would come unraveled.

"I'll be along in a minute."

Shevu waited for a moment and then came to sit down with him. Ben suspected that if he'd been a grown man, Shevu might have been harsher, but he thought Ben was still a kid, too young to be on this kind of mission whether he was a Jedi or not. In many ways, Shevu was right. But nobody was ever old enough to lose a friend and not feel it cutting through to the center of his chest. If Ben ever got that old, he didn't want to carry on.

"We don't lose many troopers in special forces. It makes it harder when we do, I think. It's hard for me, anyway."

Ben gambled on whether to speak or not. He took a breath and waited to feel everything around him shatter.

"He didn't have to *die*, sir." Once he heard his own voice, Ben just felt like he couldn't breathe, nothing worse. "He could have taken off. We could have run for it, or even been captured, and the job would still have been done."

"Ben . . . our orders were to make it look like a Corellian schism, and not to get caught or leave a trail. Can't have Jedi exposed as assassins, especially not you. We had to get you out of there."

"It didn't *have* to be me. Any trooper could have done the job. I wanted to do my duty, but if it hadn't been *me*, if Jori hadn't felt he had to protect my identity, he'd be alive."

"Ben, what do you think would have happened to him if he'd been taken back to Corellia?" Shevu lowered his voice. "You saw what we do here to prisoners. You think worse than that can't happen in Coronet?"

"So what if I had been caught? My dad would have been humiliated? So *what*? Jori's life for Dad being *upset*?"

"I could give you a list of reasons why having Corellia think their own kind did it helps the GA. But you don't want to hear that right now." Shevu stood up and beckoned to Ben to follow. He meant it. "There are anti-Gejjen factions claiming responsibility, so the mission worked fine—strategically. Now go home and take a couple of days off. If you can't stand being around your folks, or . . . or around Colonel Solo, come over to my place. My girlfriend won't mind."

It was the first time Ben had heard Shevu hint that being around Jacen wasn't necessarily the best thing for him. Ben didn't care about Jacen right then, but the rational bit of his mind that wasn't drowning in shocked grief made a note of it.

"Thanks."

"Now I've got to tell his parents. I'll have to come up with a really good cover story, and thank providence that there's no footage of him splashed all over the news right now, because that'd be a really lousy way to find out your son was dead."

Shevu sounded beaten. He was probably pretty close to Lekauf, but he'd never said. Ben had learned a lesson about being an officer today, and it was that lives were to be spent in pursuit of an objective; it might have seemed obvious, but when you worked alongside the people who might lose their loved ones because of your decisions, it acquired a whole new meaning.

"I don't think I'll ever stop feeling guilty about this," Ben said, relieved that he had so far managed not to burst into tears.

"Me neither," said Shevu. "Because it was supposed to be me who blew the ship if things went wrong."

"We never planned that—"

"You didn't. *We* did. Need to know, and all that." Shevu stopped a passing ground crew speeder and told the driver to get Ben back to HQ. "Wash that stuff out of your hair and go home."

An hour later, Ben found himself staring at his familiar reflection in the HQ refreshers, toweling his hair and wondering if Jacen had set him up.

I didn't have to do the job. Any one of us could have passed unnoticed at a spaceport.

But it was hindsight. Jacen had tasked him to do it before anyone knew where the meeting would take place. Ben still felt something was wrong, but couldn't pin it down.

He'd just lost his buddy. Maybe that made you think crazy things. When he left the HQ building and walked out into the late-afternoon sun, completely disoriented by the shifts in planetary time over the last forty-eight hours, he lowered his head and just walked aimlessly, hands in pockets.

Suddenly he felt someone's hand on his shoulder. He almost shrieked. He'd shut out everything around him. Then he found he was staring into his mother's face, and something was terribly wrong.

"Mom! Who hit you?"

"Forget that, Ben." She hugged him to her, a really desperate and crushing embrace. "I've got some questions and I will absolutely *not* be stalled this time." She had hold of his shoulders, eyes scanning his face as if she was looking for injury. "This is between you and me, I swear, not your father."

They ended up in a tapcaf in the Osarian quarter. The table was greasy and the elbows of Ben's jacket stuck to it every time he leaned on them, but nobody knew them here. Even if the food had been appetizing and not searingly hot, Ben wasn't hungry.

Mara lowered her voice. "I want to know why you've been to Vulpter."

Ben was stunned. How could she possibly know? Who'd talked? It was completely classified. Most of the GAG hadn't even been briefed on it.

"I haven't."

"You can stop the game. I know where you've been, and I have a horrible feeling I know why. The whole planet's seen the news."

Mara just stared at him, not blinking, suddenly not his mom at all. He was supposed to deny everything. He stared back, silent.

"I could ask Jacen, sweetheart, but I'm not sure I could believe him if he told me what the time was."

"You know I can't talk about my work, Mom."

"Oh, I know. I've never hidden my past from you, so I know *exactly* what your work entails. I can talk to you like a grown-up, Ben, because once you do the kind of job you're doing, you're not a kid any longer. Do we understand each other?"

Ben thought of Jori Lekauf and felt his stomach starting to knot and shake. He desperately wanted to blurt out that his buddy had died and that he wanted to roll time back to before he'd fallen into this mess, and that—that—

"Mom . . ." He couldn't get it out. She put her hand on his and squeezed. "Mom, if I tell you, will you tell me who hit you?"

"Okay, it was Lumiya. I caught her, but she got away. I gave her a good hiding, and she won't get away next time. Now—your turn."

Ben took a deep breath. This was either going to make everything better, or be the start of something disastrous. He couldn't tell: all his Force impressions had deserted him.

"I did it, Mom."

"Involved . . . or *did it?*"

Ben's mouth took over without his permission. "Folding-stock Karpaki, frangible round."

Mara actually sat back in her chair and her left hand moved as if she was about to put it to her mouth. Her right hand was still clamped tight on his.

"Okay," she said.

"Lekauf was killed, Mom." Ben couldn't remember if she knew Lekauf or not. It didn't matter. He needed to say his name and tell someone. "Jori got killed—he got killed to save my skin."

Mara busied herself sipping from the cup in front of her. Osarians liked very strongly scented herbs, and Ben knew he'd never be able to smell that aroma again without being dragged back to this awful moment.

"Why did you do it, Ben?"

"Orders. I was the best person to do it."

"Your whole company is suddenly short of snipers? Whose orders?"

"Jacen."

Mara was doing a reasonable job of not reacting, but Ben wasn't fooled. She was furious. He could see it in the whiteness of her skin, and the contrast with the yellowing bruise around her eye made it even more noticeable.

"Okay, sweetheart," she said. "Let's not tell your dad, because he'll rip Jacen's head off in the mood he's in at the moment. Can you face coming home?"

"I don't think I can sit and have dinner and not talk about this to him."

"Okay, so where are you planning on going?"

"Home. Jacen's apartment." Ben could see she wasn't keen on the idea. "Or Captain Shevu's place."

"Wherever you feel safest, Ben. I won't force you to come back with me as long as you swear you'll come to me the second you have problems, okay?"

"Okay."

"I'm sorry about your friend. I really am."

"Nobody's ever going to know how brave he was."

"I know."

"Are you angry with me? Stupid question. You must be."

"How can I be, after what I used to do?" She gripped both his hands as if she was afraid he'd run away. "This is what we made you, isn't it? We wanted you to be like us. We wanted you to be a Jedi and do your duty . . ."

Mara was quiet for a while, gazing out the window onto the sky-lane packed with traffic and clearly thinking hard.

"You still haven't told me how you knew, Mom."

She jerked back to the conversation, blinking. "No. I haven't. But I know, and I'm the only one who does. And I also know you can hide in the Force like Jacen does, and it scares me because the first time I felt it I thought you'd been killed. Please, Ben, don't hide from me. Ever."

"I wasn't, Mom. I was just trying it out."

"Okay."

"Am I going to feel bad about . . . you know, the other guy? 'Cos right now I don't care."

"I didn't," she said, seeming to understand he meant Gejjen. "Not until lately, and then it didn't feel like guilt. Just . . . not quite understanding why I did it, because being what I was didn't explain it all to me."

"I'd better go."

"You'll be okay. I'll always be there, remember. Call me."

Ben leaned forward to kiss her on the cheek. He loved her so much right then; what other mom could take news like that, horrific news, and still be there for him? He leaned farther and whispered in her ear.

"He was having a secret meeting at the port with Omas. To discuss a cease-fire."

When Ben straightened up, she smiled, but there was a real glint in her eye that said she was anything but happy.

"Thank you," she said. "I love you, Ben. Call me, okay?"

"Love you, too, Mom."

Ben couldn't stand it any longer. He walked out of the tapcaf and spent the next couple of hours wandering around, staring in shop windows and not seeing anything, before he got an air taxi back to Jacen's apartment and shut himself in his room.

It was going to take a long time to make sense of this. He slipped the vibroblade under his pillow, reluctant to let it sit as far away as his desk, and wondered what Captain Shevu was telling Jori Lekauf's family.

chapter twelve

Ori'buyce, kih'kovid.
All helmet, no head.

—Mandalorian insult for someone with an overdeveloped sense of authority

REPUBLICA HOUSE, CORUSCANT:
0001 HOURS, GALACTIC STANDARD TIME

JACEN SOLO, IN THE FORMAL UNIFORM OF A COLONEL OF THE GALAC-tic Alliance Guard, stood outside the lobby of the Republica build-ing flanked by Sergeant Wirut and Trooper Limm.

It was a real shame about Lekauf. He was a great loss. Ben had done well, but he should have been back at work right away. Jacen planned to talk to Shevu later about sending Ben on leave without clearing it with him first.

"You sure this is going to be enough, sir?" asked Wirut. "Just the three of us?"

Jacen smoothed his black gloves down over his fingers. It was one minute past midnight, and that made what he was about to do thoroughly legal, justified, and overdue.

"I don't think Chief Omas has a platoon up there, somehow."

Wirut didn't reply. Jacen was the first to admit that going to arrest the elected head of the most powerful organization in the galaxy with a couple of troopers was low-key, but he saw no point flooding the area with an entire company. Omas wouldn't put up a fight. If he did, one Jedi and two armed troopers were ample to deal with it.

Jacen opened the comlink to Niathal.

"We're in position now," he said. "We're going in."

"I have an emergency appointment with Senator G'Sil in ten minutes," Niathal said. "He's not happy about it, but I told him it couldn't wait."

"He's got no inkling of what's happening?"

"If he has, he hasn't shown the slightest sign of acting upon it."

"Okay. There's no going back now. We're committed."

"Just do it . . ."

The security guard on the front reception was a man used to seeing all kinds of uniforms wandering in and out of Republica House. The luxurious tower housed the elite of the GA, and every Senator seemed to have his or her own entourage of bodyguards as well as military visitors. Most Coruscanti knew what a GAG uniform looked like by now anyway—Jacen had made sure his secret police were anything but secret, at least in terms of their existence—but he gave the guard proper identification without being asked. There was no point being rude or throwing his weight around. The man was only doing his job.

"No need to announce me," Jacen said.

The guard checked his datapad. "You're on his admission list anyway. Go on up."

It took minutes for the turbolift to reach Omas's floor. As the cab climbed, the two troopers simply stared at the wall ahead of them. Jacen felt their reluctance, and wanted to know if it was due to a fondness for Omas or a distaste for military coups, but he didn't ask. Any army that *liked* the idea of a coup wasn't worth having. It had to be the last resort.

"How the other half lives . . . ," Wirut said as the turbolift doors

opened onto a lobby of extraordinary luxury. The air was perfumed, a pleasantly neutral woody scent, and the broad corridor was lined with niches filled with rare Naboo crystal—Omas had a weakness for that—and iridescent Shalui ceramics. "I could fit my apartment and my ten neighbors in here."

"If we put fancy pottery in the corridors of my building, it wouldn't be there long," said Limm. She cast an envious eye at a shimmering red vase that changed gradually to green and turquoise as the angle of the observer changed. "Still, his insurance payments must hurt."

"Possessions are burdens." Jacen smiled. "What you have can always be taken away, so wealth breeds fear."

"I'll willingly face that kind of fear, sir," Wirut muttered. "And a nice big SoroSuub yacht. That would scare me very nicely."

The magnificent doors to Omas's apartment were engraved bronzium, an abstract design by one of Coruscant's top artists. Jacen couldn't recall the name. It seemed a waste of talent when the doors were seen only by Omas, his inner circle, the housekeeping staff, and repair droids. Republica House had the kind of architecture and design that warranted public tours.

Jacen paused, marshaling his thoughts before pressing the bell. The troopers stood back and pulled down their visors, standard procedure when entering a building. For a moment Jacen thought they were going to stack either side of the door, but they were simply taking a pace backward, Limm keeping an eye on the corridor as a routine precaution.

Omas answered the door himself. Jacen knew he didn't have day-and-night close protection these days, but somehow he expected a droid or even a real butler to receive callers. The Chief of State looked at him with a puzzled frown, and then at the two troopers.

"Good evening, Jacen." He stepped back and ushered them in. "Wretched business, this shooting. I can't say I liked Gejjen, but it shows how careful we have to be in our line of work."

He ambled down a long hallway that made the corridor outside look like a lower levels slum. The art on the walls was breathtaking, and most of it seemed to predate the Yuuzhan Vong invasion. Some gallery curator had a very secure hiding place, then. At the end, Omas turned around.

"Can I get you good people something to drink before we sit down?"

Somehow it would have been so much easier if Omas had been hostile.

"Sir," said Jacen. "I'm arresting you in the name of the Galactic Alliance for activity likely to compromise the safety of the state."

Omas frowned slightly, as if he hadn't heard right. He walked a few steps back along the passage where the downlighters cast pools of light on velvet-pile ruby carpet.

"I beg your pardon?"

"You're under arrest, sir. We'll let you call your lawyer later, but right now it would be a good idea if you came with us."

Omas gave a little snort of amusement. "Jacen, my dear boy, this is Cal Omas you're talking to. Don't be such a prat—arrest me? *Arrest me?*"

Jacen reached in his jacket and took out a datapad. "Under the terms of the Emergency Measures Act, anyone, including heads of state, politicians, and any other individuals believed to be presenting a genuine risk to the security of the Galactic Alliance can now be detained. That's a quote, sir. The amendment to the law to include heads of state came into effect at midnight, and you *are* a head of state . . ."

Omas looked stunned rather than alarmed. Jacen was used to the GAG producing fear when they paid a visit, but amazement was disconcerting.

"I saw that amendment come through on the notifications circular yesterday," Omas said, still quite casually conversational. "Good grief. You really did it, didn't you? You actually changed the law and *planned* this."

"Sir—"

"Am I allowed to know what risk I'm supposed to pose to my own state?"

"I can show you, sir," Jacen said, and switched his datapad to the strip-cam footage of the meeting with Gejjen. He cued it up and then held the pad so that Omas could see the screen. "Please feel free to view it all and then tell me if that's *not* you in the room with two Alliance Intel officers, the late Prime Minister, and his two CorSec protection officers."

The look on Omas's face was priceless. Jacen felt a flood of relief that he had finally, *finally* made Omas realize that he was now a man with no future. Omas stared at the datapad and did indeed watch the whole meeting. Behind Jacen, Wirut and Limm waited in patient silence.

"Well," said Omas. "What can I say?"

"Sergeant Wirut will accompany you to pack an overnight bag," Jacen said. "We'll take you out as discreetly as possible."

"Secretly? Oh, I see . . ."

"No, sir, you're not going to disappear and turn up floating face-down in some sewer. This will be conducted legally and openly."

Omas stared impassively into Jacen's face and then looked past him at the two troopers. Jacen could feel the man's fear even though he looked perfectly at ease. "Sergeant, I do keep a bag packed for eventualities," Omas said, almost smiling. "If you don't trust me not to blow my brains out in the bedroom, by all means go to the fifth door on the left and pick it up for me. It's in the first closet as you enter the room. Tan leather holdall."

There was nothing worse than a dignified detainee. Jacen knew that within twenty-four hours the barracks and the CSF bar would be full of the gossip about how magnificently brave Omas had been. Wirut disappeared into the bedroom while Limm stood guard.

Omas stepped a little closer to Jacen, his face centimeters away, so close that his breath brushed Jacen's skin like a hand.

"You obnoxious, power-crazed, *ludicrous* little jerk," he said sweetly, with the smile of an indulgent grandfather. "You had Gejjen killed, too, didn't you?"

Jacen waited for him to spit in his face and still smile, but Omas conducted himself impeccably as he left. Wirut walked behind him, blaster visible but not jammed into the Chief of State's back, and Jacen led the way. It was the longest, most awkward turbolift descent that Jacen could imagine. When they reached the lobby, the security guard stared for a moment, put down his holozine, and stood up.

"Sir? What's happening?"

"Would you water the plants while I'm away, please?" Omas said pleasantly. "I'm afraid I'm under arrest."

There was a second GAG transport waiting outside. Wirut and Limm ushered Omas into it, then watched it speed away to GAG HQ. Jacen found that his hands were shaking. It was an effort to take out his comlink.

"Admiral, it's done," he said. "Time for a public announcement."

Wirut pushed back his visor and wiped his face with his glove. "That," he said, "was the hardest thing I've ever done. Next time, sir, can I volunteer for snatching heavily armed Wookiee psychopaths? It'd be a lot easier on my nerves."

Wirut and Limm joked, but the arrest had crossed an emotional line for them, and it showed. Jacen climbed into the speeder beside them and took a long route through the canyons of buildings, checking for signs that Coruscant, the heart of galactic democracy, had undergone a silent, bloodless, and thoroughly civilized military coup.

Outside government buildings and bank headquarters, small groups of GA ground forces stood guard. It looked like no more than the routine public order precautions for festival nights, except the uniforms were not the blue of CSF.

"Weird," said Limm.

"Poor old Jori." Wirut sighed. "Poor kid. He was so keen to live up to his granddad."

Jacen rubbed his eyes and realized he was in for another very long day. And the sun wasn't even up yet.

"I won't forget that," he said. "I never will."

chapter thirteen

Trading on the ISE was suspended in the early hours of this morning when Acting Chief of State Admiral Cha Niathal declared temporary martial law following the shock arrest of Cal Omas. A statement is expected in the Senate within the hour. Meanwhile, other galactic financial centers report brisk trading. KDY "A" shares closed fifty point three credits up on yesterday, and both MandalMotors and Roche Industries ended the day up more than thirty credits.

—Market News: *business headlines*

SENATOR G'SIL GLANCED AT THE HOLOCAMS THAT TRANSMITTED Senate debates to every office, restaurant, and public area in the Senate Building, then shook his head, eyes closed for a moment.

"Full house," he said. "You'd better have a good speech ready, Cha. A *really* good one."

Niathal adjusted her uniform and prepared to go out onto the

Chief of State's platform to address the Senate. Things weren't playing out quite as she'd imagined, but then battles never did, and the political arena was as prone to the fog of war as any fleet engagement. Jacen Solo, whom she expected to see strutting around the Senate, was keeping a low profile. But she'd see about that. If she was going to be shoved out front to tap-dance for his coup, she'd make sure he was visibly part of their double act. She wasn't taking responsibility for this on her own.

"It's temporary, it's for the duration of the war, and no ordinary citizens will notice an adverse impact on their lives," she said, rehearsing her key messages. "Play a bit of Omas's clandestine meeting footage, wave around the news on Mandalore and Roche, and everyone nods and says, yes indeed, Admiral, we live in dangerous times, please *do* look after us as an interim government while the Chief of State's office is thoroughly investigated."

"I *like* Jacen," G'Sil said, suddenly very quiet. "But is he reliable these days?"

"Reliable for what?"

"I would never have authorized the Gejjen business. It was . . . extreme."

"It's done. Corellia is wobbling a little, because their assorted lunatic fringes have given us a massive bonus by claiming they did it. Bothawui has been brought up short, because they probably *think* we did it but can't believe we had the nerve, and—well, I never thought I'd live to say this, but those ghastly little Mandalorian savages have been wonderfully helpful."

"Cha, I don't want to worry you, but have you noticed they're rearming? With Verpine tech, too?"

"I certainly have. Best news of the week."

"They must teach you something at staff college that's beyond us lesser mortals."

Niathal checked the chrono. She had ten minutes to psych herself up into appearing as a safe pair of hands, reluctant to take the burden of the reins of state and anxious to hand them back as soon as the current unpleasant business was over. Yes, she meant that, too. She wanted the Chief of State's post, but she wanted a genuine mandate to do it; and there was no better way to achieve that than to show she could be a responsible leader in this most extreme of situations. When she finally ran for office, the electorate would know her by her deeds.

As long as I can keep Jacen on a choke chain, of course, and he doesn't ruin it for me. If he gets out of hand . . . well, there's always Fett.

"Have you ever kept nuna?" she asked.

"Not in the apartment . . ."

"I'm told they tend to form rival groups within the flock, and they can get very territorial. Squabbles break out. Now, let wild bursas into the coop, and it's bedlam—they go into a killing frenzy, grab as many nuna to eat later as they can, and escape. They don't care which group they eat. That's your Mandalorians."

"It's a lovely analogy, but it's lost on me."

"Forget strategy. Mandalorians don't care who wins. They just want to eat, drink, fight, and maintain their self-image."

G'Sil gave her a long, wary stare. "You're the Supreme Commander. I assume you *can* assess a military risk."

"You want my assessment? Fett has no intention of expanding his small sphere of influence. Mandalorians might have been a mighty empire a few millennia ago, but they can't handle the difficult business of running a modern, complex democracy. They know it, so they just want to live their primitive warrior fantasy and revel in their reputation."

"Which is *earned*."

"I accept that they're phenomenal soldiers."

"They kicked out the Empire *and* the Yuuzhan Vong, without any help from us."

"That still doesn't mean they want to dominate the galaxy. There are fewer than three million of them on Mandalore now, and they don't have anything like a government structure that could organize them well enough to take over the GA or the Confederation. They'll always be the bursa let loose among nuna. They're opportunistic feeders."

"But Fett's a smart, smart man. Forget the Wookiee braids."

"He wants to see Jacen Solo fall a long way," Niathal said.

"I don't buy fostering galactic chaos just to get back at one man, even if it's Jacen."

"No, we've created our own chaos. Fett's just the distraction act."

Two minutes to go: Niathal sipped a glass of water and rolled her head to loosen her neck. There was nothing worse than a strained voice caused by tight muscles. She needed to sound relaxed, regretful, but authoritative. "As long as he plays bogeyman, the GA holds together, because the smaller planets are scared the Mandalorians will be back and they'll cling to us for protection."

"Or rush to the Confederation . . ."

"Not if the Confederation buys Fett's arms, and we don't. We can rob him of his neutrality, or at least the appearance of it."

G'Sil continued to look at her as if she'd arrived from beyond the Outer Rim. He was taking this coup—and she was happy to call it that in private—remarkably well. Given his position, she'd expected him to want a piece of the action.

"G'vli, will you run for the Chief of State's office in due course?"

"Will there *be* a Chief of State?"

"I fully intend to return to elections and civil rule once the war is over."

"Then no, I won't. I'm fine not being where Omas was. If a thing can happen once, it can happen twice." G'Sil steered her toward the access to the floating platform. "You need to watch your back with Jacen."

"I know," she said. "So I'm neutralizing him now. Start as you mean to go on." The word *neutralize* had several unfortunate meanings, and judging by the look on G'Sil's face, he'd thought of the worst one. "No, just tactically. Where is he, anyway?"

"He probably had some fingers he needed to break. Let me worry about finding him later." G'Sil followed her onto the platform. "Here we go."

Niathal looked down at her boots as she stepped onto the platform, and when she looked up, the sheer scale of the Senate chamber unsettled her for a split second. It was a blessing: she knew her genuine dismay would come across as humble reluctance. There was nothing worse for a new military dictator than looking too keen.

For a chamber of thousands of delegates—even with the recent secessions and defections—it was remarkably quiet. Her platform drifted serenely into the center of the massive chamber. She was looking into lights and shadows, generally unable to see faces. It was, in so many senses, a theatrical stage complete with blinding footlights.

"Gentlebeings," she began. Formal: strictly formal was the best bet, she calculated. "I never expected to be addressing you in this way, and I find myself barely prepared for it. I greatly regret the need to stand on this platform. But the need has arisen, it will be a need for the shortest period possible, and apart from the temporary leadership of the GA, nothing else will change. I stress that. There is no curfew, no censorship, and none of the other trappings of martial law. Had Chief Omas been taken ill, I would be standing here anyway, and nobody would be panicking. What's happened overnight is no more constitutionally significant than that. I've merely exercised my responsibility as the Supreme Commander to deputize for the Chief of State, on the advice of the GA security services. As soon as the general security situation with the Confederation is resolved, and I expect that to be within the short term, I'll step down and we'll hold elections for the Chief's office."

There wasn't a single lie in there. There was never any need to lie. She meant every word. There was simply information that the Senate didn't have, and everyone went through life with an incomplete picture of the galaxy anyway.

One of the representatives for Kuat signaled to speak.

"When you refer to the security services, Admiral, do you mean Alliance Intel or the GAG?"

Niathal wondered if G'Sil had engineered the question, because it was so perfectly on cue. "I'd like to share some material with you," she said. "So that you understand where the need to act arose."

It was possibly contempt of court to show the images of Omas's meeting with Gejjen; evidence like that would prejudice his chance of a fair trial, but she had a shrewd idea that Omas wouldn't be cleared by a jury, return to work with his reputation intact, and sue the GA for wrongful arrest. In his case, the arrest was verdict and sentence in one. She gestured for the images to be projected onto the viewing screen on each delegate's platform.

It was gratifying to hear the faint exclamations of surprise as the scene played out, complete with Alliance Intel officers. Niathal displayed a little dignified pain at the moment of betrayal, when Dur Gejjen discussed how to remove her and Jacen from their posts. The silence that followed was perfect.

"So, you'll understand why I felt I had to take advice from the GAG, because Alliance Intel's objectivity may have been compromised by attendance at that meeting," she said. "And while it's not illegal for two heads of state at war to have discussions, it's unacceptable for them to plan the removal of a Supreme Commander without consulting the Security and Intelligence Council."

She hoped they noted that the chair of that council was sitting at her right hand. It was time for him to do his party piece, so she sat down and let G'Sil have the floor.

"I've got very little to add," G'Sil said. "Except to say that I'm saddened to come to this. A word about the presence of GA troops on the streets alongside CSF officers. This is simply a precaution in case the anarchic elements on Coruscant try to take advantage of the situation. As in any democracy, they have the right to exist and to speak, but if any of them attempt to capitalize on the situation, then the rule of law will be upheld."

"Well, there's no need for the anarchists to overthrow the government now, is there?" said the delegate from Haruun Kal. "You got there first . . ."

"With that in mind," Niathal continued, "I intend to ask Colonel Jacen Solo to act as joint Chief of State with me. A matter of checks and balances, so that the temporary power doesn't rest with one person, and one can subject the other to scrutiny."

She let the comment from Haruun Kal pass. Nobody else picked up on it. By failing to invoke the full range of emergency restrictions she now had the right to impose, she felt she'd sent out a clear message that this really was a case of an embarrassed and reluctant military being hauled in to mind the shop because the civilian head of state had been a very naughty boy. It seemed to have worked. Either the Senate was collectively terrified, or it was 90 percent convinced, 10 percent wary.

She would settle for either.

G'Sil followed her back to her office. She sat down and felt the relief flood her.

"Next?" said G'Sil, and poured two cups of caf from the dispenser. "We have a breathing space while the Senators panic about their share prices and the Corellian administration flounders like beached daggerts."

"Reopen the stock exchange," she said. "I need to see the finance secretary at some point today to arrange for Treasury intervention if the market panics again. I'm bringing Alliance Intel under GAG command, and assigning Captain Girdun to that—"

"Oh, classic—"

"—and I want Omas's office sealed until further notice."

G'Sil looked mildly surprised. "You're not moving in there?"

"I'm not, and neither is Jacen. It smacks of enthusiasm for power rather than necessary duty. We seal it as it stands, which is best practice in terms of allowing CSF to preserve a potential crime scene." She tapped the internal comm code for Senate Building Maintenance into her desk keypad. "And nobody fights over whose chair it is."

G'Sil finally gave way to the smile that was trying to cross his face. "And what an elegant way to neutralize Jacen, should he hanker after power. Give it to him to start with."

You don't need to know we did a deal. "I don't like having opposing forces approaching from the rear, G'vli. I like them where I can see them."

"That's the first time I've heard you refer to Jacen as . . . opposing."

"We want the same outcomes," she said carefully, aware of how ephemeral alliances were in this game. "Order, stability, and peace. I don't care for his methods, that's all. Once I manage to teach him that putting citizens in camps and killing prisoners is *not* the done thing, we'll get on just fine."

"You have to see the Jedi Council, too."

"I'll see Skywalker later, but not the rest of the armed mystics . . ."

Niathal paused and sent a message to Luke that she wanted to continue the good working relationship he'd had with Omas, and that he would be welcome for an informal discussion. She'd remain cautious, though, because they seemed to represent a third and unelected power, neither civilian nor military, and every time she looked at Jacen Solo she saw just what Jedi could turn into.

"This has been surprisingly civilized," G'Sil said. "The business of the chamber is going on as usual. No riots, no protests, no counterrevolution."

"It isn't lunchtime yet."

"Nevertheless, this is remarkable."

"And we have a war going on. Even if the Corellians are spinning their wheels at the moment, Bothuwai isn't. I have crews out there on the front line."

It was simply a statement of fact. She still wore a uniform, and whatever her ambitions the service ethic was very nearly coded into her genes by now. She really did have a war to win and people to bring home alive.

"Oh, you're *good*," G'Sil said, misreading her totally. "You're *very* good. Stang, I might even vote for you on the strength of today's showing."

That was the only way Niathal wanted to remain in this post—by election; it made it much easier to hang on to it than being a dictator. She was also an officer who liked her moral lines, her rules of engagement, completely clear.

Within those, though, she believed in taking the battle to the enemy and pressing home every advantage.

"I look forward to it," she said.

JEDI COUNCIL CHAMBER

It had been a long night, and the morning's news left Luke reeling. He looked at Mara across the Chamber, noted that her injuries were largely healed, and wondered when she was going to be ready to talk to him about what was making her grind her teeth in her sleep.

Something had got to her, and the fact that she was silent and not raging about it worried him. It meant it was more than Lumiya or Alema.

"Makes you wonder what tomorrow might bring," Kyp said wearily, scratching his head with both hands as if he were shampooing his hair. "A bombshell with every bulletin."

"I haven't always seen eye-to-eye with Omas, but I don't believe he's a security risk." Luke had never handled frustration well, and age hadn't mellowed that. He could see what was happening; he knew his

history, and he had no love of military government. Nobody of his generation who'd grown up under the Empire did. "So now we have two threats—an external war, and an internal coup. Where do we concentrate our efforts?"

"Well, Niathal is well within her rights to assume power under the circumstances," Corran said. "So it's not exactly a coup, and much as we might not like it as citizens with a vote, as *Jedi* we have no business interfering in that."

"Can I say it?" Kyp asked. "Because it's just staring us in the face and nobody's mentioning it."

"Go on . . ."

"Jacen. There, I said it. Jacen, Jacen, *Jacen*. What in the name of the Force is going on here? Okay, maybe we should have taken him to task when he started kicking down doors with the GAG. Now, overnight, he's busted the Chief of State and taken over. Extreme? Out of control, my friends."

"Has he actually declared himself joint Chief of State? Personally?"

Cilghal looked up. "Admiral Niathal announced it. We've heard nothing from Jacen."

"Then maybe it wasn't his idea." Luke looked at Mara to catch her eye, but she seemed in a world of her own. "Mara?"

"Sorry." She snapped to attention, blinking. "I don't see Jacen being dragged kicking and screaming to the big office, somehow. Regardless of who came up with the idea, he's hardly rushed to decline the honor."

"He's gone to ground," said Kyp. "We've been through a whole twenty-four hours of news bulletins without seeing him. He must be chained up somewhere to keep him away from reporters."

"How would we know?" Corran asked. "He never talks to us, and he's holed up in his cozy GAG bunker when he's not out harassing Corellians."

"Time I went to see him," said Luke. "I mean *really* see him. Niathal's sent a message saying she wants to maintain the good relationship between the Jedi Council and the Chief's office. I'm taking her up on that as soon as she can clear her schedule."

Mara seemed to be concentrating on the proceedings again. "If I didn't know Corellia was in dire straits over Gejjen's death, I'd have said it was an outside attempt to destabilize the GA. If he'd still been alive, they'd have moved in on us by now."

It was an interesting thought that suddenly got more interesting in Luke's mind as he rolled it around. Mara could always spot the issue. The two events might have been coincidental, or they might not, but the assassination *was* tied up with the removal of Omas, and not only because he'd been meeting the Corellian shortly before he died. The crazier news programs were speculating wildly that Omas had been directly involved in the assassination, but Luke felt that something more convoluted was happening, and judging by the grinding-cogs expression on her face, Mara did too. She wasn't quite talking to herself, but her lips moved occasionally, involuntarily, as she stared into the mid-distance.

You used to talk everything through with me, Mara. What happened?

"You know what?" Kyp said. "We're missing an important point. As Jedi, either we're players in GA politics, or we're another instrument of the elected leadership, like the fleet. If we're the latter, then we might have our opinions, but we do as the legitimate leadership directs. If we're not, then we've got no more right to start interfering with the status quo than the Monster Raving Anarchist Party. Jacen might be completely off the charts now, but he's not acting *as* a Jedi. He's an officer in the security forces who happens to *be* a Jedi."

"When my front doors come crashing in with a GAG boot," Corran said, "that's going to make me feel *so* much better."

Kyp twisted around in his seat to jab a finger in Corran's direction. "I'm not saying we shouldn't act. Just that we need to be clear where we stand. And Niathal and Jacen are within their rights."

"There's rights," said Mara, "and there's right."

Kyp raised an eyebrow. "And the semantics thought for the day was brought to you by our sponsors . . ."

"I'm seeing Niathal," said Luke, slapping his palm down on the arm of his chair. *I should have gone with my gut so long ago. I really did take my eye off the ball trying to live up to this role.* "And before we start griping about lack of action, think about this. When it was a matter of your not approving of Ben's involvement with the GAG, it was a choice between letting him carry on and hauling a teenage boy home. Now we're talking about action against . . . what, exactly? Stage our own coup? Depose Niathal? Confiscate Jacen's lightsaber? I'm up for most things, I admit, but we have to think this through, because we might leave matters worse than before we started."

"Well, trying to talk him around is off the menu," said Mara. "So I'm sticking with going after the irritant in this. Lumiya. But let's not forget that Omas didn't exactly behave sensibly, and Niathal isn't in Lumiya's thrall. She's got her own agenda, and I don't get any sense of the dark side influencing that."

Luke knew she was right. The dynamics were complex. The best thing Jedi could do was to tackle the things that non-Force-users couldn't. Once again, he missed the clarity of thoroughly evil adversaries, or at least those he *thought* were evil.

It was hard to turn against your allies. It was as hard as turning against your own family. Now they were one and the same.

GAG HEADQUARTERS, CORUSCANT

The worst thing about waking up that morning was the few seconds of blank comfort before remembering what had happened, and then the world collapsed again. Ben couldn't stop seeing Jori Lekauf everywhere he looked. He couldn't face staying at home: he needed the company of his friends, the people who missed Lekauf, too. As he walked through the GAG security gates, and the system accepted his identicard to open the blastproof doors, every face in the corridor was Lekauf's. When Ben went into the locker room, he could hear his voice. It was a running nightmare conjured up by a combination of his Force-senses and the simple human reaction to fresh bereavement. He wanted it to stop, but he felt he was being disloyal to a dead friend for wanting *not* to see him everywhere.

Zavirk was still in the monitoring room. He looked up at Ben and tapped the MUTE button on his earpiece. "You okay?"

"Fine."

"I won't say it."

"Fine."

"And not your fault, okay? Could have been any one of us." Za-virk tapped the button again and dragged the adjacent chair closer for Ben to sit down. "You heard that the boss is . . . well, *really* the boss now?"

"Yeah."

"Should be good news for us."

Ben knew that his father would say it wasn't good news at all. He sat in the monitoring room for a while, just grateful to be among the troopers, and then wandered off to find a quiet spot. If he couldn't handle this kind of stuff without being devastated, he'd be no use in the GAG. Every other trooper here got on with it. Shevu had proba-bly had an awful conversation with Lekauf's parents, but when Ben walked by his office, he was hard at work, marking up a duty roster on the wall and getting on with things.

Okay, I'm fourteen. I could say, all right, I'm just a kid and I don't have to be tough when my buddies get killed. But I can't pick and choose when I act like an adult. I've got to get on with it, or go to school like every other kid my age.

And he was scaring his mother. She had enough problems of her own hunting Lumiya.

According to the roster display, Jacen was on duty. The time codes showed he'd been at HQ since about one in the morning. Ben couldn't feel his presence, but that didn't surprise him now. There was a time when Jacen had hidden in the Force when he had to; now he only showed himself when he seemed to feel it was necessary.

Without thinking about it, Ben found himself shutting down, too. As he walked down the corridor, the tiles still gleaming with spots of water because the cleaning droids were just meters ahead of him, he let himself merge with the matter and energy around him. The more he did it, the less he felt like he was in a trance, cut off from reality, and the more he felt like he was observing the world as it truly was, parti-cles within particles. It gave him a fleeting feeling of serene clarity. It was relief of a kind.

At the top of the corridor, a pair of doors led to the holding cells. That area was always kept shut, but today there was a notice fixed on the wall next to it that read TOP-LEVEL CLEARANCES ONLY. They were

holding Chief Omas down there. It seemed surreal. Ben carried on toward Jacen's office and he could see as he rounded the corner that the doors were open.

As usual, he couldn't feel Jacen's presence, but he could hear him talking to someone.

Who is it? Odd. I can't feel anybody else.

Jacen might have been on his comlink, but his tone of voice wasn't that slightly stilted, self-conscious one that he tended to lapse into when he couldn't see who he was speaking to. In fact, he sounded as if he was trying to keep his temper.

"You overplayed your hand," said Jacen.

"You worry too much," said a woman's voice.

That was the point at which Ben realized something was very wrong. Only a Jedi could be there and not be sensed—or a Yuuzhan Vong, and they weren't exactly frequent visitors to the GAG HQ. And the voice was somehow familiar, even though he couldn't place it.

It was dishonest to sneak up on his commanding officer—on his cousin, his mentor—but it seemed like the only sensible thing to do. Keeping himself hidden in the Force, Ben edged silently along the corridor and stood as close to the open doors as he could.

This wing of the headquarters building was deserted, and Jacen probably relied on sensing people coming and going. He thought he and his guest were alone.

"You cut it too fine," Jacen was saying. "There's being a decoy, and there's being too clever, and you crossed that line. Are you recovered now?"

"Yes," said the woman's voice. It had that slightly husky edge to it, like she used too many death sticks. "But it worked. It gave you the space to act without having her crawling all over your operation. She really thinks I want revenge for some daughter . . ."

"I sometimes think your cover stories are too complex."

"And mind-rubbing Ben about Nelani isn't?"

Ben recoiled. It was all he could do not to storm in. *Jacen. You did that?*

"He wouldn't understand why I had to do it," said Jacen.

"And that's why he can't ever be your apprentice. Get rid of him, find another one, and stop wasting your time."

"Now, there's my real problem . . ."

"I can't help you there. Whoever it turns out to be, that's the Force's decision. You'll know very soon."

"Well, I dealt with Omas, anyway. A clear path."

"Are you going to keep him here?"

"I thought house arrest might be more sensible in the long term. Republica House is easy to secure, and it makes us look like the good guys. People still like Omas."

"And here you are, joint Chief of State . . ."

"That way Niathal thinks she can keep me quiet."

"Or under control."

"She's way too smart."

"Play nicely with her. You need her to keep the military behind you."

"You're such a strategist, Lumiya . . ."

Lumiya. *Lumiya?*

Ben thought he'd misheard, or that his state of mind was making him hear what he wanted to hear, like Lekauf's voice. But he knew what he'd heard, and his first reaction wasn't one of fear or dread, but agonized embarrassment.

He'd trusted Jacen, and Jacen had *lied* to him.

He'd *mind-rubbed* him.

And they were talking about him as if he was in the way.

The fact that Jacen was knowingly talking to a Sith as if they were old friends seemed to take second place to that. For all his denial, *Jacen knew Lumiya.* And she could walk into GAG HQ and just talk to him. Jacen wasn't being conned by her; he was *chatting* casually with her about what he'd do next.

Ben found himself scrabbling for excuses that would explain why Jacen could be meeting with Lumiya and still be someone he could trust, someone with a perfectly good reason for it all.

Jacen's a Jedi. He can't be in league with her. She's done something to him. Mind-influenced him or something.

This woman had left his mother with a battered face. This woman was all he'd been taught to fear and avoid, and Jacen was talking to her in his office, as bold as anything.

Ben knew he had to tell someone, but he'd run out of people to

trust. If Jacen could be influenced like that, anyone could—except Mom. Mom wasn't in Lumiya's thrall, or she wouldn't have been in a fight with her.

Ben had to find her. He had to warn her.

That morning he'd felt like things couldn't possibly get any worse, and now he knew they could.

chapter fourteen

If you think you're going to scare us off by cozying up to the Mandalorians, Bug Boy, you've got another think coming.

—*Hebanh Del Dalhe, Murkhanan Department of Trade and Industry, to the Roche ambassador, during a disagreement on intellectual property rights*

BEVIIN-VASUR FARM, KELDABE, MANDALORE

"TOO MUCH HOLONEWS IS BAD FOR YOU," SAID THE MAN STANDING IN the doorway of the outbuilding.

Fett had spotted him coming—it was hard not to. His armor was extraordinary. There was no real need for Fett to be vigilant on Mandalore, but then Jaster Mereel had once thought he was perfectly okay among his own people, too. Safe was always better than sorry. Fett carried on cleaning his helmet, feet up on the chair.

"It's riveting," he said, nodding in the direction of the monitor that he'd propped on the table. The news anchors and commentators

had descended into a feeding frenzy about the bloodless coup. "Jacen Solo, the boy who wants to be Vader when he grows up. He finally did it."

"He probably looks in the mirror when he brushes his teeth and tells himself it's his destiny."

"And you are?"

"Venku."

He didn't have a proper Keldabe accent. If anything, he sounded like he'd spent time on Kuat, and maybe Muunilinst, too. That wasn't unusual for Mandalorians, and it was more common now that so many were flooding back to what Beviin called *Manda'yaim*.

That was the traditional name for the planet, not Mandalore. Fett had never realized that. Every day was an education that told him how far adrift he was from his own people.

"Sit down, Venku." Fett gestured to the last remaining chair in the room. He tried to think *leader* and not *bounty hunter.* "Whatever it is, get it off your chest."

Venku had the most eclectic armor Fett had ever seen. It was a custom to wear sections of armor belonging to a dead relative or friend, but Venku had no two plates that matched. Every piece was a different color. The palette ranged from blue, white, and black to gold, cream, gray, and red.

"What happened to your fashion sense? Did someone shoot it?"

Venku still stood, ignoring the chair. He glanced down at his plates as if noticing them for the first time. "The chest plate, the *buy'ce,* and shoulder sections came from my uncles. The forearm plates were my father's, the thigh plates came from my cousin, and the belt was my aunt's. Then there's—"

"Okay. Big family."

"Those who are *tab'echaaj'la* and those who still live, yes."

Fett had given up asking for translations. He got the general idea. "I'm nearly done with cleaning my bucket."

"And they said charm wasn't your strong suit. Okay, I came to tell you I'm relieved you decided to be a proper *Mand'alor.* The *Mando'ade* are coming home. You probably don't notice much beyond your own existence, but this is your purpose."

Fett had never thought of himself as easygoing, but normally he couldn't get worked up enough to slug fools if he wasn't paid to. This man didn't strike him as a fool, but he'd hit a nerve and Fett couldn't quite work out why.

"Glad I could be more useful than a doorstop."

"Which is why I'm also relieved to give you this." Venku opened a pouch on his ammunition belt—his aunt's belt, he'd said, so she must have been a typical *Mando* woman—and placed a small, dark blue rectangular container on the table. "And don't mistake this for adulation or sentimentality. You *owe* your people. There'll be someone along shortly to administer it."

Venku turned toward the door as the word *administer* bored into Fett's skull. "*Whoa* there."

Venku glanced over his multicolored shoulder. "Don't try doing it yourself. It has to be inserted into the bone marrow, and that's going to hurt like you wouldn't believe. Let someone qualified do it. It'll still hurt, but they'll place it correctly."

So this was one of Jaing's minions. He certainly didn't have his boss's sartorial style, although he did have expensive dark green leather gloves, and Fett couldn't guess what or who had contributed to those.

"Tell him we're even," Fett said. "And . . . thank him."

Venku started to say something then stopped as if he was getting a message via his helmet. Fett tilted his own helmet in his lap so he could see the HUD display that was patched into *Slave I*'s external security cam. A man tottered past the ship, clearly very old indeed from his gait but still wearing full fighting armor, and paused to look at the ship. Then he moved out of cam range in the direction of the building.

Fett would never rule out even a senile Mandalorian as a possible threat: if the old man had survived to that age, he was either unusually lucky or a serious fighter. But Fett remained with his feet on the chair, wiping the red shimmer-silk lining of his helmet with a sapon cloth, consumed with curiosity but hiding it perfectly. The old man appeared in the doorway, squeezed past Venku, and stared at Fett.

"At least I lived to see the day," he said. *"Su'cuy, Mand'alor, gar shabuir."*

It wasn't the most polite greeting that Fett had ever received, but it was certainly the most relevant to a terminally ill man. It was the

only possible way that warriors and mercenaries could greet each other: "So you're still alive." He'd worked out what *shabuir* meant, too, but he chose to take it as ribald affection rather than abuse.

The old *Mando* walked out with arthritic dignity, paused again at the door to stare at Fett, and went on his way.

"You made his day," said Venku.

"I shouldn't ask."

"Then don't." Venku sighed, then put his hands to his helmet to pop the seal. The rustle of fabric muffled his voice as he lifted the *buy'ce*. "Oh, all right, then."

Boba Fett was looking into the face of a man perhaps ten or fifteen years younger than him: dark hair with a liberal threading of gray, strong cheekbones, and the very darkest brown eyes. He'd looked much like that himself twenty years ago. The nose was sharper and the mouth was a stranger's, but the rest—it was a Fett face.

He was looking into his own eyes, and into the eyes of his long-dead father.

"I'm Venku," said the *Mando* with the motley armor. "But you probably know me better as Kad'ika. Interesting to meet you at last . . . Uncle Boba."

OSARIAN TAPCAF, CORUSCANT

"I couldn't think who else to tell," Ben said. "Or who else would listen to me if I did."

Mara wondered if he'd been crying about Lekauf or Jacen's breathtaking betrayal. He'd been crying about something, though, and he was doing a reasonable job of disguising it.

"I believe you, Ben."

"Maybe I *did* imagine it."

"You didn't." No, he certainly couldn't imagine Lumiya having a friendly chat with Jacen, dissecting their run of triumphs, and deciding when Niathal would no longer be useful.

And discussing their lies. No daughter to avenge—and wiping out Ben's memory of what happened to Nelani.

Ben had the useful ability to recall things he'd seen or heard with nearly complete accuracy. Mara's scalp had tightened and tingled as she heard her son, her precious kid, relating the exact words of that Sith cyborg and her accomplice, like an innocent possessed by a demon.

Accomplice.

Mara realized she'd shifted her position by a few parsecs. Not a vain, conceited, *naïve* victim of a manipulative Sith: an *accomplice.* Jacen wasn't weak-minded enough to fall that far and that fast unless he wanted to.

"I haven't told anyone else and I don't want to," Ben whispered. "Not Dad, either. I mean, you can tell him if you really think he needs to know, Mom, but I don't want to see the look on his face when he finds out what a moron I've been."

But I defended Jacen. When did I get stupid? "No more of a moron than the rest of us, sweetheart."

"What are we going to do?"

"I won't ask you to do anything." Mara had let her drink get cold. She couldn't swallow it anyway, even if it hadn't tasted like the *Millennium Falcon*'s hydraulic overflow, because her throat was tight with rage. "Ben, you have a choice. I told Jacen that Lumiya was trying to kill you, and he was all innocence."

"So you knew about Ziost, then . . ."

"No, I don't know anything about Ziost. But you're going to tell me."

Ben's face fell. She had to gather what intel she could, but it was also good for Ben to learn that it was all too easy to give away information accidentally. Just the word *Ziost* made all the pieces start to fall into agonizing place.

"Jacen sent me on a mission to Almania to recover an Amulet that had some dark side power. I ended up on Ziost and a ship attacked me, but I found a really weird vessel and got away."

"Just like that."

"It wasn't Lumiya, actually. It was a Bothan."

"And how did you find this ship?" Mara was trying to work out the scam. She knew what she'd done to Lumiya's ship, and that the transponder was now showing it was stationary on Coruscant. If the

last thirty-six hours hadn't been total mayhem, she'd have paid her another visit by now. "Just parked, hatch open, with the key in the drive?"

"It . . . look, I'm not insane, but it *spoke* to me."

"Ohhhh . . ." Mara had enough pieces in the puzzle now to see the rough shape of the picture that would emerge. "Spherical. Orange. Like a big eye."

Ben's face drained completely of color. "Yes."

"Tell me about it."

He struggled visibly with something. Mara guessed he'd been sworn to secrecy. It was way too late for all that loyalty bunk.

"I've *seen* the ship, Ben. It spoke to me, too. It said it thought I was the 'other one' like me, and I thought it'd mistaken me for Lumiya, but it meant you, didn't it? Somehow it picked up on our similarities."

Ben gulped in air as if the relief of being able to share the awful experience were saving him from drowning.

"I worked out how to pilot it. It communicates through the Force."

"And it's soaked in dark energies. I know. Go on."

"I don't know how it works, but if you visualize what you want it to do, it does it. It sticks out parts of itself and forms them into cannons, all kinds of weapons."

Perfect. *Perfect.* Mara was getting a better picture by the second. Lumiya could think at the ship and it'd rush to do her bidding—maybe even extrude a cable, whip it around Mara, drag her away, and nearly throttle her.

It wasn't a droid. I got bushwhacked by a living ship, a Sith *ship.*

That old, cold clarity and pitiless sense of purpose flooded Mara's body, and instead of making her gut churn, as any mother's might at hearing the kind of risk her son had been subjected to, it settled her into a calm and rational state close to transcendence. She was the Hand again, planning her move.

"So what happened to the ship between the time you found it and when I came across it the other day?"

"Where did you see it?"

"Hesperidium. When I caught up with Lumiya."

Ben's shoulders sagged. He folded his arms on the table and lowered his head onto them. Mara waited, stroking his hair because she assumed he was crying again.

He straightened up, face stricken but eyes dry. "I flew it back to the *Anakin Solo* and handed it over to Jacen."

Everything fell into place. The only pieces missing now were how she would put an end to this, but that was her specialty, and it could wait awhile until she'd made sure Ben was safe.

"Okay, I think you know how serious this is," she said. Their heads were almost touching over the table. To the Osarians who used the restaurant and who spoke very little Basic, they probably looked like mother and son having a tearful argument over homework and poor grades. They would never have guessed that it was about the fate of the galaxy.

No, it's not about the galaxy. Enough of the galaxy. The galaxy can look after its own problems for a while. This is about my child, my only child, and some Sith scum trying to kill him while his own cousin, my own nephew who should be looking after him, helps her do it.

It all became very clear and simple from that moment onward.

"Ben, will you accept a suggestion from me?"

"Anything, Mom. I'm sorry, I'm so sorry—"

"Hey, I'm the one who should be sorry." *I trusted a monster. I shouted down my husband. I ignored every single sign that Jacen was trouble.* "But you're in real danger, and it's going to be more than you can handle, so I want you to be very cautious. I want you to behave like a coward for a change. Take no risks. In fact, I'd like you to report in sick, and get as far away from Jacen as you can until I get this fixed."

Ben nodded, grim, very old eyes in a terribly young face. He really was just a kid even if he behaved like a man now. Mara was instantly so proud of him and so fiercely protective at the same time that the only cogent emotion she could identify was the instinct to seek out and kill whatever threatened him.

She could do that. It was her calling.

"I'll do it carefully," he said. "So Jacen doesn't realize I've found out that Lumiya is making him do all this."

Oh, sure she is. "That's right, sweetheart."

"I promise I won't hide in the Force from you, but . . . I might have to do it to hide from her. Or even Jacen, if she's got him so far under her control that he's . . . taken over the government."

Sometimes you had to hear someone else say it to believe it.

"Tell you what," said Mara, smiling, "why don't you show me how you do it? Then maybe I'll get a better sense of when you're just hiding, and when to worry."

Ben nodded, eyes downcast.

There would be no holds barred now. Mara would use every means and weapon at her disposal, and there would be an end to this.

They spent the rest of the day doing something that they hadn't done in a very long time: just wandering around the Skydome Botanical Gardens, talking and having fun—or as much fun as could be had with a galactic civil war in progress and a military junta running the GA. The only evidence of the huge upheaval was that the CSF officer on patrol in the plaza had a Galactic Alliance Defense Force sergeant walking the beat with him.

Apart from that, nobody seemed troubled. Mara wondered if all cataclysmic events in history were noticed only by a handful. Like Ben had said—prophetically—over lunch only days before, perhaps it had been that way during the Empire, too, and most people's lives were the same under Palpatine as they had been under the Republic. She didn't want to think it was true. Luke certainly didn't.

"Come on, Mom," Ben said. "Let's go find a nice spot on the lawns and I'll teach you how to vanish."

They said it was a sure sign of imminent old age when your kids could teach you things. It was a simple thing, hiding in the Force, but then so was dieting, and not many people could knuckle down to that and make it work, either. Ben was a remarkably patient teacher. After a couple of hours, she could manage a minute or two without needing to grab something solid.

"I'm sorry about Lekauf," she said, putting her arm around him as they walked. "I'm sorry I wasn't very kind to him. Sounds like he was one of the best."

"He did it to make sure I got away. How do I live with that kind of sacrifice, Mom?"

"By making your life count, I think, so that his wasn't wasted."

It was the closest she'd ever felt to Ben, and probably the first time they'd really related as adults. It left her feeling profoundly happy. The irony wasn't lost on her that it was in the midst of some of the worst events and greatest threats they'd ever faced. Times like this made you painfully aware of what truly mattered.

"Ben, you're probably going to see a side of me soon that isn't good old Mom." He smelled wonderfully of that indeterminable Ben-ness that she had enjoyed when he was tiny, and that was still there under the scent of military-issue soap and weapon lubricant. "But I want you to know that whatever I do, however much of a stranger you think I become, I love you, and you're my heart, every fiber of it. Nothing matters to me more than you."

She stopped to hug him, and he hugged her back rather than just submitting to the indignity as he usually did. It went on for a while.

"You know why I believe you, Mom? Because you didn't tell me to trust you. Everyone else tells me to trust them, and that's usually the cue that I shouldn't."

Mara got another glimpse of the man her son would be, and the mother she'd been so far. It hadn't worked out so badly after all.

She knew only too well what the stakes were now, and what she had to do.

JACEN SOLO'S APARTMENT, CORUSCANT

"Ben?"

Jacen looked around the apartment, but there was no sign of his young cousin. He'd probably gone back to see his parents. He still needed reassurance about the dark necessity in life, passing through that stage between being oblivious of consequences with the careless cruelty of a child, and the more sensitive but responsible acceptance that life dealt harsh and unavoidable hands to many. At the moment, Ben both felt too much and had too little life experience to handle the pain.

Jacen looked through the contents of the conservator and decided to order a delivery from a restaurant instead. There was a pattern now, he realized, and it was becoming less of his making; he'd put the pieces in place, the Force had responded, and now it was his turn to make choices when it offered them. It was a dialogue.

Lekauf was part of the pattern, too. But Jacen was still working out why it hadn't been Ben who'd died. He'd almost been sure that was the way it would end.

So I thought my destiny would let me off the hook with him. It won't.

Jacen comlinked an order for a three-course Toydarian low-fat banquet, and ran a tub of hot foaming water in the refresher. The steam condensed on the mirrored wall, and he found himself writing in the haze with his fingertip.

HE WILL IMMORTALIZE HIS LOVE.

It still didn't make sense. If it meant killing the person he loved most, as Lumiya said, then there was no question: he would have given his life for Allana. But at every turn in the last few months, he'd ended up protecting her. *You'll know when it happens.* Lumiya was certain of that, and Jacen believed it, too.

Immortalize. Make immortal. Write into history. Make permanent. Why not just kill? Maybe I translated the tassel wrong.

People read holozines in the tub to relax, but Jacen found himself behaving like a bachelor slob and eating his take-out banquet. He was exhausted. He had the feeling he was coming to the peak of a wave, struggling up the gradient, and that when he hit the crest—that final hurdle to his Sith destiny—things would ease and make sense.

Jacen laid his fork on the edge of the tub and overwrote the prophecy again in the condensation.

HE WILL IMMORTALIZE HIS LOVE.

Killing what you loved was the ultimate act of obedience and submission to higher duty. He'd seen a feature on the holochannels about a tribe—couldn't recall which, where, when—who trained their elite troops by giving them a nusito pup when they entered the cadet program. They were encouraged to bond with the pup, to race it against other cadets' nusitos, and to generally learn to love it. Then, before the cadet could graduate, he was ordered to strangle his pup. If he couldn't, or wouldn't, he was kicked out. He had to be able to put duty before emotion.

That's me. That's what I have to do.

Full of too much Toydarian sourfry, tired, and lulled by hot water, Jacen let his mind wander, and reached out in the Force to touch Allana and Tenel Ka. He risked this with decreasing frequency now. The latest attempt on their lives had been a stark warning of how precarious his family's position was. He'd never heard Allana call him *Daddy*. He probably never would.

My family. Yes, that's who my family is. Not Jaina, not Mom, not Dad; my little girl and her mother. Trust me to fall for a woman whose customs prevent her ever naming the father of her child.

He could have sworn Allana reached back at him. He was so thrilled that he opened his eyes, and then realized that it was one more chance for someone to find her and harm her. Lumiya wasn't above that. It was the Sith way. Making someone suffer and hate only strengthened their Sith powers.

He'd visit Tenel Ka as soon as he was certain that he and Niathal had consolidated the takeover and that the war would be fought more logically and with less regard for keeping insignificant worlds happy.

Got to deal with the Bothans next. Lumiya can earn her keep again.

But he couldn't keep his eyes open. He wasn't dozing, but Forcevisions wouldn't leave him alone. It was as if the Force was shaking him by the shoulders and telling him to pay attention and get on with it, because time was running out. Each time he closed his eyes, he saw the trust that Ben placed in him, and the lies he'd told the boy, and the danger he'd put him in. And Ben still kept coming back for more. He was desperate to do the right thing. Now Jacen saw him clearly, head in his hands, sobbing: *"It's too high a price."*

What was? Lekauf? No. There'd be many, many Lekaufs. Wars were full of them. It was one reason why Jacen had to put an end to fighting, any way he could.

Maybe . . . it wasn't Ben, but *about* him.

Why have I thought this over so many times? Why is it obsessing me? Because I'm denying it. Because I can't accept it's him. Because it has to be him.

It would be easy to kill Ben, because Ben trusted him. Jacen knew how bad that would make him feel. It was strangling a nusito pup.

You don't want to see the inevitable. Do you?

Jacen dried himself and spent the rest of the evening assembling

his personal armory. He examined his lightsaber and blaster, and knew that those still wouldn't be enough when Luke and Mara came after him to exact vengeance for Ben. He took out the box of assorted poisons and pathogens that could be delivered by dart or projectile, yet another range of weapons that might make it past the defenses of his most persistent enemies. He had all the bases covered: chemical, biological, mechanical.

He just wanted it all over with.

And when Ben was gone, who would be his apprentice then? Just before he fell asleep, it crossed his mind that Admiral Cha Niathal had demonstrated an excellent grasp of the rule of two.

It was just as well she wasn't a Force-user.

chapter fifteen

This has to be about more than getting tough on chaos and disorder. I need to be tough on the *causes* of chaos and disorder—greed, corruption, and ambition.

—*Jacen Solo, joint GA Chief of State, speaking at a lunch for the heads of Coruscanti industry*

BEVIIN-VASUR FARM, MANDALORE

MIRTA PUT HER FINGER TO HER LIPS, AND THE FOUR OF THEM stacked around the door as if getting ready to storm Fett's stronghold.

"I'll check," she said to Orade. Beviin winked at her. Medrit just kept glancing at his chrono as if he didn't have time for all this. "You can hide behind me if you like."

Orade licked his lips nervously. "*Cyar'ika,* when Fett says he'll break my legs, he's just looking for an excuse."

"He's a sick man, Ghes, and if you tell anyone, *I'll* be the one doing the breaking."

Ghes Orade would have faced a cannoned-up Chiss fleet armed only with a sharp stick, and laughed about his chances of survival, but he was scared stiff of her grandfather. Mirta wondered if she was doomed to have all her romances doused liberally with freezing water because everyone now knew she was a Fett. She leaned on the barn door—the building had been a drying shed—and two indignant faces turned to her.

"What are you *doing* to him?" she demanded. "Has he had a relapse or something?"

Fett was breathing hard as if he was in a lot of pain, hands clenched against his chest, face white and waxy. A woman she'd never seen before stood over him, holding a large-bore needle-tipped syringe up to the light and checking the reservoir. Another man in a ragbag of assorted armor was standing with his back to the door. He didn't turn around.

"Jaing kept his promise," Fett said, breathless. "Or he's having the last laugh and poisoning me. We'll see."

"There's a slower and less painful way of getting *this* where it needs to go," said the woman, flicking the syringe with her finger to clear air bubbles. "But there's no point messing around given the state you're in, *Mand'alor*. Direct into your bone marrow. Two shots to go."

"Just do it." He took his hands off his chest and parted his shirt. Mirta was surprised how bony he was: he looked such a fit, strong man in full armor. She never wanted anyone else to see him like this. "Is this the best Mandalore can offer me? A *veterinarian* who spends her working day with her arm up a—"

"Believe me, I prefer treating nerfs. Keep still. Or I'll miss and puncture a lung. Or worse."

"How long is this going to take?"

"*Mand'alor*, do you know what the alternative site to the sternum is for this treatment?"

"Amaze me."

"The pelvic bones."

Fett's expression was predictably blank, and he didn't say another word. He looked away, and anyone else would have thought it was casual annoyance at having his schedule interrupted, but Mirta knew him well enough by now to see he was in excruciating pain. She took the risk of stepping forward and folding her hand around his. He took it, too. She thought he'd break every bone in her fingers when the vet lined up the needle—so big that Mirta could see the hole in the tip—and pressed it hard into his breastbone, as if she were preparing a nuna for roasting.

There was an awful squelch. Orade swallowed loudly.

"If you're going to faint or throw up, son, go do it outside," the vet said irritably. "Failing that, find some analgesics. Where do you keep them?"

"Forget it," Fett said. "I need to know if you're doing me any damage."

"It's okay, *Ba'buir*," Mirta whispered. "You'll be okay."

"If the Sarlacc didn't finish me off, she won't, either."

The vet, all smiling menace, inserted the syringe in a glass vial to refill. "Last one. Shut your eyes and think of Mandalore."

Mirta glanced over her shoulder at the man in the multicolored armor. He slipped off his helmet.

"Just making sure he doesn't die before he does something useful for *Manda'yaim*," said the man. "If it works, and it should, then he'll start to show signs of recovery in a few days."

He looked a lot like Fett—and Jaing—and the resemblance was unsettling. The Kiffar part of her, the one that cared about bloodlines, told her this was her kin. Clones got around a bit during the war. She probably had a lot more genetic relatives than she'd first thought.

Fett crushed Mirta's fingers again and didn't make a sound.

The vet straightened up and opened a bottle of pungent-smelling liquid to clean her hands. "Normally, I swat my patients across the rump and let them get on with grazing. But seeing as it's you, I'll skip that and suggest you take it easy for a day or so. Expect a big bruise."

Fett gave her a silent nod of acknowledgment as she left, and fastened his undershirt. Then he looked up at Mirta. "Say hello to your uncle Venku." He indicated the man in the motley armor, who still hadn't acknowledged her. "Alias Kad'ika."

It was all making sense now. Kad'ika had to be the son of a clone trooper. There must have been a lot of them out there, and she wondered how many of them had any social graces or senses of humor, or if they all took after *Ba'buir*.

"Just doing my bit for Mandalorian unity," Venku said, slipping his helmet back on as if her close inspection was making him uncomfortable. "Wouldn't do for the *Mand'alor* to snuff it just when we're on the rise again."

He leaned over Fett and put two fingers against the pulse in his neck. Mirta expected her grandfather to flatten him for daring to lay hands on him, but he simply looked at the assorted plates of *beskar'gam* with idle curiosity and tolerated the examination.

"Your heart rate's up," Venku said. "Get some rest."

"Field medic."

"Yeah, they say I have a healing touch." Mirta found that hard to believe. Venku straightened up. "Any problems—tell the folks at Cikartan's tapcaf in town. They'll know how to contact me."

Venku made for the door. As he brushed past her, he stopped and tapped his finger against the heart-of-fire dangling from her neck. He obviously never worried about getting a punch in the face.

"Interesting," he said.

He was a chancer, a man who could obtain things—and obviously information as well. It was worth a try.

"It's a heart-of-fire," she said. "It belonged to my grandmother. I need a full-blooded Kiffar to help me read the memories imprinted in it."

He paused for a few moments. "*Mando'ade* come from all kinds of places. If I find anyone who can read the stone, I'll let you know." Then he was gone.

Orade nudged Beviin.

"Go on," Orade said. "Tell him. It'll make him happy—okay, happier. Happy people heal faster."

Fett put his armor plates back on. "What's going to make me happy?"

Beviin had the beatific smile of a man who'd finished laying up stores for the winter and just enjoyed a big meal. "Yomaget's got something to show you."

Fett grunted. He was the least expressive man Mirta knew, but he seemed vaguely disappointed. "He's got the *Bes'uliik* spaceworthy, has he?"

"Bang goes the surprise."

"It's the thought that counts." He stood up and was instantly transformed from her sick *Ba'buir* into Boba Fett, ruthless and relentless. But he didn't stride out the door right away. She took a guess that he was feeling the effects of the treatment and wasn't going to admit it, not even in front of people who knew exactly what was wrong. "Where is it?"

She gestured to the ceiling and offered him her arm.

Mirta was still looking for a reason not to hate Fett, and she was ready to look pretty deeply. She decided she could start by loving him for his sheer guts. Nothing fazed him, nothing stopped him, and nothing made him feel sorry for himself. They stood outside the barn and waited in silence. It looked like a tiny hut set against *Slave I,* laid up in her horizontal mode nearby.

A low rumble interrupted the rural peace.

Fett looked up as a dull black wedge shot across the sky and vanished behind a forested hill. Mirta lost it, but then it circled back again, came to a dead halt in midair about two hundred meters above them, and descended smoothly on burners. It landed on its blunt tail section and then extended struts to tilt through ninety degrees and come to rest horizontally like a conventional starfighter. The canopy lifted and Yomaget climbed out, slid onto the ground, and kissed the matte fuselage.

"*Cyar'ika,*" he said to the ship, running a tender hand over the skin. "I think I'm in love."

"Nice," said Fett.

"Puts the *uliik* in *Bes'uliik.*"

"Yeah, I can see it's a beast. What's different?"

"We applied the micronized *beskar* skin, *Mand'alor.* She's a toughened *shabuir* now. Care to show her to the Verpine?"

"It'd get their attention."

"If they share their ultramesh technology with us, we might be able to lighten the airframe and improve her top end in atmosphere. If we skin her completely in solid *beskar,* she's going to be invulnerable, but heavy."

"We'll keep the heavy ones. Maybe the Verpine can come up with a better fuel solution."

"Well, if you're not going to take her for a spin, I will," said Medrit. He scrambled up onto the wing and eased himself into the cockpit, looking as if he would fill it. "*Shab,* a *Mando*-Verpine assault fighter. That'll cause some sleepless nights on Coruscant."

"If we can mine and process the ore fast enough."

Yomaget looked hopeful. "We could ask those helpful insectoid chaps to lend us an orbital facility or two."

"I'll go see them," Fett said. "Got to think long-term on this. No point handing over too much to Roche early in the game."

Medrit spent the next hour taking the prototype *Bes'uliik* through its paces over the Keldabe countryside while the rest of them watched. Yomaget captured the aerobatics on his holorecorder, looking satisfied.

"Might slip this hologram out to a few contacts," he said. "We're not a modest people, are we?"

"Remind them that most of our adult population can fly a fighter, too," Fett said. "For starters."

He went back inside the barn. He didn't manage a smile, but Beviin turned to Mirta and cocked his head. "Believe it or not, that's a happy man."

Maybe he was a better judge of mood than she was. She was relieved just to hear Fett use the phrase *long-term.*

Times were changing. The rest of the galaxy might have been tearing itself apart, but the Mandalore sector—which now informally controlled Roche, if a protectorate agreement counted—was a haven of optimism after a decade or more of grim existence. That night, Mirta found the *Oyu'baat* tapcaf packed with new faces, and the singing was raucous.

If Jacen Solo, her mother's murderer, had been roasting slowly over the *Oyu'baat*'s open fire instead of the side of nerf, Mirta might even have joined in.

SENATE BUILDING, CORUSCANT

Jacen's official airspeeder brought him up to the main Senate entrance. He could have entered the building by any number of more private platforms, but he had no intention of sneaking in via the back doors; being seen counted for a lot, and he still had his heroic image to protect.

A line of citizens waited outside the doors that admitted members of the public to the viewing galleries. Some just wanted to watch the day's business, but there was a small group who were clearly protesters. It wasn't just the FREE OMAS banner that three of them were carrying among them. There was a taste of anger in the Force, vivid despite the permanent background of fear and uncertainty.

"Drop me here," Jacen said. "I'll walk."

"They'll harass you, sir," said the Gran chauffeur. "I ought to take you straight up to your floor."

"They've got a right to see who's governing them." It wasn't as if they could cause him any harm. "I find that talking to people generally clears up misunderstandings."

Jacen had expected at least one mass protest or a riot broken up by water cannon and dispersal gas. GAG intelligence showed that Corellian agents still operating on Coruscant were doing their best to make that happen. But the general willingness of the population to accept the change of regime surprised him. The stock exchange had suspended trading for a few hours, and some shares had bounced around: but the traffic still flowed, the stores were full of food, HoloNet programming was uninterrupted, and everyone was getting paid.

Unless you were Cal Omas or a civil liberties lawyer, the military junta was temporary and benign. There was a war on, after all. It was to be expected.

I ought to write a study on this. How to take over the state: smile, look reluctant, and keep the traffic flowing.

And it was just Coruscant. The rest of the GA worlds went on running their planetary business as they saw fit, unmolested, and that meant there was no need to stretch the fleet and the defense forces by

deploying them to keep order on thousands of other worlds—their own, in many cases. All Jacen and Niathal had to worry about was Coruscant, because the political and strategic reality was that Coruscant . . . was the GA . . . was Coruscant.

The rest of the Alliance is detail. I have its heart and mind.

"Good morning," Jacen said. The group of protesters stared at him with a collective, slowly dawning oh-it's-really-him expression. Even a face that had been on HNE as regularly as his took some recognizing out of context. He extended his hand to them, and one man actually shook it. Most species responded well to placatory courtesy. "I just wanted to reassure you that Master Omas will get a scrupulously fair hearing. We've let him go home, too."

When folks were worked up for yelling and seemed to want to be dragged away by CSF heavyweights, they were totally upended by having the object of their fury listen to them. Jacen's patient smile met disoriented surprise. A couple of CSF officers began wandering across, probably expecting trouble, but Jacen dissuaded them with a little Force influence and they stopped a few meters away to observe.

More important, though, was the HNE news droid trundling around the Senate Plaza. There was always at least one on duty here, just hanging around to get stock shots, but now it had an actual story. Jacen watched it approach in his peripheral vision.

"Doesn't matter how you dress it up," said the young woman holding one end of the FREE OMAS banner. "The GA is being run now by the Supreme Commander and the head of the secret police, and nobody voted for you."

Jacen managed an expression of slightly wounded innocence. "You're right, I didn't run for office, which is why I won't remain joint Chief of State any longer than I have to. Would you like to see something? Inside the building?"

The woman looked at him suspiciously. "There's always a catch."

The news droid was right behind them now. Sometimes the Force placed things in his grasp. Suddenly he realized that *everything* was being handed to him and all he had to do was react, just as Lumiya had told him, and not analyze everything.

"Your choice," Jacen said. "I just want to show you the Chief of State's office. Anyone else want to come along?"

The security guards weren't happy, but what Jacen wanted, Jacen got. He led a straggling group of protesters, day visitors, and the HNE droid through the glittering lobby and up in the turbolift to the floor of offices where the public was almost never allowed, the seat of galactic government itself.

A few civil servants in the corridor did a double take but carried on about their business. Niathal must have seen him come in on the security holocams, because she was wandering around the lobby, clutching a couple of datapads. Jacen acknowledged her with a smile and walked up to the carved double doors of the Chief of State's suite of offices.

The doors were sealed—taped shut. The bright yellow tape with the CSF logo and the legend DO NOT TAMPER was purely cosmetic, but it made the point far better than the impregnable but invisible electronic lock.

"That's Chief Omas's office," Jacen said over the head of the HNE droid. He stood back casually to let it get a better shot of him explaining earnestly to this random sample of the electorate. "It's for the elected head of state. It stays sealed until someone is elected to fill it. Neither I nor Admiral Niathal has moved in. That matters very much to us."

The thing about Mon Cals was that you could never tell if they were rolling their eyes or just taking notice. Niathal was probably rolling hers, though. Jacen could feel her amusement at his expense.

The little crowd muttered and oohed and ahhed. It was a perfect media moment. The protesters seemed at a loss for words, but Jacen was anxious that they not look humiliated.

"I hope we've reassured you." *You're up to your neck in this too, Admiral.* "And I'm glad you feel you can raise this with us, because there's no point fighting a war if we can't behave as a democracy even when things get difficult."

The jumpy security guards who'd decided to follow him showed the party out. Everyone went away either happy or at least defused. Jacen felt Niathal's gaze boring a hole in him.

"Last time I saw anything that slick and oily," she said, "was when *Ocean* leaked a whole lube reservoir over the aft weapons flat."

"Ah, but you were absolutely *right* to seal that office. *Neither* of us should have it."

"I believe in sharing *everything*."

"As do I," Jacen said.

"So let's try to address the media jointly, shall we? No point look-ing like a publicity addict, Jacen. Citizens might misunderstand your motives."

"I'm here to serve the galaxy," Jacen replied, and meant every word. "Never underestimate the power of being pleasant."

"That's fine on Coruscant, but your charm doesn't travel well." Niathal beckoned him to follow. "I have Senator G'Sil in my office, and the Senator for Murkhana, Nav Ekhat. We've hit a small snag in our new policy."

Ekhat didn't look like a woman who'd had a restful night. She didn't wait for Jacen to sit down before she launched into a tirade that had obviously been gathering steam long before he and Niathal walked in.

"I understand you're concentrating forces in the Corellian and Bothan sectors," she said, stabbing her finger at the holochart in the center of the meeting table. "Where does that leave *us*?"

"Explain your concerns," said Jacen.

"The new treaty between Roche and Mandalore."

"And you feel threatened by this."

"Given the state of our relations with Roche, yes. Are you aware that we've been having a disagreement about export markets?"

G'Sil leaned forward. "Put another way, the Verpine are accus-ing Murkhana of reverse-engineering some of their most lucrative weapons command systems, breaching their patents, and selling cheap knockoffs to undermine their markets."

"*Put another way,* Verpine don't like healthy competition," said Ekhat. "Now they've signed a deal with Mandalore for mutual aid and technical collaboration. It's the bugs-and-thugs show."

Jacen watched Niathal shift ever so slightly in her seat and felt her annoyance. Anyone who dismissed Verpine as *bugs* probably also dis-missed Mon Cals as *fish*.

"Are you expecting this alliance to threaten your security di-rectly?" Jacen asked. "Because if the Verpine were seriously annoyed, they have plenty of military hardware to make their point without call-ing in Keldabe."

"Verpine might make the stuff," she said, "but they rarely use it in anger. The Mandalorians, on the other hand, treat warfare as a national sport."

"But this is about Mandalorian iron." Niathal was working up to telling Ekhat that Murkhana was on its own. She'd probably enjoy it after that bug comment, too. "The Verpine want to produce enhanced armaments and vessels under license."

"No, they want Mandalorian *protection,* too."

"Why?" Jacen couldn't see Murkhana attacking Roche.

"They're afraid the fighting on Kem Stor Ai will spill into their backyard, and they're rich pickings that might prove too tempting for a system at war."

"I'm missing the connection."

"Mandalorian protection tends to be of the outreach kind, Colonel. It's a short step from turning out to repel the Kemi and making a . . . *disciplinary* visit to us."

Niathal got up and walked around the table, looking at the holochart from various angles. "And are you breaching the Verpine patents?"

"We don't think so," said the Senator. "But the products are very . . . *similar.*"

"You see, I'm not sure we should commit troops to trade disputes. This war is about the responsibility of member planets to commit military resources to common defense. That's one reason why the former Chief of State is *former*—because he was ready to concede part of that principle."

"As a member of the GA, we expect support when attacked."

"Roche is a neutral world," Jacen pointed out. "If you were attacked, we'd have to assess the situation, but I feel this has to be referred to the interplanetary civil courts first."

"So you're saying we're on our own."

Jacen would play the nice officer today. Niathal was doing a fine job of being the nasty one. "I'm saying that you should try to resolve this dispute by other means rather than escalate straight to saber rattling. But . . ." He thought about the talk of a new Mandalorian assault fighter. It was interesting enough on its own, but if it was a collaboration with the Verpine, the GA needed to get an idea of what it could do. He decided to disagree with Niathal. "But perhaps the presence of a GA squadron and frigate might make Roche more willing to sit down and discuss the matter again."

Niathal turned her head very slowly to stare at Jacen. He knew the risk he was taking.

"If we have spare resources, then we'll *consider* it," she said.

"Roche warned us that it'll take direct action if we don't cease production of the disputed products." Ekhat looked at all three of them pointedly in sequence as if defying them to say the word *no* out loud. Then she stood and picked up her folio case. "So sooner rather than later, please, or you'll lose another Rim world. And I don't mean resignation."

G'Sil watched Ekhat stalk out, then shrugged. "So much for the Mandalorian threat making the little planets rush to our protective arms, Cha."

"They *did* rush," Niathal said. "And that's the problem. If we're seen deploying a Star Destroyer every time some member state has a local disagreement, we'll open the floodgates, not that they're not starting to open already. Policy is to concentrate on breaking the big boys who won't play by GA rules, or we'll be putting out fires across the galaxy for decades to come." Jacen braced for impact. "And, Colonel Solo, you will *not* commit fleet resources like that without discussing the matter with me."

"I didn't commit anything. I just stated the obvious."

"And I didn't agree to it, either."

"Wouldn't it be useful to have an excuse to wander out to the Rim and take a look at those new Mandalorian fighters?"

"If they've built any yet."

"I say commit a couple of flights if we can't spare a complete squadron. If we move one of the frigates out from Bothan space, that'll bring it within range of Murkhana, at a stretch."

"Are you sure you want to provoke Mandalore?" G'Sil asked. "It's got that extra *personal* dimension now, and the last thing we need is Fett making this a vendetta against the rest of the GA. His neutrality has been a bonus, to be honest."

"I'm well aware that Fett has neither gone away nor forgotten his daughter," Jacen said. "But he's far too smart to waste his troops to fight a personal feud."

Mandalore was always a problem: always had been, always would be. It wasn't big enough to be a galactic threat, but wasn't small enough to dismiss—or remove.

Tough on chaos, and the causes of chaos.

It was being the third element in a universe of pairs that made Mandalorians disruptive. The universe was binary, bipolar, ruled by the balance between opposites, whether that was dark and light or action and reaction. It couldn't accommodate that extra pole and remain orderly. Mandalorians were an inherently destabilizing influence.

"Are you still with us, Jacen?" G'Sil asked. "You look distracted."

"Just wishing the Mandalorians would go away."

"Pay them to stay at home," said Niathal, gathering up her datapads to leave. "That's the permanent solution. As long as they have the occasional therapeutic fight to work off their aggression, they'll be happy. And that's just the females." She headed for the door. "I have fleet commanders to brief. Shame we can't approach Fett to see if he's changed his mind about staying out of the fighting."

"Isn't paying them not to fight tantamount to an insult to their honor?" Jacen asked.

"I think you're getting them mixed up with some other warmongering savages. They'd see it as protection money. They're pragmatists."

"If only all wars had such simple economic solutions."

G'Sil smiled ruefully. "Well, they've mostly got economic causes."

"Not this one," Jacen said. "It's about order. About responsibility."

Niathal and G'Sil both concealed their reactions at the same time and said nothing. He could tell they thought he was becoming eccentric, or perhaps that he hadn't quite got the hang of high-level politics. Either way, their reaction said that he wasn't playing the same game as them, and they were right.

But it was all going too smoothly. No riots, no outcry except for some of the minority media and the usual suspects in the legal and liberties community, but apart from endless media analysis of Omas's

time in office—almost as if he'd died—the vast majority of Coruscanti had treated it like a fall from grace instead of a military coup.

Having a Jedi on board did seem to make the regime change appear much more wholesome in public opinion.

"I'd expected to be storming barricades this week," Jacen said. "What did we do right?"

"We didn't suspend any normality," said G'Sil, making interesting use of *we*. "Every other politician remained in place. Just the people who administer it at the top level changed."

Order. It's all about order. This is the microcosm of the entire galaxy; the dry run for how my rule will be in due course. Quiet normality for the majority.

But Jacen was worried that it might prove to be the lull before the storm. He thought of Tenel Ka and Allana, and the impulse to visit them while he still could was overwhelming. Lumiya said he had to listen to those voices, and not think sensible things like mundane beings did.

"I need forty-eight hours out of the office," he said. "To catch up on things. Can I trust you two not to oust me while I'm away?"

Niathal didn't seem amused. "You'll return to find Boba Fett sitting in your office, but if you have to go . . . you must."

"I trust you implicitly," he said. He trusted her not to be stupid, at least. Lumiya could keep a watchful eye on the situation while he made the trip to Hapes.

Boba Fett. That was an ax still waiting to fall, and if it didn't keep him awake at night, he was certainly conscious that Fett's continued lack of bloody revenge was unsettling. Jacen put the Mandalorians on the list of things for which he'd find a solution when he was established as a Sith Lord. Vader had had the measure of them in his day: Jacen would, as well.

That, too, was in his destiny.

LUMINOUS GARDENS SPA, DRALL, CORELLIAN
SYSTEM

"So . . . still no new Prime Minister?" Mara asked.

"You're taking a big risk coming here," said Leia. "No, there's a triumvirate of the three main party leaders running Corellia until they find a new target—sorry, I mean candidate. Two dead inside a few months tends to dampen the applicants' enthusiasm."

"Well, we score for efficiency. At least we can run the GA on two."

"How very Sith."

Mara nearly choked. It wasn't funny at all. Did Leia know something?

"Mara, are you okay?"

"I think my encounter with Lumiya made me allergic to the word." With a scarf around her hair, Mara was just another middle-aged female human enjoying the resort with a friend. The two walked around the colonnade of exclusive stores and beauty salons, and Mara still found it disconcerting that anyone could be leading a normal life when hers—and that of so many others—was caught up in the turmoil of war. Normality seemed somehow obscene. "I had to see you face-to-face. You don't want Jacen to arrest you for setting foot on Coruscant, and you know he would. Where's Han?"

"He's gone on an errand with Lando. Where's Luke? Seeing as it's just us girls talking, I smell a delicate problem."

There was no point tiptoeing around it. Mara had as much evidence as she needed, but this was Leia's *son* under discussion. Leia had already lost Anakin. Mara had to be absolutely, completely certain. Ninety-nine percent sure wasn't good enough.

"Jacen," she said.

"Always is."

"I don't know how to say this to you."

"Try blurting."

"He's out of control. I mean *badly* out of control."

"Uh-huh. I admit it's challenging to have to keep tabs on your only son by watching the news coverage of his latest power grab."

"How's Han taking it?"

"Not well, to say the least. He veers between wanting to disown him again and talking about getting together to talk him around. You know, sometimes I think it's going to kill him."

Mara found that it wasn't certainty of Jacen's guilt she was looking for: it was any excuse to say that it was all Lumiya's doing, and that by removing her, Jacen could be brought back to his old self.

Whatever had happened to Jacen over the years—and that five-year "sabbatical" was still largely a blank sheet—there seemed nothing of that old self left to recover.

If this wasn't my nephew, and Leia's son, would I still be trying to find a reason not to do something about him?

No.

"You sure you're feeling okay, Mara?"

Leia was one of the few people Mara had ever truly admired. She was pretty well the only person other than Luke who Mara knew would never fall apart, however bad things got. But she still couldn't bring herself to sit Leia down and give her the full catalog of Jacen's crimes.

Yes, they were *crimes*. There was no other word for it.

"I'm going to ask you something, Leia, and if you never want to speak to me again afterward, I'll understand."

"This isn't going to end in a punch line, is it? You're serious."

"You have no idea how serious."

"Then stop dragging it out."

"Okay, do you think Jacen is susceptible enough to be controlled by Lumiya?"

I should have put the list to her first. I should have told her about Nelani, and making Ben kill Gejjen, and his little chats with his Sith buddy, and the fact that he seems to think my son is expendable.

And *apprentice*—what kind of apprentice would Lumiya be talking about? Mara faced the inevitable and hated herself for refusing to see it earlier.

"No," Leia said at last. "He's stubborn and he's his own man. She could make the difference between him doing something and hesitating, but she could never make him act totally against his will. I've had to come to terms with that, but he's still my boy, and I still love him."

It was the last thing Mara wanted to hear. She wanted to hear that Jacen was a kid who went along with the others, who got into bad company but was a good boy at heart. She wanted a reason to go after evil Lumiya and rescue deluded Jacen, because that was easy, black and white, *palatable.*

Wrong.

If it hadn't been happening within her own family, she'd never have hesitated. For a moment, she wondered if she was set on this— *this* didn't have a name yet, not a word, but she knew what *this* was— because it was her own son at most risk. *My son or yours.* It could have been selfish maternal priority, just using the rest of Jacen's actions to justify lashing out to save her child.

She tried to imagine Ben dead, and how she'd feel then. She could have stopped Palpatine, and didn't. History had taught her a lesson about hindsight, and it wouldn't give her a second chance; what was happening to Ben would happen to other people's sons, too.

"Mara, I think you should have spent a few days in bed after the fight with Lumiya," said Leia, and slipped her arm through hers. "You're not yourself at all. Let's find a stupidly expensive restaurant and forget the fat content. Take it easy for a few hours. Because I can't run on adrenaline and anxiety twenty-four hours a day like you seem to."

Leia, I'm so sorry.

I'm going to have to stop Jacen. I have to. I'm going to have to kill your son, because that's the only way of stopping him now.

"Okay, but my treat."

"You're on."

Part of Mara was appalled that she could even think it, and part was telling her that this was what happened when she forgot that Force-users' highs and lows weren't just family spats, but dynastic battles that could shake the whole galaxy. They didn't have the luxury of small stakes.

"I like the Fountain," Leia said. "They do a dessert called the Fruit Mountain. Takes two hungry women to tackle one."

"Sounds good."

It was surreal. They sat on opposite sides of the table, blue-white diya wood set with iridescent transparent tableware, and a pyramid of

multicolored fruit held together by golden spun sugar and dusted with real citrus-flavored snow was placed between them. There was a point at which Mara's eyes met Leia's as they attacked the dessert with a spoon each, and it would be a frozen moment of horror in Mara's mind forever: Leia smiled, the look in her eyes pure compassion, and Mara knew that she couldn't see the truth behind *hers*. She felt like dirt. She hated herself.

You need to know there's nothing else, absolutely nothing, *that you can do to save Jacen.*

Mara needed to confront him one last time. If anyone could stop him at the brink—the final one, anyway—then it was her, because she'd crossed from the other direction. She didn't think it would work, but she owed it to Leia—and Han.

She was planning to take Jacen from them, and they'd already lost Anakin. There was only so much pain a family could take.

chapter sixteen

The government of Bothawui is prepared to pay twenty million credits per month for the exclusive services of a Mandalorian assault fleet with infantry. We would also be greatly interested in acquiring a squadron of *Bes'uliik* assault fighters and would be prepared to pay a premium to have exclusive purchase rights to this craft.

—Formal offer to the government of Mandalore

SENATE LOBBY, CORUSCANT

"THERE YOU ARE," SAID MARA, AMBUSHING JACEN AS HE STEPPED out of the turbolift. "Glad I caught you."

He registered genuine surprise, and that gave her more satisfaction than he'd ever know. No, he hadn't felt her presence when it mattered. *Thank you, Ben. Nice trick.*

"Hi, Aunt Mara. What can I do for you?" Jacen tried to do that act of dithering on the spot, the carefully calculated body language that said he really *did* want to stay and talk, but duty was dragging him

away. *What an actor.* She could act, too, but this wasn't the time for it. "I'd love to catch up over a drink," he said, "but it's late and I've got an appointment first thing tomorrow. Can we fix a time for when I'm free? Say in a couple of days?"

"It won't take long, Jacen. It needs to be now."

Now it was her turn to take over the choreography, stepping in his way so that if he wanted to pass, he'd have to make a deliberate and rejecting sidestep. And Jacen wouldn't be that blatant, not to her. It would make her suspicious.

Too late. You've already done that, Jacen. But for Leia's sake, for Han's sake, I have to try this.

"Okay," he said.

There was something deeply unsettling about a Force-user— about anyone, really—who gave off no Force presence. It was like standing next to someone who wasn't breathing and had no pulse, a little too close to death for Mara's liking. It also pressed all those paranoid and defensive buttons, like someone whispering behind his hand in someone else's presence. It said *guilty, unnatural,* and *secret.* If the Yuuzhan Vong had been the kindest and sweetest beings in the universe, Mara knew she would have mistrusted them anyway because they didn't show up in the Force as being alive and *there.*

She steered Jacen over to an alcove. Psychologically, he might have felt more vulnerable being confronted with his acts in the middle of the lobby, where everyone could hear and see them. On the other hand, the alcove could make him feel cornered if she maneuvered him to stand with his back to the wall. Either way, she was going to get a reaction out of him. She couldn't outstrip his Force powers, but the tricks of flesh and blood put her on a more level playing field.

"You don't fool me," she said. "Not any longer, anyway."

He tried his baffled-little-boy grin. "What am I supposed to have done?"

"Remember what I was?"

"You've lost me, Aunt Mara . . ."

"This is about Lumiya. It stops here and now. You've turned into something vile, and you're too smart to be conned into *that* even by her. Beyond dark. See, I've been both sides, and I know."

"Well, I don't know what you mean. I really *don't.*"

"Wrong answer. I'll deal with Lumiya in due course, but I know what you've been doing, I don't buy the excuses that your poor parents make for you every kriffing time. So I'm going to set you a test."

"Mara, are you okay? You're not well, are you?"

"Don't even *think* about trying that one. If you acknowledge the terrible things you've done, and whatever's left of Leia's son is still functioning, then come with me right now to the Temple. We'll get the whole Council together and we'll deprogram you."

Jacen put his hands in his pockets and looked down at the floor. He still had that silly grin on his face, but it was fading a little around the eyes.

"Mara," he said, with an exaggerated softness that made her want to punch him. "Mara, I think you're forgetting that I'm joint Chief of State now, and I don't have time for this emotional outpouring, because whatever Ben's been telling you—"

He was digging himself deeper into the pit. She'd really hoped he'd step back, and she knew she was just as stupid for hoping as she'd been for turning a blind eye to his darkness in the first place.

"There's no *Ben* in this, Jacen." She stopped her finger a fraction short of jabbing him in the chest. "Leave Ben out of it. If you so much as *breathe* on him, I'll skin you alive, and that's not a euphemism. Last chance. Drop this Sith garbage now, or take what's coming."

There. She'd said it. *Sith.* Jacen's grin had vanished completely, and he looked like a total stranger. The Emperor had had yellow eyes, she recalled; they said he'd once had a kindly face with normal blue ones, but if Jacen's turned yellow, he couldn't possibly have looked any more alien to her than he did right then. There was nothing supernatural about his ambition, callousness, and arrogance.

"Good night, Aunt Mara," he said, and walked away.

She didn't watch him go. She didn't need to.

This is all your fault, girl. You should have listened to Luke. He was never fooled by all that sophistry, and you stopped him dealing with it because you couldn't deal with a teenage boy like any mom has to. The least you can do is clean up this sewer yourself.

"Okay, buddy," she said, not caring if a couple of Bith Senators were staring at her. "Okay."

There were some things she couldn't walk away from, even

though they'd tear her family apart. It was better torn than destroyed, because in time it would heal.

Jacen was going to die.

JACEN SOLO'S APARTMENT BUILDING, CORUSCANT

Lumiya had never had any problem with biding her time, but Jacen was becoming too caught up in the administrative tedium of his new toy—the Galactic Alliance—for her comfort. And her instinct told her that the Force was restless for change.

It was late, past midnight, and he still wasn't back.

He's flesh. There's something about being wholly flesh and blood that distracts you from the task, and the more flesh you sacrifice, the less heir to its limits you become. But I can't achieve what he can. The perfect balance: strength driven by passion but not confined by sentimentality.

Lumiya waited outside Jacen's apartment building, taking in the glittering night and feeling the imminence of upheaval like the oppressive air before a violent storm.

His accession to Sith Lord had to happen very soon. The momentum of events, and the ease with which they'd fallen into place, pointed to the gathering pace of the fulfillment of the tassel prophecies.

He will immortalize his love.

Lumiya no longer spent frustrating hours contemplating the meaning. It would happen, and it would become clear.

Jacen didn't appear as she'd expected. He was hard to locate, a habitual hider in the Force, so she went up to the apartment, bypassed his security locks, and sat down to wait for him. It was important that he stayed focused on the spiritual side of his progression and left the material aspect to Niathal. When he had achieved his destiny, *then* he could return to the military arena with skills beyond Niathal's, and change the course of the war.

First things first.

She almost expected to see Ben Skywalker come through the doors. Some of his clothing and possessions were still in the apartment, but he'd gone. He was too soft to stay the course, just as she'd always said; if he needed time off to weep and recover every time he carried out a necessary and unpleasant task, he'd proven he was fit to be the sacrifice Jacen would make, and too dangerously weak to be his apprentice. A Sith Lord could only function with a strong apprentice. Like a good government, a Sith needed a strong opposition to keep him sharp.

Eventually the doors opened and Jacen stood in the hallway, looking as if he hadn't wanted to find her there. He had a paper-wrapped package under one arm, and some disturbance clung to him as if he'd had a fight or an accident.

"Has anything happened?" she asked.

"Oh, a disagreement with Mara about . . . Ben. Spare me overprotective mothers."

"Well, she might have a point. The time's coming."

"You keep saying that." Jacen walked past her and went into his bedroom. She heard him opening doors and drawers as if he was in a hurry. "I'm anticipating events like a madman and looking for signs everywhere. And nothing's happening, unless you count getting rid of both Gejjen and Omas. I think that's climactic enough for one week, don't you?"

"Mundane politics."

"Maybe. Look, I've covered a lot of ground these last few weeks, and grasped every opportunity I've had to force things into fruition." The banging and scraping of closets gave way to rustling fabric, and when Jacen emerged he was carrying a small holdall. "I want some solitude to think. Keep an eye on Niathal while I'm gone."

Jacen didn't need solitude. He was quite capable of shutting out the world anytime he wanted to. The man could meditate in the middle of a hurricane. He wasn't running away; he was going in pursuit of something.

"How long?" Lumiya asked, immediately ready to calculate the maximum distance he could travel in the time available.

"Twenty-four hours, possibly forty-eight. If I stay away any longer, I don't think Niathal will misbehave, but I think Senator G'Sil might get ideas. That third element where only two can exist, you know?"

"I understand," she said.

Jacen had done this before. He would vanish for short periods, confide in nobody, and come back with a sense of melancholy about him and a little of his dark energy diminished. Lumiya had put it down

to natural apprehension about the size of the task he had ahead of him, and she'd tolerated it, but he couldn't afford to be running off again at this critical stage.

And if Jacen was in trouble, he'd never ask for help.

It was for his own good, as well as the galaxy's. This time, it was important for her to find out what was pulling him away just as he was on the brink of making everything happen. She'd follow him. She had to keep his path clear now, and remove all distractions.

"Will you have access to HNE where you're going, or do you want me to brief you on your return?"

"I don't want to be contacted," he said. "If something major happens, I'll know. Just mind the shop."

The doors closed behind him. Lumiya wandered into the bedroom to see if he'd left the package he'd been clutching under his arm. There was nothing on the bed, and when she paused to feel the tiny disturbances that showed her where objects might have been hidden, there was no trace of anything beyond items taken: just a change of clothing, and the small necessities men needed. Jacen seemed to like plain antiseptic soap, a discovery that she found both touching and funny; Jacen was moving ever closer to self-denial. He didn't have to indulge that nasty Jedi habit. She'd have to help him be a little kinder to himself when he'd made his transition.

The apartment was more austere than it had been a few months before. Every time she came here, there was one less comfort and fewer personal touches than the last. There were now no holoimages of family and friends to be seen. He hadn't even stuffed them into a cupboard to avoid their accusing glances that asked what had happened to good old Jacen.

But it wasn't altogether a bad sign. Perhaps he was washing away the old Jacen and preparing for the one he would become. So if he needed to do that by wearing sackcloth and brushing his teeth with salt, that was fine. She shut off the lights, checked that the apartment was secure, and made her way out of the apartment building to the walkways of Coruscant.

She slipped through the back alley and into the disused warehouse where she'd hidden the Sith meditation sphere. Ben Skywalker did have his uses; even insects had a vital role in the ecology. The ship would come into its own now.

Lumiya might not have been able to find Jacen when he vanished into the Force, but the ancient red sphere somehow could. She could feel its curiosity and even a little excitement. It wanted to be useful again, to serve. It extruded its boarding ramp without even being asked.

Follow Jacen Solo, she thought, and pictured him in her mind so that the sphere didn't get distracted by Ben. It seemed fascinated by the boy. *Follow the Sith-Lord-to-be.*

He was going to succeed.

BEVIIN-VASUR FARM, MANDALORE

The hard red soil was baked solid like pottery clay, and it shattered at the first blow of his vibroshovel. Fett stared at a stark white tracery of bones beneath, highlighted by the harsh sun.

"Why did you leave me here, son?" asked Jango Fett. Where was he? There was no face, nothing at all. But the voice was *right there.* "I've been waiting."

"Where are you, Dad? I can't find you."

"I waited . . ."

"Where are you?" Fett was shouting for his father, but his voice was a kid's and the hands he could see clutching the shovel were an old man's, veined and spotted. Panic and desperation nearly choked him. "Dad, I can't see you." He started tearing aside the hard dirt, and the gritty particles jammed painfully under his fingernails. He kept digging, sobbing. *"Where are you?"*

Fett woke with a start. His heart was pounding; sweat prickled on his back. Then it faded and he was looking at the chrono on the far wall. In the weeks since he'd brought his father's remains back to Mandalore, he'd had that nightmare far too often. He swung his legs over the side of the bed and tested his weight on them, waiting for the pain to start gnawing at the joints.

It wasn't so bad. In fact, he just felt a little stiff around his lower back, as if he'd been digging. Maybe he'd acted out that nightmare.

He bounced on his heels a few times to see what happened. There was no pain. He didn't even feel that nausea that had been so routine, he'd forgotten what it felt like to wake up without it.

Apart from running a temperature, he felt better than he had in days—months, in fact. He was *alive*. He wouldn't believe he was in the clear until the nerf-doctor came back with the test results, but he knew something fundamental had changed.

So you didn't poison me, Jaing.

He went to the refresher to shower, if a torrent of cold water from an overhead cistern could be called that, and shaved with an ancient fixed blade that nicked his chin. Where the Sarlacc's acid hadn't left smooth, glossy scar tissue, there was still stubble to tackle, and these days most of it was pure white and hard to see. He shaved twice a day anyway. These were the unguarded, naked times when he allowed himself to think of Ailyn and other painful things, because he had to look himself in the eye, and he wasn't a liar. Lying wasn't just bad; it was stupid. Lying to yourself was the most stupid thing of all.

And now that he wasn't so preoccupied with his own death, he could think about the deaths of others. There was a lot of unfinished business. He'd start with Ailyn.

She was a stranger when I opened that body bag. A middle-aged woman. Not lovely like her mother. Old before her time, exhausted, dead. And still my baby, my little girl. I don't care if you tried to kill me. I really don't.

Killing was his trade. He didn't enjoy it, and he didn't dread it. The only person whose death he knew would make him feel good and not just competent was Jacen Solo.

Better that you rot than die. I can wait. Thanks for motivating me to survive.

I'm back.

Fett checked his face in the mirror for missed beard, double-checked with his fingertips, then lowered his helmet over his head. The world became sharp and fully comprehensible again with all the extra senses built into his armor. At a time when other men had failing eyesight and unreliable hearing, Fett could see through solid walls and eavesdrop kilometers away. There was a lot to be said for smart tech. He flexed his fingers in his gauntlets, finally feeling complete and girded against the world.

Yes, I really am back.

He rode the speeder bike into Keldabe and hammered on the

doors of the vet's surgery. She had her name on a durasteel plate: HAYCA MEKKET.

A man leaned out of the open upper window, looking bleary-eyed, and stared down at Fett. He disappeared again. "Sweetness," he bellowed. "It's your special patient."

The vet appeared at the window. "I suppose I've got to open early, especially for you."

"Haven't you got any letters after your name?"

"Nerfs can't read. Why bother?"

"Got my results?"

"Yeah."

"And?"

"The cell degeneration's stopped. But the lab tech over on Dawn said we shouldn't breed from you." Somehow she was easier to deal with than Beluine. "You know that needle was for banthas?"

"Felt like it."

"You're a hard man, Fett. I'm glad you're not dead."

"How much do I owe you?"

"A quilt. A nice, thick red one."

Fett went back to *Slave I* and caught up with the news. Murkhana and Roche were heading for a showdown: it was a good opportunity to show what a single *Bes'uliik* could do, if the Verpine wanted to invoke the treaty.

Fierfek, I did it again. I'm going to live.

If nothing else went wrong, he'd have another thirty years, maybe more. Most people would have been overjoyed at the reprieve. But Fett found he was actually glad that he'd come so close to death again, because it had a way of sharpening him up and making him think harder. He liked the risk; he liked beating the odds.

I suppose I should tell Mirta.

Now he felt he could ask her what Ailyn had taught her over the years to make her hate him so much. What he really wanted to know, though, was where Ailyn had learned her hatred. Most kids from divorces didn't pursue a homicidal feud across half a galaxy.

But it could wait an hour or so while he had a decent breakfast.

He'd enjoy it today. He was going to *live*.

chapter seventeen

I find it interesting that Taun We has never held it against Fett for attacking Kamino. Either he's her favorite unfinished project, or there's something else we don't know.

—*Jaing Skirata, musing on the motives of Kaminoans*

"IT'S REALLY KIND OF YOU TO PUT ME UP, SIR." BEN TRIED TO TAKE UP as little room as possible on Captain Shevu's sofa. It wasn't just awkwardness about intruding on someone's privacy; Ben found himself trying to hide—not *in* the Force, but *from* it. Ideally, he'd have gone home with Mom, but that meant Dad, too, and he simply couldn't face him yet.

"You're not really afraid of your dad, are you?" Shevu handed him a plate of breadsticks filled with fruit preserves, which was a weird combination but he seemed to leave the proper cooking to his girl-friend. "He seems such a nice guy."

"He is," said Ben. "But did you ever think your parents knew everything you were thinking, and everything you'd done wrong, just by looking at you?"

"All the time."

"Jedi parents really can—well, nearly."

Shevu's opinion of Jacen showed on his face now that he was off-duty. "I think Master Skywalker would be angry with the person who made you do it, not you."

"Oh, he's angry enough with Jacen."

"Sorry, I shouldn't put you on the spot about your family. It's not fair. Forget I said it."

"I think I did the right thing for the wrong reasons."

"Well, beats doing the wrong thing for the right reasons—classic excuse, that one. I was a cop. I know . . ."

"Do you want to stay in the GAG?"

"I miss CSF, actually. I miss catching real criminals and showing tourists the way to the Rotunda." He wandered into the kitchen, and there was a banging and clattering of dishes. He came back with a glass of juice and drank it in two gulps. "You sure you're all right?"

"Oh, yeah. Look, I'll be out of your way as soon as I can."

"No rush. Shula thinks it's great that you wash the dishes."

Shevu's girlfriend said he was a "nice polite boy." Ben thought that providing a safe haven for him was worth help with the chores, at the very least. "I can Force-dry them, too."

Shevu laughed and handed him the remote control for the lights. Ben got the feeling that Shevu was happier keeping an eye on him in the aftermath of the assassination because he didn't approve of the Jedi habit of letting "children" carry weapons and fight. As far as he was concerned, Ben shouldn't have been serving in the front lines before he was at least eighteen. He was just too polite to say that he thought Jedi made bad parents.

Poor Mom.

Ben slept. He had a few odd dreams about Lekauf that woke him up, and the grief when he woke up properly and remembered his comrade was dead was painful. He lay wondering about Lekauf's folks, and how they were coping, and then he thought he drifted off again because he could hear—no, he could *feel* a voice in his head asking *where he was.*

He sat up. He knew he was fully awake, because he could see the environment-control light on the wall, winking faint red every ten seconds. It took him a while to work out why he knew the voice but couldn't put a face to it when he shut his eyes again.

It was the Sith ship. He didn't know where it was, but it was calling him. It wanted to know where he was.

Sith sphere, color orange, no index number, last known registered owner: Lumiya. Ben decided to treat it like a stolen speeder, the way Shevu would. *I owe Jacen this. He'd never have done these things without Lumiya twisting his mind. Shows he's not half as clever as he thinks he is.*

Mom would probably try to talk him out of it. But they'd reached an understanding now that he had to do things his own way, because she couldn't expect anything else from him, given his pedigree.

Ben pulled on his clothes, left a scribbled flimsi note for Shevu, and set off for the GAG compound to liberate an unmarked long-range speeder.

The nice thing about being the secret police was that provided you signed out the kit, nobody asked you what you planned to do with it. And it was legitimate police business to catch criminals.

It was only when he fumbled in his pocket for his ID that he realized he'd left his vibroblade at Shevu's. He hoped he wouldn't need his mom's luck tonight.

SKYWALKERS' APARTMENT, CORUSCANT

Luke was asleep when Mara got back, and she was relieved. It saved a lot of awkward questions. She peered through the doors, counted the seconds between rasping snores, and decided he was out cold.

Good.

She slipped past the bed and selected her favorite working clothes:

dark gray fatigues with plenty of pockets for storing small weapons and ammo. She had no idea how long it would take to run Jacen to ground, so she opted to pack for a mission—as much as she could cram into her backpack.

I've got to stick on his tail now. I've got to strike when I can.

She could track Lumiya, and he was still in touch with her. If she hung around Lumiya, then she'd eventually get Jacen where she wanted him—away from the genteel, constitutional way of doing things on Coruscant. Jacen had said he had an appointment, too, and while it might have been another of his lies, the chances were that he'd want to tell Lumiya that Mara was on to them.

I'll save you the trouble.

She made a conscious effort not to see Leia's face in her mind's eye, and somehow she'd erased poor Han from this altogether. It wasn't that fathers' feelings didn't matter, but she had a better idea of the pain Leia would go through; however old kids got, the memory of them as newborns never faded.

It might be true for dads, as well. But Mara only knew what a mother felt, and that was bad enough.

She checked her datapad for the transponder trace. Ben's showed he was still at Shevu's, and so he was one factor she didn't have to worry about. Lumiya's transponder indicated she was heading for the Perlemian node just off Coruscant. If Jacen wasn't with her, Mara thought, she might well get a lead to one of her bolt-holes; in the assassination business, every scrap of data on a target's habits and movements was valuable. It would be worth the journey, and the technician at the base was used to Jedi booking out flight time in StealthXs. She didn't have to fill out any forms that said her mission was to kill the joint Chief of State.

Mara closed the inner doors to keep the light in the hallway from waking Luke, and paused at the apartment's front entrance. *Okay, I'll risk it. If he wakes up, though . . . it'll be another argument.*

She put down her pack and tiptoed back into the bedroom, leaned over Luke—still snoring like a turbosaw—and kissed his forehead as lightly as she could. He grunted.

"Sorry I never spotted it," she mouthed at him. "But better late than never."

Luke grunted again, and his eyelids twitched. Mara debated whether to give him a little Force-touch deep in his mind and see if she could get him to smile in his sleep, but decided she was pushing her luck, and Jacen probably had a head start on her. Lumiya definitely did.

Mara paused at the doors and left a flimsi note stuck on them.

Gone hunting for a few days. Don't be mad at me, farmboy . . .

There was no need to say who the quarry was. She'd have a hard enough time explaining when she returned.

SITH MEDITATION SPHERE, PERLEMIAN TRADE ROUTE

"Hush," Lumiya said aloud. "I have no idea if he can hear you."

The meditation sphere had developed an annoying habit of asking her questions. It wanted to know why there were *so few*. Lumiya wasn't sure where to begin with such a vague question. The ship had been buried on Ziost for more time than it wanted to remember, it told her, and now it was curious to know where *all the dark ones* had gone.

"It's a long story," Lumiya said. "We haven't been in the ascendant for a long time. Jacen Solo will change all that."

What about the others?

"Oh, Alema?"

She comes and goes, broken, but sometimes very happy.

It was a good description of Alema's almost bipolar moods— murderous, bitter obsession punctuated by highs of . . . murderous triumphant obsession. The sphere was very attuned to feelings, it seemed. Maybe it could sense darkness anywhere, like a homing beacon, so that it could go to the aid of Sith in difficulty. "I told her to tail Jacen, but I should have known better than to rely on a psychiatric case. But who else is there? Apart from me, that is."

Plenty of little darknesses. The two with my flame.

Lumiya repeated it to herself. *Flame.* "Ahh . . . red hair? Mara Jade Skywalker. She was the Emperor's Hand, an agent for the dark side, just like me. The boy is her son."

You darknesses should never fight. So few of you. I stopped her fighting.

"You certainly did." It was fascinating that the ship could still sense the dark side in Mara, even though she'd abandoned her roots. But to taste it in Ben, too . . . it might have been in his genes, or perhaps the ship was reacting to his new career as a state assassin. Like mother, like son; Lumiya almost thought she'd written off Ben too soon. "Do you sense dark ones near?"

The broken one is looking for the Lord-to-be.

"If she looks as if she's going to interfere, remove her—dark or not." Lumiya had told Alema to track Jacen, but now wasn't the best time for Alema to interfere. "Jacen Solo is our priority."

The ship went quiet. It was impossible to get an accurate sense of speed in a vessel with no instruments in hyperspace, but she could measure the duration of the journey on her chrono, and the ship could tell her where its equivalent location was in realspace.

Past Arkania. Past Chazwa.

Where was Jacen going? Not Ziost, unless he was taking an extraordinary route. He'd be brushing the Roche sector, if he dropped out of hyperspace, and for a moment she wondered if he was simply panicking about the possibility of the Roche-Mandalorian arms deal turning the war in the Confederation's favor, and going to the Verpine to undermine the pact: but that was routine work for minions, for his admirals and agents, and she'd be annoyed if he was wasting his energies on *that*.

He leaves hyperspace, the ship said at last.

"Where is he?"

Hapes Cluster.

"Follow him."

Perhaps he was going to enlist the Queen Mother's help. The Verpine seemed to be troubling him; that meant Lumiya hadn't heard the full story about the arms deal.

"This is beneath you, Jacen." She sighed. "*Priorities.* You really can't delegate, can you? That's one thing that your grandfather *could* do."

Jacen was heading for Hapes itself. Lumiya encouraged the Sith sphere to leave more distance between them by imagining a cord

stretching to a hair's thickness. Eventually Jacen reached the edge of the Hapans' security area, and slipped through.

He lands. He has an entry code.

Lumiya debated whether to use the code to follow him more closely, then decided against it. She didn't know if that would attract attention. "Maintain position until he leaves."

She decided to sit it out, and hoped she wasn't misjudging the situation and that Niathal and G'Sil weren't now declaring the Glorious Third Republic or some such nonsense. The trouble with the small people was that they often left little in the Force for her to feel at this distance, and Coruscant's citizens were so passive and compliant that there would be no great disturbance for her to detect even if Niathal declared martial law in Jacen's absence. It was nothing that couldn't be put right on her return, but she'd have to explain why she'd been *goofing off,* as Ben might call it, and Jacen would become petulant and uncooperative.

Jacen's like a moody teenager at the moment. When he makes the transition to Sith Lord, he'll settle down fast.

And she'd be no more use to him after she found him a replacement for Ben Skywalker. Lumiya accepted that her days were numbered.

She lost herself in meditation, wondering who might be Jacen's apprentice to come, when an explosion of feeling shook her as if she'd been grabbed by the shoulders and kissed by a total stranger. The Sith sphere reacted, too, a great soaring excitement that seemed to bounce between her and the ship's bulkheads.

"What's happening? Ship? What is it?"

But she already knew: it was Jacen, slipping out of his permanently repressed Force state and allowing himself intense, overpowering emotion for the first time in ages. The image the ship threw into Lumiya's mind was one of gulping down an icy glass of water after weeks in a burning desert. The sensation was intense enough to bring Lumiya to the point of gasping.

He has love, said the ship. *He has loves there.*

So Jacen Solo had a lover.

Stupid boy.

He could have had any number of lovers—*after* he achieved his full power. Passion was fine, attachment could magnify strength, but running around the galaxy for a secret assignation smacked of a teenager's total surrender to hormonal crisis.

Jacen, you're thirty-one, thirty-two, and a grown man doesn't have to sneak light-years away for a little romance, not even one in your position.

Unless . . .

Lumiya could think like Jacen now, even if his more vulnerably human side caught her wrong-footed.

Hapes. This was Hapes. And it involved something he'd kept secret *even from her.*

His lover was part of the Royal Court, then, the epicenter of paranoia when it came to alliances of any kind, because indiscretion often meant a blade between the ribs or a sprinkling of poison in the wine. *That* would explain a secret dash across hyperspace at sporadic intervals.

And Queen Mother Tenel Ka was a Jedi to whom Jacen had been close for years. It was conjecture, but Jacen wouldn't consort with a palace maid. He was conscious of his lofty station in life; he would be drawn to a Jedi queen.

Lumiya risked searching the Force more closely for him to try to get an impression of exactly where he was. The sphere said he was in the palace itself, and although the tidal wave of emotion that had burst through had ebbed, it was still powerful enough to focus on. She shut out everything else—even her constant obsession, Jacen's destiny— and just opened her mind to the most basic impressions. His Force presence could be strong enough to drown out everyone else's around him. Now that he thought he was unseen and undetected, his presence was as deafening as a shout.

Lumiya couldn't even feel the ship around her.

The sense she was wrapped up in now wasn't taste or sight or sound, but . . . *touch.*

There was something soft, silky, and furry in her hands—Jacen's hands—and it yielded when he closed his fingers. It meant nothing to her, and *then*—then she understood.

"Ship, you said *loves.*"

Two, the ship said. *Yes, two.*

The ship could detect Force-users, and it felt there were two more on Hapes, two more whose link with Jacen Solo had to be kept secret at any cost, and who would have an emotionally overwhelmed Jacen clutching something soft and covered in silky fur . . .

A toy. *A soft toy.* Jacen had come back to the apartment with a plain package gripped tight under his arm, and left with it. He'd bought a cuddly toy for a child he loved with his entire being.

Lumiya snapped herself out of the connection, and managed to stop short of beating her fists on the stark red deck of the sphere in sheer frustration. The ship might have taken it the wrong way.

Oh, Jacen, you had a child with Tenel Ka.

Lumiya now understood his fear and desperation. She thought of all the conversations she'd had with him about *immortalizing his love,* and suddenly realized who was in his mind when he looked so utterly tortured and desperate as she explained that he had to destroy what he loved most.

It explained everything. Lumiya never thought she could pity someone again enough to weep, but she found her vision blurred by tears that threatened to spill down her cheeks.

She settled in for a long wait in a state of mental silence, not even wanting to occupy herself with getting to know this extraordinary ship. She'd need to be there for Jacen after this. It seemed insultingly banal to kill time when he was about to make a sacrifice that almost no mundane being—or Jedi—would understand or forgive.

Yes, it was a very high price indeed.

chapter eighteen

The Roche government has given Murkhana twenty-four hours to cease production of weapons command systems that are allegedly in breach of patents, or face what it describes as "immediate enforcement." GA Chief of Staff Niathal tonight warned Roche against military action and said GA fighters would be patrolling the system in a peacekeeping role.

—*HNE news update*

HAPES

MARA DROPPED OUT OF HYPERSPACE STILL PUTTING TOGETHER scenarios to explain why Lumiya had gone racing down the Perlemian to the Hapes Cluster shortly after a GAG StealthX was signed out of the GA Fleet hangar by Colonel Jacen Solo.

There was no sign of the StealthX. If Jacen wasn't making himself detectable in the Force, Mara couldn't spot the stealth fighter any better than an enemy could. But ideas were forming in her mind.

Either Lumiya was fermenting more trouble to break the Alliance, in which case Hapes was a wasted journey, or she was meeting someone here like Alema—*sorry, Jaina, I'll try to bring her back alive for you, but no promises, not in this mood*—or . . . she was pursuing Jacen.

Or . . . maybe she'd found the transponder and was back to playing tag.

Mara thought it was odd that the ship hadn't spat out the tiny device, given that it was smart enough to throw a line around her neck to save Lumiya's tin backside.

It could have killed me easily enough, too. But it didn't.

Mara disliked reasoning in a vacuum. She didn't quite trust the crazier things that crossed her mind lately. But maybe the ship still saw her as a dark sider. It would be academic soon, but the thought that she might still have that tang of darkness about her produced some mixed emotions.

Yeah, I'm going to kill my sister-in-law's son. On the dark scale of ten, that's a twelve.

Now that her anger had ebbed, she was beginning to wonder what she was doing here. The Hapans would wonder that, too, if they managed to spot a StealthX hanging around their system unannounced. Lumiya's transponder showed that her ship was sitting in a cluster of asteroids, but she wasn't showing up on scans.

What was she waiting for?

Mara ran a discreet check on her instruments. If she went active on sensors, she'd give away her position, so it had to be a case of passive detection only.

She was watching, or waiting, and how the Hapans hadn't taken an unhealthy interest in the sphere was anyone's guess, but Lumiya had a talent for evasion.

Follow the credits. But in this case, follow the Sith.

Mara shut down as many systems as she could afford to do without and waited. The temptation to launch a spread of proton torpedoes took some resisting, but until Mara worked out what Lumiya was waiting for, the Sith had a stay of execution.

It had to be Jacen that Lumiya had followed, although how she'd managed that Mara wasn't yet sure. Maybe Tenel Ka had summoned him, to intercede and get him to drop that stupid warrant on his parents. That didn't explain Lumiya riding escort, though, or why she'd tailed him for eighteen solid hours.

It was staring Mara in the face, whatever it was. She knew that. She was missing a piece again. But all she needed was to locate Jacen, not work out his pension plan.

I could just comm Tenel Ka and ask . . .

However tightly the Hapans controlled access to their space, a thirteen-meter piece of stealth technology drifting between planets was just a speck of dust. Mara was effectively hidden, and so was Jacen. If he was on the surface, she might—just might—detect him when he took off for a moment, but that meant going active and attracting attention.

Think. Think.

She could wait until he reentered the Perlemian Trade Route, but that made the assumption that he was returning to Coruscant the way he came. *I don't have infinite oxygen, either . . .* There was an easy solution, but it would blow her cover.

An hour later, she was ready to use it. She opened the secure comlink and readied herself for a little social engineering.

"Hapan Fleet Ops, this is GA StealthX Five-Alpha requesting assistance." That would cause a flap, but it had to be done.

"Five-Alpha, this is Hapan Fleet Ops. We don't like surprises, even from allies."

Oops. This *was* paranoid country. "Apologies, Fleet. I'd like to stay off the chart, but can you confirm that Chief of State Solo is unharmed and that his vessel is undamaged?"

There was a brief silence. Knowing Hapan Fleet Ops, they were checking her out to be sure she was a GA pilot and that her transponder—now obligingly active—matched their security code list.

"Confirmed, Five-Alpha. His ship landed in the Fountain Palace compound without incident. Should we be aware of any special security issues?"

Ahh . . . definitely visiting Tenel Ka, then. Probably explaining himself: *Believe me, Your Royal Highness, I had no choice, I had to depose Omas . . .*

"Fleet, he's not aware that we have concerns for his safety and that we've put close protection on him in transit. He thinks he can handle it himself. Discretion on your part would ensure he doesn't try to shake me. I've detected a vessel following him but I lost it in your

space. Unknown origin, ten-meter red sphere with distinctive ocular front viewscreen and cruciform masts and vanes."

Mara's warning displays were lighting up: Now that the Hapans had a fix on her transmission, they were checking out the StealthX with sensors while they had the chance. She could have blocked them, but she let them probe around to keep them happy.

"Understood, Five-Alpha. We'll give you a heads-up when he makes a move. If we detect the sphere, do you want us to detain or neutralize?"

"Your space," she said. *Have this with my very best wishes, Lumiya.* "I have no orders to detain. Feel free to neutralize."

"Copy that, Five-Alpha. Unless you flash us in the meantime, we won't ping you until the Chief of State takes off."

They were such nice, helpful people, the Hapans, even if they *were* paranoid. And they understood plots, assassins, and keeping their mouths shut. Mara shut down all noncriticals and meditated in darkness, marveling anew at how very vivid and exquisitely beautiful starscapes were without the gauzy filter of an atmosphere.

She allowed herself one quick glance at her datapad to reassure herself that there was one thing she didn't have to worry about.

Ben's transponder said he was still safely on Coruscant.

GAG SHUTTLE, TAANAB SPACE

Ben had learned a lot from his GAG comrades about tailing suspects discreetly, and one basic trick was to overshoot an exit and double back. He dropped out of hyperspace and headed back Coreward to Taanab, not Hapes, even though he was sure the Sith sphere was there.

He could feel it, but he couldn't detect it conventionally; he could have spoken to it, but he stayed shut down in the Force to avoid Lumiya's attention. He tried to work out why she was interested in Hapes, and failed, but there was nothing of Jacen that he could feel, just a trace of his own mother. The closer he ventured toward Hapan space, the more powerful her presence became.

Don't tell me we're both following Lumiya.

He'd have some explaining to do. But it didn't matter: he'd happily take being grounded for a year and even sent to Ossus as long as he could keep an eye on his mom right now. He set a course for the freight corridor and dropped out into realspace again, merging with the convoys of transports then with a group of ore haulers. Running a loop had also served another purpose: almost like listening to the source of a sound, Ben made a mental map of the silent voice of the Sith sphere and got a good sense of where it was in physical space. It was close to Hapes itself.

And—he felt it now—so was his mother. She'd found Lumiya, then. She'd beaten him to the target.

Ben savored a brief fantasy of emptying the shuttle's cannon into the sphere, felt strangely sorry to destroy the ship just to finish Lumiya, and wondered if all boys went through a stage of feeling aggressively protective toward their mothers. Maybe that went with finding it so hard to deal with fathers as you grew up. It was that alpha-male thing.

Come off it. How many guys your age—or any age—have to worry about their family being attacked by Sith and insane Dark Jedi? This isn't normal life. The rules are different.

Ben got as close to the Sith sphere as he dared. As far as he could tell, it was holding its position, but when it moved—he'd go for the kill. Then his mom would know he was there whether he made himself detectable in the Force or not, because the GAG shuttle was about as stealthy as a brick.

If he could avoid killing the Sith ship, he would. For some reason, it bothered him more than killing a real human being, which he'd done too many times now.

FOUNTAIN PALACE, HAPES

Jacen said good-bye to Allana, finding it freshly painful not to be able to call her his little girl.

"Nice fur," she said. She refused to be parted from the stuffed tauntaun and hugged it to her with both arms. "What's his name?"

Jacen squatted down level with her. She was Force-sensitive and smart, but if she'd realized who he actually was, she was too well

schooled in survival to say. He liked to think that it was a knowledge they both shared, and that she understood why he couldn't be Daddy—not yet, anyway. It was a sobering thought for such a little girl.

"What do you want to call him?"

"Jacen."

"That's lovely. Why Jacen, sweetie?"

"So when you don't come to see us I can talk to him instead."

A father's guts were made to be twisted. Jacen reached the stage of wanting to just turn and run when he took his leave of her and Tenel Ka, so he could avoid that hesitant parting a step at a time, looking back over and over again and thinking: *What if this was the last time I ever saw them?* He *did* think it. It was morbid, but a measure of how important they were to him that he tested just how devastated he'd feel without them. At least as Chief of State, he had a much better reason for more frequent contact with an allied monarch.

And he'd come through this visit without his destiny bursting in and creating a moment that told him he had to kill them. He listened for that whisper of fate, dreading it, but there was only silence.

It would only have caused him pain, nothing more. Sith ways were logical; never pointlessly cruel. Whatever sacrifice he still had to make, it would have productive *meaning*, however hard.

Jacen, the tauntaun, who was there for Allana when he wasn't around, would always hurt a little, though.

Tenel Ka walked with him in silence to the StealthX in the compound.

"You're not happy about Omas, are you?" he said.

She did that gracious tilt of the head, the one she must have learned to cover her real reaction when she was being bored senseless by guests at a diplomatic reception.

"It's very different, being the focus of government after you've enjoyed the relative freedoms of being a deputy," she said. "I hope it doesn't turn out to be a mistake for you."

"I can always steer the attention to Niathal."

"Make sure you both have different ambitions. It's far safer than both wanting the same thing."

"That sounds like the kind of advice I should wake up sweating about in the small hours."

"I think the phrase is *lonely at the top*, Jacen Solo." She indicated the blaster, lightsaber, vibroblade, and toxin darts in the belt around his waist. "I see you're getting used to the Hapan level of mistrust . . ."

"Like you say, it's lonely."

He didn't look back this time. Now that his brief respite was over, the fresh memory of Mara haranguing him—had he handled it right, did she have enough on him to destroy all he was working for?—flooded back in along with Ben's face.

I want it over with. I can deal with it. I just can't stand not know-ing where and when and how.

The StealthX lifted clear, and Hapes dwindled into a sumptuous quilt of gardens and canals again. He had a good idea now of what he'd face when Ben was gone: Mara, an animal robbed of her young with all the primeval wounded rage that went with it, and Luke—he had no idea how Luke would react, only that a man who could bring down the Empire, and whose blood was closer to Vader's even than his own, wouldn't be paralyzed by grief.

Jacen was now more afraid of the Skywalkers discovering Allana's parentage than of the Hapan nobles. He could probably protect her from the Hapans if he had to, but it would be far harder to protect her from the vengeance of Luke or Mara. Allana was his weak point.

But nobody knew, and it would stay that way until he was certain he'd eliminated every threat she might face. He wasn't taking chances. He was going to create two of the most lethal enemies any being could have.

"Hapan Fleet Ops to StealthX One-One, safe return," said the voice on the comm. They had never said that before: being Chief of State had obviously upped their anxiety status to triple-red or some-thing. But he was perfectly safe here. He was still visible in the Force, still all warmed bittersweet feelings, and for a little while he could af-ford not to care.

As Jacen accelerated toward the hyperjump point, he could have sworn a vessel was close to him. He felt something in the Force for a moment, but it was gone again. He checked his instruments: nothing. If the Hapes Cluster hadn't been such a maze of hazards, he'd have jumped the moment he passed the planet's upper atmosphere.

It must be something in the Hapan water. You were never this jumpy.

But there *was* something out there, and while he hated the impre-

cision of the phrase *something dark,* that was the best he could do: something hostile that was trying hard not to be. He hoped it was Hapan, and that they were just trying in vain to track him out of their space. He should have been able to sense that clearly, though, an ordinary vessel flown by ordinary people.

This wasn't ordinary. He planned for the worst.

If he angled the StealthX right and shut down the head-up display, he could see a panoramic rear view reflected in the viewscreen. Sometimes he needed to see with his eyes to be certain. He killed the display and shifted his focus, and for a moment all he saw was velvet void.

Then the stars winked out.

"Lumiya?"

Silence.

She could hide in the Force, too. She thought he was letting his concentration wander. She probably couldn't resist finding out where he was going.

If she'd followed him here, then she *knew* about Tenel Ka. She'd use it.

"It's okay, Lumiya, I know it's you."

But there was still no response. That wasn't like her.

"Lumiya, I can't let you live now, you realize that?"

For a moment, even in this crisis, he found himself measuring her death against his prophecy. Was it Lumiya after all? Was *she* the sacrifice? What could there possibly be about her death that would kill something he loved?

"Lumiya, last chance . . ."

Then a searing white beam flooded his cockpit and blinded him for a second; he rolled instinctively to break, suddenly aware it was a landing light so close on his tail that the vessel must have nearly collided with him. How did the proximity sensors miss it? How did *he* miss it?

His Force-senses were flooded instantly with someone else's ice-cold anger. The comm crackled.

"Game over, Lumiya," he said, targeting his aft cannon.

"You bet it is," said Mara.

chapter nineteen

She logged out Five-Alpha at 0036 hours, sir, and she didn't file a flight plan.

—GA StealthX technician, Coruscant, to Luke Skywalker

HAPES CLUSTER

JACEN COULDN'T FIRE.

It wasn't regard for Mara, because his first instinct was to lock on and press the button, but she was so close that the detonation would have taken him with her. StealthXs had sacrificed shielding for sensor negators. It was only at times like this—times that should never have happened, *would* never have happened—that it was a problem.

He jinked left, and she matched him, and right, and left, and still she was so close on his tail that he braced for impact out of reflex, arms locked out on the yoke.

There was no advantage: same starfighter. No edge: she was as good a pilot. No refuge: they were in open space. It was down to who hated more, and who was more prepared to die to take out the other.

All Jacen could think of was that now it was Mara who'd followed him here and knew about Tenel Ka. Her threats over Ben seemed irrelevant. He had a whole new problem.

His comm crackled again. He braced for a stream of vitriol from his aunt. But it was someone else's voice.

"I have her, Jacen."

Lumiya. Savior, maybe, but she shouldn't have been here either. So Lumiya and Mara probably knew about Tenel Ka and Allana; and Lumiya certainly knew that he couldn't let either woman live with that knowledge. Now he had two assassins on his tail, and he couldn't trust either of them not to kill or betray him.

Laser cannons flared across his port side and he felt the impact in the airframe, but he was still in one piece. He smelled smoke. Brilliant white light filled the cockpit. Lumiya—*if* she was targeting Mara, *if* she wasn't trying to kill him in some bizarre Sith test—had the same problem: Mara was flying so close that any explosion put him in her blast radius, or would send her debris punching through his shields at this range.

Jacen did what he'd done many times: he simply dropped away by looping through ninety degrees. He needed to put a second of space between them, and he also needed to come back at her with an advantage.

Mara might have sent a message to Luke by now, revealing everything. She wanted maximum damage. His secret was as good a missile to be used against him as any ordnance.

As he climbed out of the loop, Jacen looked up through the canopy, desperate for any reflection or hint of movement. StealthXs had never been designed to fight one another. Their almost complete lack of sensor trace made tracking Mara impossible. That was why she was so close on his tail, too. They couldn't detect each other reliably, except through the Force, or by spotting silhouettes against the starfield.

And Mara seemed to be able to dip in and out of the Force, just like him. *Just like Ben.*

He should never have taught Ben to do it.

The fact that Mara hadn't said more than four words was the most disorienting thing of all. Now he needed to get her onto ground of his choosing. He could feel Lumiya somewhere off to starboard, moving at high speed, and he had no idea what the Sith sphere was capable of in her hands. All he knew was that it was obsolete—and old tech and brute force could often bypass more complex systems.

"Canopy," he yelled. Ben's report had said he'd used a magnetic accelerator in the Sith sphere. "Lumiya, crack her canopy. Weak shields."

He didn't have to explain it to her. Suddenly he could see an orange ball accelerating toward him on a collision course and he flipped ninety degrees just in time for it to pass under him. The next thing he heard was Lumiya's voice saying, "Hull breach, she's venting atmosphere."

As Jacen came around again in a loop, orienting by feeling Mara in the Force once more, he could see a thin white trail moving at high speed toward the center of the cluster. Mara was hit, a slow leak either in the canopy or straight through the skin into the cockpit, and she was trying to land before a crack spread and became an explosive decompression. Even with a flight suit, her chances of surviving that were slim.

She was heading for Kavan. That suited Jacen fine. Once he had her on the ground he could take her, because even if she called in support, who would respond to someone in a battle with Jacen Solo? Not the Hapans. Who would believe her? People many hours away.

He felt no violence or malice at all, but then he never did in combat. He just felt an overwhelming desire to win and survive, and all other emotions were pushed into the background.

He turned his attention to Lumiya.

"It's okay, Jacen," she said. "I know what you have to keep secret. I'll make sure it stays that way—"

"You certainly will," he said, and locked all eight proton torpedoes on the Sith sphere. "This is what you taught me to be."

Jacen fired on her, and felt no triumph or shame, only temporary relief.

But he saw no explosion, no white-hot ball or glittering cloud of slow-tumbling debris. His onboard sensors picked up nothing.

Where was she? Was it a kill or not?

He'd have to trawl for wreckage later. Right now, his priority was to silence Mara Jade Skywalker.

HAPAN SPACE

Ben couldn't feel his mother, but he knew she wasn't dead. She was hiding, just as he'd taught her. Lumiya was here in the Sith ship, though, streaking away on his starboard side, and he wasn't going to break off the pursuit now. She was the key to this. She'd be the key dead or alive. Ben knew he was capable of doing either.

The ship was speaking inside his head, just as it had before. It might have been talking to itself or addressing both him and Lumiya, but it was deeply unhappy.

He has tried to cause irreparable damage.

"Ship, shut up," Lumiya said. Ben could hear her, too, as if the ship's thought processes were an open circuit. "He has to survive. We don't."

The rule of ages is that I must not be targeted.

The sphere had clearly decided enough was enough, and looped back in the direction from which it had come. Ben could see it in his forward screens and on sensors, but he could also see it in his head. The general impression was that it was rolling up its sleeves and going back to knock ten bells out of whoever had fired on it.

"Ship, break off."

I do what I must.

"Ship!"

Ben's drives were screaming trying to keep up with it. There was no real up or down in space, but it was like plummeting in the slipstream of a raptor.

"Ship, my mom's down there," Ben pleaded. "She didn't fire on you."

Masters may use their ships to fight but not involve apprentices.

"Ship, Jacen made an error. Do it for me, so I can find my mom again. Please—don't fire."

The sphere decelerated dramatically.

Who is the enemy? the ship asked. *Unless I know, I can do nothing except evade and protect.*

"That's right," Ben said. Shevu had told him that *humoring* nutters, as he called it, was an essential police skill. Keeping them talking was what it was all about—and if Ben had the ship, he had Lumiya. "Ship, what's your task?"

Once I fought. Now I educate and protect apprentices.

"What do you believe I am?"

Apprentice.

"Who's the one within you now?"

Apprentice also.

Ben was starting to form a picture of the sphere's view of the world. It had been buried on Ziost for centuries and possibly millennia. It had reacted to him when he was being targeted from orbit and running for his life with a terrified little girl.

"Ship, what do you mean—educate?"

I teach apprentices to fight.

Ben could sense Lumiya communicating with it. The ship was responding strongly in his mind, but there was a second stream of soundless words running almost like interference on a comlink from overlapping frequencies. She was urging the sphere to fire on Ben, to ram his shuttle, to kill him.

Yes. I am now for apprentices, so they learn and come to no harm. I used to be for Masters at war.

It made sudden sense to Ben. "You're a Sith training vessel." It would see him as an apprentice because he *was* one, in a way, but Lumiya confused him. "Why do you think the woman in you now is an apprentice?"

Because she knows so little of me. Like you.

Ben accepted he wasn't an intellectual like Jacen, but he could grind through options, eliminating things as he went, just like his mom. He could work out *anything* by just asking question after question.

"The woman apprentice in you had us shot at when we left Ziost."

We shot back.

The ship recognized him, and it decided that both he and Lumiya were novices who needed its advice and care. It had stopped his mother from killing Lumiya on Hesperidium because that was its job: teaching apprentices to fight. Ben wondered how many chances it gave Sith apprentices before it decided they were weaklings who deserved what they got.

There was no way he was going to talk it into killing Lumiya—he wondered how it would do that—and she was having no luck getting it to attack him, either. Ben was in no real danger. But his mother was, and not from that ship. Someone else wanted her dead.

He needed to find her. He dropped toward Reboam, and the Sith sphere escorted him, with Lumiya impotent within.

Ben had caught a Sith. And now he had no idea how to use her to his advantage.

KAVAN, HAPES CLUSTER

Mara set the StealthX down in the middle of nowhere and reminded herself that being the target or the assassin was simply a state of mind.

No doubt Jacen thought he'd forced her to land so he could finish her off. She thought she'd ditched to get him where she could use her fighting skills to better advantage.

It was a matter of who found who first.

I can stop this anytime I want.

After all she'd seen and heard, there was still the Mara within who couldn't really believe her nephew was dangerously and irredeemably evil.

If you don't do it, who will? And who'll blame you for not acting while he could be stopped? Palpatine, Palpatine, Palpatine . . . your lesson in twenty-twenty hindsight.

So here she was, telling herself that she was going to go through a very bad time after she killed him, but it had to be done. And Jacen was probably thinking the identical thing. They were the same. No moral high ground; just a leftover equation that said all other things being equal, Mara preferred to see Jacen dead than Ben, or Luke, or herself. Survival: there was nothing wrong with surviving.

Luke now kept reaching out to her in the Force, increasingly anxious, trying to find her, but she didn't dare reach back. There was no telling what Jacen could detect. When she wanted to be found by Jacen—he'd know all about it.

She grabbed her bag and everything from the cockpit that could be used as a weapon, then found some cover while she consulted her datapad for charts and surveys of Kavan. It was honeycombed with ruined monuments and tunnels. *Fine. If I get him in a confined space, he can't use all his Force skills, but I can make the most of what I've got.* She decided to make her way into the maze of buried passages and get Jacen to follow her.

She was nowhere near any centers of population, so she was also a long way from any help. She didn't intend to summon any, anyway. Not until it was time to remove the body.

She secreted all her weapons in her jacket, belt, and boots, and sprinted for the first tunnel she saw. It was getting easier by the minute to disappear into the Force for as long as she needed. But now she needed to be visible, a beacon for Jacen to lure him onto the rocks.

Come and get me, Colonel Solo.

chapter twenty

From: Sass Sikili, negotiator of Roche
To: Boba Fett, Mand'alor

Murkhana has failed to respond. Because they have failed to re-
spond, and we fear this will encourage others to ignore our
patents, we request your support, so that the point may be made
that we take our patents seriously. I would very much like to see
the Bes'uliik *in action; our metallurgists have been looking at*
ways to produce lighter beskar *structures, so when you pound the*
Murkhana factories to dust, we will be inspired to be more inven-
tive. This is very good for business.

JEDI TEMPLE, CORUSCANT

LUKE MET JAINA ON THE STEPS OF THE JEDI TEMPLE. HE WAS DASH-
ing out as she was dashing in. He caught her arm and steered her
back down the path.

"Where did she go, Jaina?"

"Uncle Luke, I swear I'm not covering for her. I don't know and she's not answering any of her links. Why are you worried?"

Luke held the crumpled flimsi in his fist. *Gone hunting for a few days.* Mara had signed out a StealthX just after midnight two days before. He shoved the note in his pocket. The feeling of dread overwhelmed him.

"Come on," he said. "I have to go look for her. Something's wrong. And Ben's gone, too. I've had the worst feeling, like she's walking into a trap."

Ben wasn't just missing; Luke could no longer feel him in the Force. And now he couldn't feel Mara. He'd called everyone, including Han and Leia, and he didn't kriffing care if the GAG detained him for contacting Corellian agents with a warrant out for their arrest.

He expected Jacen to show up to issue a warning, but Niathal said Jacen was away on "business." The GAG StealthX was gone again. The man came and went as he pleased, it seemed.

I can imagine. Jacen was permanently invisible in the Force now, that was for sure. Luke hailed an air taxi, and they headed for Starfighter Command.

"I've spent more time there since I left the military than when I was in uniform," Jaina said.

"Can you feel her, Jaina? Can you feel Mara?"

She looked slightly to one side of Luke, defocused, and shook her head slowly. "Nothing."

"I haven't felt her now for hours."

When they reached Starfighter Command, they headed for the chart room. Luke found that he could look at charts and pick up strong correlations in the Force—something Ben had proved to have a talent for, too. He stood in front of the banks of holocharts and tried to relax enough to let the Force steer his attention. He made an effort to put out of his mind where he thought she might have been heading.

After a while, when the glowing lines and clusters of dots began to blur and lose their perspective, he found himself drawn to one sector in particular.

"I'm sure she's in the Hapes Cluster," he said at last.

When Luke had first felt Mara drop out of the Force, it was so sudden and uncontrolled that he thought she'd been killed. It woke him in a panic. The three seconds of pure agonized paralysis lasted until she faded back in again, and again, and he worked out that she was doing it deliberately.

"Ironically, it would have been better if she'd taken a regular X-wing," Jaina said. "The starfighter techies say it's almost impossible to locate a StealthX by any of the usual search methods."

She was right. Unless someone happened to eyeball Five-Alpha or Mara had left a transponder or comlink active, the starfighter would simply vanish.

A visual search was all that was left—that, or finding Mara herself. Luke headed for the hangars, and Jaina followed.

"How do we recover StealthXs that ditch, then?" Luke asked, trying not to vent his frustration on hardworking ground crew.

The technician stepped back from the starfighter. "Rescue beacon or the Mark One pall of smoke and flame, sir," he said warily. "The GA asked Incom to make them very hard to detect, and they did."

"Okay, I'll stop harassing people with work to do and go out there myself." Luke reminded himself that Mara was hunting Lumiya, and so he *had* to expect her to use every trick in the book. That didn't stop him from worrying. "After all, I'm the one who shook Lumiya's hand, and not her throat . . ."

Then Mara was suddenly *there*, not just back in the Force but magnifying her presence, as if she wanted to be found. She was defiant, unafraid, and spoiling for a fight. She'd found Lumiya all right.

"Why's she *doing* that, though?" Jaina had her own hunt—for Alema. Now she was keen to help find Mara. "It's like she's taunting her."

"Or she's in trouble and she wants me to find her."

"No." Jaina closed her eyes for a moment, concentrating. "Doesn't feel like a call for help. Feels like . . . a fight."

Luke decided to warn Tenel Ka that he was on his way purely as a precaution. *Eighteen-standard-hour transit.* Given the number of planets in the Hapes Cluster, it would probably take even the Hapans a lot longer than that to find a StealthX, but the more eyes that were out looking out for Mara, the better.

Luke tried to appear casual as he climbed into his cockpit. Jaina stood looking up at him.

"I know I'm officially out of the service," she said, "but if someone authorizes it, I'm happy to join in. Please."

Luke gestured to the ground crew. "Thanks."

"It's Lumiya we should be worrying about." Jaina was trying to reassure him. "I can see Aunt Mara going in for braided scalps like Fett. Red ones. Does Lumiya dye her hair, do you think? Will the stuff have icky gray roots?"

Luke knew she was trying to make him laugh, and he tried to oblige. But just hearing the name *Fett* reminded him that pretty well every member of his family, Solos or Skywalkers, was at the top of someone's must-kill-today list.

Luke didn't want or expect to be loved by everyone. He just wanted to wake up one morning and find his loved ones left alone to get on with their lives.

When Mara came home—scalps or no scalps, war or no war—he was going to book a vacation for the two of them, somewhere soothingly uneventful. He balled the flimsi note she'd left for him and wedged it into a gap in the cockpit fascia. The StealthX's drives whined into life.

It wouldn't be Hesperidium, though.

KAVAN

Jacen had expected to have to deal with an angry Mara *after* he killed Ben, not before.

He was still looking for meanings and patterns in the events around him, and he now saw in himself a certain desperation to try whatever was placed in his path to see if that did the trick and sealed his Sith status.

Will I notice? What does it feel like?

How will I know?

There had to be something that changed the fabric of the galaxy—a tipping point. Meanwhile, Mara was challenging him, pinpointing herself in the tunnels that ran deep under the Kavan countryside, thinking she was still an A-list assassin and that she could take someone who had complete mastery of the Force.

She *was* a superb assassin, but her Force skills were crude compared to his. Once Jacen removed her, it would be easier to deal with Ben. And Luke . . . he'd cross that bridge when he had to.

Jacen checked his belt, pockets, and holster, and decided to oblige Mara. Lumiya and Ben seemed to be elsewhere having their own showdown. Now it all fitted. Lumiya had to be silenced for what she knew, and Ben would do it. It was tidy. It was a food chain.

Jacen loaded four poisoned darts into an adapted blaster and slipped the others into slots on his belt, wondering how he could think such things so calmly. He approached the tunnel mouth with slow care. While he could sense the layout, Mara had vanished from the Force again. There was about a meter of headroom as he edged carefully along the central tunnel, and he could see horizontal shafts at about hip height branching off. It had been built to drain storm water; in harsh winters, local Kavani had once made emergency homes down here.

Jacen stood and listened.

"Okay," he said. "I know you can hear me, Mara. You can still back out of this."

His voice echoed. There was no response, just as he expected, so he began walking deeper into the maze of drains, lightsaber in his right hand and blaster in the other. The only light around him now was a green haze from the glowing blade of energy.

"I could," he said quietly, "go back, block the entrance to this complex with flammable material, and set fire to it." She could hear *him,* all right: he could hear water dripping slowly deep in the tunnels. Sound was magnified, even if it was hard to pinpoint the origin. "And the fact that these tunnels have vents means the chimney effect would smoke you out, asphyxiate you, or barbecue you."

Silence.

He held his breath, listening.

Crack.

His right knee exploded with blinding pain as Mara cannoned out horizontally, Force-assisted, from a side conduit and caught his leg on the joint with her boots, ripping the tendons. As he lost his footing in the narrow passage, screaming, he found himself wedged for a second and groping for support. He lashed out with his lightsaber, shaving powdery brick from the wall. Mara dropped to the muddy floor to dodge the lightsaber, then sprang up and sprinted away down the tunnel.

It wasn't a good start. Jacen swore and made himself run after her, willing endorphins to numb his leg and telling himself that he knew she was setting up a trap. She wanted him confined, pinned down, penned.

If she thought tunnels would even the odds, she was wrong. He'd bury her here.

Mara found the perfect trap at the end of one of the culverts. She could hear Jacen's running footsteps and she had a good fifty meters on him.

From here, the vaulted ceiling became lower, and even Mara had to run at a crouch. It wasn't the place to swing a standard lightsaber. The tunnels were in poor condition, and the brick arches were starting to sag and collapse in places.

So he wouldn't oblige her by revealing his physical position in the Force. *Fine.* She spotted a rusty metal sheet about half a meter wide and laid it carefully across the tunnel floor, propped on stones so he'd tread on it and give her an audible warning when he reached that point. An intense Force shake of the brickwork and arches in front of and behind the metal plate weakened them, and then she stopped them from collapsing by Force pressure.

Hold 'em up. Wait for him to hit that plate . . .

Going after Jacen would never work. He could never be allowed to set the agenda. He could come after *her.*

Trap, immobilize, kill.

It wasn't pretty, and it wouldn't capture the public's imagination like a lightsaber display at the academy, but her training was in destruction. Jacen's was in deception.

She could hear him breathing, and the irregular *vzzzm-vzzzm-vzzzm* of his lightsaber as he stalked, jumping and turning to be sure she wasn't behind him. Then she could hear that he wasn't swinging the blade so much; the short staccato hums and buzzes told her he was running out of room.

She was trapped too, of course, unless she counted the ventilation shafts every fifty meters. But when she said she was leaving here over his dead body, she meant it.

She felt the beginning of a compassionate human thought about Leia, but killed it stone-dead. It would weaken her.

Jacen's boots crunched over bricks. He was impatient. She was in his way, holding him up when he wanted to get on with something.

Crunch . . . crunch . . . crunch.

If she'd timed it right, he was close to stepping on that rusty plate.

Clang . . .

The rumbling began. She brought down both sections of tunnel, before and behind, with a massive exertion in the Force that made her breathless. She didn't hear him call out. Even in the damp conditions, clouds of fine debris filled the air and made her choke.

Mara waited, one hand over her mouth and nose, shoto drawn, and listened in the Force.

There was whimpering and the *chunk-chunk* sound of the last falling bricks. She didn't expect that weight of debris from a low ceiling to cause impact injury, but to engulf and immobilize him. He wouldn't be dead—yet.

She waited in silence, a nonexistent presence herself, until she could hear no more movement.

Okay. Let's see what I have to do to end this.

An arm was all that protruded from the rubble. Through a fist-sized gap, she could see the wet, blinking glint of an eye and blood-stained face. A hand reached out to her, fingers splayed, bloody and shaking. Other people might have felt an urge to take that hand, the most distinctively human of things, but it was an old, tired Sith stunt, and she'd used it herself too many times.

She took her blaster and leveled it at the eye, one-handed, forefinger resting on the trigger. She had the shoto ready in case a coup de grâce was called for.

She felt as detached and steady as she'd ever been as the Emperor's Hand.

"Tell my mom I'm sorry I failed her," Jacen whispered.

"She knows," Mara said, and squeezed the trigger.

chapter twenty-one

Nu kyr'adyc, shi taab'echaaj'la.
Not gone, merely marching far away.

—*Mandalorian phrase for the departed*

KAVAN

THEY SAID THAT THE HUMAN BODY WAS CAPABLE OF EXTRAORDInary feats of strength when in extremis. For a Jedi, it was something else entirely.

Jacen Solo wasn't ready to die, not now, not so close to his ascendance, and not in a stinking drain like vermin.

He deflected the energy bolt with one last surge of the Force and sent the rubble erupting off his crushed and bleeding body like a detonation. Bricks hammered the walls and rained fragments, knocking Mara flat like a bomb blast. She made an animal noise that was more anger than pain and flailed for a moment as she tried to get up.

The effort froze Jacen for two vital seconds. But he knew if he

didn't get up *now* and fight back, Mara would come in for the kill, again and again, until he was worn down and too weak to fend her off.

He scrambled to his feet, staggering more than standing, and suddenly understood.

It was *Mara* who had to die to fulfill his destiny.

Killing *her* was the test: the words of the prophecy were meaningless, and at a visceral level he *knew* that her death was the pivotal act. He didn't know how, and this wasn't the time to stop and think about it. He surrendered totally to instinct for the first time in ages. Whatever guided a Sith's hand had to guide him now.

But he was hurt, and badly.

Ben . . . he didn't know where Ben fitted into this, but now he knew he did, as surely as he knew anything. Jacen didn't care, because he knew he had to kill Mara *now* and nothing else would make sense until he did that.

He fumbled for his lightsaber and thumbed it into life again. Mara was already back on her feet, coming at him with the shoto and vibroblade, brick dust and black-red blood snaking down her forehead from a scalp cut. She leapt at him with the shoto held left-handed, fencing-style, seared the angle of his cheekbone, and caught him under the tip of chin with the vibroblade as he jerked back.

She shouldn't have been able to get near him. He had total mastery, and she was just athletic and fast. He pushed back at her in the Force, sending her crashing against a wall with a loud grunt, but she kept coming at him, one–two, one–two with the shoto and the blade, and he was being driven back, his strength ebbing. He needed space to fight.

He drew his dart gun and fired one after the other, but Mara scattered all four needles in a blur of blue light. They fell to the ground. He turned and scrambled through the collapsed brick, using the Force to hurl debris up at her from the floor of the passage while she leapt from block to boulder to chunk of masonry, until she Force-leapt onto his back and brought him down.

They rolled. This wasn't a duel: it was a brawl. She thrust her vibroblade up under his chin and he jerked his head to one side, feeling the tip skate from his jaw to his hairline as it missed his jugular. He couldn't draw the weapons he needed. He was losing blood, losing strength, waning, flailing his lightsaber to fend her off. It was almost useless in such a close-quarters struggle. Mara, manic and panting, flicked the shoto to counter every desperate stabbing thrust.

"Ben . . . I'll see you dead first . . . before . . . you get . . . Ben."

Jacen was on the knife-edge between dying and killing. They grappled, Force-pushed, Force-crushed: he threw her back again, trying to Force-jolt her spine and paralyze her for a moment, but somehow she deflected it and bricks flew out of the wall as if someone had punched them through from the other side. She almost Force-snatched the lightsaber from his hand, but even with his injuries he hung on to it. He *wouldn't* die. He *couldn't*, not now.

"You can't beat me," he gasped. "It's not meant to be."

"Really?" Mara snarled. "I say it is."

Then she launched herself at him—unthinking, a wild woman, hair flying—and he Force-pushed to send her slamming against a pillar in midleap. But the battering he'd taken and the ferocity of her relentless attack had blinded him to danger from another quarter. As he lurched backward to avoid her, his legs went from under him and he stumbled into a gaping crack opened up by the subsidence. He fell badly: red-hot pain seared from ankle to knee. His lightsaber went flying. Pain could be ignored, but the moment it took him to get to his feet again was enough for Mara to right herself and come back at him with the shoto and plunge it into the soft tissue just under the end of his collarbone.

Lightsaber wounds hurt a lot more than he ever imagined. Jacen screamed. He summoned his own weapon back to his hand and Mara crashed into him, knocking him flat again and pinning him down. Her vibroblade stopped a hand span from his throat as he managed to grab her hair and drag her face nearer and nearer to his lightsaber. She struggled to pull back, hacking at him with the shoto but blocked by his dwindling Force power each time.

Her vibroblade grazed his neck. He fumbled in his belt for a dart. She jerked back with a massive effort, leaving him clutching a handful of red hair, and the only thing that crossed his mind as she arched her back and held her arms high to bring both shoto and vibroblade down into his chest was that she would never, ever harm Ben.

Jacen stared into her eyes and instantly created the illusion of Ben's face beneath her. She blinked.

It gave him the edge for that fraction of a moment. It was long enough to ram the poison dart into her leg with its protective plastoid cone still in place.

It was just a small needle, ten centimeters long. He stabbed her so hard that the sharp end punched through the cone and the fabric of her pants.

Mara gasped and looked down at her leg as if she was puzzled rather than hurt. The dart quivered as she moved, and then fell to the floor.

"Oh . . . it's done . . ." Jacen said. The shoto fell from her hand and she made a vague and uncontrolled pawing movement with the vibroblade. It caught him in the bicep, but there was no strength behind the blow, and she dropped the weapon. "I'm sorry, Mara. Had to be you. Thought it was Ben. But it's over now, it's over . . ."

"What have you done? What the stang have you *done* to me?" But she was already losing her balance as the poison paralyzed her, and she slumped to one side as he got to his feet, staring up at him more with shock than rage or fear.

"The prophecy." It didn't matter now: the toxin—complex, relatively painless—was circulating through her body. "Don't fight it. No healing trance. Just let go . . ."

Mara tried to get up but sank back to sit on her heels, with an expression as if she'd forgotten something and was trying to remember. She crumpled against the wall. Jacen had never felt such relief. It didn't have to be Allana, or Tenel Ka, or even Ben. It was over, all *over.*

"What?" Mara said. She tried to put her fingers to her lips, shaking, but her hand fell back to her lap. She looked at them as if expecting to see blood.

Jacen suppressed his instinct to help her. "It's my destiny, Mara—to be a Sith Lord, and bring order and justice. I had to kill you to do it. You're going to save so many people, Mara. You've saved Ben. You've saved Allana, too. It's not a waste, believe me."

"You're . . . as vile as he was."

Jacen could hardly understand what she was saying. "Who?"

"Palpatine."

"It's not like that," he said. He had to make her see what was happening. It was important. He owed her that revelation. She'd made the sacrifice, although he was now starting to wonder what that meant for whatever love he had to give up. "It's not about ambition. It's about the galaxy, about peace. It's about building a different world."

She stared back at him, and now he could see—and feel—her disgust. He wasn't sure if it was aimed at him or at herself.

Jacen hurt. He was starting to feel the full extent of his injuries, and he needed to heal himself. He also needed to get out of this tunnel.

Mara was breathing heavily now, one hand slack in her lap but the other still clenching and unclenching as if trying to form a fist to give him one final punch. Her vivid green eyes were still bright with relentless purpose. He knew he would try to forget them every day of his life.

"You think . . . you've won," she said, slurred, but utterly lucid and unafraid. "But Luke will crush you . . . and I refuse . . . to let you . . . destroy the future . . . for my Ben."

Jacen sat and waited, almost expecting a prophecy from her to help him make sense of what he'd done. But after a few moments, he felt the final discharge of elemental energy that every Force-user would notice and comprehend.

Ben was the last word she ever spoke.

KAVAN

Lumiya felt the Force shift subtly like tectonic plates in motion. She hadn't realized that the decisive moment would feel quite like that.

"Ship," she said, "The new Dark Lord needs me. Follow him."

Then she left to prepare for death, intending to die well.

KAVAN

Ben suddenly couldn't hear the voice of the Sith sphere. His own name—*Ben, Ben, Ben*—drowned out every other sound, even though deep in his head, it was quieter than a whisper, a summons and a farewell for him alone. He forgot about Lumiya, and stumbled toward the source of the voice, blinded by tears.

"Mom!" he yelled. *"Mom!"*

PERLEMIAN TRADE ROUTE

In the cockpit of his StealthX heading for Hapes, Luke Skywalker felt a hand brush his hair, and as he reached out involuntarily to touch it, he knew his world had ended.

chapter twenty-two

I don't know what's happening, *Mand'alor*, but the amount of secure GA comm traffic flying around the Hapan Cluster now has to be seen to be believed. Major panic ongoing. Stand by.

—*Goran Beviin, surveillance expert, reporting back from the nearby Roche asteroid field prior to launch of the* Bes'uliik

GAG STEALTHX, LAID UP ON ZIOST

J ACEN REALLY DIDN'T KNOW WHERE ELSE TO GO.

He stared at the cockpit panel facing him, knowing that he should have been back on Corsucant at least twenty hours ago, and that Niathal would be cursing him roundly.

He was alone, in creased black fatigues, in agonizing pain, and—hungry.

This wasn't the ascension of the Lord of the Sith that he'd expected. He wondered what ordinary people thought happened when the course of history swung on a single pivotal act. They probably

didn't envisage that their future was now in the hands of a tired, sweaty man who kept thinking he needed a shave, and almost unable to believe that he'd—·

Killed Mara Jade Skywalker.

Killing didn't get any easier. He was just getting better at it.

But it still didn't make sense. He rubbed his cheek, and the stubble rasped audibly under his fingers. Mara *hadn't* been the most precious thing in his life. In recent weeks, she'd changed from being his only friend to just someone else who didn't trust him and was getting in his way.

She was his aunt. She was *family.* When his role in her death became known—it had to be *when,* but not now, not anytime soon—the shock and hatred would tear apart what was left of the Skywalker and Solo families. Maybe even Niathal, and all the others who understood that securing peace was a dirty business, would be disgusted.

I just killed my aunt. I grew up with her. She was there for me. We fought a war together.

I have to face her son. I have to face Ben.

What have I done?

His stomach rumbled. How could he possibly be hungry at a time like this?

He will immortalize his love.

Stupid knotted tassels, all kinds of ancient Sith prophecies that would come to pass when the new Dark Lord was ready to take up his mantle and usher in a golden age of justice, order, and peace. The key had been turned—and this was what the prophecy was supposed to mean—by Jacen killing *what he most loved.*

He'd killed Mara, and Nelani, and Fett's daughter, and chaotic unjust democracy, and he loved none of those. He'd tried to kill Lumiya more than once. She seemed to think that was part of the job description for Sith acolytes.

So Jacen didn't believe it. And if Mara hadn't been trying to kill him to begin with, he would have seen it even more as a life thrown carelessly away.

The fabric of existence didn't seem to have changed enough. That shift should have been cataclysmic, and although he was too much of a pragmatist to think he could raise his fists to the sky and call down lightning to energize a mighty soul, he expected to be able to taste the spiritual and existential transformation.

He was afraid. However certain he'd been a few hours ago that Mara was to be the one destined to die, it didn't make sense in the context of the prophecy. He didn't feel different, either. Did that mean he still had to kill someone else? He'd been so certain it would all be over now. The sense of anticlimax was almost enough to make him sob.

Then he felt a presence. He leaned his head against the side of the cockpit canopy, and gazing up at him from the nightmarish planet surrounding his fighter was Lumiya.

Jacen popped the seal. "I'm surprised you could be bothered to come and find me, after what happened."

"You now need to be seen." Lumiya had a new serenity about her. As ever, she still seemed to take no offense at him for trying to kill her again. "Your new existence has started, Dark Lord."

"Really?" The pain in his shoulder gnawed at him like an animal tearing his flesh. "I don't feel very lordly."

"I assure you it's done. I felt it."

She might have been humoring him. He shifted in his seat to ease the assortment of bruises. "I'll be looking for further proof."

"Stop arguing with the Force and pay attention to what you have to do next. Luke Skywalker arrived at Hapes a couple of hours ago and they're looking for evidence. And Niathal is griping bitterly about your being AWOL."

"They won't find me."

"That's not what I mean. Your trip to the Royal Court, a subject I will take to my grave by the way, needs to be smoothed out in terms of credibility. Sooner or later, it'll emerge that you were in the Hapes Cluster, and that Mara knew that."

"How?"

"May I alarm you?"

"Can you alarm me any more? Is it possible?"

"Mara had a conversation with Hapan Fleet Ops while in Hapan space about your presence on Hapes. I intercepted it, which is one reason why I was able to come to your aid."

"Wonderful."

"And she even gave them a description of the Sith sphere as a possible hostile. I think that stacks up to a scenario needing a plausible explanantion."

Lumiya was right. Jacen needed a cover story, if only for Tenel Ka.

"This is going to tax even my creativity," Jacen said. "How widely known is this?"

"There are no secrets in the galaxy, Jacen, only varying sizes of distribution lists. The Bothans will have it, the Mandalorians will have it . . . and Alliance Intel will have it, and they don't love you at all these days."

"Well, if I weren't a Sith Lord fresh out of the box, I'd be borked."

"Don't joke. *Never* joke about this."

"I could say quite legitimately that I was visiting Tenel Ka as Chief of State because of the continuing embarrassment about my parents."

"And what about your wretched physical state?"

"Ah. I'm hastening the healing trance as much as I can."

"What about Mara's body?"

"I left it where it was."

"She didn't become discorporeal? She left her remains?"

"I think so. Does that surprise you?"

Lumiya seemed to consider something, breaking her intense gaze. "I always thought she'd become one with the Force somehow."

"Well, who knows. And here I am about to say they'll never trace the poison back to me, but does it matter? One day soon, they'll all have to know."

"And by then it'll be too late for them to do anything to you." Lumiya turned as if to walk away, and then seemed to change her mind. "My ship has been *noted,* Ben didn't see you on Kavan, and I'm almost certainly the prime suspect for Mara's death. This all enables me to do the last service I can for you."

"Which is . . . ?"

Lumiya's most unnerving state was when she was being gracious. It told Jacen that she knew something he didn't.

"To buy you time to consolidate your hold on the galaxy," she said. "By making Luke believe it was all my doing."

"Don't you think you should be hiding from him?"

"No. You might say that's *my* destiny."

"That smacks of a death wish."

"My work and my life are done, Jacen. I'd really welcome a rest."

Death seemed a very routine commodity lately. Jacen wasn't comfortable with that. He had a sudden urge to embrace life. Deep in him, for all the boy inside that still expected a lightning bolt to mark his passage into Sith maturity, there was a feeling of optimism, green and fresh. It took him aback.

"By the way, Alema is still prowling," Lumiya said. "If you spot her, she'll probably be coveting the Sith ship to pursue her vendetta against your parents. I have no doubt you'll see her around."

Jacen wondered if Sith left wills; Lumiya certainly seemed to have thought hers through. She studied him with her head on one side for a while, eyes disturbingly green and not unlike Mara's, and then she walked away into the icy fog.

He meditated for an hour or so to hasten the healing process, and then set off for Coruscant—via Hapes.

FOUNTAIN PALACE, HAPES

"Luke . . . Luke? *Luke.*"

Tenel Ka had to repeat his name three times before he could manage to lift his head to look at her. The elegant brocade sofa felt as if it were swallowing him whole, and maybe that would have been for the best.

There was an insulating gauze of numbness holding Luke together, and it took triple repetition to penetrate it—the first to stop him thinking that he hadn't even said good-bye to Mara and was asleep when she left; the second to stop him racking his brains for the last words he'd said to her, which he couldn't recall; and the third to stop him seeing in his mind's eye her scribbled note that he'd balled up and used to plug a hole in his cockpit console, and that he had now lovingly smoothed flat and would keep with him for the rest of his life.

Gone hunting for a few days. Don't be mad at me, farmboy . . .

"Luke, Jaina's here."

"Thank you, Tenel Ka . . ." As long as he stayed numb, Luke felt he would function. He would gather his thoughts, see that the rest of

the family was coping, and then he'd act—when he knew what to do. "I can't thank you enough."

"Luke, I have all my guard deployed searching the cluster."

Jaina walked in briskly, face grim and eyes a little swollen. She dropped down on her knees and pressed herself into Luke's lap, cuddling him in silence. He hadn't really needed to call: they'd all felt it.

"Still no sign of Ben," Luke said, stroking Jaina's hair. "And I can't even guess where he is."

Jaina knelt back on her heels. "I can't feel him, either, Uncle Luke."

"He'll be okay, sweetheart. I'd know if . . ."

Luke didn't finish the sentence. He knew now exactly how Ben's death would feel to him in the Force. Ben wasn't dead.

Luke waited for a call back from Leia and Han. He *knew* Leia had sensed Mara's passing: after that moment when he'd felt the lightest of touches on his hair, and he turned his head, he'd had the sensation of meeting Leia's eyes.

She'd call. He'd keep calling anyway.

Tenel Ka's regal composure flickered for a moment. "Jacen was here earlier."

"What?" Jaina suddenly regained that edge in her voice. "What do you mean, *here?*"

"He paid a visit yesterday," Tenel Ka said. "I don't know where he is now, but—"

"Would Hapan Fleet Ops have logged his vessel's movements?" asked Jaina. "Any scrap of information might help."

Jacen must have felt the death like anyone else, and there was a good chance he'd actually been here while Mara was pursuing Lumiya in this very system. But he was "busy" on GAG business. Luke seethed in silence.

Tenel Ka nodded, all gracious calm again. "I'll have the captain get all the available information for you."

Tenel Ka strode out. Jaina's expression was murderous.

"Don't say it," said Luke.

"He's a total stranger," Jaina said. "There. I had to, or else I'll have an aneurysm trying to stifle the urge to punch him out when he finally bothers to show up."

Luke hugged Jaina, feeling dwarfed by the grand stateroom, and his comlink buzzed. It was Leia.

"Hey," she said. Leia didn't just touch him in the Force, she *enveloped* him. "We're coming back as fast as we can. I'm so sorry. I am so, so sorry."

It sounded as if Han had wrestled the link from her. "Kid, you just hang in there. Don't do a thing. Leave it all to us. Is Ben okay?"

"Missing again."

"He'll be fine. Don't you worry. We're coming."

There wasn't much else Han could say, and he never mentioned Jacen. Luke put his comlink back in his pocket.

The silence felt like pressure building on his eardrums. His breathing seemed to fill the room. *What was the last thing I said to her?*

"You know pretty well the last thing Mara and I talked about?" Jaina said suddenly. She was doing exactly what he was—replaying final conversations. Tears welled in her eyes. "Nothing important, like how much I loved her and what she'd done for me. Just how much energy I waste in stupid games with Zekk and Jag, like a dumb sulky teenager."

"Don't do this to yourself."

"Takes . . . *this* to make me grow up." Jaina didn't seem able to say the words: *Mara's death.* "Everything's changed now."

"I know. I know."

"It's Lumiya."

"We don't *know* that."

"You're reasonable to the last, aren't you, Uncle Luke?"

"None of us is thinking straight at the moment." He didn't need Jaina going off on an impulsive quest for vengeance. He had to focus—somehow. "Why don't you call . . . Zekk? Jag?" He hadn't a clue which of the two men she'd want to turn to now. "They need to know, too."

Jaina brushed the tip of her nose discreetly with the back of her wrist, and seemed to take an unnaturally fixed interest in the ornate carvings on a chair leg nearby. "I'll *inform* them, but I'm done with all

that personal stuff. I'm going to concentrate on one thing, and that's making Lumiya pay. If I'm supposed to be the Sword of the Jedi, then it's time I took it seriously, and there's *nothing* that's worth my time more than this."

The duty captain of the guard came in later with a datapad on a bronzium platter and held it out to Luke. When he hesitated, Jaina took it and pored over it. The expression of I-told-you-so on her face told Luke that it wasn't going to be comfortable news.

"You want the short version, Uncle Luke?"

"Up to you."

"Mara shows up after Jacen, in Five-Alpha, and asks Ops to keep an eye out for an orange spherical ship with cruciform masts, because our new Chief of State might be under threat."

Luke always tried not to be swayed by circumstantial evidence, because two and two frequently proved to add up to anything but four. But he didn't know if they'd find any other evidence. He didn't know if they'd ever find Mara's body—or even if she'd left mortal remains. He couldn't ignore this.

"Jaina," he said. "I think you have to leave this to me."

"What was it you said about none of us thinking straight?"

"I don't want anyone acting on half the facts."

"What's it going to take, then?"

"She's—she was *my wife*. I insist that I handle this myself."

"You shouldn't have to."

"I *want* to. Don't take this from me."

Jaina actually flinched. Luke didn't think he'd snapped at her. Maybe his pain was so intense that the sudden burst of it then had touched her in the Force.

"Okay, Uncle," she said quietly. "But you just say the word, and I'll be there."

There was still no sign of Jacen by the time Luke had tried unsuccessfully to sleep for six hours. He'd dropped off the charts, as Jaina put it. And Ben had not reappeared. Ben, at least, had good reason.

The search for Five-Alpha resumed early in the morning.

KELDABE, MANDALORE

The fourth *Bes'uliik* off the production line rolled out of the hangar to meet the scrutiny of a small crowd of silent, armored men. They'd folded their arms in that typical go-on-amaze-me *Mando* way, but as soon as the fighter came alive and sent dust pluming with its downdraft, they all applauded and yelled, *"Oya!"*

Yes, they thought it was okay. Fett watched it with a certain pride. The higher frequencies in its drives made his sinuses tingle.

"Who says defense procurement drags its feet?" said Medrit. He didn't seem bothered by the noise, even minus his helmet, but then blacksmiths had often been deafened by their trade. "Record time."

"Only another half a million of these," Fett said, "and we'll be in business."

"It's never about numbers, *Mand'alor*. Never was."

There was something about the fighter—its effortless hover and tilt, combined with the distinct throbbing note of its propulsion—that made it exceptionally attractive. Fett doubted if it would have looked quite so pretty if it was pounding your city to molten slag. He planned to claim the offer of a test flight.

Mandalore was *resurgent,* as Beviin liked to say, and it was gathering pace. A steady stream of Mandalorians was returning from diaspora. A few hundred thousand in a week was nothing for a trillion-body city-planet like Coruscant, but Mandalore was now creaking with the influx.

"You'd think a big empty planet like this could cope with a few immigrants," Fett said.

"Poor infrastructure." Medrit craned his neck to watch another *Bes'uliik* take off. "Got to fix that. Four million was always a nice stable population until the crab-boys messed everything up."

"How many incomers, worst scenario?"

"Impossible to tell. But you asked for two million to come back, and I dare say we'll get that."

Fett still marveled at the ability of people to uproot themselves, but then *Mando'ade* were traditionally nomads—and even he was happier in *Slave I* than with a roof over his head. "I'm always touched

when people do things without my needing to hang them out of windows."

"Sometimes," said Medrit, "you have only to ask. Go read the *Resol'nare*. The six basic tenets of being a *Mando*. One is to rally to the Mandalore when called."

"Handy," said Fett. "But it doesn't always happen."

Fett had begun to see the recurring parallels between Mandalore the world and Mandalore the leader, and why the two terms had become synonymous in the outside world. He'd always called himself a figurehead, a reminder of what Mandalorians seemed to think they should be, social template as well as someone to hang the blame on: but it came true. He was recovering, and so was the nation. Mandalore seemed to move inversely to the rest of the galaxy, which was busy going down the tubes and ripping itself apart yet again. But that was good for business if you sold arms and military skills, so the correlation was expected.

"Time to celebrate," Medrit said. "A little, anyway. Come on, everyone's heading to the tapcaf. First round's on you."

As he walked, Fett reflected that he was as close to satisfied with life as he'd been in a long time, except for the few nagging loose ends that had loomed large when he was dying, and still hadn't gone away.

One of them was Jacen Solo.

It always came down to Jedi and their schisms in the end.

"It's true, I tell you. She's been *murdered*." Beviin was holding court in the *Oyu'baat,* a tapcaf that brewed a sweet, sticky *net'ra gal* and never ran out of narcolethe. "Big search going on in the Hapan Cluster. *Serious* trouble."

Fett visited the 'caf once a week partly because Mirta said it was good for morale, but mainly because Beviin asked him to. Fett wanted Beviin to succeed him, even if most expected him to groom Mirta.

"Cabinet in session, then?" he said.

The chieftains and neighbors who drank here had become Fett's cabinet, and if there was any serious attempt at government going on—*Mando'ade* regarded that as a deeply unhealthy and *aruetyc* thing—then it would only be tolerated over a *buy'ce gal* in the tapcaf.

"Welcome to the foreign affairs committee," said Beviin. "Mara Skywalker's missing, presumed dead."

"How do they know she's dead if the body disappears in a puff of smoke?" Carid muttered. He was playing a four-way board game with Medrit, Dinua, and Mirta that used short-handled stabbing blades. Fett watched from the sidelines, never able to work out the rules. "They do that, don't they?"

Fett thought of his lightsaber collection. "Sometimes."

Carid, using his helmet on the floor as a footrest, winked. "So where's the forensics?"

Dinua stabbed her blade into the board, and there was a murmur of *"Kandosii."* "They sense it all in the Force."

"I'd joke, but I hear their son has gone missing, too." Carid tutted loudly. "What kind of parents *are* these Jedi?"

Fett wouldn't have traded places with any of the Solos or Skywalkers. They were a tragically unhappy dynasty, and even if sympathy was something nobody paid him to have, he understood the loss of a parent, and a child.

"Any mention of Jacen Solo?" he asked.

"That name has cropped up."

"There's a surprise."

"Mentions of a *Lumiya,* too. Alias Shira Brie."

Now, *there* was a name from Fett's past. Some things never went away. "It all ran better under Vader."

"I'm still waiting for justice for my mama," Mirta said quietly. "Because if nobody else can be bothered to slit Jacen Solo's throat, I will."

She hadn't mentioned that in a while. Everyone—*everyone*—was waiting to see what retribution Fett had devised for the Solo brat. The longer he waited, the more sadistically *just* they expected it to be. But Fett could see something different in Mirta's eyes: if her grandfather was the most efficiently brutal bounty hunter in the galaxy, why hadn't he brought her Jacen Solo's hide?

The Jedi were right about one thing. Raw anger was a poor basis for action. He'd teach her cold patience, the best legacy he could bequeath her.

"Medrit," said Fett, "I want to send Han Solo a gift."

"Nice carbonite table?"

"Proper *beskar* crushgaunts, so he can throttle the life out of his vermin spawn. And maybe a couple of armor plates and a small blade."

"Gift-wrapped, signed *Please kill your son before we have to*?"

"Just *With deepest sympathy*."

It was as deep as Fett could manage, anyway. It must have been terrible to have such a disappointment for a son.

HAPES CLUSTER

Luke thought it was prudent for Corran Horn to take over the Jedi Council in his absence. He wasn't sure he could trust himself. It all felt very academic, even on a good day, and today was as far from one of those as he could imagine.

But apart from the fact that he was now minus everything good in his heart except Ben, Luke felt like his old self for the first time in years. He felt clarity. He knew what he had to do, and there were no gray areas or ambiguities about who was right and who was wrong. For all his pain, the sense of clean focus gave him something to cling to.

And old voices called to him.

He cruised the Transitory Mists in the StealthX, wondering if it had been a phantom effect of the region's ionization and sensor-scrambling phenomena that had guided him here. He magnified his presence in the Force again.

The comm alert broke his concentration for a moment.

"Luke," said Corran's voice. "This is kind of hard to ignore. Everyone's getting anxious to saddle up and lend you a hand."

"There's only one person I need to respond, my friend. And she's coming. But . . . thanks."

"What do you mean, *She's coming*?"

"Lumiya. I can feel her strongly now."

"It's a trap, Luke."

"For me *and* her, then."

"She's making it too easy."

"Corran, don't worry about me . . ."

"You know any one of us would gladly do it for you."

"I do. And that's why *I* have to."

Lumiya was here; Luke could feel her because she wanted him to, he knew that. He wondered how many times she'd passed by him unnoticed and undetected, and congratulated herself on her stealth. He thought of the hand offered to him after they last fought, and how he hadn't detected any ill will. That level of skilled deceit would have been impressive if he hadn't felt so sickeningly betrayed by it—betrayed by his own gullibility.

Mara used to say he bent over backward to see the good in everyone.

"I won't be trying too hard today," he whispered. "In fact, not at all."

He didn't even miss Mara right then. To miss someone, he had to accept that they were gone so he could yearn for them. Mara was still there, just frustratingly silent and unseen, and he dreaded the moment when he finally said to himself, *Yes, she's gone, she's really gone, and she isn't going to walk through the doors and complain how crowded the skylanes are these days.*

The Transitory Mists were bandit country, rife with piracy, and Luke didn't care. He maintained a steady circuit off Tepheron. Eventually, the feeling of someone darting through his peripheral vision became one of someone in the same room. He rotated the fighter 360 degrees in each plane, ignoring his sensors and his Force-senses for the moment because he wanted to see this thing coming, to look it in the eye and take in the entirety of it in the fundamental way of a grieving husband, not a Jedi Master.

"I knew you'd find time for me," he commed.

Had she heard him?

His comm crackled. Lumiya's voice had never aged. He hadn't noticed that before. "I saw no point in running, Luke. Let's finish this."

The ship was exactly as he'd imagined: rough-skinned, red-orange, so organic in appearance that it might have suited the Yuuzhan Vong. The angular masts and webbed vanes at its cardinal points lent it an edge of predatory grace.

"I had to make sure she died," said Lumiya. "But you'll understand that, sooner or later."

She didn't open fire, and the sphere didn't move. Luke considered taking one kill shot, but he'd done that before, and a pilot called Shira Brie had survived the appalling injuries he inflicted to be become the cyborg facing him now. No, she had to die for good.

The sphere rotated to face Terephon and began to pick up speed, on a straight course for the planet. Luke set off in pursuit and the two ships accelerated, pushing their sublight limits in what Luke started to feel was a crash dive.

Oh no, Lumiya, you don't get away with a suicide run. You're mine.

He stayed within his thoughts: he had next to nothing to say to her now. The sphere was streaking ahead of him, pulling away. He hung on it, closing the gap, calculating how long he had to intercept before it hit the upper atmosphere and plummeted to the surface, robbing him of every closure he needed.

And justice. Don't forget that. It's about paying the price for Mara's life.

The StealthX edged nearer its manual's recommended safe velocity. Luke brought the fighter alongside the sphere, dipping one set of wings in warning to make it clear he'd intercept her. Maybe she didn't realize that he had tractor capability: she would now. Luke dropped back behind her and applied enough traction to slow her and get her attention. He could have sworn something protested. It was the ship, complaining deep in his mind about the rough handling.

Lumiya seemed to get the idea and decelerated. Luke broke contact before they hit atmosphere, and followed her down, buzzing her to force her to land on a flat-topped mesa overlooking a typically spacious Hapan-style city nestling among trees and vast gardens.

He jumped out of the cockpit and waited for her to leave the safety of her vessel, standing with his lightsaber in both hands. Eventually an opening formed in the side of the sphere, and she emerged. Would the ship attack him as it had Mara? It made no move. He couldn't even feel it now.

"Come on, Luke, try to finish the job. Mara would have wanted that, yes?" Lumiya reached up to her face and tore away the veil that covered everything but her eyes. Then she reached behind her back and slowly drew out her lightwhip. "And this isn't to make you feel shame for the extent of my injuries. I just want you to see who you're fighting."

"I'm seeing." Luke drew his lightsaber and temporary comfort flooded him. "And this ends here."

He knew the lightwhip by now. He'd relied on the shoto as an extra weapon in the past to counter the whip's twin elements of matter and energy, but he was flooded with a new confidence that he could take her with just the lightsaber that had always stood between him and darkness. Holding it two-handed over his head, he rotated it slowly, stalking around her.

Lumiya raised her arm to flick the whip and get the momentum for the forward stroke. And then she cracked it, sending forks of dark energy crackling into the ground at his feet, making him jump back before he sprang forward again and brought the lightsaber around in a right-to-left arc that she parried with the whip's handle. He leapt out of range of the whirling tails again and again, then she paused and he edged closer again.

"You hate me that much?" he asked.

"I don't hate you at all."

"You killed her. You killed my Mara."

"Nothing personal." She looked as if she was smiling, but the movement was around her eyes rather than her cybernetic mouth. "Just doing what I swore an oath to the Emperor to do. To serve the dark side. Oaths matter, Luke. They're all you're left with in the end."

She drew back her arm and brought the lightwhip crackling through the air, missing Luke by centimeters. He lunged at her again and again, driven back each time. She'd slow sooner or later.

But so would he.

Then, as she began to raise her arm again, he ran at her, so close in that she couldn't get the whip traveling at its maximum lethal speed. He forced her back, step by step, as she tried to maintain the distance she needed.

One—two—three—four; she blocked him, handle held this way, then that, using the whip like a short lightsaber to deflect him, but

Luke didn't pause or shift direction to wrong-foot her. He drove her like a battering ram toward the edge of the mesa, pushing her within meters, then a step, of the edge.

Lumiya held the whip handle in both hands like a staff and blocked his downward sweep. For a moment they were locked in a stalemate, pushing against each other and grunting with the effort, with only the sounds of exertion because they had nothing left to say to each other.

Her rear foot began to slide backward as she struggled for purchase. The edge of the mesa was cracked and fissured. The smooth glittering stone began to crumble.

Luke reached out and caught her hand as she fell, whip tumbling and bouncing down the steep rock face into oblivion. He leaned back, all his weight on his heels, knuckles clenched white with the strain of holding her weight, and for a second he wanted to see her face dwindling as she fell to her death, mouth open in a scream, but that wasn't the way to end this.

"I'd never let you fall," Luke said, and pulled her back to safety. As she straightened up, he looked her in the eyes—calm, eerily calm—and swung his lightsaber in a single decapitating arc.

Now he could breathe again.

KAVAN: STORM WATER TUNNELS

Ben sat in the tunnel with his mother for a long time, and that fact in itself was the start of his investigation.

At first, he deluded himself that she was in a deep healing trance, even though the Force never lied, and the void that had opened in it would have been felt and understood by every Jedi.

He'd run straight to her side, through country he didn't know, and found her. He wanted to think she wasn't dead because she was *there,* still much as he'd last seen her except for the blood and scrapes of a new fight.

So he sat with her, waiting.

He wanted to clean her face and make her beautiful again, but his

GAG training said not to remove evidence, not to tamper with a crime scene.

Ben the fourteen-year-old son, lost and grief-stricken, willed his mother just to be in a deep trance. Ben the lieutenant knew better but didn't mention it to his child-self, and was careful to note everything around him, take holoimages, make notes of smells, sounds, and other ephemeral data, and begin to form a logical sequence that would tell him how his mother had met her death.

He was still sitting there, taking in every pore of her skin and every speck of brick dust on her jacket, when he heard someone picking his way over debris toward him.

He couldn't feel the person in the Force.

"Hello, Jacen," he said, and turned to look at him.

Jacen's mouth opened slightly while he stared first at Mara—a long, baffled stare—and then at Ben. He reached out his hand to him.

"It's okay, Ben. It's okay. We'll get whoever did this. I swear we will."

Ben was still shut down, hiding his Force presence, but Jacen had found him. It was time to go to his father. He wanted to be with him now.

Maybe the killing of his mother had left a mark in the Force that Jacen had followed. Ben considered the possibility that he was too upset to notice it himself.

He made a careful note of it anyway.

chapter twenty-three

Lawyers for former GA Chief of State Cal Omas have slammed the Justice Department for the delay in bringing charges against him. Omas, currently under house arrest, is said to be pressing for a public trial. A GAG spokesman said today that investigations were still ongoing.

—HNE news bulletin

THE OYU'BAAT, KELDABE, MANDALORE

VENKU—KAD'IKA—CAME UP TO FETT AND MIRTA IN THE TAPCAF and gestured over his shoulder.

"He says he'll do it," said Venku. "He didn't want to tell you he could read the stone there and then, in case he couldn't. He hates disappointing people."

The old man who'd come to stare at Fett with Kad'ika the other day walked slowly across the tapcaf. He peeled off his gloves and held out a frail hand dappled with age.

"I can do it," he said. "Let me hold the stone."

Mirta looked hesitant, then took off the necklace to hand it to Fett.

"You're Kiffar by origin, then," Fett said. Mandalorians came from any number of species and planets, but adopting the culture didn't erase their genetic profiles. "Saves me a journey."

"I . . . know the planet."

"What's your price?"

"Your peace of mind, *Mand'alor*. Nobody should search in vain for the resting place of loved ones."

Fett wasn't expecting that. The hand still held out in front of him was surprisingly steady. Fett held the heart-of-fire by its leather cord and lowered it into the man's palm before sitting down and trying to seem unconcerned.

The old man folded his fingers around it and stood staring at his fist, his breathing slow and heavy.

"She was very unhappy, wasn't she?"

It was a good guess. It was inevitable, in fact. The old man probably said it to all the wounded and lonely souls he came across. Charlatans and con men relied on the reactions of others. Fett said nothing to help him take a lucky guess, and there was no expression to betray him.

"And she found it hard to ever trust another man."

Fett still sat in silence, one boot on the chair. Sintas had never trusted anyone. Bounty hunters weren't the trusting kind, so it was a safe, easy deduction dressed up as revelation.

"Her worst days were when your daughter learned to talk, and asked where *Dada* was."

Fett was starting to tire of this. He shifted in his seat, ignoring the voice that whispered it was probably true. How would he know, anyway? He couldn't verify it. He and Sintas had parted by then and he saw nothing more of Ailyn.

Not until I saw her dead body.

"She thought you still cared when you recovered the hologram for her."

Now that wasn't a guess. It was specific. And it was . . . true. Fett didn't dare look at Mirta. The inn was absolutely silent: the popping

and crackling of the tapcaf's log fire sounded like battlefield explosions.

"She said you were far too young to know what you were doing, and you said you only needed to know that she was beautiful, that she was a terrific shot, and that you could trust her as much as you could trust any woman."

Fett's scalp tightened and prickled. It was *exactly* what he'd said, and it was too stupid and juvenile a line for anyone to make up on the spot. *No, he has to have information, he has to be putting on a show, he got the information from someone . . . but how?*

The man took a deep breath and hesitated before speaking again.

"You told her that you'd make Lenovar pay for what he did to her, and she tried to talk you out of it—"

It was too much for Fett. "Enough." He thrust out his hand, palm up. "So you can read the stone."

Venku lowered his chin. Even without sight of the man's face, Fett knew the expression behind the visor was fearless and protective anger.

The old *Mando* took a gentler approach than his bodyguard. "Just tell me what you want to know," he said. "I know these things can be painful."

Mirta didn't give Fett a chance to answer. It was just as well: he couldn't bring himself to say it. To onlookers, he was just being typically silent and surly.

"I want to know how she spent her last hours," Mirta said. "I want to find her body."

The old man put the heart-of-fire on the table while he removed his helmet. He had a fine-boned, thin face and a wispy beard that was whiter than his hair, which still showed traces of sandy blond. He was sweating: picking up the memories and traces of time embedded in the stone's molecular structure seemed to be exhausting him.

And he didn't have a Kiffar facial tattoo. But then neither did Mirta, despite the fact that Ailyn had embraced the Kiffar culture completely. In some lines of work, a permanent identifying mark had its drawbacks.

"It doesn't give me the memories in order," said the veteran. "It's all random, like flashbacks. I see images, hear sounds, smell aromas, and so on. Making sense of it isn't easy."

He laid his helmet on the table and picked up the stone again, this time pressing it between both palms. Venku put a steadying hand on his shoulder, and Fett felt inexplicably uneasy.

"Do you want me to . . . find acts of violence?"

Fett glanced at Mirta, not for agreement but because he couldn't help it. Her brow was creased in a little frown. Dry-eyed; focused. Not a pretty girl, but a good strong bone structure.

"You'll find plenty of that," she said. "She was a bounty hunter."

"You're not in here, Mirta . . . ," said the old *Mando,* eyes tight shut.

"She died before I was born. I want to know who killed her."

There were a few more people now in the tapcaf than there had been. Fett indicated the door with a jerk of his thumb. "*Out.* I'll let you know when you can finish your drinks."

I want to know who killed her, too. It's too long ago, but I want to know.

"She wore this all the time." The old man looked almost in pain, and Venku squeezed his shoulder. "She was angry a lot of the time. Scared, too. There are so many people passing through here . . . but I keep coming back to a chart of Phaeda. Red skies, and someone she was following. Resada? Rezoda?"

Mirta didn't blink. She seemed transfixed. "Grandmama didn't tell anyone where she was going, or who she was hunting."

The man opened his eyes and took a rasping breath. "Phaeda. Whatever it was, it happened on Phaeda." He jerked back and stared at the stone. "And she fought to hang on to this. She fought *hard.*"

Fett managed not to swallow. He was sure they'd all hear it. "She lost."

"I want to know," said Mirta.

Venku stepped in. "He's had enough. Maybe later." He retrieved his helmet and tried to steer the old man away. "Come on."

"I don't know about the when," the old man said, pulling from Venku's grasp, "but I know it's Phaeda. I'm sorry. I'm really sorry."

He handed the stone back to Mirta, placing it in her cupped palms with both hands as if it were a live fledgling. Fett had never been comfortable around that mystical kind of thing. He simply observed.

"It's okay," Mirta said. "You've told me a lot, and I'm grateful. Let me buy you an ale."

"Maybe another day, *ner ad'ika*," Venku said. "But thank you."

Mirta watched the door close. As she turned back to Fett, the door opened again and disgruntled drinkers filtered back in, giving the two of them a wide berth.

"Well? Was he right, *Ba'buir*?"

Fett shrugged. It had shaken him, like all the painful memories that flooded back without his permission. "On the nail."

"Well, we can follow that lead."

Fett dreaded what else the old man had seen in the stone. *Old man.* He was only ten or maybe fifteen years older than Fett. "I don't think I've ever been to Phaeda."

The tapcaf owner lined up fresh ales on the bar. "I see you've met Kad'ika, then, *Mand'alor*."

"Yeah. Fascinating."

"The old man with him—don't see him around much. Gotab, I think. I used to think that was Kad'ika's father, but apparently not."

The name didn't mean a thing to Fett, but he filed it mentally under subjects to investigate later. *Phaeda.* He'd scour *Slave I*'s databases, maybe hack into the Phaeda archives. Mirta was examining the stone closely.

"Must have cost every credit you had, *Ba'buir*."

She passed the heart-of-fire to Fett and he turned it over in his fingers, touching the carving on the edge. Only the most skilled cutter could facet the uncut stones without shattering them, let alone carve them.

"It's rare to find one with all the colors in it. They're usually red or orange, but the light ones with the whole rainbow . . . they cost."

"I saw a blue one once," Mirta said.

"I was sixteen. I couldn't afford a blue one."

Fett could afford one now, any number of them, even the rarest of deep royal-blue stones that showed their incredible range of multicolored fire only in bright sunlight. But he no longer had a lover to give them to. It had been a very long time.

"Tell me something about Ailyn," he said. "Was she ever happy?"

Mirta chewed over the question. "I don't think so."

The only thing Fett knew about his own daughter beyond the people she'd killed and what she'd stolen was that she had never been happy, never called him *Dad,* and that she'd taught Mirta to hate him. He still hadn't questioned the girl about that. The time never felt right.

"Were *you* ever happy?" Mirta asked.

Fett never considered if anyone wondered if he was happy or not. There seemed to be a blanket assumption that Boba Fett coasted along on a narrow path of dispassion, never angry, never happy, never sad.

"I was happy as a kid," he said at last. "I stopped being happy on Geonosis and I never bothered trying again."

But he'd been angry, all right: angry, grief-stricken, terrified, lonely, and hostile. He'd run through all the negative emotions at full intensity in those days after his father's death, crammed in the spaces between doing what he had to do to survive, when he needed to be all cold logic. It was a switch he had to throw, off and on, off and on, until one day it didn't switch on again, and the pain was gone. So were the joy and the love.

If he did what his dad wanted, it might come back. If he did an honorable job, and tried to at least understand the remnant of his own family, he stood a chance of recapturing some of what was ripped from him in that arena on Geonosis.

"Drink up, *Ba'buir,*" Mirta said. "I want to go and do some digging about Phaeda."

GALACTIC ALLIANCE WARSHIP OCEAN,
ON STATION JUST BEYOND CORELLIAN SPACE

"It's *awfully* good of you to join us," said Admiral Niathal. Jacen walked onto the bridge and tasted the mix of emotions around him, ranging from vague interest to nervousness. "I was very sorry indeed to hear of your loss."

Jacen nodded politely. She sounded as if she really meant the condolence, but then she was pretty good at hitting the right note. He was visiting *Ocean* in his capacity as Chief of State to try out a little hearts-and-minds on a gathering of the various ally worlds. There was nothing like a meeting on a suitably mighty warship to show folks what was at stake. The Confederation was now planning a major push against the Core Worlds, intelligence suggested, so Jacen hoped everyone was paying attention.

Life was going on much as before. Recent days seemed to have been a lot of sweat for nothing. If he needed any more answers to Sith philosophical questions, he was on his own. Lumiya had managed to commit suicide-by-Skywalker. Jacen might not have been part of the Jedi Council, but the GAG were very efficient interceptors of messages.

Uncle Luke did it. He actually did it. Like my dad—you never know how far they'll go, do you?

"So," Jacen said, "Corellia seems to have been very quiet in my absence."

"They were waiting for your return—that push on the Core looks imminent. They'd hate you to miss anything." Niathal, annoyed or not about his extra day or so of absence, seemed to have an air about her of someone who was suddenly more comfortable with her new role, as if she'd taken advantage of his back being turned to forge fresh alliances and consolidate her power. It was almost like a fragrance; the aura that surrounded the love of power was something Jacen knew very well indeed. "The triumvirate is still doing the day-to-day running of affairs, but I've got our Intel folks and political analysts reading the signs about who might replace the dear departed Prime—" She stopped abruptly, and this time she was genuinely rattled. He could feel it. "I'm so sorry. That was grossly insensitive of me under the circumstances."

"It's okay." Maybe there was a gentler side to Niathal after all. If there was, he'd exploit it to the hilt. "Can't tread on eggs and suspend all normal conversation about deaths. The best thing we can do to honor my aunt's memory is to win for her."

"Indeed."

"Murkhana seems tense. We're past the deadline, yes?"

"We're keeping a watching brief on that. Might well be Mandalorian psych tactics. Eight X-wings on standby to keep the peace is the price of GA harmony. On the other hand, if the Mandalorians *do* show up to support their Verpine allies by halting disputed production in their own inimitable way, then at least we might get a *very* useful look at the capabilities of their new assault fighter."

"Some might think," he said quietly, "that we'd prefer to see them attack Murkhana than not."

"I never turn down intelligence, Colonel Solo."

"Very wise, Admiral Niathal."

Jacen wandered over to the bridge holochart that showed the entire Corellian theater. They still had a lot of ships. There was a limited action going on on the Coreward side of the chart. It always struck Jacen as overdetached to show real-time life-and-death struggles as charmingly aesthetic and silent graphics.

"Is this current?"

"Yes, sir," said the officer of the watch. "Updated once a minute."

"I think we're missing something, Lieutenant," Jacen said, dipping his fingertip into the maze of light to make his point. "Look, what you have here is actually a flotilla of corvettes, and *this* Destroyer here will move into *this* position, because she's actually operating a—"

He trailed off, aware of the raised eyebrows and puzzled looks he was getting, but bathed in the growing warmth of revelation.

I can see all this.

"Can we check that out?" the officer of the watch called to a colleague. "Colonel Solo is rarely mistaken."

Colonel Solo, Jacen thought, had just had the epiphany of his life.

It's true. Lumiya was right. Oh, this is exquisite. I was blind before. How did I ever think I could succeed as a commander without this?

Lumiya had promised him a battlefield awareness and judgment that made ordinary battle meditation look like a finger painting—to sense and coordinate by the power of his mind and will alone, a power that only came to fruition in the Master of the Sith.

It's me. It really is. It was Mara's sacrifice after all, I accept that now.

But I still don't understand the prophecy. And I don't like what I can't understand.

He was a Sith Lord. Now his work could truly begin.

It had happened.

And it was *beautiful.*

JEDI COUNCIL SHUTTLE, HAPES CLUSTER

Luke was grateful for something he still couldn't understand.
He paused before he walked through the doors to the compartment, taking a few deep breaths. Cilghal looked up as he came in, and moved as if to leave.

Mara—no, Mara's *body*—lay draped from the neck down in a plain white sheet on an examination table. Luke had steeled himself for something terrible, imagining her horribly disfigured or her features contorted; but she simply looked as if she were sleeping on her back, pale and peaceful, her red hair smoothly tidy in a way it never was when he watched her as she slept.

"It's okay, Cilghal," he said. "I don't need to be alone with her."

"Oh, yes, you do, Luke," she said softly. "And I can come back later."

"I don't understand it," he said. "But I get to hold her one last time, and I wondered if I ever would. I can't tell you how grateful I am."

He couldn't see Cilghal's face now. His eyes were hot and brimming. She patted his arm.

"You thought she would become discorporeal," she said.

"We talked about it once or twice. I thought she might choose that when the time came. I'm glad she changed her mind."

"She certainly made sure we had evidence." Cilghal paused for a second, inhaled sharply, and started again. "It was poison, one I've never seen before. But don't doubt that she also wanted you to be able to say good-bye."

Cilghal turned and hurried out.

Luke couldn't speak or even look away from Mara, and he spent a long time staring into her face. If her eyes had opened, and she'd asked how long she'd overslept, he wouldn't have been surprised. He lifted the sheet to clasp her left hand, and it was just the chill that made him flinch. After a while the skin felt warm from the heat of his own body.

Cilghal needed forensic evidence for the record. But Lumiya had killed Mara, and Lumiya had paid the price. There was no investigation to follow.

Yet that meant there was no need for Mara to remain now, and

Luke was torn between wanting never to take his eyes from her and re-calling how Yoda became one with the Force: then he might *really* see her again. But he understood so little of those elements of mysticism. Right then, he was grateful to settle for watching her.

"You really did want to see me, didn't you?" he whispered, and leaned over to kiss her. He wondered if she would vanish in the next instant. He didn't dare look away, and knew that it was only stopping him from accepting that she was gone. Even when he felt Ben walking toward the compartment, and heard him walk softly across the deck, he didn't turn around. He reached out his left arm so Ben would walk up to him and accept the embrace while Luke watched over Mara.

"Hey, sweetheart," he said to her. "It's Ben."

"I'm sorry you couldn't find me, Dad," he said. "I just had to go to her and be there."

It was the first time Luke had spoken to Ben since before Mara had left: it felt like the first time in ages, in fact. Luke tried to think about what it must have been like for Ben to stand guard over his mother's body, alone and scared, but he was still too mired in his own grief and shock.

"Dad . . . I know she's telling us something. I've been thinking about it all the way back."

Poor kid. Luke didn't quite understand what he meant, but they could talk it through later. He was proud of his son's strength and dig-nity. Ben could take the other news, too. He did a man's job now.

"Anyway, I got Lumiya."

"Yeah?" Ben sounded surprised. "What do you mean, *got?*"

"I killed her. I won't dress it up. I owed it to Mara to give her jus-tice."

Ben was totally silent. Luke felt a small disturbance around him and his muscles stiffened.

"Dad . . ."

"I know, legal process and all that, but legal process . . . Lumiya said she had to . . . well, a life for a life. That's all."

"Dad . . . Dad, it wasn't Lumiya."

"It was. She said . . ."

What exactly *had* Lumiya said?

"No, no, it can't be, because I was right next to her at the moment

Mom died, nowhere near the scene. We'd landed on Kavan, both of us. She was still in the Sith sphere."

Luke heard Ben's voice from a long way away, and everything was upended again.

It wasn't her. It wasn't Lumiya.

"Dad, take it easy, okay? We'll find who did it." Ben grabbed his shoulders. "Dad, that's why Mom stayed. She stayed so we could find evidence. We don't know who did it yet. Forget about Lumiya. You just got to her first—I was going after her *before* Mom died. You did the galaxy a necessary service."

No, he *hadn't*. Luke didn't feel he had done that at all. He'd killed Lumiya—evil as she was—for something she hadn't done. That *wasn't justice*.

Luke found himself sinking to his knees. "I killed the wrong—"

"*Sith.*"

"I killed *the wrong person*. But she said—"

Ben put his hands on either side of his father's face, suddenly years older than Luke. "Look at me, Dad. It's not good to do this here. Let's talk elsewhere."

"Ben . . ."

"What about all the other people she killed and had killed? She's not worth your anguish, Dad. Save your tears for Mom, 'cos I will."

Luke managed to hang on for a few more minutes. When he couldn't stand it any longer, he strode off to his cabin, shut the hatch, and sobbed and raged in private until he was spent. He'd thought he was bearing up well, holding in all those tears, and then something like Lumiya added a straw to the scales and the floodgates opened. He hated her for that. He'd wanted to weep for Mara, his grief untainted by anything connected with the evil that had led to her death. He didn't want Lumiya intruding in this moment, and yet somehow she had.

Whoever had killed Mara was still around. He could focus on bringing them to justice, and that meant he had something else to hang on to while he struggled with grief.

But Lumiya had done it again.

She'd fooled him one last time, manipulated him one last time, thwarted him one last time, and it broke something deep, deep inside him.

chapter twenty-four

Message to: Hapan Fleet Ops
Originating station: Terephon

Unregistered and unidentified ship notified to us by Jedi Master
Skywalker has been removed without authorization from Tu'ana
City. Please advise Master Skywalker that we regret this act of
theft while the vessel was in our jurisdiction, and will meet any
claim for compensation.

MANDALMOTORS LANDING STRIP, KELDABE, MANDALORE

BOBA FETT MESHED HIS FINGERS TO PUSH HIS GLOVES BACK TIGHT on his hands, and looked up at the open cockpit of the *Bes'uliik*. Under his visor, he allowed himself an intensely private, broad grin.

Beviin applauded, laughing. "*Mando* boys on tour! Come on, *Bob'ika*, take that jet pack off before you get in or you'll have a nasty involuntary ejection at altitude . . ."

Spirits were high. Fett hadn't led a Mandalorian strike force since the *vongese* war, as far as he could recall. There might have been others, but that was the big one, the one that counted.

There were cheers of *"Oya manda!"* as *Bes'uliik* prototype fighters were rolled out from the hangar. People were taking holorecordings and pointing out the finer points of the airframe to their kids. The mood around Fett felt like a heady blend of nostalgia and optimism for the future, which was perhaps inappropriate considering that they were about to violate Murkhana sovereign territory—only temporarily, of course—and bomb a couple of its factory complexes into Hutt space.

It was all being done considerately. He'd made a point of sending a warning to factory staff and residents in the likely blast zone to evacuate well in advance. It wasn't as if the *Mando* flight was sneaking in and hammering them without decent notice. *Mando'ade* weren't savages, after all. Well, not recently . . . and only to *vongese*, if they were.

Besides, Fett wanted decent HNE coverage of the new fighter in action. It was worth an armored division in terms of deterrent. There was nothing sloppier than finishing an engagement before the media had a chance to set up and record it.

Dad would have loved this.

Fett was due to be the last pilot to embark, so he watched the other pilots getting into their cockpits. Beviin had been looking forward to this like a kid before a birthday. Medrit lifted up their grandchildren, Shalk and Briila, so the kids could slap their handprints on the fuselage in paint. It was a discreet light gray, although Shalk insisted a good *verdyc* blood-red shade would have been heaps and *heaps* better.

"Ba'buir," called Mirta. "Hey, hang on! *Pare sol!*"

Fett turned. Mirta was running across the field, datapad clutched in her hand, and Orade ran with her. Either she thought *Ba'buir* was so senile that he wasn't capable of returning alive from a simple bombing raid in the hardest fighter on the market, or she wanted to do something unforgivably sentimental. He braced for mild embarrassment.

But she didn't look like she was about to have a sentimental moment. She looked—distraught.

Fett automatically did a quick scan around the crowd to make sure everyone whose survival mattered to him was still there and in one piece. Mirta was clearly bearing bad news that couldn't wait.

Ah well. It happens.

"Ba'buir," she panted. "I want you to be really calm about this."

Fett said nothing, and just pointed to his visor.

"I'm not sure how to tell you this." She brandished the datapad as if she wanted to show she had evidence, and that she wasn't kidding. "It's . . . I don't know . . ."

"Spit it out."

"You know I started going through the Phaeda stuff?"

"Yeah."

"I did a search of all the archive material for names like *Resada* and *Rezoda.*"

Fett could see he was going to have to drag it out of her a grunt at a time. "Yeah."

"Rezodar, gangster. Dead gangster, in fact. Died around thirty-eight years ago. *That's* the name stored in the heart-of-fire."

Fett noted Orade looking at Mirta as if he was more worried about her than about Fett's wrath for once. "That's going to be a significant date, I assume."

"It is. I found he had an outstanding estate, which is what Phaeda calls leaving stuff of value without a will or anyone to claim it. The state can't claim it, so they store it. The state lawyer's really annoyed about still having to store stuff, and he says if we want to file a claim, he'll be a happier man. It'll take some time."

Fett wasn't sure that news of a very dead scumbag's leavings was worth interrupting his *Bes'uliik* moment. But Mirta wasn't the drama-queen kind. This had to be something about Sintas's death that would make him very, very *focused.* She'd worked out that he'd been touchy—and then some—about slights to Sintas, even if he had left her.

"Mirta," Fett said firmly. He rarely used her name. "Just tell me the seriously bad bit."

She handed him the datapad. The screen was already set to show images of what was stored in Rezodar's lockup, all numbered by the inheritance court division. Fett thumbed through them.

"Just look for the carbonite slab, *Ba'buir*."

Fett didn't like the sound of that.

When he got to it, he couldn't quite make out the contours, so he magnified the image.

Oh, fierfek . . .

He wanted to blurt out something, but no sound came anyway, and nobody was any the wiser with a man in a helmet. His legs threatened to give way. He handed the datapad back to her, taking a deep, slow breath to try to control the tremor in his guts.

"What do you need from me to get this released?" Fett was sure his voice was shaking. "Credits? Signature?"

"Is that *it*?" Mirta demanded.

"Just tell me." *It can't be true. It can't be.*

"I can do it myself." She looked hurt, which wasn't easy for a hard-faced girl like that. "A thousand credits."

"I'll pay." Fett could hardly believe the words that were coming out of his mouth, all in the voice of a calm stranger. "She was—she's my ex-wife, after all."

Sintas was *alive*.

Sintas Vel, his first and only wife, was alive, provided nothing had gone wrong with the carbonite process.

She was going to have quite a bit of catching up to do with the galaxy—and her shattered family.

Ailyn, what can I say?

"Okay." Mirta was all sour grit again. "Play the hard man in front of your *burc'yase*, but I *know* you by now."

Fett had decided to visit the refresher before the sortie. Now was a very good time. "I bet you do."

He strode off, same as ever, because that was what everyone expected, then shut the refresher doors and leaned his back against the wall. He slid all the way down it and squatted there, head in his hands, shaking.

Sintas was *alive*.

He waited a few minutes, then got to his feet and walked out onto the landing strip to join his *Bes'uliik* as if nothing had happened.

CAPTAIN'S DAY CABIN, SSD <u>ANAKIN SOLO</u>

I *see it now.*
   I know what I loved most and what had to be killed.

Jacen had laid on his bunk for hours, trying to slot the last piece into the puzzle that tormented him. It was the prophecy. It didn't fit.

He will immortalize his love.

It was only when Jacen considered that *he* might not refer to himself that he started down a complex path that showed the prophecy in its multifaceted complexity. It didn't just have one meaning: it had many.

And this is why I'm now Lord of the Sith.

There'd been no pyrotechnics, and no cataclysmic shift in the Force; and yet, from where he stood now, Jacen looked back and saw a landscape that had changed utterly. It had changed footstep by footstep, act by act, death by death, a change so gradual and incremental that he hardly noticed its passage until—

Until *now.*

He wasn't the same Jacen Solo who was shocked when Lumiya had told him he was destined to be a Sith Lord.

If he looked back far enough, Jacen saw its beginnings in Vergere's oddly concerned avian eyes as he suffered physical torment that had changed him forever, showing him that there was nothing he couldn't endure and pass beyond if his will wanted it.

And he'd killed not a *person* he loved, but something precious whose absence he was going to find very hard to handle. It was already searing a hole in him. It had *mattered.* And it still had the appearance of being alive, but it was walking dead.

What he'd loved and yet killed was Ben's admiration and devotion to him. Jacen had grown to love that adulation—and he had loved robbing Luke of the role of adored father and mentor.

He will immortalize his love . . . where immortalize *means "dead."*

And Ben—he knew Ben well enough to realize that he would never rest until his beloved mother's killer was caught, and that she would always be that perfect icon of beauty and courage to him.

Ben's love's immortal now. It'll last as long as he lives, unchanging, like his vision of Mara. And—like the hatred and venegeance he'll feel for me when he learns what I did. That'll live forever, too.

Jacen got up and looked at his reflection in the mirror on the bulkhead again. He'd studied it as if looking for changing symptoms, hour by hour, to see if his Sith status were manifesting itself in his flesh. He didn't look any different.

But he kept seeing Ben's face as he walked up to the boy in that tunnel and found him keeping vigil over his dead mother. His eyes . . . they knew something was waiting to be revealed, something that would rip him apart.

Mara made Ben start wondering why she didn't become one with the Force. Sooner or later, he'll find out. You played your part in my destiny, Mara.

And when Ben finally found out that it was Jacen who'd killed her, he'd hate him more than he could even begin to imagine. Jacen had injected a slow poison into Ben's love for him, as surely as he'd poisoned his mother, and seeded a terrible and wonderful hatred. A Sith *needed* that magnificent well of loathing to achieve greatness. Ben would eventually become greater than his Jedi father could ever be.

In the meantime, Jacen's war continued, now on the wider political stage as well as in the GAG.

He picked up the black GAG helmet that he rarely wore, rotated it between his fingers, and felt an odd queasiness in his gut as he put it on. It was standard GAG trooper issue, flared jaw section with a dispersal-gas-proof filter, the visor a single shallow V-band of toughened duraplast, just a basic tool of the job. It wasn't much different from the functional helmet troops had worn for decades.

But I don't need this, do I?

He stood in front of the polished durasteel bulkhead. The black outline in front of him was smeared and hazy, a mere impressionist suggestion of what he was. He could hardly look. He was everything his enemies said he was. He was embarrassed; yes, the embarrassment overshadowed any guilt.

He had killed, and killed again, and killed Mara Jade Skywalker, who was both family and friend. Friends . . . now he had none left except Tenel Ka and Allana, and they would come to hate him when the truth was known.

I've sunk as low as I can, in the eyes of ordinary people.

But now the only direction is . . . up.

Jacen thought of a brief conversation with one of the GAG troops, a former police officer from the Coruscant Security Force. Most murders, the officer had said, were committed by family and close friends. The random killing of strangers was relatively rare, even in the seediest quarters of the violent, lawless lower levels.

I'm not so unusual, then.

Jacen took a breath and stepped two strides sideways. He was now looking into the mirror set into the bulkhead of his day cabin again; crystal clear, sharp, merciless. He gazed at an image of all-encompassing black. He knew what people said behind his back: that he was trying to emulate Vader.

So? I'm proud of my grandfather, but not blind to the weaknesses that brought him down.

But that was wounded pride speaking. *I have to be beyond that now.* He had to be beyond fear of small consciences and even beyond the hatred that would make Ben Skywalker a strong, worthy, and terrifying successor to the title of Dark Lord.

But that would be years in the future. Now was the time for a man who'd once been Jacen Solo to shoulder that responsibility for the galaxy's sake.

Jacen took off the helmet, looked into his own eyes, and didn't flinch.

"Caedus," he said. "My name is Darth Caedus."

about the author

KAREN TRAVISS is the author of *Star Wars: Legacy of the Force: Bloodlines* and two *Star Wars:* Republic Commando novels, *Hard Contact* and *Triple Zero,* as well as *City of Pearl, Crossing the Line, The World Before, Matriarch,* and *Ally.* A former defense correspondent and TV and newspaper journalist, Traviss has also worked as a police press officer, an advertising copywriter, and a journalism lecturer. She has served in both the Royal Naval Auxiliary Service and the Territorial Army. Since her graduation from the Clarion East class of 2000, her short stories have appeared in *Asimov's, Realms of Fantasy, On Spec,* and *Star Wars Insider.* She lives in Devizes, England.